The Missing Mother *of* Rose Cottage

The
Missing
Mother
of Rose
Cottage

Cathy Hayward

Published by Lake Union Publishing, Seattle

www.apub.com

Amazon, the Amazon logo, and Lake Union Publishing are trademarks of Amazon.com, Inc., or its affiliates.

EU Product Safety contact:
Amazon Media EU S.à r.l.
38, avenue John F. Kennedy, L-1855 Luxembourg
amazonpublishing-gpsr@amazon.com

ISBN-13: 9781662540288
eISBN: 9781662540271

Original cover design by Emma Rogers
Cover adaptation by Will Speed
Cover image: © David Lichtneker / Arcangel; © Vilor © Ortis © AYIKU / Shutterstock; © AJI T / Adobe

Printed in the United States of America

For Katy

Chapter 1

JOANNE

AUGUST 2021

Mike enveloped Joanne in a massive hug, though she could tell he was being careful not to crush her growing belly. He smelled of her childhood. A tang of aftershave and, somewhere in the background, oil from the car mechanics'.

'We're both so pleased for you, love,' Mike said, drawing back from the front doorway and looking at her. Despite his broad smile, there was an anxiety in his eyes. 'You look well.' It was more of a question.

'You do, chick, blooming,' said her stepmam, Lou, hugging her in turn. 'But you're carrying it well. No one would believe you're five months gone already.'

Joanne's husband, Alex, came up behind her and rested his hand around her waist. 'Come in, both of you. And we'll show you the photos from the hospital, you'll love them.'

'Photos?' Lou squealed. 'You've got photos?'

'Well, the scans. But they're incredibly lifelike,' said Joanne. 'It's like the baby's actually there. Come through. I've got them on the kitchen table.'

They walked down the narrow hallway into the kitchen. Spread across the table were four 3D images of a fully formed baby. Lou picked one up.

'Oh, that's amazing, it's so lifelike.'

Mike hung back.

'Dad, don't you want to see? It's your new grandchild.' Joanne smiled up at him.

Mike smoothed his hand over his almost bald head, then nodded. He stared at the photos for a long time. 'Beautiful.'

'He? She? really is gorgeous,' said Lou. 'Did you find out what you're having? A boy or a girl?'

Joanne shook her head. 'No, we want it to be a surprise.' She smiled up at Alex, who grinned back at her. This baby was already bringing them back together, she thought. Making them a proper family at last.

'I don't like surprises,' said Mike, his eyebrows drawing together.

'Oh Mike, don't be silly,' said Lou. 'And it's not your surprise anyway to like or not, it's Jo and Alex's.' She went forward and put her arm around Joanne's shoulders. 'How are you feeling, love?'

'I just feel relieved. I feel I can finally start to enjoy the pregnancy now that we've had the five-month scan. Before then, I couldn't let myself think about it too much, in case it all went wrong again.' An image of the pools of blood from her most recent miscarriage flickered across her mind. The silver bracelets slid down her arm as she rested her hand on her belly, which was finally becoming slightly rounded.

'Don't even think about that now. You're going to be absolutely fine this time. In a few months, you'll have a beautiful baby in your arms and you won't even remember all that.' Lou smiled at her and looked down at the scan pictures. 'You deserve this.'

'That's what Dr Petzold said. He said we'd forget all the IVF and just think about the baby.' It would be strange not seeing him again, she realised, having been in and out of his surgery for years. 'Our little lockdown baby. Our last-chance baby.' *In so many ways*, she thought. She tucked an escaped curl back into her hair, which was piled on top of her head.

'I think it's amazing, the scans they do these days,' said Lou, touching the putty-coloured figure.

Joanne looked over her shoulder. 'I'll have another scan at twenty-eight weeks – just because of the IVF and my age.' She laughed lightly. 'Geriatric mum.'

'Oh, don't be daft,' said Lou. 'The main thing is that you've got the all-clear.' She handed the scan back to Joanne.

'I can tell them in the shop now. The midwife gave me a form to hand in, so I can get maternity pay. The girls will all be so pleased for me.'

'That's why we're here, love,' said Mike. 'Now that you've got that all-clear, we've got some baby bits for you. Come and give us a hand, Alex.'

'Oooh, exciting!' said Joanne. 'What is it?'

'Just you wait and see,' said Lou, grinning. 'You're going to love it. I'll make us some coffee.'

'Thanks, Mam.' Joanne watched Alex follow her dad down the hall and out into the sunshine. Something in him had changed today. Relaxed, maybe. As if he'd been holding on to something, and seeing the baby on the screen had allowed him to release it. They'd never talked after the miscarriages, just quietly held on to their grief separately and focused together on the next time. Always the next time. And then the next time. Seven babies slipping away, year after year. And that was when she'd been able to get pregnant at all. The months of trying, waiting up for Alex to come back from a twelve-hour night shift when he'd held patients' hands as they lay dying, and then insisting they made love because she was ovulating. The two-week wait and then instead of two blue lines on the pregnancy test, one big fat negative and a heavy period. Not surprising that they'd struggled, that their marriage had struggled. It wasn't quite how they'd imagined their future would be when they'd met fifteen years ago on a karaoke night in a pub in town.

The coffee machine released an ominous shriek. 'Oh that silly thing,' said Lou. 'You'll have to show me how to work it again, it just doesn't like me.'

'I'll do it, Mam, you get the milk.'

Lou bustled around getting out mugs and putting a bag of sugar on the table. Joanne took a deep breath like they'd taught her in the mindfulness class. This was the next time. It was all OK. She measured the coffee into the portafilter and slipped it into the machine, focusing on the feeling of the gritty coffee on her fingers. 'I thought I might start a range of baby jewellery for my online store,' she said. Think positive, they'd taught her. Think of things other than having a baby.

'Like christening bracelets?' asked Lou.

'Yeah, that. But also jewellery for mams. Personalised silver necklaces with charms with their baby's birth dates on. Or baby feet and handprints on if they're local and I can do the moulds.'

'That's a lovely idea, chick. I'm so proud of you. Maybe you could persuade Mandy to stock some of your bits in the shop. Or maybe get your own shop one day.' She watched Joanne froth the coffee and then took the mug from her, sliding it onto the table.

'That's the dream, isn't it. My own shop.' Joanne touched her stomach. If she'd been able to get pregnant straight away, she'd probably have had her own shop by now, she thought. Instead, she'd had to stay on at Mandy's all these years holding out for maternity pay, knowing it would be difficult to take time off if she had her own place. Years of life being on hold – as Alex had steadily risen from being a student nurse to now a specialist cancer nurse. She crossed her arms over her chest. But she didn't regret it, it was all going to be worth it. 'Me and my little girl behind the counter of our own jewellery shop full of lovely things. Hopefully, one day.'

'Or boy.' Lou raised her eyebrows. 'You sure you didn't find out what you're having?'

Joanne shook her head, smiling as Mike came back and slid a box on the table. Alex followed with another, and they disappeared back down the hall.

'What's all this?' Joanne opened up a flap of the box and underneath were neatly folded baby clothes. She drew out a lemon-coloured wool cardigan and brought it to her face. Underneath the staleness, she could smell her father held between the threads.

'Oh, I remember you in that one,' said Lou. 'Isn't it tiny? It must have been when I first met your dad.'

Alex came into the kitchen with two white wooden frames, followed by Mike with two side panels, which caught on the door jamb.

'And what's that?' asked Joanne, smiling. Lou rested her hand on Joanne's shoulder.

Mike looked up at her. 'It's your old cot, love. The one you slept in as a baby. I thought you might like it for your baby. Keep the tradition, like.'

Joanne touched the side rail of the cot, the paint flaking beneath her fingers. She frowned. Somewhere, a memory floated of her holding on to this bar and shouting. But the more she concentrated on it, the more it slipped away just out of reach. She stroked the wood. She was sure she'd bitten this and sure enough, underneath her fingers she could feel small indentations. Tiny teeth marks. She definitely remembered her half-brother, Patrick – born four years after her – in this cot, rattling the bars for attention. She used to stand there and taunt him with toys.

'Of course, we can sand it down, love. Make it good as new.' Anxiety threaded through Mike's voice.

'I'll clean it up so it's properly shining,' said Lou. 'And you'll need to get a new mattress.'

It wasn't always white, Joanne thought. There had been cartoons on the end. She went to the end boards that Alex was holding and turned them round. On the other side there was a faded Bagpuss. Joanne traced her finger around his face. It had been bright pink, she remembered now.

'We'll sand that off, love. It's probably toxic paint.' Her father again.

Joanne looked up at the three of them, watching her. 'I remember this,' she whispered. 'I'm so glad you kept it.'

Mike sighed and his face eased into a sad smile. 'Your mum would have wanted you to have this,' he said quietly. 'This was her cot when she was a baby. Grace's mum and dad gave it to us when she had you.'

Joanne closed her eyes, holding on to the side rail. She had so few things of her birth mother's. Just the one picture of her wedding to Mike, which she kept in a drawer so as not to upset Lou. Occasionally, she took it out and studied the smiling face of the woman who looked so like her but she'd never met, who had slipped out of this world as Joanne had entered it. She shivered and folded the memory away. She mustn't dwell on that. Not now. Focus on the positives.

'You all right, love?' Alex said.

Joanne opened her eyes and smiled at the concerned faces looking at her. 'Yes, sorry. I just remember this cot. It took me back.' She touched the silver scar that wound its way lazily up her neck, like a river.

'Maybe we shouldn't have brought it over,' said Mike, watching her and rubbing his head again.

'Don't be silly, Dad, it's perfect. I love it.' Joanne smiled, genuinely this time. 'I'd love our baby to have the cot that I had, and my mother before me.' It felt strange saying *mother* out loud. She so rarely used the word. She'd always called her stepmother Mam.

'Let's get it upstairs then, and Alex can put it together. Give us a hand, Alex, and we can shift those boxes too.'

'Now that we've had the scan, we can start getting the baby's room ready,' said Joanne to Lou as the men disappeared up the narrow staircase, banging the cot against the walls.

'It's so exciting, Jo love. You really deserve this after everything you've been through. And Patrick has a load more stuff from his two that he can bring over. Toys and the like. Your baby won't want for nothing.'

Joanne thought of Patrick's house round the corner, their two busy toddlers. It was hard to believe that she would soon have a baby too. After all those years of hoping, it was finally happening.

'Come on,' said Lou. 'I'll take this box, let's follow the men and you can start getting that nursery ready.'

Later, after Mike and Lou had left, Joanne sat on the little window seat of the box room unpacking the two boxes of clothes while Alex rubbed down the cot ready to paint. She looked around. They hadn't changed the swirly seventies wallpaper since they moved in just after they married, more than ten years ago now. They hadn't wanted to jinx it. She'd been using the room as a workshop for her jewellery making, trying not to think about what it might one day become as she hammered out silver bangles on the anvil. The room had been waiting, just like she'd been waiting, for so long, since she'd gone off the Pill on their honeymoon. But now they could finally start preparing for the baby. Her eyes sparkled.

'I thought we could paint this room a light yellow. It gets the morning sun, so it'll be lovely and bright. A frieze around the top. Of birds and animals.' It was a conversation they'd had many times before. The paint was in the shed, untouched from when he'd bought it eight years ago. The frieze sat rolled up in the bottom of the chest of drawers, bought when she reached the twelve-week point in her second pregnancy, only to miscarry three weeks later.

Alex nodded and grinned at her. 'I'm doing nights next week, so I've got four days off after. I'll start then. Then all the paint smells will be gone by the time the baby arrives.' He walked over to the window seat and dropped a kiss on her head. 'I'm so proud of you.'

Joanne turned her face up, her eyes soft. 'We made it in the end.'

Alex closed his eyes and sighed. 'Yes.' He swallowed and walked back to the cot.

'I'll buy some fabric for some curtains and maybe a new pad for this window seat and start on them.' Joanne took out another cardigan, a pale blue this time, and stacked it with the others next to her. Underneath was a terry-towelling jumpsuit she vaguely remembered. She'd worn this on the beach, she thought, until it was so tight she could hardly walk.

'I'll rub that down and repaint it,' Joanne said, looking at the old chest of drawers in the corner. 'Then I can put these clothes in there once I've washed them.'

Alex shook his head. 'I don't want you painting anything. You know what the doctor said. Take it easy. I'll do it when I've painted the room.'

'Yes, nurse,' she said lightly, and he rolled his eyes at her.

Joanne stroked her belly again. *Stay in there*, she thought. If she lost this baby, there would be no more chances. Not at her age. And anyway, they'd used up all her stored eggs. The decent ones, at least. Just the tired old ones were left, buried at the bottom of the freezer, like out-of-date peas. 'I'll get some lining paper for the drawers then. And start on a quilt once I've done the curtains. Mam has that pattern.'

Alex put the sanding paper down and slid the cot against the wall. 'This will be perfect,' he said, looking down between the slats. 'It's hard to believe our baby will be sleeping here in a few months' time.'

Their eyes met and they both smiled, almost shyly. There was so much left unsaid, she thought, but maybe that was the best way. Mam said that, in a long marriage, it was better that some things were hidden.

Joanne reached into the box and drew out a cream cardigan with a Fair Isle design picked out in pink around the top. If they had a girl, this would be perfect. She was about to throw the empty box on the floor when a square slice of paper slipped out from under the cardboard flap. It was face down, but she realised from its size and shininess that it was a Polaroid photo. Joanne picked it up and turned it over. An unlined version of her dad's face grinned back at her, his arm resting on the shoulder of a woman with curly dark hair piled on top of her head, strands wild about her face. It was like looking in a mirror. Grace. My birth mam, thought Joanne. Then suddenly Lou's face came to mind and she felt a stab of guilt. Lou was her mam.

Joanne's stomach flutter flickered up to her throat, suddenly making it difficult to breathe. 'Alex, look. I've never seen this photo before. Why has no one ever shown this to me?'

GRACE

NOVEMBER 1974

'I'm late,' I whispered to Susie, leaning towards her sewing machine and waiting for her reaction.

She screwed her face up. 'Late?' Her eyes widened and she took her foot off the pedal, the needle slowing down. 'Oh, *late*. Oh my God. Grace!' she squealed, and she covered her mouth with her hand.

Mrs Cornford snapped round to look in our direction and we both ducked our heads.

'How late?' Susie said out of the corner of her mouth, making a show of rethreading her machine.

'Two weeks,' I whispered, tucking a curl behind my ear so I could see her better without being obvious.

'But you're never late,' Susie said.

I bit my lip to stop myself from smiling. 'I know.' There was a fluttery feeling in my belly. Maybe that was the baby. *If* there was a baby.

She raised her eyebrows. 'Do you feel different at all?'

I shook my head. I'd examined every sensation I'd felt over the last few days but there was nothing to suggest that I was pregnant. My clothes still fitted and I hadn't been sick like Jackie Wright was when she was expecting.

Mrs Cornford levered herself up from her desk and walked towards our line. I looked back at the machine and carefully fitted the double-grooved foot, took a piece of cord, turned the bright blue damask over its length and slipped it under the needle. Out of the corner of my eye, I could see her getting closer. She passed Maisie, who sat with a mouthful of pins at the end of the line. Then she moved on to Ethel, who always bit her lip as she sewed, leaning over her back to watch her stitching. She stood directly behind me as I jammed my foot on the pedal until the entire length of cord was enclosed and then I released it from the machine, snipping off the ends.

'Very nice, Mrs Bennett.'

'Thank you, Mrs Cornford,' I murmured, picking up another piece of damask, feeling her move to stand behind Susie, hands on her overstuffed hips. Susie was the untidiest seamstress in the upholstery factory. Her space was always littered with discarded pins, stray pieces of fabric, old threads and handfuls of padding.

Susie felt her presence too, because she dropped her chalk. It slid under my chair and I leaned down to pick it up, handing it over to her with what I hoped was a sympathetic look.

'There's enough wasted fabric here to make an entire three-piece suite,' Mrs Cornford said, her voice carrying over the rattle of machines. 'If you carry on like this, Mrs Carter, I'll make sure Mr Rogers docks it from your wages.'

Out of the corner of my eye, I could see the blush rise up Susie's neck. 'I'm sorry, Mrs Cornford,' she said. 'I'll try harder.'

'Make sure you do.' She waddled off down the line, her dark button eyes missing nothing.

We both knew Mr Rogers would never dock our wages. He was best friends with Dad, who worked next door in the factory's joinery section. And Mrs Cornford knew that too, which annoyed her all the more.

When Mrs Cornford had returned to her paperwork, Susie glanced over to me. 'Have you told your mum?'

I shook my head. 'Not even Mike. I thought I'd go to the doctor first. Make sure I'm right. I don't want everyone getting all excited and it's just me getting my dates wrong.' I looked down at the fabric, which was beginning to bunch, and took my foot off the pedal. I knew I didn't have my dates wrong. I'd been over and over them. My visitor came like clockwork, every twenty-nine days. And it should have come fifteen days ago. But it hadn't. If I'm honest, I had been wondering if it would happen. Mike and I hadn't always been that careful in the four years since we were married. He'd wanted to wait for a bit, but I couldn't wait to start a family.

'I bet you don't have your dates wrong,' Susie said. 'You were always better at maths than me.' She gave a little smile. 'Oh my God, Gracie, you're going to have a baby.'

I giggled. She was as excited as me.

The bell rang and we all leaped up, abandoning our cushions mid-stitch to grab our coats. Mrs Cornford pursed her lips as we all rushed for the door. 'Fifteen minutes, please. Not a second more. Especially you, Mrs Carter.'

We threaded our way through the throng and found our usual perch in a small patch of weak winter sunshine.

'God, I hate her, Gracie,' moaned Susie, taking out a packet of Silk Cut, lighting two and passing one to me. 'She's always telling me off.'

'Oh Suse.' I took a deep drag and slipped my arm round her shoulders. It was true. Mrs C did seem to have it in for her. 'Just try to keep your head down. Don't do anything to provoke her.'

'But I don't. She just picks on me. You could make the same mistake as me, and she wouldn't notice or would just be really nice about it.'

I nodded. 'Just ignore her. Who cares what she thinks anyway? She's ancient.'

Susie laughed. 'Yeah, her face is like an old piece of wrinkled linen.'

'She needs a good iron.' We both giggled and took another drag.

'Actually, I'd say she's more like suede. Liable to age quickly.'

I snorted and smoke puffs came out of my nose like a dragon. 'What about Mrs Beatty?' I asked, taking another pull.

Susie put her head on one side. 'Hmmm. How about leather? Hard-working, long-lasting and . . .'

'A bit of an old cow?'

'Grace Bennett!' said Susie. 'I didn't expect that from you.'

I smiled. I liked making her laugh.

'What about Linda?' I asked.

'It's got to be a red satin,' Susie said after a pause. 'Glossy, elegant, but a bit slippery.'

I smirked. 'Valerie would be a pair of denim jeans. Sturdy and—'

'Common!' shrieked Susie, and we both doubled over in laughter.

'We should stop being so mean,' I said, not really wanting to stop at all but starting to feel a little sick. I stubbed out my ciggie on the wall. 'Let's think of nice things.'

Susie nodded. 'My mum would be a tweed. Hard-wearing, warm, and comforting.'

'Awww, I love your mum,' I said. 'My mum would be a burgundy velvet. Warm and cosy to cuddle up with.'

Susie smiled. 'Your sister Emily would be a pale cream silk. Smooth and elegant but difficult to handle.'

'God yeah, I don't miss living with her, that's for sure. I've never known someone so difficult.'

Susie touched my arm. She knew how hard things had been with Emily at times. The darkness of her moods followed by a sudden energy where she'd tidy the house incessantly and shout at anyone who so much as dirtied a mug. 'Though I'm getting on with her much better since we don't live together any more. Mike doesn't steal my mascara or borrow my clothes like she did. Though he's been a bit off recently. Preoccupied.'

'Imagine when you tell him you're having a baby,' said Susie, her whole face smiling. 'He'll be so excited. Everyone will be, Gracie.'

'I don't know for sure,' I said. 'Until it's confirmed by the doctor, I don't want to get my hopes up.' I tried to stop myself smiling but the truth was I couldn't wait to tell the world.

'Will you two girls stop gossiping out there and get back to work.' Mrs Cornford's voice was like a scissor blade cutting through fabric. 'Didn't you hear the bell?'

Susie stubbed out her ciggie on the wall and we scrambled to our feet. There was another flutter in my tummy that I thought might be the baby. I reached down to stroke it.

Susie grinned. 'See, you're definitely expecting. I've seen all pregnant ladies do that,' she whispered as we walked back inside.

I looked down at my flat stomach and thought of the tiny baby in there beginning to grow. I couldn't stop the smile taking over my face. Mike would be so excited when I told him.

Chapter 2

Joanne

August 2021

Joanne stared at the photo, drinking in the way Grace was smiling at her dad rather than into the camera. She must have loved him, she thought. It was a strangely intimate look. Alex squeezed next to her on the window seat of the little box room.

'What is it?' he asked. 'I thought it was only all your old baby clothes in those boxes.'

'It was, but this was at the bottom, hiding underneath the flap. Look – it's a picture of my birth mam with Dad before I was born.'

The couple were standing on a seafront, the sea a faded blue in the background, windbreaks crisscrossing the beach. Grace was wearing a long orange and brown patterned maxi dress and little heels. Her mother's hair was piled on top of her head, just like Joanne wore hers now. Despite the excess of hair, she was dwarfed by Mike.

'Your mum was tiny, wasn't she? You take after her. And your hair is identical,' said Alex. 'She was beautiful, just like you.' He stroked the scar on her neck, something he'd started doing not long after they first met, almost fifteen years ago, when she'd accused him of hating it.

Joanne glanced up at him and smiled. It was a long time since he'd last said that she was beautiful. Underneath the picture, loopy handwriting in blue fountain pen had written Us waiting for baby Joanne or Justin, May 1975, Brighton beach. She traced her fingers along the text. 'This must be her handwriting. I've never seen it before.'

'May 1975,' said Alex. 'She would have been pregnant with you.'

Joanne let out a breath. 'Of course.' And now she could see the way the dress disguised her mother's growing bump. 'That's me in there,' she said, smiling up at Alex.

Alex slipped his arm around Joanne and they both leaned over the photo. 'Which means I would have been called Justin if I'd been a boy,' said Joanne. 'How funny to think that. That once they were there, happy and healthy, all excited about me being born.'

Joanne closed her eyes. Suddenly it all felt too much. The first tears trickled on to her cheeks. 'She never knew whether I was a boy or a girl. Joanne or Justin. She never got that chance.' She held her small bump, as if drawing in the baby to comfort her.

'Oh Jo,' said Alex, putting his other arm round her and enveloping her in a hug. 'Don't get upset. Lou has been more than a mam to you.'

Joanne opened her eyes and sniffed loudly. 'I know. It's just so sad seeing this photo, how happy they both look. I've never even seen her handwriting before. And to see that they'd planned names for if I was a boy or a girl. Just as we're doing now. But a few months later she was dead. Having that baby killed her. I killed her.' Joanne sniffed again and took a tissue out of her maternity jeans pocket to blow her nose.

Alex scratched his beard. 'Jo, you didn't kill her. She died in childbirth, it's a different thing. They didn't have all the technology for giving birth in those days. It's completely changed now. Just like the way we used to treat cancer patients is so different to what I now do every day on the oncology ward.'

Joanne nodded slowly and looked back at the writing. Her own mother had written those words.

'Wait, this was in Brighton?' said Alex, leaning forward. 'Were you born there? I thought you were a born and bred Berwicker. You've been deceiving me – you're a southerner all along.'

Joanne laughed, suddenly glad that he was trying to lighten the mood. 'I am a proper northerner. I was born in Brighton, that's true. I've always known that. My dad came up here after my mam died. I think I was a month old or something when we came to Berwick, and we stayed here ever since. She's buried down there.'

'Hmm, you're still a soft southerner.' Alex laughed, kissed the top of her head and got up, picking up the empty box. He turned it upside down and sliced down the base of it with his thumbnail. As he started to fold the box flat, several more Polaroids fell onto the carpet. Joanne slid off the window seat and bent to pick them up. Her throat suddenly felt thick again. She felt Alex grip her shoulders as she turned them over.

A young woman was holding a tiny baby, wrapped in a white shawl. In the background was the metal frame of a hospital bed. The woman's long curly hair was spread across the pillow and around her face. She was looking down at the baby in her arms. It was unmistakably Grace. And she was holding what could only be a baby Joanne.

Alex's mouth hung open, and he turned to Joanne, who was clutching her chest. 'Give it to me.' Joanne grabbed the photo and brought it close to her face. 'That's Grace, isn't it? That's Grace and me.' Joanne looked up at Alex. 'I don't understand.' She took small, shaky breaths, trying to squeeze air into her lungs.

'Nor do I,' said Alex, looking down at the photo.

On the back of the photo, the same looping handwriting had written:

Born: 5.35am, 11 July 1975 at Royal Sussex County Hospital, Brighton

Weight: 7 lbs, 6 ozs

'My birth mam didn't die having me,' Joanne said dully, her arms suddenly feeling weak. The photo slipped down her lap and Alex caught it. 'Why would Dad say she did when she didn't?' She screwed up her face and covered it with her hands as tears slipped down her cheeks.

'Maybe she didn't die immediately. Maybe it was the next day, or something like that. That can happen. So it was just easier to say in childbirth.' He swallowed, looked around the room and then back at the photo. 'Maybe the loopy handwriting isn't your mam's. It could be her mam or a friend, or something.'

'Then why would she write 'Us waiting for baby' on the first photo. That's not Dad's writing, so it must be Grace's. She was alive long enough to write down the time I was born and my weight.'

Alex was silent. He picked up the other Polaroids from where Joanne had dropped them on the floor. One was of Grace, still in the hospital bed but with an older woman sitting on a chair next to her and a younger woman crouching behind. Underneath, in different handwriting – spiky, with a biro – someone had written *Mummy and me with Granny* and *Susie*.

Joanne crossed her arms over her belly.

Alex slowly turned over the next photograph. It was of a couple standing in front of a small cottage, roses around the door, like a child might draw. They were holding a baby wrapped in a shawl. The baby's face wasn't visible, but the man and woman were undoubtedly Mike and Grace. Grace's hair was loose down her back, the curls framing her face. Mike was wearing a patterned tank top and had long sideburns.

'That must be them bringing me home from hospital. That's us outside the cottage they had in Brighton,' said Joanne slowly. 'They brought me home, Alex. Grace never died. At least, not in childbirth.' She started to cry properly now, her chest heaving, her mind roiling with confusion. 'What the hell happened to her?'

Alex gently put the photos next to him on the window seat, before sliding his arm around Joanne's shoulder again. He stroked her shoulder. 'Don't get upset, Jo. I'm sure there's a simple explanation—'

Joanne exhaled, a bubble blowing out of her nostril. 'Don't get upset?' she said, louder than she'd meant to. 'How the hell am I supposed to feel when it turns out I've been lied to about something so important, all these years?' A sharp pain flicked through her stomach, making her wince.

Alex's eyes darted to her belly. 'What's the matter?'

'Nothing.' Joanne shook her head. 'Just a twinge. Let's look at the photos again,' she said, leaning across Alex for them. She wiped her hand under her nose and sniffed.

But Alex covered the photos with his hand. 'No, we need to stop. You're going to make yourself ill. And my baby ill. I'm sure it's just a misunderstanding.'

'Alex, please—' said Joanne, trying to grab the Polaroids.

'No, Jo,' said Alex, standing up and holding the photos firmly in his hand. 'I get you want to know more about this, but it isn't all just about you.' He sighed. 'I know it's mostly about you,' he corrected himself. 'But it's my last chance to be a dad too. Everyone focuses on you. But I'm here too. I'm going through it too.' He pulled at his beard.

'You're not really going through it though, are you?' she said, a wave of anger making her sound harsher than she'd intended. 'You're not the one who had the daily injections, who had to take all those pills, who had everyone peering at your bits all the time and sticking things up inside you.' She grimaced at the memory of the doctor and his dreaded ultrasound probe, and stared at Alex. 'All you have to do is look at porn and wank in a jar. Then it's job done and hope for the best.' She turned away and walked out of the box room.

'I might not have to do much physically,' he said, following her down the stairs into the kitchen. 'But everyone focuses on you, looks after you, asks after you.' He shrugged. 'Nobody ever asks how I feel. It's all completely out of my control.' Alex's shoulders slumped.

'It's out of my control too,' said Joanne dully, her silver cuff bangle clanking against the kitchen counter.

'But it's happening in you. It's central to you,' Alex said, gesturing towards her. 'I'm not even part of it. I've wanted this for so long.' He glanced at her. 'We've wanted this for so long,' he clarified. 'I just don't want to risk anything. Please put this out of your mind for now. I can see how it affects you physically – you all tense up. You look stressed. I bet you anything your blood pressure is up. You just need to leave it. For now.' His eyes were soft, begging.

Joanne crossed her arms above her bump. 'I'm sorry you feel that way. But this is happening to me, it's largely about me. And my baby—'

'*Our* baby,' emphasised Alex.

Joanne ignored him. 'It's me who has struggled to become a mum, not you. There's nothing wrong with you. Your sperm is merrily swimming around, desperate for action. It's my insides that are twisted and now ancient.' She screwed up her face, willing herself not to cry any more. Not to prove him right.

'Exactly, it's our last chance.' He held his hands out. 'For both of us to be parents. I don't want you to be worried about this. Go round and see your dad and ask him if you want to. I'm sure he'll explain it all and then you can relax. Just don't get stressed. Think of our baby.' His voice was suddenly hard.

Joanne nodded, closed her eyes and took a deep breath. 'I'll go there now.'

'I'll come with you.'

She shook her head. 'No, I want to do this on my own.'

GRACE

JANUARY 1975

'They must know we can't afford to buy much,' I said, as we slipped into Hanningtons' children's department behind two women, one pushing a huge Silver Cross pram.

'I know, but it doesn't harm to look. I want to get you a present now it's all confirmed by the doctor and everyone knows your news. If I really saved up—'

I laughed and rolled my eyes at Susie. She was hopeless at saving. Even if she had the money in the first place.

But I loved it in Hanningtons too. Crisp white cotton dresses with the most delicate broderie anglaise sleeves on padded hangers, the matching knickers underneath, the smallest sailor suits with stiff white collars. Stacks of bonnets in the softest wool. Piles of delicate muslin cloths in different colours. Even nappies looked expensive here – the softest terry towelling in front of a picture of a smiling baby. The sort of place where you could pretend for a moment that you were rich and you could wave your hand and buy anything.

The sales assistant, a girl we knew vaguely from school, looked up and gave us a small smile and then went to greet the women with the pram. She knew where the money was. We walked past the shiny expensive prams lined up as if for inspection, not daring to touch the polished handles, past the racks of cotton vests, swaddled in plastic, to the baby equipment area. We both loved the cribs, the bath stands, the baby bouncers, the changing boxes and even the special lidded nappy buckets. Susie stroked the bath stand.

'Don't even think about it,' I said. 'You know what your mum will say.'

Susie smiled. 'Use the sink, you don't need no baby bath.' She did a perfect mimic of her mum and we both laughed.

'Mike would say the same thing.' We walked into the maternity clothes section.

'He's going to be a good dad, isn't he?' she said, with her thinking face on.

'Yes. He said initially that he wanted to wait a little, but he's always wanted his own family. He tries to pretend he's not as excited as me, but I know he is. Sometimes I catch him just looking at nothing at all and I know he's thinking about the baby.' I sighed. 'But I think it makes him sad, that his mum and dad aren't around any more, to see the baby when she comes.'

Susie touched my shoulder, her face soft. 'He's a good man, Mike,' she said. 'A really good man.'

She was right. I still felt a little tingly and excited when I woke up next to him, like I needed to pinch myself to make sure I wasn't dreaming. He'd been the quiet boy at school, who sat at the back and wasn't very good at football. But his best friend, John, who he'd known since infant school and who Susie had fallen in love with as soon as she clapped eyes on him in junior school, brought him out of himself. The four of us had been a little gang in juniors and then gone up to the senior school together. Things had been weird for a couple of years as our friendships with Mike and John developed into romances, but by the time we left school, we were very much a foursome again. When Mike proposed soon after we started work at the furniture factory, Mum and Dad made us wait until I was twenty-one, just to make sure that we were sure. But I'd always known he was the only one for me. He had a really strong sense of right and wrong, even then, such as when he stood up for the Indian boy who hardly spoke any English and was being bullied. 'It weren't right,' he said afterwards as he held his hand underneath his bleeding nose, having taken one of the bully's punches. Mike and I were married just before Susie and John. Susie's parents had made them wait too.

We walked away from the bath stand. 'If you could buy anything, what would you go for?' she said, looking around. 'Money's no object.'

I glanced over the dresses and the little cardigans. There'd be no point buying something I could make myself, that'd be a waste. The bath stand, though. I couldn't make that. And I'd never known anyone to have anything like it. 'The bath stand,' I said. 'I could put it in the bathroom next to the bath and put the baby's lotions on the shelf underneath. It'd look lovely.' I carried on looking around, imagining my perfect nursery. A wooden cot with a lacy white canopy. A specially designed changing table with the drawers underneath. A wooden rocking chair filled with plump cushions for feeding the baby on. And then, in the corner, there was a pile of small square books wrapped in paper and cellophane. On the cover there was a cartoon baby waving goodbye to a stork and the title *Baby's Record Book*. I picked up the display copy and turned over the first page. *My Mum and Dad*. There were gaps to fill in information about the parents. About how you felt, expecting a baby. What did they expect you to say? Of course everyone would say how excited they were. I flipped over the next stiff page and there was a page for the baby's arrival – the time and hospital name – then the baby's weight and height over the first few months, the eye and hair colour, and when she took her first steps. Imagine having a book like this and writing down every detail of the baby's life.

'Look, Suse,' I said, turning back to her. She was still fingering the maternity dungarees. 'Look at this.' She wandered over and I handed her the book. 'It's got sections where you can write in your baby's weight and when they get their first teeth and everything.'

Susie flicked through the first few pages. 'That's such a great idea. Look, you can get your photos developed and then put them in here.' She turned over another page. 'Oh look, Your *Baby's First Christmas*. Look at the drawings. They're really sweet.'

'I'm going to buy it,' I said firmly.

'Really?' said Susie. She flipped it over and her eyes widened. 'It's quite expensive.' She put it back on the table.

'But I'm never going to be able to afford that baby bath and I'm making almost everything else. This will be about the only thing I'll buy new.' I smiled and picked up a wrapped book from the pile and slipped it under my arm, imagining myself sitting next to the cot, recording when my new baby fell asleep on her first night. 'I can't wait to show Mike.'

Susie looked at me. 'I have some news of my own.'

'Oh?' I glanced at her and realised her face was quivering, like a balloon about to pop. My stomach did a flip, which I knew wasn't the baby.

'You remember when you said you were late, all those weeks ago?'

I nodded and stared at her. Was she?

She must have seen the question on my face because she grinned. 'I am too!'

'How late?' I said, a big smile spreading across my face.

'A month,' she said, closing the baby book and handing it back to me.

'A month!' I squealed. 'How have you kept this secret for a month?' I could feel my mouth hanging open as I stared at her.

Behind Susie, the older saleswoman looked over at us, her lips pursed.

Susie sighed. 'Well, I'm not so organised as you. I didn't realise that I was late for the first fortnight. It was only when we went to the club that I realised I hadn't had my visitor since before the last time we were there. I went to the doctor last week with Mum and they confirmed it yesterday.'

I hugged her, burying my face in her blonde hair, breathing in the smell of her shampoo. 'I'm so pleased for you,' I said, drawing back and looking at her. Her face was infused with happiness. 'You're going to be an amazing mum.'

'So are you,' she said. 'I'm just so glad we're doing this together.'

I laughed and took her arm. 'We've always done everything together, so why should this be any different?'

We started to walk away.

'True,' said Susie, laughing, then turning back. 'Hold on,' she added over her shoulder as she grabbed another baby record book off the display. 'I'll have one too, then we can fill it out together.'

'Brilliant,' I said as we linked arms again. 'I've got loads of patterns for baby clothes that you can borrow. Mum gave them to me. Some of them are quite old but they're lovely. Little matinee jackets and the sweetest little bootees. And I think there are some in the library too, if we can tear ourselves away from Mills & Boon.'

Susie squeezed my arm. 'I can't wait to get started, but Mum says I should wait a bit. Just to see. Not to tempt fate.'

'Oh, don't be silly, Suse, you'll be fine.' I just wanted us to be sitting together, knitting for our babies. 'And as my baby grows out of things, I can pass them on to you. When are you due?'

'The doctor said mid-September. Imagine if the baby came on my birthday!'

'A double present,' I said, counting on my fingers. 'So yours will be two months younger than mine. That's perfect.'

Susie picked up a cream broderie anglaise dress and stroked the collar.

'What do you want to have? Boy or girl?' I asked her, already thinking about two little girls in matching outfits being best friends, as Susie and I had been. 'I think mine's a girl,' I said. Susie was still looking at the dress. 'Mum's made me promise only to knit lemon and white but I'm desperate to do a pink bonnet at least. But she said it'll be a waste of wool if it's a boy.'

'I'd like a girl too,' Susie said, taking the dress off the rack and holding it against her flat tummy. 'Imagine buying dresses like this for them. We could have matching girls, like twins. Just like we were at school.'

I laughed, feeling warm inside. My little girl was going to grow up with my best friend's little girl, a ready-made best friend. And if Susie had a boy, they could get married and Susie and I would be real family. Or was that naive? I squeezed her arm and looked back at the dress. 'Even if we both have girls, I can't see us being able to afford even one of those dresses. But I could try to copy it on my machine at home.'

We joined arms again. 'C'mon then,' she said. 'Let's pay for these baby books and then go home and start finding some patterns.'

Chapter 3

Joanne

August 2021

Joanne closed the front door behind her and walked down the street. The shouting from the rowers on the river grew louder as she rounded the corner and the glistening ribbon of the Tweed came into view. In front of her, the viaduct stretched across the river, the sun shimmering through the arches. The rowers were passing underneath it, through water made liquid gold by the sun. She walked on and then turned back away from it at the next street and was in front of her mam and dad's front door, the red paint slightly peeling in places. She knocked and immediately let herself in.

The layout was exactly the same as her and Alex's home. A front room, a rarely used dining room, a kitchen and bathroom on the ground floor and then three small bedrooms upstairs. She'd grown up in this house and most of the furniture hadn't changed. The Formica kitchen table was still there, the old bench seats covered with sticky plastic.

'Oh, hello, love,' said her dad, looking up from the local paper.

'Fancy a cuppa, love? I was just putting the kettle on.' Lou always had a pot of tea on the go.

'Thanks, Mam.' Joanne slipped on to the bench opposite Mike. She needed to get it out straight away or she was going to lose her nerve. 'Dad, I wanted to ask you something.'

Mike folded the paper in half and slid it away from him. He looked up at Joanne.

'When did Grace die?' The name felt foreign in her mouth. Joanne watched as a cloud seemed to cast a shadow over Mike's face.

He pressed his lips together and shook his head slightly. 'Oh Jo, we've been through this. You know Grace died having you. I was worried giving you that cot would set you off. We should never have done it.' He looked up at Lou, shaking his head.

Lou put the teapot on the table with the mugs and slid on to the bench seat next to Mike. She stirred the tea in the pot and then started pouring.

'It's not the cot, Dad. I found something in the boxes.'

Mike looked up. 'Found what? What have you found?' Lou slid Joanne's old fairy mug across the table to her and then covered Mike's hand with hers and gave it a squeeze. But he didn't seem to notice.

'I found some old photos, Dad. At the bottom of one of the boxes.' She wished now that she'd brought them with her. 'Polaroid photos of you and Grace. One in Brighton on the seafront when she was expecting me.'

Mike looked at his hands for a long time. 'I remember that,' he said slowly. 'Grace wrote on it – the names we were thinking of calling you when we were decorating the box room.'

Joanne tapped the floor repeatedly with her foot. 'And after she had me.'

Mike smoothed his hand over his head and nodded.

'There's pictures of Grace holding me, Dad. How could she have held me if she died having me?' Joanne's voice cracked at the end, and she looked down into the sludgy tea.

Lou gasped. 'Mike?' She looked over at Joanne and bit her lip.

'She died a few days afterwards,' he whispered.

'A few days afterwards?' Joanne shouted. She stood up suddenly and the chair tipped, falling backwards on to the lino. 'I've always thought of her dying on my birthday and it's always made me sad to celebrate my birth on the day she died.' She gulped, and pushed the tears down. 'I thought all this time that I was the cause of death. That she'd died giving birth. It made me so worried to have children in case the same thing happened to me.'

Mike had his hands over his ears, his head bowed. 'Don't shout so.'

'How did she die?' said Joanne, looking down at him, her hands planted on the table either side of the mug.

'I think it was a fall. A head injury as a result of a fall,' he said softly.

'You *think* it was a fall? You don't actually know how your wife died?' Joanne knew she was shouting again.

'Jo, calm—' Lou got up and moved round the table to rest her hand on Joanne's shoulder. 'The baby—' Her face was creased with concern.

'Things were different in those days,' whispered Mike. 'They never told you nothing. But her death was caused by the birth, which is why I said that.' His eyes darted towards Joanne and Lou and away again.

'So you lied to me.' Joanne closed her eyes. 'When did she die then? What date? What date should I remember my mother on if it wasn't my birthday?' She opened her eyes again and glanced up at Lou. 'I'm sorry, I—'

Lou shook her head. 'Don't be silly, love.'

'I-I-I can't remember.' Mike spoke so quietly Joanne could hardly hear.

'What?'

Lou had picked up the chair. Joanne could feel her guiding her to it to sit down.

'You've forgotten when Grace died?' Joanne heard the sneer in her voice. Mike was looking down at his white knuckles.

'Let me refresh your memory. There's a picture in that book of you and Grace taking me home. You're standing outside a cottage. She was out of hospital and she looked fine. So what happened?'

Mike shook his head and closed his eyes.

'Dad! Tell me. I need to know. You lied to me.'

'She had a fall and hit her head, love, not long after the birth. That's all I can tell you.' He ran his hand over his head, again smoothing down his non-existent hair.

'How do I even know that's true?' Joanne waved her hands and knocked over the fairy cup that she'd drunk out of for as long as she could remember. 'She looks fine in the picture outside the cottage. Not like someone who would have a fall and die.' The pale liquid sloshed over the side of the table as the cup rolled off and smashed on the floor, shards skittering across the room.

Lou leaped aside as Joanne stormed off down the corridor, slamming the front door on her way out.

◆ ◆ ◆

Joanne sat with Alex in their front room.

'I can't believe that Dad'd lie to me about this. About something so important.' She sighed. 'All these years I've hated celebrating my birthday because I thought it was the day Grace died, and it wasn't at all.'

'It does seem odd,' said Alex, his arm around her. 'I can't think why he would do that. But look, he's a good man. He must have had some reason. Don't let it spoil things. Not when we've just had the all-clear. I don't want you worrying when we should be celebrating. We always tell patients that stress is the worst thing you can do to your body. Listen to Nurse Alex.' He tried a smile.

'I'm not worrying,' she said. 'I just want to know what happened to my birth mother. Please give me those photos back. I want to look at them again.'

But Alex shook his head. 'No, love, not now. Let's just let the dust settle a bit. I really don't want you getting that upset again. Think of the baby. You know what the doctor said. No stress, no excitement. Rest. Listen to the nurse,' he tried again.

Again Jo ignored him, deflecting his attempt at humour. 'Oh, come on, they're my photos. It's my right.' Her eyes flicked around the room, looking for the square photos with the loopy handwriting.

Alex scratched his beard and looked down. 'I don't want to fight with you, Jo, but you should leave this. If your dad said that Grace died of a head injury, then accept it.'

'I can't.' She shook her head. 'He's lied already, he could still be lying.'

Alex sighed. 'Your dad's not the lying type.'

'Well, I'm going to find out for myself. I saw on the telly that you can get death certificates off the internet now. I should be able to find out from that when she died.'

Alex sighed again, his eyebrows squeezed together. Joanne glanced at him. 'Then you can put it to rest?'

'Yes,' Joanne said, nodding.

Alex sighed and stroked her shoulder. 'I'll get the laptop. Hold on.'

Joanne thought again of the picture of her mother in hospital, holding her. Even her eyes were smiling. She'd looked beautiful. Happy. Healthy. How could she have simply died a few days later?

Something flickered in her tummy. Joanne looked down. Was it wind, or was it something more significant? The baby's way of letting her know that she was OK. Or he. Joanne smiled and stroked the top of her bump, but the feeling didn't come again. She'd wait before she told Alex, she thought. Just in case it wasn't. She gave a small smile.

Alex dropped back on to the sofa with the laptop. After a Google search, they had the right website and Joanne tapped in her mother's name, 1975 as the year of death and Brighton as the location. 'That's wide enough that it'll come up,' she said, pressing the find button.

A short list of names appeared on the screen. All Bennetts who had died in 1975 in Brighton. Eric Walter, Harriet Louise, James Jackson. But no Grace Bennett.

'That's odd,' said Joanne, twiddling a curl around her finger.

Alex looked at the screen. 'Why don't you try searching wider, in case she died outside of Brighton. We know that I was born in the Brighton hospital but they lived just outside of Brighton I think.'

Joanne nodded and typed in the details. A long list of Bennetts came up. They scrolled through the list but there were no Graces.

They both sighed. 'How about focusing just on Brighton but expanding the date range?' Alex said.

'But we know she died just after I was born. In July 1975.'

'OK, but maybe recording her death slipped into 1976 for some reason.' Joanne slid the laptop across to him. He accidentally extended the range to 1977 and had clicked find before he realised his mistake.

'Sorry, there'll be too many now. I'll go back.'

He'd finished speaking when a list of about twenty names came up on the screen. *Grace* leaped out at them straight away. 'Look,' said Joanne, her heart thumping. 'Grace Bennett. Oh—' She scanned across and saw the date. 'June 1977. That can't be her.' She sighed and her shoulders dropped. They must be looking in the wrong place.

'Hold on,' said Alex. 'How old would your mam have been when she died? In her twenties, yeah?'

'Yes, she was twenty-five when she had me.'

Alex counted on his fingers. 'So she was born in 1950.'

Joanne nodded without thinking, wondering again if the bubbly feeling in her tummy was the baby.

'Then this could be your mam,' said Alex, pointing at the screen. 'It's just the death date that doesn't match up. But how many Grace Bennetts could there be who were born in 1950 and died in Brighton in the mid-seventies? It's too much of a coincidence.' He slid the computer across to her.

Joanne turned to look at the screen, a funny feeling in her stomach that she knew this time had nothing to do with the baby. Alex was right. It was too much of a coincidence. She clicked on the link and up came the full name, Grace Elizabeth.

She looked up at Alex. 'Her middle name was Elizabeth, that's why my middle name is Elizabeth too. That must be her.' Tears formed in her eyes. 'But June 1977. Surely they wouldn't have waited that long to report her death?'

Alex slipped his arm around Joanne again. 'I'm sure there's a reasonable explanation.' But his voice didn't sound so sure.

'Dad lied about Grace dying in childbirth, then he said she died a few days later, and now it turns out it might actually be a few years later. And he was really funny about how she'd died. It was almost like he wanted to hide it.' Joanne's eyes narrowed into a frown. 'He's hiding something. I know it.'

Alex shifted on the sofa and scratched his beard again. 'I'm sure it's nothing. But if you want to be sure, why don't you order her death certificate? They must have the cause of death on there. They did with my dad last year. Then we can finally put this to rest and focus on our baby.'

Joanne nodded and passed the laptop back to Alex, who started typing away. She walked over to the mantelpiece and looked at the photo of her and her dad on her wedding day. They were standing outside the church. He had his hands clenched, ready to walk her down the aisle. She glanced at her father's face and quickly turned away.

GRACE

MARCH 1975

Mum looked like she was sucking a lemon. 'It's bad luck, Gracie love,' she said for the umpteenth time. 'Everyone says you should never bring the pram or the cot into the house until after the baby's born. It's bad luck.'

'Who says that?' I mumbled, glancing up from the pattern.

'Everyone,' she said, pursing her lips into a circle of disapproval, her knitting needles click-clacking louder than usual. 'It's a portent of doom.'

I rolled my eyes. *What rubbish. As if when you put a cot together could affect the health of your baby.* 'A what?'

'A portent of doom. Something bad will happen.' She pursed her lips. 'When your dad and I said we'd give you your old cot, we meant that we'd get it put together while you were in hospital having the baby. Not now, months in advance.' She'd said that before too.

'But Mum,' I said, picking up the stitch, 'I want the cot up now so I can measure it and start making sheets and blankets for the baby.'

'I could have given you those measurements without assembling it all,' she grumbled, but her voice was softer, the sharp edges smoothed away. She mouthed numbers as she counted along the stitches.

There was a thud from upstairs followed by a gruff 'damn'. We both looked at the ceiling and then at each other. Mum raised her eyebrows. 'Thank goodness Mike is there to help your dad.'

I smiled. It was a truce of sorts. I looked back at the blanket. Striped lemon and white, and so, so soft. Against my cheek, it felt like a wisp of cloud. In a few months, it would be tucked round our little baby. I picked up the stitch and tried to get back into the rhythm of it. I wished I was better at knitting. Susie had already knitted way more than me. Sewing was always more my thing.

Mum hummed under her breath. 'Are those new?' she said eventually, looking at the latest pile of Mills & Boon.

'Yeah, I picked them up from the library with Suse after work yesterday. Mike said I need to put my feet up more, so this gives me more chance to read.'

'I'm not sure you need much encouragement to read, love.'

I laughed. 'True.'

'You'll be there with a baby and a bottle in one hand and a book in the other.'

The stitch slipped again and, as I pulled, the whole row and then the two before it unravelled.

'Sugar.'

'Careful, or that whole blanket will fall apart,' said Mum, looking over.

'Grace,' Mike's voice called down from upstairs. 'It's ready.' Mum put her knitting aside and carefully picked up my stitch.

We went upstairs. The door to the box room was closed and Mike stood outside, a grin splitting his face.

'I want you to close your eyes and I'll guide you in.'

I smiled and did what I was told.

'No cheating now. Put your hands over your eyes like a blindfold.'

I covered my eyes with my hands, and he took my arm and I heard the click of the door as it opened. It was cooler in the box room and smelled of chemicals. They must have the window open. Mike steered me across the room. 'OK, open your eyes.'

Directly in front of me was the cot – huge, grand, and smelling of fresh white paint. The tears surged up and filled my eyes before I could stop them. 'Oh Mike, it's beautiful.' It looked just like new. Even better than some of the ones in Hanningtons.

He hugged me to him, and I wiped the tears on his shirt. 'And there's more,' he said, turning me around. On the opposite side of the room was a chest of drawers with a strange-looking lid. I'd seen these in Hanningtons too. You lifted the lid and then changed the baby's nappy on it. I'd seen the price tag too. I spun round. 'How did you get this?'

Dad stood smoking by the window. 'There was a defective one in the factory. The wood had all splintered down the back and inside. They were throwing it out. So I said I'd take it home and fix it up. They didn't mind.'

Under the lid were different compartments for changing the baby's nappy. 'You put your clean nappies here, and the liners there,' said Mum, pointing. 'Then you'll have a bucket to the side for the dirty ones to soak in. Your pot of zinc and castor oil cream goes here. To prevent nappy rash,' she added, to my questioning look.

'It's amazing,' I said, stroking the top. 'Did you know?' I asked Mum.

She nodded, a small smile lighting her face. 'We all want the best for this baby.' She walked over to the cot. 'Granny has an old nursing chair we could put next to the cot for giving the baby his bottle.'

'Her,' I corrected her.

She snorted. 'You'll get what you get. I don't want you being disappointed if it's a boy.'

'I'm certain it's a girl,' I said, feeling the bubbly sensation that I now knew was definitely the baby.

Mike slid his arm around my shoulders. 'Happy?' he said, pushing his hair out of his eyes.

'Very happy.' I smiled into his chest as he hugged me again.

After Mum and Dad went home, I stood in the baby's room watching the last of the spring sun filter through the cot's bars and cast stripes across the bare mattress. I held on to the side rail, feeling the small indentations under my fingertips – bite marks and scratches from me, Gerry and Emily. I had no memories of sleeping in this cot. By the time I'd have been old enough to remember, I was on a little truckle bed and my sisters were in here.

The end of the cot looked too white, too bare. It'd be nice to decorate it. Susie and I had seen some transfers in town – bright ones of Bagpuss, which would look pretty.

Soon Mike's and my baby would be lying on this mattress, gurgling and smiling. I picked up the baby book from the shelf and slipped it out of the cellophane wrapper. It had that new smell. Like when you get a book from the library that nobody's borrowed before. The rabbit on the front cover smiled down at the baby rabbit she rocked in a cradle.

On the first page, there was space for a photo of Mike and me. There were some wedding ones we could use, that we didn't put in the album. But it might be nice to have a new one. Perhaps of me pregnant, with Mike hugging me. We'd taken a picture on the Polaroid camera at the weekend when we'd gone into Brighton for fish and chips. I went into our bedroom and took it off the dressing table. For once I liked the way I looked. The heels went well with the dress, though they'd been murder to wear.

I picked up the pen and balanced the book on top of the chest of drawers, writing Mike's and my name in my best handwriting.

My mother's name: Grace Elizabeth Bennett

My father's name: Michael Roy Bennett

'Oh, there you are,' he said. I smiled up at Mike as he came into the room. 'I should have known you'd be in here hiding away.'

I showed him the book. 'I thought I'd start filling this out. The baby record book.'

He nodded and stood behind me, his arms around my waist, reading the text. 'We should start to think about names,' he said. 'I know it's early, but—'

I'd been waiting for him to say something about names. I didn't want to be the one to bring it up first. I nodded and touched his hand where it rested on the blank page of the book. The space where we'd write our choices of baby names.

'Do you have any ideas?' he asked, kissing the top of my head.

'Well, I—' I swallowed. What if he didn't like the name I'd chosen?

'You have, haven't you.' I could hear he was smiling.

I nodded. He spun me round. 'I might have known you'd already chosen, Mrs Bennett,' he said, laughing. 'So, tell me, what are we calling this baby?'

'I've only chosen a girl's name, to be fair. I'm sure it's a girl.'

'And?'

'Joanne,' I said, watching his face.

A slow smile spread across it. 'Joanne. Joanne?' he said. 'Joanne,' he said again, testing it out. 'Joanne. Joanne. I like it. She could shorten it to Jo if she wanted.'

'You can choose the boy's name, if you like,' I said, kissing him on the lips.

'I've been thinking about that. What do you think of Justin? Or maybe Paul?'

I shrugged my shoulders. 'Either is good with me.' It didn't matter what boy's name we chose, it was definitely a girl.

'Justin means just and fair. Paul means humble. I can't make up my mind between the two. I thought we could have my dad's name – Roy – as the middle name, whatever we chose.' I smiled and touched his cheek. He never spoke about his dad, who had died when he was young, followed by his mum in his early teens.

The spine creaked as I turned the page. I'd wait until he'd decided to write it in the book. On the bottom of the Polaroid, I wrote Us waiting for baby Joanne or Justin, May 1975, Brighton beach. Justin sounded better than Paul.

'*How do you feel about having a baby?*' I asked, reading the text and then turning my neck to catch his expression.

His chin seemed to quiver a little. 'It's all I've ever wanted,' he said. 'To marry you and have a family. Ever since that first time we went out to the Seven Sisters.' He wiped his hand over his face. 'I know I don't often show it, but I can't wait to hold it, look into his' – he looked at me and smiled slightly – 'or her eyes, see him smile. And know he's part of us. I know I said I wanted to wait a bit, but now it's happening, well, I couldn't be more proud of you.'

The tears pricked my eyes again. Mike never spoke like that. He was far more extroverted than me, always the one to strike up conversations with strangers, the life and soul of any party. But he never talked about his feelings. I looked down and started to write. He stood over me, watching me, gripping my shoulder.

Chapter 4

JOANNE

AUGUST 2021

Alex came down the stairs and popped his head round the corner of the front room. 'I'm off to work, love.'

Joanne muted the TV, jumped up and gave him a hug. 'Have a good shift. See you in the morning.'

'Promise me you'll relax and not think about any of this.' He held Joanne at arm's length and frowned at her.

'I promise,' she said, smiling widely, holding up three fingers. 'Brownie's honour.'

He laughed. 'Were you ever a Brownie?'

'No.'

He laughed again and kissed her on the forehead. 'Night, love.'

'Night.' Joanne sank back into the sofa and waited for the sound of the front door to click shut. She stared at the muted TV, watching the team of builders putting the finishing touches to an accessible bathroom, and counted to a hundred. Then she got up and went upstairs to their bedroom. She stood in the doorway and glanced around. The photos were in here somewhere, she was sure of it. Unless he'd taken them to the hospital with him. Where would he have hidden them? They were small enough to be any-where. She had to put herself in his shoes.

She knelt down next to Alex's bedside table and opened the top drawer. A jumble of sunglasses, phone chargers, old bits of electrical wire, batteries and old tissues. Next drawer down she knew was socks and pants. She slid her hand underneath them. Nothing. His section in their chest of drawers held nothing more exciting than some T-shirts, shorts, faded scrubs, and a couple of hoodies. She opened their wardrobe, but there was only a black suit he'd got last year for the funeral, a couple of shirts with a black tie draped around the hanger. Underneath were boxes of shoes – she opened them up but there was no sign of the photos. Joanne stood on tiptoe and ran her hand along the top of the wardrobe. It touched a book, and she smiled, a nervous feeling in her tummy, which she knew was triggered by the prospect of seeing the pictures of herself. With a grunt, she managed to lever the corner of the book over the top of the wardrobe and grab it. As it fell into her hands, she realised it was a book for first-time dads. She flipped it over and read aloud to the silent room:

'*Learn what to expect from the moment you find out that your significant other is pregnant. Starting with the stuff she will need to birth a healthy beautiful baby. Like what foods are best for her, what medical exams she will need, and everything else you should do to make it easier for her.*'

There was a bookmark. She flipped it open at the page. It was a postcard of a painting. Joanne turned it over. *The Bathers*. Paul Cézanne. From the National Gallery. It was blank on the back. Odd. She'd never known Alex talk about art and he'd certainly never been to the National Gallery. They'd never even visited the Berwick one. The postcard had been holding open a page about preparing your home for a new baby. So very Alex. She shook out the book but there were no photos inside. She slid the book back on top of the wardrobe. She'd wondered how Alex had known so much. It was just like him to hide it though.

Joanne knelt and looked under the bed, but it was just suitcases covered in dust that hadn't been touched for ages. She stood up and went into the baby's room. The sunset was streaming through the small window, streaking the room red and pink. The only new thing was the baby mat she'd bought in the sale yesterday. She glanced in the spare room, opening the built-in cupboard, but there were only paint tins and sheets ready for Alex to decorate the nursery.

She stood in the kitchen and mentally tracked through the down-stairs rooms. If she were Alex, where would she hide something? A place Joanne would never think to look? The bathroom door creaked as she opened it and sat on the loo. She seemed to be in here every five minutes at the moment. How much worse was it going to get before the end? She might set up home in here. She leaned over her knees to make sure she'd got the last of the wee out – a trick the midwife had taught her – and it was then she noticed a few specks of sawdust on the lino by the bath. The screw on the bath panel looked like it had been undone. Joanne pulled up her knickers and trousers in one go and flung open the cupboard under the sink, grabbing a screwdriver. She carefully undid the screw, wedging open the bath panel. Slid between the wooden bath panel and the metal bath was an envelope.

Joanne lifted it out, dropping the screwdriver and screw on the bathroom floor. She sat cross-legged, leaned back against the bath and opened it. A small stack of Polaroids was inside. Her parents stared out at her, her father grinning broadly as he gripped Grace. Joanne covered his face with one hand, tracing the loopy handwrit-ing with the other. Standing in front of the cottage, holding a baby Joanne, Grace looked healthy. Rosy cheeks. Bright eyes. Very far away from being about to die. And if it was her death certificate that she had found online then it was possible she had died months and months later, long after they'd arrived in Berwick.

The spiky handwriting – the one that couldn't have been Grace's – had scribbled Joanne's weight in her first, second, third and fourth week on the back of the picture from the hospital. But then it stopped. Underneath the three photos were two others she hadn't seen. Grace was holding the baby Joanne while sitting on a mustard-coloured sofa, the edge of a brown-and-orange-patterned wallpaper in the background. She was staring blankly at the camera, neither frowning nor smiling. The baby was crying but Grace didn't seem to notice. Underneath, the spiky handwriting said *Mummy and me, seven days old, at home*. She looked . . . Joanne couldn't think of the word. Not unhappy, but definitely not happy either. Empty, almost. Joanne swallowed, her mouth dry, and turned over the page.

The final picture was of Grace sitting cross-legged on a multicoloured rag rug, the baby in her lap. Baby Joanne was gazing up at Grace, who was staring at something out of shot.

Joanne chewed on her lip. On the back of the photo the blue fountain pen was back, but the loopy handwriting was erratic. Scribbly. Confused.

Joanne read it aloud.

My most precious

Red

Joanne

Mustn't touch

Rory

Irasa

No No

Love

The writing became more and more difficult to read, the letters just a swirl of squiggles and strokes on the page. Joanne squeezed her eyes together in an effort to decipher the words.

She looked at the back of the photo of Mike and Grace before she was born. It looked like it'd been ripped out of something. There was a film of glued paper stuck to the back, as if someone had pulled it out in a hurry. But out of what?

She flicked back to the picture of Grace holding her in hospital and stared into her eyes. 'Oh Grace,' she said through her tears. 'What does it mean? You didn't die having me at all, did you? What happened to you?'

GRACE

APRIL 1975

'It's going to be such a lovely room,' said Mum, looking around the baby's room. 'What a lucky baby. None of you lot had your own room when you were little. When you came along, we were living at Nanna Florrie's and only moved into our own place after Gerry was born. You all slept together and got on with it.'

I tried to stop myself rolling my eyes. She said that every time she came round. 'Well, the baby will be in with me and Mike to begin with, but I wanted him or her to have their own space. I want it to be perfect.' I touched the side of the empty cot. *I must get on with making the sheets and a quilt. There was so much to do.*

'Is this the fabric for the curtains?' asked Mum, picking up the gingham from the window seat.

I nodded. 'Yes, Mrs Cornford has been giving me loads of bits and bobs. Offcuts here and there for the quilt and then yesterday she gave me this whole bolt. I reckon I could get a small pair of curtains out of it, a cushion pad for the window seat and maybe even a sheet or two.'

Mum sat down on the seat and spread the material over her lap. 'It's beautiful. I love the red. You could take a few squares of this for the baby's quilt and then mix and match with the other offcuts. That way it'll all look matching. Gingham's good like that.'

'That's a good idea, Mum.' It *was* a good idea. I wanted it all to be right. I smoothed my hand over the gingham, imagining it in a quilt.

'I'll buy you some nice padding for the quilt and some lining for the curtains. Make them nice and thick to keep out the light.'

'Thanks, Mum.' I smiled. 'That's really kind. The other thing I was thinking of is a rug,' I said, looking at the moth-eaten carpet. 'The carpet's really old in here and obviously we can't afford new. But I could make a rug to cover over the worst of it.'

Mum wound up the fabric and knelt down to feel the carpet. 'Hmm, there's not much life left in it, is there? Old Mrs Jenkins used to make nice wool rugs, you could ask her.'

'Actually, I was thinking of a rag rug. Y'know, those rugs that are made from bits of old clothes and—'

'Of course I remember rag rugs. We used to make them during the war. We had them all over the house.'

'I could get some hessian from work and then use some of the offcuts plus some old clothes. I reckon if I asked around, I'd get enough to make a rug large enough to cover the floor.'

Mum got up from the window seat. 'In my day, you only had rag rugs when you were poor and couldn't afford nothing else. You've got your own house and everything. It's not right.'

'Oh, Mum.' I laughed, standing and slipping my arms around her waist and giving her a hug. 'You are daft sometimes. No one cares about stuff like that any more.' I broke away and looked around the room. 'I think it's exactly what this room needs. And it'll give me something to do in the last few months when I'm not working.'

'You need to enjoy this time, Gracie,' said Mum, frowning again. 'You're going to be busy enough when baby arrives. And then baby two and three and four. Enjoy the peace and quiet while you can.'

I laughed. But I knew what she was trying to say. I'd always been someone who was easily overwhelmed. When we did exams at school, I panicked myself into paralysis and couldn't remember anything at all. When other people were revising, I'd sit there with a novel and pretend it wasn't happening. Even when I'd first learned to sew, I found remembering all the different stitches and methods terrifying. I'd get it wrong and then cry and cry. Thinking about all the things I'd have to remember as a mum gave me a pain in my chest. The same lump of panic I had with the exams.

Mum turned around, slipped a curl behind my ear and put her hands on my shoulders. 'You're going to make a wonderful mum,' she said, her face soft like cashmere, pulling me into a hug. 'I can't wait to see you with the baby.'

I breathed slowly while I waited for the slight panic in my chest to die down. *I will make a wonderful mum*, I repeated to myself.

Chapter 5

Joanne

September 2021

The envelope was waiting on the mat when Joanne got back from the shop the following week. Her feet ached after standing at the till all day and she was about to step over the post to get to the sofa when she saw an unfamiliar postmark – and then the inscription General Register Office. Her swollen ankles forgotten, she picked up the envelope and started tearing it open as she walked into the kitchen.

She slid the clean, crisp piece of paper out of the envelope and scanned down the text. It was all as they'd read on the website. Grace Elizabeth Bennett had died on 27 June 1977 at Egremont Hospital, Brighton. The cause of death was listed as extradural haematoma. She googled it. 'An extradural haematoma is a collection of blood in the space between the skull and the outer protective lining that covers the brain,' she read. 'It usually occurs because of a head injury.' That was what her dad had told her.

Joanne narrowed her eyes. What did that mean? And was this Grace Bennett definitely her mother? The maiden name was listed as Turner, but Joanne had never known what her mother's maiden name was so that didn't help, although she could easily find out. She'd never really asked, happy to have Lou, who treated her as her own.

But then she scanned down to the bottom of the document. Under the section entitled *Informant* was a scrawl she'd recognise anywhere. Her father's signature. Joanne shivered. Suddenly, everything felt very heavy and she sat down in the kitchen chair, staring at her father's name. *Michael Bennett, husband.* He had not only known about her mother's death, he had been the one to inform the authorities. He had been openly lying again when he said she had died a few days after Joanne was born. It was almost two years later.

Joanne closed her eyes and focused on drawing breath into her tight chest. There would be a reasonable explanation, there had to be. But if he'd lied about when her mother had died, what else had he lied about?

She checked her watch. Her father would be down the Rotary by now. Joanne let herself out of the house and walked the few streets to her old family home. Even when she stood inside the front door, she listened for a moment for the sound of his voice before walking into the kitchen. Lou was busy ironing.

'Hello, chick,' said Lou through a haze of steam. 'I was hoping you'd pop round. It's been a while since we've seen you. You all right, my lovely?' She reached across and turned down the radio.

'I'm OK, Mam.' Joanne touched the bag with the death certificate in it.

Lou set the iron on its end, where it puffed away like a dragon, and gave Joanne a big hug. 'You're getting bigger by the day. There's a noticeable bump there now.'

Joanne smiled. It was true. In the fortnight it had taken the death certificate to arrive, her belly had popped out. Customers had been commenting on it in the shop all week. 'Mam, can I talk to you about something? Something important?'

'Of course you can, chick. You can talk to me about anything.' She was flushed from the heat of the iron. 'Let me just turn this off and get us a cuppa.'

Joanne slid on to the bench seat, her thighs sticking against the plastic. Lou busied herself moving the ironing board out of the way and making a pot of tea. She put the mugs on the table with a plate of Jammie Dodgers. 'The twins were round earlier and they didn't finish these, so we can have them.'

Joanne picked one up and started nibbling around the edges, saving the jam centre for last. Finally, Lou sat down and poured the tea and passed a mug across to her. 'Now, what's up?' Her soft eyes beamed at Joanne, and she suddenly felt a stab of guilt for asking her about Grace's death. But who else was there to ask? Her father didn't want to talk about it and was implicated in some way. Lou was the only person who'd been around at that time – or at least soon after.

'What happened the other week with Dad, I didn't mean—'

'Oh, don't worry about that, chick. Your father knows things are tricky at the moment. He's not upset with you. We all just want you to be happy and healthy.'

Joanne nodded. 'Did you know my mother? It's so odd saying that. I don't want to call her Grace, as that's so impersonal. And you're my mam.'

Lou smiled again and covered Joanne's hand with both of her own. They were hot from holding the mug. 'It's OK. I know what you mean. It's natural you want to know about your birth mam. I'm surprised it's never come up before now.'

'Well, I always thought she'd died when I was born. In childbirth. But now to discover'

'It was only a few days later though, weren't it? I know that feels different to dying in childbirth, but your dad wasn't trying to hide anything. He just didn't want to cause you pain.'

'It was more than a few days, Mam. It was almost two years.'

Lou's mouth sagged. 'What d'you mean, two years? Your birth mam died following childbirth. Mike always said she had.'

Joanne reached into her bag and took out the photos. She put the picture of Mike and Grace before she was born to the back and pushed the pile towards Lou. 'Look,' she said, pointing. 'This is me and my birth mam in the hospital with her mam.'

Lou picked her glasses off her chest, where they hung on a beaded chain, and slid them on to her nose. A small circle of steam bloomed on both lenses. She looked at the picture and a faint blush started to creep up her neck. 'This is you and Grace?' she asked.

Joanne nodded. 'These are the photos I found. Underneath all those baby clothes.'

Lou put the photo on the table and looked at the next one – the picture of Mike and Grace standing outside the Brighton cottage. Her smile wavered and she looked up at Joanne.

Joanne slid out the death certificate, still in its Do Not Bend envelope. She passed it across to Lou.

'What's this, chick?' Unease threaded through Lou's voice.

'It's Grace's death certificate.'

Lou was scanning the paper, her hand beginning to shake. 'But it can't be. It's the same name, I'll give you, but this Grace died in June 1977. Your dad was here. He'd been living in Berwick for a long while by then.'

Joanne bit her lip and reached over to touch Lou's free hand. 'Read further down. Where it says *Informant*.'

There was a pause. 'Oh God.' Lou dropped the certificate on the table, where one side of it soaked up the moisture from the bottom of the mug, so she hastily picked it back up again. 'But it can't be. Mike was here then. He moved here in August 1975 – or was it September? I remember him coming into the garage. His car had broken down, and he asked if he could borrow our ramp. Just to have a look under it. I remember holding you that first day while he looked at the car.' Lou put the certificate down again and got up, refilling the kettle and wiping down the already clean counter.

Joanne watched her and sighed. Then she picked up the death certificate again, rereading the simple words written by an unknown hand. Tracing her father's signature. Why had he lied? What was he hiding?

Lou slipped back on to the chair, covering her mouth with her hands. 'I don't suppose it could be a different Grace—'

Joanne knew she was trying to find any explanation other than that Mike had lied all these years. She looked down at her hands.

'I just don't understand why he would lie about it. Say his wife had died when she hadn't.'

Joanne nodded her head slightly and reached across to touch Lou's hand.

'The thing is—' Lou stopped and looked down again. 'He wasn't keen at first. I mean, he avoided me for a long time. Friendly enough, always polite but nothing else. Dad said to him once that I was a bit keen on him – I was so embarrassed – but Mike just gave him that sad smile of his and never said anything else. But in June 1977 – I remember it because that Rod Stewart's "I Don't Want to Talk About It" was playing all the time and I loved that song – he asked me out. I was flabbergasted. After all that time, just as I'd given up. I said yes straight away. We went to the cinema on our first date.' Lou glanced at the death certificate again. 'That would have been just after Grace died. I always wondered why he'd changed his mind. I guess I know now,' she said quietly.

'Why do you think Dad would have lied about Grace dying?' Joanne watched Lou's face.

Lou shook her head. 'I don't know, chick, I'm sorry. It seems . . .' She paused and looked at the ceiling. '. . . out of character. I don't think he's ever lied. About anything.'

'Except this,' said Joanne, trying not to think about her father's face when he'd admitted that he couldn't remember when exactly Grace had died. Yet he'd signed the death certificate. 'Where was she, my mother, for those last two years of her life? When my dad was up here, with me. With you.' She glanced at Lou.

'Oh God, Jo, I'm so sorry you had to find this out, especially in your condition. Let me speak to him. I'll find out what happened and then perhaps the two of you can talk it through.'

Joanne got up from the table. 'Thanks, Mam. I'll leave you to it,' she said, looking at the ironing board.

Lou nodded, worry deepening the lines across her forehead. She passed Joanne the photos and the death certificate. 'I'm sure there's a perfectly innocent explanation,' she said weakly.

Joanne hugged her. 'Bye, Mam.' At the front door, she turned. Lou was pressing the skin underneath her eyes. She'd seen her do that only a few times before – at her mam's funeral and each time she'd miscarried. It stopped her crying.

GRACE

MAY 1975

It was finally warm enough to sit outside for lunch again. 'Just in time for your last day,' said Susie, sitting on the wall and unwrapping a sandwich that she had taken out of her bag. She bit into it and the slightly off-putting smell of sandwich spread drifted over. She turned, her mouth full. 'I'm going to miss our lunches. It's not going to be the same when you're gone.'

'It's only a couple of months until you'll be leaving too.' Susie's belly was just beginning to show, though you couldn't tell through the smock I'd made for her. 'Who d'you think you'll have lunch with when I'm gone?'

Susie made a face. 'Linda? Valerie? I don't know. I think I'll just keep myself to myself. Do more reading.'

I took a bite of my corned beef sandwich. 'It'll go by quickly. Perhaps I can come and meet you, just until the baby comes?'

She smiled. 'That'd be nice, but you'll be busy preparing Mike's dinner, won't you, and washing his socks.'

We laughed and I poked her in her side. 'I'm going to miss this place.'

'You're going to miss the free stuff.'

I rolled my eyes. 'I didn't think I'd ever say that. But now it's come, I will. Even Mrs Cornford. She's been so kind about all the offcuts.'

'Don't get weepy on me,' Susie said, her head tilted to one side.

'I'm not. But I'll really miss earning my own money. Having to ask Mike for it will be strange. And I'll miss the people.'

Susie nodded, chewing. 'I told you though, you should do your own thing. You're an amazing seamstress. Once the baby's old enough.'

'Grace Bennett Dresses,' I said, waving my hands at my imaginary shopfront. 'I will. It could be good pin money.'

'More than that, I reckon. Brunswick Furniture Brighton now, London and Paris next.' Susie folded up her sandwich wrapper and slipped it back into her bag, taking out her Silk Cut. I wondered how she still had the stomach for them.

'Maybe,' I said, taking a bite of my apple.

'Definitely. I'll be your first customer.'

'I already make almost everything you wear,' I said, munching.

'True,' said Susie. 'But I'll start to pay you once you're rich and famous.'

We laughed and watched the lads at the back of Marks and Spencer across the road heave the boxes off the delivery lorry. Eventually, the lorry drove away, belching smoke, and the boys sat down and lit up again. Susie was right. I'd love to set up on my own. Once the baby was old enough. My own shopfront with a mannequin wearing the latest dress I'd made. I'd sit in there with a sewing machine and take commissions.

'Oh, I meant to say,' said Susie, trying and failing to blow a smoke ring. 'My mum has a big bag of scraps for you. For your rug. Some old tea towels, that terry-towelling suit I used to wear, lots of old bits. She's been saving them since I told her about it.'

I pulled my mouth into a smile. 'That's great, thanks.'

Susie put her head on one side. 'What's wrong? You don't sound great.'

I sighed. 'It's just that I have so much fabric, bags and bags of offcuts. You can hardly move in the baby's room for it. And I haven't done anything with it yet. It's like a jumble sale in there. Everyone's been so kind but—' I leaned over my belly and put my head in my hands. Susie's hand was warm across my back. 'I don't know where to start.' I tried to gulp back the tears.

Susie gripped my shoulders and turned me to face her. 'Don't be silly, Gracie. I'll help. We'll do it together. Let's start this weekend. And once we've made a start, you'll be able to do a bit more when I'm at work and I'll help in the evenings.'

I nodded and tried to swallow.

'You know what it's like,' she said, her voice like a wool blanket flowing around me. 'It's like every pattern we ever do. You start with all that fabric and the paper pattern and it's always hard at first. But as soon as you get into it, into the swing of it, you're fine.'

I sniffed and looked in my pocket for my hanky. Susie was quicker and got hers out of her sleeve. 'Here.'

I wiped my eyes and then blew my nose. The seagull who'd been eyeing up my crusts flew off in fright. 'I know you're right,' I said.

'I'm always right.' She sounded just like her mum.

Another lorry pulled up outside the back of Marks and Spencer. The boys stubbed out their ciggies, stood up and stretched.

'Sorry I cried like that,' I said, turning to face her again. 'I don't know what's wrong with me.' I blew my nose again. 'I was so relieved to be pregnant so I wouldn't have that awful PMT for a few months, but it's even worse. I'm so up and down. Sometimes I don't know how I'm going to cope when the baby arrives.'

'Don't be silly.' Susie wrinkled her nose, ground her ciggie under her foot and lit another. 'I've cried loads since I got pregnant. John despairs. He thought at the start that he'd done something wrong. Now he just rolls his eyes and makes me a cup of tea.'

I laughed, feeling lighter.

'And we'll all be around to support you with the baby. Me, Emily and Gerry and your mum.'

'True.'

'Oh,' said Susie, looking down at her belly.

'Are you OK?' Susie's forehead was concertinaed like the pleats in a skirt.

'I think I felt something. A fluttering feeling.' She stroked her belly.

'Like a butterfly trapped inside you?'

She nodded, her eyes sparkling.

'That's it, that's the baby. Quickening, they call it.' I clapped my hands. 'Exciting.'

She was silent – I could tell she was waiting to feel it again. 'But it only comes and goes to begin with. It won't be long, y'know, and we'll be sitting like this with our babies in prams.'

'I can't wait,' I said. 'I'm just so glad we're going through this together.'

We smiled at each other. 'C'mon, we should be getting back. Mrs C won't let you be late, even on your last day.'

We scrambled to our feet, and she slipped her arm into mine as we walked back to the factory for the end of my last shift.

Chapter 6

Joanne

September 2021

However hard she listened, Joanne couldn't quite hear what Grace was saying. She understood some words, but they didn't make sense as a sentence. Love. Baby. Mum. She snatched at the words, devouring them greedily, screwing up her face to hear better. Young, soft skin touching hers. As real as her own hand. 'Grace, I can't hear you,' she murmured. Alex leaned over her, shaking her shoulder.

'It's OK, Jo,' he said. 'It's just a dream.'

Joanne ignored him, pushing him away and looking back at Grace. She was fading, her hand becoming less solid, her words muffled as Alex broke in.

'Jo, Jo.'

She shook his hand off her shoulder and opened her eyes, but the space where Grace had been was empty.

'For God's sake,' she said, lying on her back and closing her eyes to prevent any conversation.

'It was just a dream,' he said again, quietly this time. The mattress shifted as he lay down again and made himself comfortable.

His breathing changed quickly and within a minute she knew he was asleep again. Joanne turned over into the same position, willing Grace to come back. What had she been trying to tell her? It had felt comforting, but also a warning. She lay waiting but Grace didn't come back.

The memory of her hand, her words, lingered all day. In the shop, as she wrapped up tiny parcels of jewellery, she thought again of Grace's hand on hers. The soft squeeze. The sound of her voice – gentle, soothing. She wanted to tell her mam about the dream – if that was what it had been – but they'd heard nothing from her dad or Lou since she'd showed Lou the death certificate. They usually saw each other most days.

Later that evening, she sat with Alex in front of the TV. 'How long do you think I should leave it?' Joanne asked Alex, stroking her bump, now beginning to fill her maternity jeans.

Alex didn't look up from his phone. 'I'm sure he'll pop round soon.'

'But it's been ten days,' said Joanne, tapping her foot on the floor.

The TV hummed away, a celebrity cook trying to teach a group of keen amateurs to make a risotto. Joanne watched for a few moments and then glanced again at the envelope with the death certificate still propped up on the mantelpiece. She sighed and looked around the room. The coffee table was piled up with the small cream boxes she had put together for the silver bangles and earrings she was making for the Christmas fairs. She seemed to start earlier and earlier every year to meet demand. Though she wasn't sure how many of the fairs she was going to do this year – she'd be almost having the baby by then. Maybe Alex could go instead, or her parents. Her eyes flicked back to the death certificate.

'Alex, can you look at me?'

Alex put his phone down on the coffee table with a sigh and swivelled to face her. 'He's probably just busy, love. You know he still pops down to the mechanics', and there's the Rotary.'

Joanne nodded. 'It's not Monday, so it can't be Rotary. I think he's avoiding me. I can't remember the last time I didn't see him for this long. Either of them. Mam's always coming round with something. Especially since I've been pregnant this time.' She glanced down at her belly again.

Alex looked directly at Joanne. 'Have you tried calling him, or going round? You've always done that too. Maybe he thinks it's odd that you haven't popped round since you stormed off.'

'True,' said Joanne, nodding. Maybe that was it. 'I'll call him now. They're bound to be in at teatime.'

She picked up her mobile and clicked on her parents' landline number. It took a while to connect but then rang and rang. 'No answer,' she said after a while, still letting it ring. 'I'll try his mobile. Just on the off chance.'

Joanne ended the call and called her dad's mobile. He had a tiny little Nokia phone, which he rarely turned on. It went straight to voicemail – a disembodied voice asking her to leave a message. There was no point. Instead, she tried Lou's mobile, but that rang for a bit and then went to voicemail.

'Nothing from either of them,' Joanne said to Alex, who put down his own phone, a frown playing in his eyes.

'I'm sure he's not avoiding you. He's your dad, after all. He's probably still a bit awkward about all this stuff with Grace—' Alex looked at her. 'D'you want to go round there? Chat to him face to face. That might be better than the phone?'

Joanne nodded and stood up. Alex was at her waist height, and he kissed her stomach. 'Hello, little one, Daddy's here.'

They laughed, breaking the tension. Alex stood up next to Joanne, cradling her face in his hands. 'You look so beautiful. I know what they mean by blooming now.'

He went to kiss her on the forehead, but Joanne kissed him on the lips. 'You're going to make an amazing dad. Only ten weeks to go.'

They slipped out of the front door and walked down to the River Tweed. The rare heatwave was holding and people were sitting all along the river on benches, enjoying the early evening summer sunshine with bottles of beer and wine. Joanne felt uncomfortably hot – it was true what they said about pregnant women always being warm – and loosened a little the silk scarf she often wore.

They turned away from the river and were soon standing outside Mike and Lou's front door. Joanne glanced at Alex, who nodded. She turned the door handle, but the door didn't open. She pushed it again, but it was stuck. Alex tried it, but the same thing happened.

'It's locked,' said Joanne, feeling a knot tighten in her belly.

'It can't be,' said Alex. 'They never lock their door. Except at night.' He checked his watch.

They rang the doorbell, Joanne shifting from foot to foot. Nothing happened. Alex rapped on the window of the front room and Joanne tried to peer through the net curtains. The room was empty, but on the coffee table sat two full mugs of tea, the steam rising up from the surface, and the TV was showing the same celebrity cooking show they'd been watching earlier.

'They're in,' said Joanne, her heart beginning to thump. 'Look.' She nodded towards the window. She imagined them hiding in the hall, trying to avoid her. The thought made her heart contract.

Alex peered in and nodded, then knocked on the door. 'Lou, Mike. It's us. You all right?'

There was no response from inside. But the old man who'd lived opposite for as long as Joanne could remember came out. 'What's up, you two? Can't get in?'

Joanne shook her head. 'The door's locked, Mr Dixon.'

'It can't be,' said the old man, shuffling across the cobbles. 'They never lock it.' He tried the door and frowned, his skin rippling across his face. 'Well, that's odd. I've never known that in all my years.' The old Northumbrian burr wound through his voice.

He stood with them around the door, waiting. Soon, another neighbour, Mrs Stewart from number 42, joined them, wearing an old housecoat and carrying a duster.

'They're definitely in,' she said. 'Mike popped up to Bridge Street for something earlier, but he came back about twenty minutes ago. Lou's been in all day.'

The four of them stood staring at the door and each other. Eventually, Mr Dixon spoke. 'Perhaps we should call the police. In case there's something wrong.'

Joanne's eyes darted to Alex, who shook his head. 'Nah, I don't think we need to do that, Mr Dixon. Look, if you don't mind, Mrs Stewart, I'll go through yours and climb over the wall. Then I can get round the back.'

Mrs Stewart nodded, her eyes glinting. 'Come right this way, young Alex.'

They'd just started walking away when the front door opened a couple of inches. Lou's face squeezed through the gap.

'She's here,' shouted Mr Dixon. 'Janet, it's all right now. Lou's here.'

Janet Stewart dropped her head and turned around.

Lou looked pale, with puffy purple circles under her eyes. 'I'm sorry, chick, it's not a good time,' she said to Joanne, her eyes downcast.

Joanne dashed forward so there was only a few inches between them. 'What's happened, Mam, you look awful.'

Lou just shook her head.

'But Mam, I've been waiting to hear from you, and Dad. About Grace, about the death certificate,' she whispered, feeling Mr Dixon and Mrs Stewart's eyes on her, even from where they'd moved back. 'It's been ten days.'

'I know.' Lou's shoulders dropped. 'I've spoken to your dad about it. It's all OK. There's nothing to talk about. There's no mystery.'

'Of course there's something to talk about,' said Joanne, louder this time. 'Dad lied. He told me Grace had died having me, and instead she died two years later. He lied, Mam.'

'I know, chick, but he had good reason. I know you can't appreciate that now, but he did. Please believe me.'

Joanne put her hand on the door frame, as if to push her way in. 'So he's told you what happened?'

Lou nodded slowly and looked at her feet.

'What, and you're not going to tell me? Grace was my birth mother. I deserve to know why Dad lied about her death. She was still alive when I was almost two. I missed out on a chance to know her.'

Joanne heard a sharp intake of breath from Mrs Stewart and Mr Dixon clearing his throat. She didn't want to have the conversation on the street. Lou looked up to the sky and sighed. She reached through the door frame and put her hand on Joanne's shoulder. 'It's not as simple as that, Jo. Your dad doesn't want to tell you in your condition. He says it's not something you should know right now. And I agree. I'm sorry, chick. We'll tell you more after you've had the baby. But it's nothing to worry about.'

Lou tried to close the gap of the door, but Joanne had wedged her foot in it. 'That's so unfair, Mam, I deserve to know.' She started to cry and wiped the tears away with her hand. 'Mam, tell me.'

Lou shook her head sadly and looked up at Alex, who was standing behind Joanne. 'Please don't ask him, Jo. Please understand. You might not want the truth.'

'I might not want the truth?' Joanne was shouting now. 'What d'you mean? Of course I want the bloody truth. That's exactly what I do want.' She could see tears easing out of Lou's downturned eyes. She'd hardly ever seen her mam cry.

'What's going on?' A loud voice behind her made Joanne step back and turn round. Her brother was striding along the street, his hands in the pockets of his overalls.

'Oh Pat, I was just trying to get into Mam and Dad's.' A thin sheen of sweat covered her flushed cheeks.

Patrick reached the door and put his arm around Joanne's shoulders. He leaned towards his mother. 'What's going on, Mam?'

'I'm sorry, chicks, I just can't. This is between Joanne and Dad. I can't explain, I'm sorry.' Before either of them had a chance to say anything, she'd shut the door and they heard metal grating as the bolt was slid across.

Patrick faced Joanne, rubbing his chin. 'What's all that about, eh?'

Joanne closed her eyes. Although her brother knew that Lou wasn't her birth mother, it was never something they'd talked about. 'I found out that my birth mam didn't die when she had me, but two years later. But Dad won't say why.'

Patrick grunted. 'But that's old history, Jo. Mam brought you up, you don't need to be bothering them about all of that now. Especially not now,' he said, glancing at her stomach.

'You don't understand. I need to know what happened.' Joanne clenched her hand into a fist and banged on the door. 'Mam? Dad?' Her voice caught. Why wouldn't they tell her? How could they keep it secret? She had a right to know.

'But Mam's your mam,' said Patrick again. 'Whether or not she actually gave birth to you. What difference does that make?'

'It makes all the difference,' said Joanne, her shoulders slumping.

A few more people had gathered nearby, seeing what was going on.

She flinched as Alex took her arm and snatched it away from him. 'Dad,' she shouted again as she banged on the door. 'Dad, let me in.'

'Come on, Jo, we need to go home,' said Alex into her ear. 'It's time to go.'

Patrick stood next to him, worry written across his forehead. 'Jo, you're making a scene, look,' he muttered, gesturing at the crowd.

'I want to find out what happened to Grace, to my mother,' insisted Joanne, her breathing shaky. She stood with her hands on her hips staring at the closed door, her eyes narrowed, her whole body rigid.

'Jo—'

Bang. Bang. Bang. Joanne hammered on the door again. 'Dad, let me in. I've got a right to know. She was my mother.' A splinter of pain knifed through her. 'What did you do to her?'

GRACE

MAY 1975

'Let's move the cot and the chest of drawers into the other room,' said Mike. 'Then we'll have more space to lay all this stuff out.'

'Good idea.' John grabbed the other end of the cot and they carried it into our bedroom. Despite all the bags full of fabric, the room felt empty without it. Susie was emptying one of the bags on to the floor.

'You've got so much material here,' she said, turning round. 'I see why it was all a bit overwhelming.'

'I just didn't know where to start,' I said. 'Thanks for helping. I feel much better with you here.' It was true. The lump that had been growing in my chest had melted away, making it easier to breathe.

'Don't be daft, that's what friends are for. Oh look! My old terry-towelling suit.' She held up a stained and faded scrap of red cloth. 'Mum said she'd put that in the bag.'

'I remember you wearing that.' I smiled at the memory. 'Bognor, we must have been about four or five. You wore it until you had to fold yourself double to get into it.'

'And then I couldn't stand up straight. Mum had to hide it in the end to stop me wearing it. I can't believe she kept it all this time.'

The boys came back in and lifted up the chest of drawers. 'Be careful, there are some things inside that,' I said.

Mike blew me a kiss and they disappeared out of the door.

'I love organising the drawers.' I smiled at Susie. 'Putting in the clothes I've made so far. Piling up the tiny squares for the nappies.'

'I'm the same,' she said, her eyes lighting up. 'All I've got is that first matinee jacket I made and some hand-me-downs from one of Mum's friends, but I can't stop looking at them. I went to a jumble sale yesterday with Mum. I picked up loads of weird old jumpers to unpick and reknit.'

'Lemon and white?'

'Lemon and white.' She pulled a face. 'There was a lovely pink wool, but I didn't dare.'

The bags were all empty and a sea of red covered the floor, worse than the factory ever looked. I sighed. 'Where shall we start?'

'Well, what do you want to do with the rug?' Susie asked, her hands on her hips, looking down at the mess. 'Are you planning a design or . . .'

'I thought it would be random, just to add colour to the room, really, and cover this carpet.'

'I reckon we sort by shade for now,' Susie said. 'So, the light reds over there and the darker ones over here, then we can start cutting.'

I threw an old pink towel across the room. Susie held up a deep-burgundy wool coat, with moth holes so large you could fit your finger through them.

Mike came back in carrying the hessian. 'Where d'you want this, love?'

'Oh, just put it in the corner. We'll lay it out once we've got all this sorted.'

John put his head around the door. 'You OK if Mike and I pop up to the track?'

Susie looked up and smiled. 'Yeah, see you two later. Grace and I thought we'd all have tea here, when you're back.'

Mike came in and dropped a kiss on the top of my head. 'Lovely. We'll treat you both to a couple at the Seven Sisters afterwards. There's a darts evening tonight.' They clattered down the stairs, the front door slammed, and we could still hear them through the window talking until their voices finally faded.

I passed Susie a pair of scissors. 'The library book said to cut strips of fabric about one and a half inches by two and a half inches. Let's place all the strips into these bags, then we can get rid of the stuff we don't want in the other bags.'

Susie sat cross-legged on the floor and started to cut.

My back was beginning to ache, the baby's weight pressing down on my hips. I leaned against the window seat for support. It was a nice rhythm, cutting the fabric and then putting it into piles. You didn't need to think like we did at work. Or worry that you were going to make a mistake. Inside me the baby swam, pushing against the confines of her private pool.

'Strange thinking that I'm not going to be back at Brunswick again.'

'I can't wait till I leave,' said Susie. 'Mrs C will be at me more than ever without you there. Only two more months. I'll be finishing just before you have your baby, so I can help out.'

'I hadn't thought of that,' I said slowly. 'That'll be great.' I let out a long breath. It would be good to have her around. I kept wondering how I would cope with a new baby. I'd hardly ever held one before. I threw aside what was left of a rust-coloured T-shirt.

'So what are you going to do with your time?' Susie said, cutting up an old red sock. Who on Earth wore red socks?

I waved my hand around the room. 'This rug, mainly. And don't tell my mum, but I've got a baby dress pattern. I'm going to make a couple more.'

Susie laughed. 'Your mum will go mad if she finds out. If you have a boy, I'll have them for my girl.'

'I'm having a girl,' I said firmly. 'Let me show you. The dress is so sweet.' I opened the window seat and dug down under the blankets, where I'd hidden it from Mum.

'Oh, that's gorgeous,' said Susie, fingering the broderie anglaise collar. 'It's just like the ones in Hanningtons.'

I nodded and gave a small smile.

'You copied the pattern, didn't you?' She looked at me, her eyes dancing.

'I didn't copy, I just made a few good guesses.' I tried to hold on to the smile, but it grew across my face.

'Grace Bennett stealing. I never thought I'd see the day.' She held it up in front of her, the delicate whiteness standing out against her dark smock.'

I crossed my arms. She could be so irritating sometimes.

'Don't look so cross, I was only joking.'

I smiled again. Susie handed me back the dress. It was hard to believe that in a few months I'd be slipping tiny arms through those holes. Inside, the baby did another somersault. I slipped it back into some paper and then between the blankets. I picked up a worn blanket and started cutting it into strips.

'What shall we do for tea?' she said.

'I've got some boil-in-the-bag haddock – there's enough for us four.'

'Great, I'll bring round some potatoes to chip.'

We were quiet for a long time. Just the snip-snip of the scissors, and the rustle of the old bits of cloth as they were discarded. Finally, there was no cloth left. Both Susie and I stood up, stretching out our backs. 'Crikey, I ache,' I said, the stiffness spreading through my shoulders. 'I'll make us a cup of tea.'

'Ooh yes, I'll just tidy this lot up, ready to start on the rug.'

Downstairs, I put the kettle on and read a few pages of the newspaper while I waited for it to boil. The lead story was about a coach crash up north, which had killed a load of pensioners. The brakes had failed and the coach had fallen off a bridge. I shuddered and turned over the page. Another woman had been raped in Cambridge and police were warning all women in the city to be careful. I flicked over another page. A husband in the West Country had murdered his heavily pregnant wife but doctors had managed to deliver her live baby. Christ. I threw the paper in the bin and turned back to the kettle.

Susie had laid out the hessian by the time I brought the tea up. It was huge, stretching from the door to the window frame. 'It's going to look brilliant,' she said. 'It'll make this room so colourful.'

I set the teas down. Susie immediately picked hers up and took a sip. 'So how do we do this then?'

I sat next to her, picking up my latch hook and the side of the hessian. 'I had a go on a spare piece of hessian,' I explained. 'You push the hook through a loop of the hessian, making sure it goes all the way through to the other side of it.' I turned it over to show her. 'Let the latch fall open on the other side and fold each strip of cloth in half around the hook on this side.' I looked up at her. Her face was the picture of concentration. 'Fold the two ends of the rag over each other inside the hook and flick the latch closed on top of them.' I pulled the hook back through the loop of hessian. 'Then you just pull it back like this and open the latch.'

'OK, I think I get that. Let me give it a try on a corner.' She picked up a strip of scarlet cotton and, with her tongue between her teeth, began to wrap it round the hook.

I moved over to the other side and started to do the same with a cherry-red wool. Soon the hessian had red edges. As we worked, the redness spread slowly inwards, like a blood-soaked hanky.

Chapter 7

Joanne

September 2021

The cooking show on TV was just finishing; the young actor from *Emmerdale* hadn't made it through to the next round and she was crying on the shoulder of the celebrity chef. Joanne switched it off. She couldn't focus on it anyway. Her mind kept racing through the events of earlier in the day, outside Dad and Lou's.

Alex touched her arm uncertainly. 'I'll make us a cuppa,' he said, disappearing into the kitchen.

Joanne picked the envelope off the mantelpiece and sat down heavily. She slipped out the death certificate and reread the details she'd already memorised. *What happened between Dad arriving in Berwick and Grace dying?* thought Joanne. What had happened that made Lou look so shocked when she heard about it more than forty years later? She felt her heart contract with pain again. She didn't want to think about it, but she couldn't think about anything else. She hadn't been able to think about anything else since she'd first found the photos.

Joanne opened her phone's photos and looked again at the picture of her and her mother when she had just been born – she'd photographed each Polaroid before carefully putting them back in the envelope and the envelope back behind the bath panel, where Alex had hidden it. They both looked so young. At least, compared to Joanne and Alex, having a baby in their forties. A lifetime later. Geriatric mother.

Alex came back in and set the two mugs down on the coffee table. He sat on the sofa and put his arm around Joanne. 'I'm sorry it didn't work out as you hoped, Jo,' he said, pulling his beard.

Joanne nodded, picking up the death certificate.

He opened his mouth again as if to say something else, but closed it and looked away.

She stood up and went to the mantelpiece. She opened her phone again, looking at the pictures, tracing her finger over her mother's face and then flicking through to look at the strange writing. It still bothered her what it meant. It was as if it was some sort of secret message from mother to daughter that she didn't have the code for.

'What was Grace doing for those two years while my dad was up here, getting together with Mam?' Joanne looked down at the photo again. 'She looked perfectly healthy when she left hospital. What happened so that, within a month, Dad left Sussex and came here – about as far away from Brighton as it's possible to get? Where was Grace? Was she well? Ill? What was she doing? Did anyone even know?'

'What are you looking at?' said Alex, standing up, his eyes narrowing.

'Nothing,' said Joanne, quickly flicking out of the photos app. 'Just thinking about those pictures we found.'

'I told you to leave it alone, love, it's causing you a lot of stress.' He went behind her and slipped his arms over her bump. She wondered if he was also looking at her phone.

'It's OK, I feel fine,' she said brightly.

'C'mon, come and sit down. Put your feet up.'

She allowed him to guide her back to the sofa. She picked up the death certificate again.

Alex looked at her and sighed. 'Why don't you try to get your mam on her own again? Try tomorrow, when your dad's out. I reckon you could persuade her to tell you. You know how close you two are.'

Joanne raised her eyebrows. 'I thought we were close,' she said. 'But I wonder now. She's just taking his side without even asking about me, or thinking about how I felt. I don't think it'd make any difference me going round there again.' She sniffed. 'And I don't want to give her the satisfaction.'

'Don't say that, Jo, she's your mam.'

Joanne put the death certificate back on the table and leaned back into the sofa. 'Not my real mam,' she said, her mouth twisted.

'She *is* your real mam, Jo. She brought you up.'

'Only because now it seems my dad did something to my real mam.'

Alex glanced at her but said nothing.

'I dreamed of her last night. Grace.' She hadn't planned to say anything to Alex – wanting to keep Grace to herself. But suddenly she couldn't stop it tumbling out. 'It was really confused but she was there, talking to me, but nothing she said was making sense.'

'That happens in dreams, doesn't it. Things don't make sense.'

'It was just so comforting though. Hearing her voice, seeing her like that.'

Alex picked up the death certificate. 'So Grace died in Egremont Hospital in Brighton,' he said. 'If your dad and mam won't tell you what happened, then maybe you can find out yourself. There must be records. Or people who knew her when she was there.'

'You're right,' said Joanne, suddenly sitting up straight. 'There must be a way of finding out what happened. Not just through Dad. Or Mam. There would have been people who knew her.' She thought back to the photos. 'There was that photo of my parents outside what I think was their home. A cottage with roses around the door. Someone would have taken that. And there was the lady in the photo next to my mam and me in the hospital. She was called Susie. We could go to Brighton, find them and ask them.'

Alex drew his eyebrows together. 'Well, I meant hospital records or something. Research that we could do on the internet. Not actually going to Brighton to talk to people. Not now, in your condition. C'mon, be sensible.'

'Don't be daft, Alex, going down there is a perfect idea.' Joanne tightened her fists. 'If Dad won't tell me why she died two years after I was born, then I'll find out myself.' She stood up, her arms clenched at her side, and looked down at him. 'And I know where you've hidden those photos. I want them back. It's my only link with my mother.' Scans of the photos weren't the same as something her mother had actually touched. Written on.

Alex dropped his head. 'I should have known you'd find them. You're so determined sometimes.' He stood up. 'I'll go and get them.'

GRACE

JUNE 1975

Sweat ran down my cleavage and soaked into my bra. I shaded my eyes with my hand and half squinted at the sun. I slipped my hand under my hair, lifting it up to let the air reach my neck. That was better.

'Stop looking so grumpy.' Mike smiled at me and pulled my arm through his.

I couldn't help but smile back. 'Sorry. I'm just feeling so bloom-ing uncomfortable. And why's it so hot? Surely it's never this hot in June?' I couldn't seem to take a full breath. There just didn't feel like there was room for my lungs now.

'You usually love the heat.' Mike looked down at the beach, frowning. I could hardly see the pebbles for the towels between the dads hiding behind the striped windbreaks, the mums sunbathing on flowery patterned towels and the groups of kids playing. Old ladies held their hats, their flabby arms swaying. But however much breeze there was, it didn't seem to cool me down.

'It won't be long. It could be almost any day now,' he said. 'And you heard what your mum said. A nice long walk could be just the thing the baby needs to make an appearance.'

I nodded, though the last thing I felt like was a long walk in the scorching sun. My ankles were like two bulging shopping bags. The drawstring dress, whose pattern had promised to take me right up to my due date, was digging into the top of my belly. The baby kept pushing its feet against the fabric. I wanted to be at home, my feet up, finishing off my book.

'How about we walk up and get some fish and chips and have a sit-down on the beach and then get the bus back. We could stop at the Seven Sisters for a beer. Have a little treat for a change.' He grinned at me, and I knew he was already imagining the crispy cod batter with a saveloy on the side.

My throat gagged at the thought. I shook my head. 'I can't fit fish and chips in here,' I said, pushing down at the top of my belly to give my lungs more space.

His face pinched. 'An ice cream then?'

A cool lolly against my cheek, my tongue. Bliss. Suddenly, it was the only thing I wanted. And I wanted it now. I squeezed his arm. 'That'd be nice.'

'Cool you down,' he said. 'Let's walk up to Marrocco's and get an ice cream. You can have a rest and then we can get the bus.'

The promenade stretched out in front of us, dotted with couples of all ages arm in arm and children weaving in and out of them. The tarmac shimmered in the heat. 'Marrocco's is so far,' I said. 'There are closer places.'

'But none with ice cream as good as Marrocco's,' Mike said, crossing his arms. 'Come on, you never know, it might bring on the baby. A nice long walk, your mum said.' He took out his ciggies and offered one to me. I shook my head. He rolled his eyes and then lit one for himself.

He was trying to be helpful, I knew that. I undid my hair and re-tied it to keep it properly off my neck and followed him. In the sea, girls bobbed about on lilos. How blissful it would be to dip my feet in the cool water. 'Let's have a paddle first.'

Mike grinned at me. 'OK, race you to the sea.'

I laughed and waddled behind him on to the stones. As we crunched through the sunbathers and windbreaks, I spotted a large area free of people close to the water's edge. Perfect. 'Mike, look. Let's sit down over there.'

He nodded and went ahead as my elephant ankles stumbled against the shingle. By the time I reached him, he was standing stock still, staring straight ahead. Stretching from his feet to the water's edge were hundreds of silvery mackerel, lying on their sides. Some were being washed in and out with the tide, the waves giving life to their dead bodies. Others lay further up the stones, left behind by the water, gasping their final breaths in the heat. Their eyes panicked, glassy. I thought of the battered fish lying in the heated cabinet at the chippy and retched. As I bent over, one of the fish seemed to wriggle towards me in his death throes. I shrieked and stumbled backwards.

Mike grabbed my arm. 'C'mon, let's find somewhere else to sit.'

Chapter 8

JOANNE

SEPTEMBER 2021

'Isn't it warm?' said Joanne as they walked hand in hand along the Brighton promenade in the early evening sun. On the beach, families with young children were interspersed with groups of teens swigging from beer cans. Seagulls circled overhead, eyeing up discarded chip wrappers and children's ice creams. Beyond them, paddleboarders glided along on what looked like a sheen of golden silk. Joanne and Alex bought fish and chips and polystyrene cups of tea and sat down on one of the benches overlooking the beach.

After just a few mouthfuls of the buttery cod, her belly felt taut against her jeans. 'I'm full already,' she said, pressing her bump away from her ribs. 'It feels tight, like a drum.'

Alex's eyes widened and he stared at her belly before reaching out and touching it. 'It does,' he said, his head jerking towards her. 'Is that normal?'

Joanne bit her lip. 'I don't know. Maybe it's the baby changing positions or something. There must be less space in there now.' She looked down at her belly.

'All the same, I don't think we should walk far,' he said, tension strung through his voice. 'Let's go back to the B&B after this.' He kissed the side of her head. 'We need to keep you well rested.'

Joanne looked at him and offered a small smile. 'I know.' They kissed on the lips. 'You taste of that yucky sauce,' she said, wiping her mouth. They rarely kissed on the lips now, she thought. He always seemed to kiss her forehead. Like her dad did.

'Tartare sauce. Nothing like it.' He grinned and stuffed another sauce-coated chip in his mouth.

'I wonder where my parents lived when they were here,' said Joanne after a while. 'Perhaps they walked along the beach together when she was pregnant and sat and ate fish and chips. They could even have sat in this very spot.' She looked at the old wooden bench, flecks of green paint a reminder of what it had once looked like. It could easily have been around in the 1970s.

'I can't believe you've never been to Brighton before,' said Alex, dipping a chip in more sauce. 'I came for a stag years ago, and there was something before that too. A birthday party, perhaps.' He took a bite of fish. 'Especially as you were born here.' He glanced at her belly.

'The hen dos I've been to were all in Newcastle or Edinburgh,' Joanne said, swallowing a small spoonful of mushy peas. That seemed to go down better than the chips. 'And Dad never wanted to talk about those days. I always thought that my birth mother died having me so there didn't seem any point really, in coming here, digging all that up.' She sighed and looked out to sea.

An old lady sat down at the opposite end of the bench and smiled at them both. She reached into her bag, brought out a flask and slowly poured herself a cup of tea.

Alex waved his arms defensively at a seagull perched on the railing, checking out his chips. 'Somehow, I can't see your dad in Brighton. He seems so at home in Berwick.'

'I suppose it was different here in the seventies,' said Joanne. 'Everywhere was. And he was younger then, too. He must've liked the busyness of it.'

'True,' said Alex. 'So where shall we go tomorrow?'

A dull ache began in Joanne's back and she shifted against the bench. 'I don't know really,' she said, taking a sip of tea. 'I've got the address of where the hospital was. It's quite a bus ride away but I'd like to see where she died.' Alex squeezed her hand. 'I don't know after that. I'd love to be able to find out where their house in Brighton was, but the photo isn't much to go on.' Joanne reached into her bag for the now well-thumbed Polaroids. 'I didn't see anything cottagey on the walk down from the station. It looks quite rural really, not in town. Maybe it's on the outskirts somewhere.'

One seagull, bolder than the rest, scuttled forward and grabbed at a chip that had fallen from Alex's paper. 'Blimey,' he said, covering the remainder with the top of the wrapper. 'I thought he was going to go for the whole thing.' They both laughed.

'Excuse me, dears, I couldn't help overhearing,' said the old lady, leaning over. 'You're looking for someone? Perhaps I can help, I've been here all my life.'

Joanne smiled and edged towards her, the dull pain prodding her back. 'Oh, are you sure? Thank you. I'm looking for my mother, Grace Bennett. She died here when I was young—'

The old lady clicked her tongue and nodded sympathetically.

'In the seventies. I don't know much about her, but I'd love to find out where we lived and be able to visit the house where—' She stopped and found it hard to swallow.

The old lady put her cup down on the slats and inched across the bench towards Joanne. 'Show me the photo, dear, and I'll see if I recognise your mother.' She glanced at Joanne's neck. 'That's a very pretty necklace you're wearing.'

Joanne's hand flew to her pebble-link metallic collar necklace, one of her bestsellers. 'Thank you.' She slid along the bench and handed the old lady the Polaroid. 'This was my mother, and' – she paused – 'Dad and me. I think it's taken when they first brought me home from the hospital.' She glanced at her father's smiling face and her eyes hardened.

The old lady delved into her bag and brought out a pair of reading glasses, which she perched on her nose. She peered at the photo. 'My, you're the spitting image of your mum, aren't you. I would have thought you were the same person.' She looked up at Joanne and her face softened into a smile.

'Yes, Dad always said that,' she said, her face expressionless.

The old lady studied the photo again. Joanne watched her face for any sign of recognition. She finally looked up. 'I didn't know your mother, dear, I'm sorry. Brighton was a big place even then. But I don't think that house is in Brighton. I'd say it was one of the villages just along the coast. Seadean is my guess.'

'Seadean? How far's that?' Joanne glanced over her shoulder at Alex.

'It's not far from here, half an hour on the bus. It's a tiny place, a hamlet really. Just a collection of cottages, a cafe and a pub, the Seven Sisters I think. Some of the cottages are brightly painted now – the hippies took over.' She pursed her lips. 'But in the seventies, it was all Sussex flint and white paint. It could be there.'

'Oh, thank you, that's really helpful.'

'Of course, it's probably been repainted by now. Something ghastly. What you need is someone who lived in Seadean or thereabouts in the nineteen-seventies who might recognise your mum.'

'True.' Joanne nodded slowly. 'Do you know anyone who might be able to help?'

The lady shook her head. 'No, all my friends are dying off or have gone batty and can't remember what day of the week it is. But my daughter lives just along the coast from Seadean, another village called Rottingdean, with her family, she might, I suppose.' She took a sip of tea from the flask's plastic cup. 'There's quite a well-known community group there where they share news and leftovers and things like that. She uses it all the time. It's on the internet. Facebook.'

Joanne nodded.

'You could try that. Someone will have been here when your mother was alive. Someone will know her.'

'That's a great idea,' said Joanne, smiling at the old lady as she drained the last of the tea and packed up her flask.

'Well, I must be on my way. If I sit down too long, I seize up.' She slowly levered herself up with her stick and got to her feet.

'Thank you so much,' said Alex, getting up too to see if she needed any help.

'You're both very welcome. Good luck with your search.' She tottered off slowly down the promenade towards the ruined West Pier, around which starlings were weaving intricate patterns in the air.

'That's such a great idea,' said Joanne, already taking out her phone. 'Let me see if I can find the Facebook group she meant.'

Alex was looking at the map on his phone. 'She's right. Seadean isn't far from here. Just a short bus ride from the B&B. We could go up there tomorrow morning and have a look around. See if we can find anything that looks like the cottage.' He pressed his lips into her hair. She smiled distractedly as she scrolled through the search results, ignoring the prodding in her back.

'Here it is,' she said, pointing at her phone. 'Seadean Community Notice Board. That must be what the old lady meant. Look at all the cute little cottages!'

'Oh yeah. They're just like the photo.'

'OK. I've joined the group.'

Alex leaned over her shoulder. 'What are you going to say?'

'Hmm, I don't know,' said Joanne, taking a bite of a cold chip and looking at him. 'I could post up this picture of Grace, Dad and me and say something like "Do you know this woman?"'

Alex laughed. 'Sounds like a wanted poster.'

Joanne laughed, took a sip of the now cold tea and started typing. Alex looked out to sea, his hand resting on her leg. After a while, she handed the phone to him. 'What about this?'

Underneath the photo of her parents holding her outside the cottage, Joanne had written:

Do you recognise these people?

These are my parents, Mike and Grace Bennett, with me as a newborn baby in 1975 standing outside a cottage we believe is in Seadean. I'm looking for news of my mother. If you knew her or my father, then please get in touch. Thank you.

'I think that's perfect, Jo. Go for it.' Alex smiled and pulled her towards him. 'Just think who might see it.'

'I know. Imagine.' A rush of adrenaline surged through Joanne as she pressed *Post* then slipped the phone back in her bag. She turned towards Alex, a grin lighting up her face. He leaned forward and kissed her lips softly, cupping her face with one hand. Joanne smiled into his eyes as they drew apart. 'Watch out,' she said. 'That gull is getting closer, he's after your chips.'

Alex flapped his arms, mimicking the gull, making Joanne bend over with laughter until the ache in her back made her wince.

'Are you OK?' Alex had frozen, arms in mid-air. He let them drop sharply. 'You look like you're in pain.'

'It's nothing, just a bit of backache,' said Joanne, reaching round to rub her spine.

'C'mon, let's walk back to the B&B,' said Alex, standing and stretching. 'You should rest after that long train journey. We can put something on the TV.'

A group of seagulls were waiting for scraps a couple of metres away. 'This lot are quite threatening. They're huge!' said Joanne, giving them a wide berth.

They walked past the gaudy pier where the queue for the doughnut stall snaked around the corner, and then turned inland to the B&B tucked away in a side street.

Once in their room, Joanne started pulling off her clothes, rubbing her back again to ease the ache when Alex wasn't looking. 'I'm so tired. It must be the travelling,' she said, yawning.

'Maybe the sea air is more tiring down here,' said Alex. 'I'm knackered too.'

Once in her nightie, Joanne plugged her phone in to charge, and then noticed a message on the screen. She gasped.

'Alex, look!'

Joanne's Facebook post had received lots of likes already, a few people wishing her luck and suggesting which cottage it was. A post at the bottom from someone called Susie Carter said, *I was your mum's best friend since infant school. I've been waiting to hear news of you for years. I'll send you a private message.*

Joanne read it out and started to cry. 'I'm finally going to get some answers. Find out what Dad—' She took a shuddering breath. 'What happened to her.'

GRACE

JULY 1975

The sun streamed through the window, making patterns on the finished rag rug. It seemed to burn into the reds and oranges, making them even more vibrant. I should have closed the curtains to stop it fading the colours. But then it would only fade the new gingham curtains instead.

I slid down the wall. The sun couldn't reach under the window seat. I stretched out, my puffy hand reaching into the sun's rays for a moment before I pulled it back. Sitting cross-legged seemed to be the most comfortable position. It almost felt as if the baby's head was resting on the floor, though the doctor had promised me it was a bit more complicated than that.

My last day before being a mother. Tomorrow I'd have a baby in my arms. I could feel my heart skip every time I thought about it. A bit of excitement and a lot of nerves. I glanced over at the cot. Everything was ready. It had been ready for weeks. Mike had been tripping over the hospital bag in the hall since May. Who was I kidding, getting it ready so early? May!

And it was all going to be perfect. I had always wanted to start the pains just after Mike had gone to work and then for him to find out when he got home that he had a daughter. Just in time for visiting hour. And now that's exactly what was going to happen. Or at least what they said was going to happen. Induction sounded amazing.

But I felt so tired. Mum said it was normal. It was the hottest summer for decades, they kept saying on the radio. My hands were so swollen I hadn't worn my wedding band for weeks. I was like a giant hippo.

I shifted on the cushion and picked up the book again. I still wasn't sure about it. I preferred romances and there was something a little sinister about this book. But it was a good distraction from the waiting. Annabelle's life was so exciting. Parties, balls, satin dresses, helicopter rides. The aristocracy. A few pages back, hadn't there been a duke? And there were dowager countesses on every page. Countless nannies to look after her children. Her husband, Rory, sounded divine – those dark eyes, the hair flopping over his face. I flipped over the page. Scotland sounded less hot than Brighton. I bet there wouldn't be a heatwave up there. And girls like Annabelle didn't get as big as this. I bet she'd hardly noticed when she was pregnant.

I uncrossed my legs to ease the pins and needles and turned another page.

'Helloooo.' Susie was climbing the stairs. I read to the end of the paragraph and then put the book down as she walked through the door.

'How are you?' She slipped down and sat next to me, both of us leaning our backs against the base of the window seat, just like being at school again. 'Tomorrow's the big day!'

I fanned myself with the book. 'I know. It's finally happening!' I sighed. 'And I'm so glad. I'm just so tired. I can't sleep at night. I'm so big that I just can't get comfortable.' Poor Mike, I know I kept him up half the night trying to find a position that I could sleep in.

Susie's hand was soft and cool as it covered mine. 'You'll be OK. Once that baby's in your arms, you'll forget about these last few days of pregnancy.'

I nodded. 'They're worried that I'm so big, apparently. Especially as my ankles and hands have swelled up. But this time tomorrow—' I felt like I was sitting on a coir mat at the top of a helter-skelter, about to let go and plummet round and round into my future life.

Susie gave me an awkward hug. One huge bump and her growing one. 'That's so perfect. Oh, Gracie. I'm so excited for you. You make sure Mike tells us as soon as he hears.'

'I will. He's under strict instructions. They said I should have the baby by the early afternoon and be ready for visiting hour in the evening.'

'It sounds so easy. Hopefully I can visit the following day.' She picked up the corner of the rug. 'This looks great here. You did an amazing job. I wish I'd done one at the same time now.'

'I feel like this rug has been all I've done for the last few months, but it's been worth it,' I said, running my eyes over the neatly rolled lines of fabric, which went from salmon pink by the cot to burgundy red by the chest of drawers. 'This time next year, the baby could be walking on it.'

'Oh my God, what a thought! Both our babies can play on it. How many did you say you wanted? Four?'

I nodded. 'But I'll let you know how I feel after tomorrow.' I looked down at my tummy. 'What happens when you get induced?' I said. I hadn't realised I was going to say it. I hadn't realised that I was even thinking about it, but there it was. Floating around the room.

Susie shrugged. 'I dunno. Didn't the doctor say?'

I shook my head and wiped the film of sweat off my forehead. My hands were already clammy so all it did was make me hotter. 'He just said we'll induce you tomorrow morning and you'll have the baby by the afternoon.'

'Well, that sounds simple, doesn't it? I hope they induce me too. You'll have to tell me everything. Every detail.' Susie levered herself up and peered over the side of the cot. 'It's all ready, then.'

I laughed. 'I've been ready for months.'

'You know what they say will make the baby come?' Susie said, smiling cheekily.

'What?'

'You know.' She winked. 'I overheard my mum talking about it with your mum. You and Mike.' She nodded towards my belly.

'Oh, for God's sake, Suse, that's the last bloody thing on my mind. And his. I can barely move, let alone anything like that.'

Susie grinned. 'I'm sure you could if you tried.'

I smiled at her despite myself.

Susie stretched out her arms to me. 'C'mon, let's go for a walk. Our last walk together before you're a mum.'

Chapter 9

Joanne

September 2021

Susie Carter was exactly like her Facebook profile photo. Small, blonde and very smiley. She was waiting on the decking outside the cafe in the centre of Seadean the following morning when Joanne and Alex turned the corner. The sun emerged from behind a cloud and it was suddenly very warm.

'Susie?' panted Joanne. 'I'm so sorry we're late. I didn't realise Seadean was so hilly.' She rested her hand on her back to push down the persistent ache, and tried to get her breath back. She knew the butterflies in her tummy were nothing to do with the baby. She was going to get some answers from this stranger.

Susie's mouth had fallen open and she was staring at Joanne intently. 'You look so much like your mum,' she said eventually, her eyes bright. 'Literally the same. You could be her. The spit.' Susie reached out and touched Joanne's hair. 'Your hair is identical. Oh gosh, it's like being transported back in time.'

Joanne smiled. 'I didn't realise I looked so similar to her until recently. We only had one photo of her at home and her hair was all tied up there.'

'Oh.' Susie knitted her eyebrows together and paused. 'I have loads of photos of your mum. Tons. Right from infant school through to—' Susie stopped and looked down. Joanne's chest tightened. 'Anyway, let me give you a big hug. The last time I did this, you were a babe in my arms.'

There was something incredibly comforting about being hugged by this woman, Joanne felt, as Susie enveloped her in her pink fluffy jumper and the scent of clean washing. As close to hugging her own mother as she'd ever get. She closed her eyes.

'This is Alex, my husband,' said Joanne as Susie released her. Susie smiled and hugged him as well.

'Shall we get a cup of tea and then we can chat,' said Susie, nodding at the cafe.

'Yes, let's,' said Joanne, as she followed Susie inside and they all settled down and ordered.

'Y'know, I wouldn't have seen your post normally,' said Susie. 'I'm not on Facebook much. But one of my neighbours, who's lived in the same street as me since we were at school, she spotted it. Not someone your mum and I hung around with, but anyway.' Susie made a face. 'She came round and said, "Isn't that that Grace that you was friends with at school?" and I said, "Yes it is." I couldn't believe that you've come back after all this time. I was so excited.'

Joanne liked her immediately. 'Well, I'm expecting a baby myself, so it seemed like the right time to find out more.' Joanne glanced at Alex. They'd agreed they wouldn't say anything to Susie about the timing of Grace's death until they found out how much Susie knew.

'Ah, I thought you might be expecting, but I didn't want to say nothing in case I was wrong,' said Susie, laughing. 'You never know these days and people get ever so offended. It can't be your first though, surely? Not at your age.'

Joanne frowned. The coffee grinder crunched through the silence.

'Oh, sorry, love,' said Susie above the noise. 'I don't mean to offend. I was just surprised. My daughter's exactly your age and her children are teenagers now. Two girls.' Susie made a face and then smiled up at Joanne. She seemed so warm and genuine that Joanne smiled back.

'It is rather late,' Joanne admitted. 'We started just after we got married ten years ago and then had problems.' She shook her head. 'Anyway, it's all fine now. I'm due in December,' she said, getting her answer in first to the inevitable question.

Susie gave a wide grin. 'That's so exciting. Your mum would be so proud of you. But tell me, where do you live now? You're not local, I can tell that.'

'We're in Berwick-upon-Tweed, right up by the Scottish border. I've been there all my life.'

'I thought he'd go far away,' muttered Susie, looking out of the window and nodding.

Joanne looked at her profile, her breath quickening. So her dad had been escaping from whatever had happened. She was about to ask what Susie meant when the waiter appeared with a tray of tea and pastries. They went through the rigmarole of laying it all out on the table and sharing around the croissants and pains au chocolat.

The cafe windows were steaming up. Joanne felt a sudden flush of heat across her face. She unwound her silk scarf and slipped out of her cardigan. Susie glanced at her neck and then looked down at her tea, her hand trembling as she stirred in some more sugar. She was blushing.

Joanne hated people looking at her scar. For years she had been called 'Scarface' at school, so she ended up almost always covering it with her handmade necklaces or thin silk scarves, but there was something different about the way Susie had looked at it. As if she was looking *for* it, not *at* it.

'It was an accident, when I was very little. I ran into a barbed wire fence—' said Joanne.

Susie nodded. Joanne looked at the scarf, wound up on top of her cardigan. She wished she hadn't taken it off now.

'I like your necklaces,' Susie said, gesturing towards Joanne's chest.

She smiled. 'Thanks, I made them myself. I work in a clothes shop but make jewellery for an online store. I'd love to have my own shop one day.'

Susie's face broke into a smile. 'Your mum was creative too. She was an amazing seamstress. Made all her own clothes, and for other people as well.' She looked down at the table. 'When she gave up work when she was pregnant with you, she'd talked about wanting to start a dressmaking business, have her own shop. If she was around now, you could—'

'That's really weird. I dreamed of her again the other night. She was making a dress, sewing up the hem. A royal-blue one with polka dots.'

'Yes, she had one just like that. She made one for me too,' said Susie. 'I wonder what happened to that.'

Joanne glanced at Alex, but he didn't seem to have heard. She then reached forward so her bump was pressing against the table, shifting her buttocks to try to alleviate the twinges in her back. 'So, Susie, tell me more about her. What was she like as a person?' The flickering feeling in her tummy intensified. She picked up a croissant and took a bite, mainly to give herself something to do with her hands.

Susie seemed to collect herself. She looked up, a big grin splitting her face. 'Oh, Grace was just wonderful. Our families lived a few doors down from each other so I've known her for as long as I can remember.

We went to the same school all the way through – she was the clever one, always had her head in a book, I used to copy her work – and we even worked in the same factory together, making covers for three-piece suites.' Susie picked up her mug and took a sip of tea. 'She met Mike around the same time I met John – at school – and we were bridesmaids at each other's weddings. John and Mike were best man for each other. We were in and out of each other's houses all our lives. We even got pregnant at the same time – well, I was due a couple of months after your mum. My daughter's forty-five now and she lives in London with her family.'

Joanne took a sip of tea. 'And you all lived in the village?'

Susie nodded, smiling. 'Oh yes, just around the corner. I'll show you the cottage your parents lived in if you like. Rose Cottage. The one in the photo you put on Facebook.' She started slicing up a pain au chocolat.

'I'd love that,' whispered Joanne, finding it difficult to swallow. Rose Cottage. She bent down and fiddled in her bag, squeezing her eyes shut to stop the tears. Alex put his hand on her back. Eventually, when she was sure the tears had backed down, she picked the envelope with the photos out of her bag and pushed it across the table to Susie.

Susie dusted the pastry off her fingers and picked it up, taking out the photo of Grace and Mike outside the cottage, smiling. 'Oh, she was a beautiful girl, was your mum. Your mum's mum took this photo. It was when they came back from the hospital after having you.'

'I thought it might have been,' said Joanne, pressing her lips with her fingers.

Susie was looking at the photo, a faraway expression on her face. She put it back on the table and sifted through the envelope, drawing out the picture of Mike and Grace before Joanne was born. She turned it over, touching the rough back. 'This photo was in a baby book, you know the type where you write down a baby's weight and first steps and things. We bought those books together, your mum and me. In Hanningtons. It was a department store in town, ever so posh. It's closed down now.' She looked at the next photo of Grace, Joanne, the grandmother and Susie herself in the hospital. 'We look so young.'

'We started filling the baby books out together and thought we'd do the whole book together.' She sighed and put the photos on the table. 'But of course that didn't happen.'

'Do you have any other photos of her? I only have what's here – and a wedding photo that my dad kept.' Joanne shifted in her chair, trying to move the ache.

'Really?' Susie wove her eyebrows together again. 'But Mike must have had a load of photographs when he left.' She shook her head.

'What was he like, my dad, then? What were they like together?' Joanne held her breath and watched Susie's face. Out of the corner of her eye, she could see Alex sitting completely still. This was it. Susie would know if there'd been arguments, or—

But Susie's face was beaming. 'Oh, they was a lovely couple. Meant to be together, right from the start. I don't think they ever looked at anyone else. It was always Grace for Mike and Mike for Grace. Like two lovebirds. Inseparable.' Her face darkened. 'Until things changed.'

The trembling spread up through Joanne's stomach and into her chest and arms. 'What do you mean?' Her breath shortened as she watched Susie pause and look down at the table, where she started picking at a dried bit of ketchup.

'Y'know, it's not just me who remembers your mum,' she murmured. 'There's a few of us girls from school who are still around. And your Auntie Gerry, your mum's sister. She lives nearby—'

'My aunt?' said Joanne, her eyes wide. 'I didn't know I had an aunt.'

'Really?' said Susie, slurping the last of her tea, looking up at last, her eyes questioning. 'Did Mike not tell you about your family?'

Joanne shook her head and pushed away the half-eaten croissant. The smell was making her feel sick. 'He said that his parents had died when he was young.'

Susie coughed. 'Well, yes, Mike's family had passed, of course. But not your mum's family. Gerry lives up by the village war memorial, but your Auntie Emily emigrated to Australia in the seventies. We haven't seen her since. But I hear from her now and again.'

'Two aunts?' said Joanne, her mouth still hanging open. Alex's hand gripped hers under the table. More lies. She closed her eyes. She wanted to know the truth, but the thought of hearing the words was terrifying. Once they'd been said, they couldn't be unsaid.

Susie nodded. 'And your grandmother. Your mum's mum. Kathleen. She died a few years ago now, but she often talked about you and wondered what happened to you. Surely Mike told you about – about everyone?'

Joanne looked up and rubbed her hand over her face, shielding her eyes. Why had her dad kept so much secret? Why did he hide from her the life he'd had in Brighton? The family she had.

'I'll give Gerry a call once we're finished here and she can pop round. You shouldn't be hearing all this just from me.' Susie stopped and looked out of the window. The 'all this' hung in the air between them.

'There was lots of us here then who've been wondering for years what happened to you. That's why I was so pleased to see that message.' Susie took a deep breath. 'Now, tell me about you. What you've been up to all these years. What Mike's been up to? John still misses him, I know.'

But Joanne wanted a few questions of her own answered before she told Susie about her own life. She glanced at Alex, who raised his eyebrows a fraction. She turned back to Susie. 'There are two sets of writing on those photos. What looks like it might be Grace – loopy writing in blue fountain pen – and then spikier writing in biro. Do you know who that might be?'

The whole of Susie's face lit up. 'That's me, the spiky writing. Mine was always terrible compared to Grace's. We always used to joke about it. If I needed anything written out nicely, I'd ask her to do it for me.' She flicked through the photos until she came to her own handwriting and shook her head. 'Embarrassing, really.'

'But why did you write on the photos? Why didn't Grace do it?'

Susie's smile started to slip. 'Well, of course, she wasn't well after she had you. I knew she'd want a record of you when she got well, so I took the photos and put them on the dresser in your room so she could put them in the book when she got better.' Susie turned over the photo of the three women and baby Joanne in the hospital and ran her fingers along the lines where she'd written Joanne's weight. 'I'd forgotten I'd weighed you every week,' she said quietly. 'Until—' She swallowed.

Joanne watched her face intently as she flipped through the remaining photos, scanning the text and staring at the photos. 'Ah, that rug.' Susie shook her head and put the photos back in the envelope, handing it back to Joanne. 'You ready to come and see more? I have hundreds of photos of your mum.' She pushed her empty mug away and got up to pay. 'No, I insist.' She flapped at Alex, who was digging around for his wallet. 'I've wanted to see you for so many years, little Joanne. This one is on me.'

They walked slowly up the hill into the village, Joanne trying to ignore the ache in her back, which was slowly crawling its way underneath her belly. Susie chatted all the way. 'Just down that road is the school your mum and I went to. Here's the church hall where your mum and dad, and John and I, had our wedding receptions, just a few months apart.'

Joanne stopped and took a picture on her phone, trying to imagine her dad celebrating here, walking out with his bride on his arm. It was so hard to imagine him with anyone but Lou. But he'd had a whole life before he came to Berwick. A life that he'd never talked about. Was it just out of respect for Lou, or something else?

They walked along a few more streets, the picture postcard cottages shimmering in the sunshine. 'This is our road – Windmill Lane. I'm just along here,' said Susie, pointing out a turquoise cottage with a weathered bench outside nestled among delphinium and foxglove spires. Cheerful clusters of daisies, cornflowers and lavender bordered the path.

'I lived there from the day I was born – John moved in with my parents after we married – and I bet I'll die in that place.' She smiled. 'And just a few doors down, the yellow one, is where your mum and dad lived.'

The once yellow walls of the cottage were mottled with patches of peeling paint and streaks of mildew. Paint flaked off the windows showing the bare wood beneath.

'It's a rental,' explained Susie. 'Students from the universities in Brighton live there now. I can never get used to that.' In every other way, it was identical to all the others in the lane. A small wrought-iron gate led up a paved path to the front door. Whereas Susie's garden was full of flowers, here tangled weeds and grass bordered the path, flattened in places with a recycling bin full of beer bottles and plastic milk cartons, and a black bin bag. The large window next to the front door, which Joanne guessed would be the front room, was covered with a sheet. Two small windows upstairs would be bedrooms, she guessed. A seagull pecked at a discarded burger box. Joanne took out the photo of her parents in front of Rose Cottage. Except for the colour, it was an exact match. This was where Grace had lived, where she'd probably written the baby book and then taken her home after she was born.

Alex put his arm around her shoulders. 'We found it.'

Joanne nodded. 'I wish we could go inside, see the rooms. Compare them to the photos.' She flicked through the photos to the one of her mum on the sofa holding her, and glanced up at the window. That had happened metres away. She was so close to the truth.

'Go and stand in front and I'll take a picture of you with the photo, standing in the same place as your mam and dad.'

Joanne nodded and stood by the door. Alex went into the road, through the parked cars, to take the picture.

'Take one without me in it too,' she requested. She wanted to imagine her mum and dad standing in front of it now, welcoming her in for a coffee. Celebrating the news of their grandchild. She could see Susie on the opposite side of the lane, chatting animatedly into her phone.

'How are you feeling?' asked Alex, returning to her. 'I'm worried about you with all this walking and stuff.' He slipped his arm into hers.

Joanne tried to ignore the pain in her back. 'I'm OK. I know this is what I wanted. But it's strange being here. Walking in her footsteps.' She paused and looked up at Alex. 'I wish Mam and Dad were here too, doing this with me.'

Alex nodded and pulled her towards his chest, holding her tightly and stroking her hair. 'It'll be OK. They'll come round.'

Susie had crossed back over the lane and was waving her hands excitedly. 'I've just spoken to your Aunt Gerry. She's so amazed that it's actually you. She's on her way over. Come on in and have a sit-down while we wait for her. She won't be a minute. I'll put the kettle on. Then we can have a proper chat.'

GRACE

JULY 1975

The water was scorching, like stepping into a simmering saucepan. I looked up at the nurse and she nodded encouragingly. 'A nice warm bath and an enema and then we'll get you started,' she said, her blonde bob swinging as she talked.

A red flush was spreading up my legs as I obediently lowered myself into the bath. It was like being back at school, being told what to do.

'What will happen now?'

'It will all be fine,' she said, as she checked the temperature and went out of the room, her rubber shoes squeaking on the faded lino. She came back a moment later with a glass full of orange liquid. 'Drink this,' she said, standing over me with her hands on her hips. I tried to take a sip and gagged. It tasted like the petroleum jelly we rubbed on our lips and eyelashes.

'Do I have to?' I asked, looking up at her.

She nodded. 'Orange juice and castor oil. It'll help to bring things on.'

I closed my eyes and drank the concoction, feeling it slither down my throat. I gagged again.

She leaned across me and opened the tap. A deep gurgling rose up from beneath the floor, shaking the taps. After a long wait, the water spewed out irregularly, spitting and jerking its way into the bath. I quickly moved my feet away from the taps.

A bar of soap, greyed with age, sat on the ledge, small black hairs matted into its crevasses. I was glad I didn't need to wash. I'd had a bath before I left home. I closed my eyes again and thought of Mike, bringing me the cup of tea that morning and sitting on the edge of the bath to kiss me. He'd be at work now. Thinking of me and what was happening. Waiting for news. I knew Susie and Mum would be waiting to hear from him.

The nurse turned off the taps. 'I'll leave you to relax for a few minutes and then we'll bring you in.' She smiled and closed the door quietly.

I tried to lie back and relax but the heat of the water made it difficult to think about anything. At the top of the door was a window. Silvery lines threaded through the green glass. How did they get them there? The baby squirmed in my belly, pushing against its tight confines. What must it be like to be stuck inside, hardly able to turn or move? Waiting to see what happened next. Perhaps the baby was as excited as me about her arrival. I stroked my hand over the enormous bump rising out of the silvery liquid. I could feel something – a hand or a foot, just under my rib. It was crouched in position like a sprinter, ready to spring into the world.

The door opened again and the midwife stood there, the light shining off her blonde hair. 'It's your time, Mrs Bennett.'

She handed me a much-washed pink towel as I struggled out of the bath. It was a relief to be out of the scorching water. Once I was dry, I wrapped my dressing gown around my belly and followed her down the corridor. Grunting, and the occasional scream, punctuated the air. I glanced at the closed doors and looked away.

There was an open door at the end of the corridor and I followed the midwife through it. It was a small, almost claustrophobic space, dominated by a bed. 'Up you get,' she said, sounding for all the world like I was a small child. I clambered on and attempted to lie down. It was as hard as an ironing board.

'By the time you're out of here, you'll have a beautiful baby,' she said. 'Now, we'll start with the enema and shave you to get you ready, and then the doctor will induce you. Move on to your side.'

As I turned over, I felt more people enter the room. They lifted up my dressing gown and nightie and I felt hands on me. Janet at number 34 had warned me about the enema. I screwed up my eyes tight and thought about Bognor. Susie and I sitting on the pier eating Flake 99s. I bit my lip as I felt something in my bottom, but Janet was right, it didn't hurt that much. You just had to try really hard not to break wind. I focused back on Bognor. Ice creams. The glorious feel of sand and how Susie used to cry when she was little and the sand rubbed between her toes and gave her such blisters she couldn't wear her jelly shoes. Oh no, my bottom had made a really bubbly sound. How embarrassing. Skimming stones across the water. Dad got to seven jumps. Susie's dad made eight and I knew our dad was a bit cross about that. The smell of sausages on the caravan grill. Being allowed to sleep in the same bed as Susie for a fortnight. Though we didn't sleep much.

'All done, Mrs Bennett. Now turn on to your back and we'll just tidy you up.' That hadn't been half as bad as I'd thought. I took a deep breath and smiled. It was all going to be OK. Despite my huge belly, I felt strangely empty inside. But it was a nice feeling.

The nurse propped me up into a half-sitting position and fitted my feet into cool metal stirrups. She took a razor and in a few stripes removed my pubic hair. As she turned away, I felt down there. It felt smooth. Bald. Susie and I had done that when we were teenagers, when we hated the look of the dark curly hair. The itching had lasted weeks. We'd never done it again. But I supposed that in a few days I'd have better things to focus on than itching.

'Now, here's the doctor to induce you.' She touched my hand and turned away.

A thin man with a pair of thick glasses took my hand and introduced himself. 'Delighted to meet you, Mrs Bennett. I'm Dr Somer. Let's get this baby out, shall we? And you'll be able to call your husband with the news once he's back from work.'

I smiled up at him and nodded. He opened up my dressing gown and without saying anything slipped something cold into me. I gasped. I hadn't been expecting that. I looked at him, wanting him to say something, explain what was happening, but he didn't. He just turned around and beckoned over a younger man who'd been standing by the door. They both peered at me down below. 'If you look through the speculum, you'll see that the amniotic sac is visualised. See?'

'Yes, sir,' said the younger man.

'Now, I want you to pierce the sac,' he said, handing the younger man a long, thin instrument.

Pierce? I turned to ask the nurse what was happening, but she had her back turned and was fiddling with something on the side. I could only see the top of the men's heads, although I could feel their hands down below.

'Um.' I tried to speak but nothing came out. I took a shaky breath and thought I might cry but then there was a sharp pain and I gasped and then realised in horror that I'd wet myself. Wee pooled on to the thin sheet and then spread out across it. I tried to close my legs to hide it, but there was still something inside me down below.

'Feet in stirrups, Mrs Bennett. Keep your feet in the stirrups.' It was the older doctor again. He didn't look up. 'You'll see here that the amniotic fluid is slowly escaping, allowing the presenting part to descend safely into the pelvis.'

'Yes, sir.'

'Right, remove the speculum, and let's pop next door and you can have another go.'

There was a strange sucking noise and then both men stood up. 'Clean up Mrs Bennett, will you,' the older doctor said in the direction of the midwife. Then both men turned to the door and were gone.

The midwife took her turn between my legs and started wiping up the wee with a warm flannel. 'I'm so sorry, I don't know what happened. I've never done that before,' I said.

She smiled and patted me on the shoulder. 'Don't worry, Mrs Bennett, it's all perfectly normal. That's your waters breaking.'

I nodded, although I didn't really know what she meant. She rinsed the flannel in the sink and then took out two large belt-type things, which she wrapped, with difficulty, around my stomach. 'These are the transducers. They'll monitor the contractions and your baby's heartbeat so we know exactly what's going on inside you.' There was a note of pride in her voice. I smiled, because I think that was what she expected me to do, but the belt was too tight against my belly. My skin was already stretched like a drum.

'I'm going to leave you for a bit and see how you get on,' she said. 'Here's the bell if you need anything.'

She closed the door quietly behind her and I leaned back on the bed. *This is it.* I glanced down at my stomach, but nothing seemed to have changed. I touched myself down there again and smiled. I couldn't wait to tell Susie, she'd laugh so much. I wondered what she was doing. Waiting for news, I suppose. Knitting. Maybe she would do a rag rug too. I knew she was thinking about it, though she'd left it a bit late.

A sharp pain – a little like a stitch but further down – ripped through my thoughts and I pressed the bell. No one came. Another pain started almost straight away, and I pressed the bell again. The baby was coming, I could feel it was. I'd had several more pains by the time the midwife appeared. 'How's things coming along, Mrs Bennett?'

I grunted and pointed at my belly. 'It hurts,' I said. 'Lots of pain.'

'Good, good,' she said, patting my shoulder again. 'Now what I want you to do is to count the gaps between the pains. Can you do that?'

I nodded. 'But there aren't really any gaps,' I said.

She didn't seem to hear but started closing the windows. 'Ring the bell if you need anything,' she added as she slipped out of the door.

Without the slight breeze, the room was stifling. I lay back on the rock-hard bed and tried to remember the panting they'd taught us in the relaxation classes. The pain built again and I pressed the bell, biting my lip through it. The midwife didn't come back. This was ridiculous. Why were they leaving me like this? I tried to get up, but the belt things pinned me to the bed. There was a constant pain in my back. Something was going wrong. I pressed the bell again. A woman was shouting through the wall, but I couldn't make out the words. 'Shut up,' I shouted back. I wanted her to stop. I slammed my hand on the bell but the door stayed shut.

I took my feet out of the stirrups and tried to push them away. I wanted to get up. To walk. It was agony, like the vice Mike used in the garage, gripping me constantly. Pushing, pulling. Constant. I pressed the bell repeatedly. The door stayed shut. The world turned red and black then red again.

The woman next door was screaming. I shouted at her to keep quiet. The noise was distracting.

A hand was on my shoulder. 'Mrs Bennett.' At last. 'Trying to get off the bed is strictly forbidden. You must stay in this position, so we can monitor you.' It was the same nurse as before, her perfect blonde bob mocking my wild curls, now damp with sweat. 'And please try not to make so much noise. It's upsetting for the other mums.' I wasn't making any noise.

I moaned quietly again as the vice turned another notch. 'But you're not monitoring me. I'm in agony.'

She looked at the monitor. 'You're progressing very well, Mrs Bennett. It won't be long and you'll have your baby.'

'It hurts,' I roared at her. I wanted to punch her, to kick her until she stopped smiling and being so pleasant.

'Would you like some pain relief? When you're induced, it can come on quite quickly.'

I looked at her, my mouth open, and nodded. Thank God.

She busied herself in the corner of the room and then came back next to me. The pain was now constant. 'Now, you'll feel a slight scratch.' I closed my eyes and what could only have been a spear pierced my side. I shouted something I didn't understand.

'That's the pain relief,' she said.

I opened my eyes and realised there were more people in the room. They crowded around my bed, watching me. It was the older doctor again.

'You're doing very well, Mrs Bennett. It won't be long now.' Then he was gone. The same nurse was still there but there was another woman with her. The rhythmic thud of the monitor suddenly stopped. I hadn't heard it until it wasn't there.

'Oh God, there's something wrong,' said the other nurse. She looked older – grey hair and creases around her eyes and mouth.

'Oh, don't worry about that, it does that sometimes,' said the blonde one, readjusting it. The noise thudded back. It sounded like a heartbeat.

A sharp pain gripped my mouth this time, and blood filled it. I pointed at it, unable to talk.

The nurse shook her head. 'You can't eat during labour, Mrs Bennett.'

I opened my mouth and blood dribbled down my chin. I smeared it across my face and held it up to the light.

The nurse leaned over me. 'All that gritting your teeth and you've gone and broken one.' She handed me some wadding. 'Put this between your teeth. It'll stop any further damage. You'll have to see a dentist afterwards.'

The vice turned. It all went black again. Beautiful, soothing black. I dreamed of the stork from the baby book above me. He was holding the baby up high, gently lowering her into my arms. The baby was soft, slightly moist like a rose petal. She looked up at me and gurgled. The stork drew the white cloth into its beak, slipping the baby into my arms. Then it rose up and flew away, its beating wings covering us in a gentle breeze.

Then the light snapped on and a voice was shouting, 'She's back.' I tried to turn my head to look for the stork but there was nothing beyond the brilliant light. Maybe I'd died and this was heaven. But it still hurt too much. Perhaps it was hell.

There was more talking beyond the light, but I couldn't hear what they were saying. There were hands down below and it felt as if they were forcing me open. 'You didn't say it was breech,' someone said. Breech? The woman next door was still shouting, saying the most terrible words. I wanted her to stop but I couldn't find my voice. It seemed to have sunk down inside me.

'Forceps,' someone said.

Make it end. I could feel myself shaking.

I looked for the stork, but he still didn't come. Just the redness of the pain moving from bright vermilion to the darkest burgundy and back again. Like the rag rug. *Stop, stop.*

'Episiotomy.' That voice again. The doctor they called 'sir'.

People were racing around, the door was open. The screaming was louder than ever.

'Where is all the blood coming from?' someone shouted.

The burgundy slipped into black and I turned to look for the stork. But he wasn't there. Instead, my mother's grandmother, who I'd only seen in photos, was holding out her hand and reaching for me. 'Welcome,' she was saying. She folded me into her arms. I stayed there for a long time, and when I finally opened my eyes the room was dark. The shouting had stopped and a baby was crying. I tried to sit up.

'Be careful, Mrs Bennett,' said the nurse. 'You've had a difficult time of it. Don't move for now, you're all stitched up.'

'The baby,' I whispered.

'A beautiful baby girl.' The nurse smiled, laying me back on the bed. 'Congratulations.'

A girl, I'd always known it. I reached my arms out to the sound of the crying but the other nurse was already wrapping her up. I could see a slip of pink flesh as she carried her from the room.

'I want to—' I reached out my arms towards the nurse. But the door shut behind her.

'My baby.' Someone – was it me? – started to howl.

'You need to rest, Mrs Bennett. You've had a difficult birth. We'll take care of Baby.'

'But I need to phone my husband to tell him. He'll be back from work and waiting to hear.'

'It's the middle of the night, Mrs Bennett, he'll be fast asleep. I'll give you something to help you sleep.'

I shook my head and tried to sit up. A dark pain reached up from below. 'My baby—' I said.

A scratch in my arm, and then the blackness covered me like a blanket. I looked for my great-grandmother, but I was alone.

Chapter 10

Joanne

September 2021

The cottages in Seadean were completely different to the one she'd grown up in in Berwick, thought Joanne, like something from a painting. Funny to think her dad had lived in a place like this but ended up in Berwick.

'Come in, come in,' said Susie, leading them into a front room and indicating a floral sofa where a tabby cat was lounging in the sunshine. 'Move off, Tigger,' she added, sweeping the cat away.

Joanne sank into the soft fabric next to Alex and stroked her belly. The baby's kicks had been more pronounced recently. Reassuring nudges. But it had been still for a few hours now, the ache spreading across her back like melted butter in a pan. She wondered if the baby could feel her pain. She pushed away the thought and looked around the room. Two armchairs stuffed with cushions sat either side of a wood-burning stove. The bookcase in the corner was crammed with paperbacks.

On the wall was a print of a painting that seemed really familiar to her, although she couldn't think why. And then it came to her.

'That painting,' she said, turning to Alex and pointing at the wall. 'You had a postcard of it as a bookmark in that dads' parenting book.'

Alex stared at the picture in its white wooden frame. He seemed to be lost in thought for a moment and then to come to. 'Oh, a patient gave it to me. You know what they can be like towards the end. Wanting to say thank you. They can easily get attached to you.' He gave a little laugh. 'She gave me this as a thank-you. Said she'd seen it in the National Gallery many times and it was her favourite painting. She loved the colours, said that through his use of colour, the bathers blend into the landscape.'

But Joanne was hardly listening. In the centre of the mantelpiece was a wedding photo of a lovely young couple, but it was the woman standing next to the bride who caught Joanne's attention. Grace. Joanne made to get up, but Susie stopped her.

'You stay there, in your condition. I'll bring over the photo.' Susie reached up and brought the silver frame down, blowing off imaginary dust. 'This is my wedding day. John and me. Your mum was a beautiful bridesmaid. Just look at her.' Susie handed Joanne the frame.

It was like looking at her own reflection, Joanne thought. But one in peach frills. Grace was holding a little flower basket and smiling from ear to ear. Joanne could see that she'd tried to tie her hair down by pinning it back and under, just as she herself sometimes tried, but it was all a little fruitless. It sprang out of the side of her head, framing her beautiful face.

Susie was rummaging in the bottom of the cabinet, muttering to herself. 'I know they're in here somewhere. Ah, here they are.' She drew out a couple of slim photo albums and put them on the table in front of Joanne. 'These are the old albums my mum had when we were children. There are loads of photos of your mum and me in them. I think there's a few more, hold on.'

Alex reached forward and picked one up, opening it for Joanne. The pictures were stuck on the page behind a thin sheet of brittle plastic. Two small girls stood smiling on the beach wearing matching terry-towelling shorts suits, buckets and spades against their legs. They were unmistakably Susie and Grace. Joanne traced her finger on her mother's face, her curls already wild.

'Blimey, you're so like her,' said Alex, staring at the photo and then at Joanne.

Susie squeezed on to the sofa on the other side of Joanne, sandwiching her in the middle. 'That's your mum and I down on the beach. We must be, what, six or seven then. That next one is me and my brother.' She turned the page. 'Oh, here's your mum and me on sports day. You can see your mum's mum in the distance, look. With the blue dress.' Joanne squinted at a faded figure in a row of other women.

They flicked through more pages. 'This is us on holiday,' said Susie, laughing at a picture of herself in just knickers, standing on the steps of a caravan. 'We always went together, the two families. Down to Bognor for the week with the caravan, because there's sand there.'

'It sounds just like your holidays as a child, Jo,' said Alex. 'And mine,' he added. Joanne nodded, unable to take her eyes off the pictures.

Over the page there was a photo of two women standing in the caravan's tiny kitchen. Both had headscarves on; one had a cigarette glued to the corner of her mouth. 'That's my mum with the fag, and next to her is your grandmother. She was a lovely lady.' Joanne stared at the face and felt her heart contract.

The doorbell trilled and Susie bounced up. 'That must be Gerry.' She disappeared into the corridor.

'You OK?' whispered Alex, his hand around Joanne's shoulder. 'This isn't too much for you, is it?' She could hear the anxiety in his voice.

Joanne shook her head. 'No, I need to be here, to see this. Now we're having a baby, it's more important than ever that I know where I'm from, so that when she's old enough I can share it with her.' Joanne heard the sob in her voice before she felt it, and swallowed. Alex stroked her shoulder. The ache grew and she struggled not to wince. The murmur of whispered conversation drifted through the door. There was a pause and then a tall woman with closely cropped blonde hair walked in. Her eyes flitted to Joanne and widened, and her hand flew to her mouth. Then she broke into a smile. 'You're not wrong, Susie. She's so like her.'

Joanne stood up, pushing the pain away, smiling uncertainly. She felt Alex gripping her hand beside her.

The woman walked forward. 'I'm Gerry. Your mum's older sister.' She stood in front of Joanne and then suddenly embraced her, her hands gripping Joanne's shoulders.

'The last time I held you, you were a foot long. I didn't realise it would be another forty-odd years until I held you again.' Aunt Gerry bit her lip and held Joanne at arm's length. 'You look so much like her, it's uncanny. As if Grace has come back to life. Everyone must tell you that.'

Joanne forced the corners of her mouth into a smile. 'Not really. Nobody I grew up with knew her, apart from Dad, of course, and he never spoke about Grace at all.'

Gerry glanced at Susie standing by the door and raised her eyebrows a fraction.

Susie dipped her head in response and then clapped her hands. 'Right, let's get some tea. I'll leave you in here while I sort it out.'

As they moved to the sofa, Joanne caught Gerry glancing at her neck, covered by the scarf. She brought her hand up to adjust it, suddenly self-conscious.

Alex took one of the armchairs as Joanne and Gerry sat on the sofa. 'I'm so thrilled to see you again, dear little Joanne. We waited so long for news . . .' She trailed off, opened up a large shoulder bag she'd brought with her and took out another photo album. 'When Susie said you were here, I thought I'd bring this. I got it from Mum's house after she died.' She opened it gently. 'It's all old family pictures.' On the first page was the same image of Joanne being held in the hospital by an older woman next to Grace.

'That's Mum, your grandmother. She was so excited to be a grandmother. You were her first grandchild.' Gerry paused. 'Which made your leaving all the harder.'

Joanne could feel the tightness growing in her chest, competing with the ache below.

Aunt Gerry turned over the page and there were more photos of a baby Joanne at home. In one, a younger Gerry was holding her, looking slightly uncomfortable. 'I'd never held a baby before. I was worried about dropping you, I think.' She laughed. 'This is your grandfather, my dad. He was so proud of your mum having you.'

Susie bustled back in and Alex helped her lay out the teapot and mugs. Joanne could feel his eyes on her, watching, worrying.

Joanne pored over the pictures of the people who looked so like her but hadn't even been names in her consciousness until now. How strange that all these people had existed all along and she hadn't even known about them. But then she suddenly thought maybe she'd felt the lack of something but had never known what it was.

She glanced up at the dyed blonde head next to her. 'Do you have children, Gerry?'

Gerry's eyes flitted back to Susie, who looked away. 'No, it wasn't for me, after Grace. And your Aunt Emily, in Australia, she didn't have any either. She went travelling after—' She stopped and took a breath. 'After everything that happened.'

Did they mean her dad leaving? Did they know what had happened to Grace? wondered Joanne. She pressed her lips together. She was desperate to ask them how much they knew but it suddenly felt too massive. From the looks passing between Gerry and Susie, she had begun to feel that something really terrible had taken place and she was scared now of what she might find out. She was determined to ask them, but it felt important that she waited for just the right moment or, like her mam and dad, they might just clam up.

Susie picked up the teapot and started pouring. 'We should tell Emily about Joanne. She'll be so excited. Perhaps we could get her on the computer.'

Gerry looked at her watch. 'It'll be nine p.m. in Sydney, it's not too late to call her now if we do it quickly.' She reached into her bag, brought out a phone with a cracked screen and started dialling. Joanne tried to pull a deep breath into her lungs. It was all happening too fast. Too many people, too many secrets.

Susie grinned at Joanne, her eyes alight.

'So how come Emily ended up in Australia?' asked Alex as Gerry fiddled with her phone. Joanne closed her eyes, grateful he'd taken the conversation on. From not knowing anything, it suddenly felt she was going to know too much. She pressed her hands on her belly.

Susie looked at her hands. 'She left Brighton not long after Joanne and her dad did. It all seemed to affect her even more than the rest of us.'

Joanne frowned. *It all.* What was the *it all* that had affected her so much she moved to the other side of the world? And her dad fled to the other end of the country? Where had Grace been in those two years? Not here with her family, it seemed. What did they know? If they'd known Mike had . . . She blinked. If they'd known he'd *hurt* Grace, then surely they wouldn't speak about him like this.

There was the familiar FaceTime beeping from Gerry's phone and Susie continued, 'So she took off. And travelled. I know people do that all the time now, but they didn't in the seventies, not where we were from anyway. We never went anywhere, so it was quite a thing.' Susie pressed her lips together. 'She ended up in Australia a few years later and she stayed ever since. She married an Australian chap. Gerry's been out there a few times to visit her over the years—' Susie nodded towards Aunt Gerry, who was speaking into the phone, an intense frown drawing all her wrinkles together. 'But Emily's never been back. I knew she wouldn't when she left . . .' Susie trailed off.

Joanne glanced towards Gerry, who had taken the phone away from her ear and was brandishing it at her.

'And here she is. Your Aunt Emily. All the way from Sydney.' The lined face of a grey-haired woman filled the screen. Emily clearly wasn't as familiar with hair dye as Susie and Aunt Gerry.

'Oh!' The kindly face on the screen drained of colour.

Joanne tried to smile as Gerry scooted along the sofa to sit next to her, their faces pressed together so Aunt Emily could see both of them.

'Isn't she the spitting image, Em? I couldn't believe it.'

Aunt Emily nodded, her eyes still wide.

'Hello,' said Joanne uncertainly. It was like being a child again, when Lou had paraded her in front of numerous cousins many times removed. They'd talked about her as if she wasn't there – gossiped about where she'd come from, why it was so sad that her mam had died, prodded and poked her dress, commented on her hair, sympathised about her scar.

'Little Joanne. I've often thought of you and wondered how you were.' The voice had an Australian twang.

Joanne stared at her. 'It's been amazing to discover that I have a family, people who knew me and wondered about me.' She knew she sounded robotic. Alex got up from the chair and slid down next to her, gripping her. She felt herself lean against him and let out a breath.

'And who's this? More family?'

There was a pause. Alex glanced at Joanne and then answered, 'I'm Alex, Joanne's husband.'

'What does that make you to us, second cousin-in-law? I'm never sure how it works.'

Alex laughed and shook his head. 'I don't know either.' Joanne felt his eyes on her. He stroked her shoulder and she leaned further into him. He felt solid, real.

'We all wondered about you, Joanne, and talked about you,' said Aunt Emily, her voice tinny through the phone. 'I'd love to visit and see you.' Gerry looked at Susie and raised her eyebrows slightly before looking back at the screen. 'Your mum was such a character, such a lovely girl. We all miss her.' Her voice was full of emotion.

'We do.' Susie nodded. 'But we keep her alive and have done all these years. Just talking about her, talking about the times together.'

Gerry nodded, smiling.

'It's strange,' said Joanne slowly. 'In my house we never talked about Grace, and yet here everyone did.' She looked at Alex, who bobbed his head. 'If only I'd known.'

'Well, of course it was awful for your father,' said Gerry, her mouth turning down. 'We're not surprised he moved away afterwards. People are funny about that sort of thing.' Out of the corner of her eye, Joanne saw Susie shake her head slightly at Gerry, as if to warn her.

'What do you mean?' said Joanne, looking in turn at the three women. She could feel Alex stiffen beside her.

But their faces suddenly closed. Aunt Emily appeared to freeze on the screen. Susie shook her head. 'Oh you know, it was tough for him, what happened to your mum. It was for all of us.'

Joanne frowned. Whatever had happened maybe hadn't been to do with her dad. They were sympathetic towards him, not accusing. Maybe he hadn't . . . ? She couldn't form the words now, couldn't follow the thought. Had she really convinced herself he had something to do with it? But it still didn't explain how Grace had died just two years later.

They chatted some more on the phone, her aunts sharing memories of Grace. Eventually, they said goodbye to Emily. Gerry stood. 'How long are you both in Brighton for?'

'Well, we just came down to find out more about Jo's mam's family. I guess we'll go back tomorrow, or the day after? We've both got work,' said Alex, looking at Joanne for confirmation.

She nodded. 'But I'd like to hear more. Not just about Grace – Mam. But about Dad. About what happened at the end. Before they left.'

Susie and Gerry shared a glance, which Joanne had been waiting for. She knew Alex had seen it too.

'Look, I appreciate that this has been a shock today,' said Susie gently. 'Why don't you come round tomorrow, and we can chat more. Gerry?'

Once again, Joanne caught the silent conversation between the two women. 'I can do that,' Gerry said eventually.

Joanne nodded. 'That would be good.' They'd tell her tomorrow, she was sure of it. Or a version of the truth. A version they'd agree on as soon as she and Alex left.

They stood and exchanged numbers, hugging their goodbyes.

Joanne and Alex walked a few doors down and stood outside her mum and dad's old cottage. Alex enveloped her in a hug. 'Jesus, I wasn't expecting all that. Are you OK?' he asked, his mouth sagging. 'That was a lot to take in.'

Joanne sniffed, her face buried against his chest. 'It was so amazing to see them, to know that they were thinking of me. To see the photos, but—' She drew back and looked at Alex.

'I know what you're going to say,' he said, tucking a curl behind her ear. 'There was so much they didn't tell us.'

'Yeah.' Joanne bit her lip.

'I thought you might ask them directly what happened.'

She blew out a long breath. 'It just felt too much to ask straight away. The first time we met them. I didn't want to spoil it.'

Alex nodded his head slowly. 'But whatever it was, they don't blame your dad. I thought that was pretty clear.' He stroked her cheek.

Joanne looked him in the eye. 'No. And thank God.' She swallowed and looked down. 'I didn't realise how much I was worried about that.'

'Given what you knew, it was understandable. But you know your dad, he's a decent man. He'd stop the car on a motorway rather than run over anything. I don't know anyone as soft as him.'

Joanne closed her eyes. 'I know.' She looked at the cottage. 'But this is where it all happened. So we're closer to the truth than when we first arrived in Brighton.'

'We'll find out tomorrow,' he said, taking her arm and walking back down the lane to the bus stop back to Brighton.

Joanne went with him, ignoring the pain that hugged her back and gripped her belly.

GRACE

JULY 1975

A voice worked its way into the darkness. I pushed it back but it forced its way through my consciousness, like a splinter. 'Mrs Bennett, Mrs Bennett.' The blackness started to grey, even though I grasped on to it. I cracked open my eyes and squinted against the brightness. 'Mrs Bennett, we have your baby. It'll soon be visiting hour, you need to be ready.'

'Oh.' My baby. I pushed myself up and felt a seam below start to stretch.

'Careful, careful. You've got internal and external stitching down there. Let's get you on a ring. It'll make it more comfortable for you to sit.' It was a different nurse from before, younger, smiling. She grunted as she lifted me up by the shoulders and centred me on the rubber ring, the sort we used to take to Bognor. The seam below eased, though I felt like a small child sitting on it. What was it like, stitching flesh? Was it hard like leather or yielding like silk?

'Thank you.' I looked past her at the other nurse, cradling a baby. My daughter. I reached out my arms and they gently slipped her into them, just like the stork, carefully positioning her head against my arm. She felt solid, real but also like a wispy cloud.

'Joanne,' I whispered. 'Hello.' Her cheek was of the softest cream silk, strands of fine downy hair like delicate silken threads poking out from underneath the woollen bonnet I'd made when she'd been a tiny baby inside me. Her eyes were closed, her head the only visible thing outside the shawl. I started to unwrap it. Underneath, she wore a white cotton one-piece. Between the poppers, I could see the corner of the terry nappy. Who had slipped her arms and legs into this? How long had I been asleep? I bit my lip as I looked down at her birdlike mouth. I'd already missed out on some of her life.

'Keep the baby warm,' the older nurse said disapprovingly. She moved towards me and tucked the shawl around Joanne until she was like an Egyptian mummy again, before walking away down the line of beds. The room was full of women, all sitting up in bed cradling babies. Joanne shifted in my arms but didn't wake. I couldn't stop staring at her, memorising every perfect feature, willing her to open her eyes. It seemed impossible that this baby, this person, had come from me.

A bell rang. I heard the rumble of male voices and an energy ran around the ward. Women sat up straighter in their beds. The one opposite rearranged her dress and combed her fingers through her long, dark hair. The woman to my right expertly cradled her baby in one arm and reapplied her lipstick with the other. I stared at Joanne and wondered if Mike would have preferred a boy. They always said men wanted their firstborn to be a boy.

The sister opened the door at the end of the ward. Men flooded through in a flurry of noise and colour. Mike was at the back of the group, his eyes darting around the room trying to locate us. I wanted to raise my arm, but I worried I'd drop the baby. I sat there and watched him glance at all the other women before his eyes settled on me. His whole face relaxed into a smile and he strode towards me. Us. He slid into the chair by the bed and touched my arm. 'When I didn't hear last night, I was so worried. But they called first thing. And they wouldn't say whether it was a boy or a girl.' His eyes showed the tightness of a sleepless night. He picked at the pink ribbon on the cot. 'It's a girl?'

I nodded. 'You didn't want a boy? You're not disappointed?'

'Oh Gracie, of course not. And I know you wanted a girl.' He stood up and slid his arm around my shoulders. The seam stretched again and I bit my lip. 'Are you all right?'

'Just a bit sore,' I said, blinking back the smarting. I couldn't tell him about the stitches. What an awful thing.

He nodded. 'She's beautiful,' he said, staring down at Joanne, his face softening. His rough hands looked somehow wrong on her smooth cheek.

'You're still happy calling her Joanne?' I said.

'Well, we can't call her Justin or Paul. That would be odd.'

I laughed. He was always good at making me laugh.

The sound of gurgling babies and chattering couples filled the room but Joanne stayed asleep. My eyes kept flitting between Mike and Joanne's faces.

'Was it OK then? Having her? It took much longer than they said. We were all worried.'

I thought of the stork slipping the baby into my arms and whisking the sheet away. I didn't want to remember the red and the blackness. Particularly the red. 'It was fine. She's here now, that's the main thing.' I traced the tiny arcs of hair that would become her eyebrows. 'I'm sorry you were worried.'

Mike shifted in his chair and leaned his elbows on the bed.

'Ah, Mr Bennett.' The older nurse again. Mike jumped back, as if he'd been stung. She straightened the edge of my sheet. 'Mr Bennett, I'm the matron. Your wife had a tricky time of it in the delivery room so we're taking especial care of her. But please don't worry, she's in the best hands. And look at your daughter. What a beautiful baby.'

I drew my lips into the smile I knew was expected. 'I'm absolutely fine,' I said to Mike, seeing his concern. 'I've been asleep since I had her. I've no idea of the time. What time *is* it?'

But Mike wasn't looking at me. 'Am I allowed to hold her?' he asked the matron, almost shyly.

I dug my fingers tighter into her shawl, but the matron was already slipping her arms under Joanne's head and bringing her towards him. 'Of course, Mr Bennett. We encourage our fathers to support our new mums now.' She settled Joanne in his arms, making sure her head was supported by his arm, her shawl properly wrapped. 'She'll need your help once she's home.'

My arms felt heavy, empty, useless. I picked at my thumbnail.

Mike was stroking the side of the baby's cheek. 'She's just like you,' he said, not looking up. 'Beautiful.'

The baby's eyelids were starting to flutter and, almost in slow motion, she opened her eyes and fixed them on Mike's face. 'Gracie, look.' He glanced at me. 'She's awake.' His mouth gaped.

A spit of something dark surged through me. I should have been the one she saw first. That was how it was supposed to be. I pushed it back down and focused on her eyes. She was fixated on Mike. 'Her eyes are so dark, so blue. Do you think they'll stay that way?' he asked.

I shrugged and the movement caused a spasm of pain down below. 'I dunno.'

'Do you want to hold her again?' he asked, standing up awkwardly and trying to pass the baby to me like a parcel. Matron's eyes followed us. 'I'll take a picture of you both to show the others.'

Mike settled her back in my arms just as Matron had done with him, and took out the Polaroid camera. I fixed a smile on my face and stared at the lens. He clicked it and then sat back down, putting the camera on the side and holding the picture waiting for it to appear. Joanne had closed her eyes again. Her tiny fist was hovering outside of her mouth. Did babies suck their thumbs this young? I stared at her, willing her to look at me.

'You're so amazing, Gracie,' Mike said, touching my arm. 'Everyone sends their love. Your mum can't wait to visit. Susie says she was up all night worrying about you.'

Susie. What would I tell her about what happened? I didn't want her to know the full horror of it when she was so close to giving birth herself. Maybe that was why Mum had never warned me. *Just a few hours of pain and it's all worth it in the end.* That's all she'd said. Not being torn apart, being hanged, drawn and quartered in some barbaric medieval act. I shifted on the ring and swallowed the wince.

'Your dad, John and I are going to the Seven Sisters later to wet the baby's head.'

I nodded. I tried to imagine sitting in the bar of the Seven Sisters with a Lambrusco. It felt like something I'd done in another world.

'I'll pick up the pram tomorrow, get it all ready for when you both come home.' He reached over and touched my arm. 'Anything else you want me to do?'

I looked at him. He suddenly seemed very far away. I shook my head.

'I'll tell everyone how well you're doing. How beautiful the baby is.'

I nodded. Was I doing well?

'Look, look at the two of you.' He held up the picture in front of my face – a woman holding a baby was slowly emerging. I didn't know her.

The bell rang. It must be the end of visiting time. I felt my shoulders drop and took a deep breath. Why did I feel relieved?

Mike got to his feet and dropped a kiss first on Joanne's blanket and then on my forehead. 'You've made me the happiest man alive, Gracie.' His eyes melted, like chocolate in the sun. 'Thank you. I'll see you both soon.'

I lifted my mouth into a smile and watched him join the crocodile of husbands walking down the ward to the door. At the end, he turned and raised a hand and was gone.

Joanne was still asleep in my arms, her head heavy. There was a clock opposite I hadn't noticed before. Six o'clock. Early evening. That was right, they'd always said visiting hour was early evening.

Chapter 11

Joanne

September 2021

Joanne didn't realise it was blood at first. She woke to the sound of
the seagulls screeching overhead and thought the dampness on the
sheet was sweat. The room was clammy, the weather close. It was
only when she reached down between her legs that she realised it
was coming from her. In the split second it took her hand to wipe
her thighs and look at the colour of the liquid, she'd gone through
the options. She'd wet herself. She'd heard that pregnant women
did do that sometimes, but surely not in the sixth month. Her
waters had broken. It was way too early for that. If it was her waters
now, she'd spend the rest of the pregnancy in hospital while they
tried to save the baby. She pushed the alternative out of her mind
but as she brought her hand up to the weak dawn light, the liquid
smeared on her hand looked black. Menacing.

'Alex,' she gasped, her heart already thudding, the dread clutching her throat. She knew it had all been too good to be true. She'd
never be a mother. 'I'm bleeding.'

Alex sprang to life immediately, pressing the switch so the bed
was drenched in light. It looked like a murder scene. Blood was
smeared across the sheets and duvet, veining across her thighs.

'Fuck,' he whispered. 'I'll call an ambulance.' He leaped out of bed.

Joanne lay back on the pillows, holding herself between her legs as if she could somehow keep the baby in with her hands. Blood pooled in her cupped fingers. She squeezed her eyes shut, concentrating on feeling the baby move, knowing that any movement would mean it was OK. But it was still, silent. She'd been so certain this time. To get to the five-month scan, to see the baby fully formed. She closed her eyes and turned on her side, curling into the foetal position, pulling the duvet over her head. The dread settled over her, cold grief gripping her heart. This had been their last chance.

Someone drew back the duvet and gripped her shoulders. 'We're just going to move you on to this stretcher, love. You don't need to do anything. Just relax.' The voice was kindly. Someone who knew what they were doing.

Joanne let herself be moved. Kept her eyes shut. She didn't want to see any more blood. See any more pieces of her disintegrating baby. Didn't want to see their sympathetic faces. Alex's disappointment. They strapped her to the stretcher and the air changed as they moved out of the room and down the stairs. She squeezed open a swollen eye and saw the B&B lady standing in her pink dressing gown, rags in her hair, hand over her mouth. She closed them again and the seagulls were suddenly louder as they came outside. And then they were inside the ambulance. It smelled clean in there. Like a tube of antiseptic.

Hands pulled away the blanket and examined her. She'd lost all sense of privacy during the years of IVF, so the probing hands didn't worry her. She felt a hand grip hers – Alex's – and then they were moving. The sirens ripping apart the morning air, louder even than the seagulls.

'Don't tell Mam and Dad what's happened,' she said. 'I don't want them to know. To worry.'

Alex was silent.

It seemed only minutes later and she was being taken out, the morning air cool against her face before she was once more inside. Under strip lights this time. She closed her eyes tighter and curled inside herself again.

More hands. More kindly voices. Alex was talking. Hands were pulling the blanket away. 'Joanne, love.' Something was cold and wet on her tummy. *Ultrasound gel*, she thought. They were going to look inside and see the dark, gaping hole where her baby had been. She pushed it all away and slipped into the blackness. Grace was suddenly there, holding her like she was a baby. She turned into her and breathed in the smell. It was different from Mam. A softer scent. Like roses. She was stroking Joanne's face, whispering to her. She couldn't quite hear what Grace was saying. But she was smoothing it all away.

It seemed a long time later that Alex was stroking her face. She was propped up now. In a different room. The lights were softer here. Like sunshine. She opened her eyes. He was smiling at her.

His face was different. Taut. His eyes swollen. 'The baby's fine, Jo, it's OK.'

Joanne glanced down at her belly. It was still rounded. She looked up at him.

Alex nodded. 'It was just a small bleed. It looked far worse than it was. But the baby's OK.'

Warmth came flooding back into her chest. 'Are you sure?' Joanne whispered. She pushed the blackness away, back into the corner of her mind.

'How are you doing in here?' A nurse pulled the curtain closed behind her. 'Ah, you're awake now, back in the land of the living.'

Joanne smiled and took a deep breath. It was OK. The baby was OK. Grace had made the baby live. 'Hello.'

'Hello, Mrs Shaw. Has your husband told you the good news? Your baby is fine, but we're going to keep you in for a day or so, just to monitor you. We can't have you bleeding like that all the time.' She smiled and jotted something down on the clipboard at the end of the bed. 'But there's absolutely nothing to worry about.'

Joanne closed her eyes in relief and lay back on the pillows. Grace had been here, while she was asleep. She was sure of it. It had been Grace who had saved her baby. The nurse chatted away and Joanne nodded and tried to listen, but her thoughts felt far away.

When she'd gone, Joanne turned to Alex. 'Will you call Susie and tell her what's happened? Perhaps she could come here to chat.'

Alex looked at her, his face still pale. 'I'll send her a text. But don't you think we should drop all this for now? That what happened yesterday, meeting Susie and your aunts, brought all this on?'

Joanne wrinkled her nose. 'I was just tired, that's all. You heard the nurse, the baby's fine.' She reached down and stroked the curve of her belly. She could feel Grace, nearby. 'It's just a chat, that's all. What harm can it do? I want to find out what happened to her, to Grace. And Susie and Gerry know what happened, I'm sure of it.'

Alex shook his head. 'Jo, you've got to think of the baby. Our baby,' he emphasised. 'We could have lost it today—' His voice cracked and he looked away.

Joanne nodded, remembering the blood on the sheets. Would the B&B take them off before they got back? And then Grace was in her mind again, really vivid and present. She was standing in front of the little yellow cottage. She seemed to be beckoning Joanne in. 'But I just want to talk to Susie. Just once more. To see what she knows about Grace.'

Alex pressed his lips into a hard line. 'Jo, this is all we've ever wanted. Our baby. Our family. Years we've waited. Don't risk stressing yourself out now. We're so close to having her. Just a few more weeks.'

Grace was still there. She'd opened up the front door and was walking through it, turning to reach for Joanne.

'Just one conversation, Alex, just one. Please.'

'What about your mam? She should know that you're in hospital.'

Grace was shaking her head.

'No, I don't want her or Dad to know. Not after everything that's happened.'

'But we know they had nothing to do with Grace's . . . disappearance.'

'They're still keeping secrets from me. I need to know what happened.'

Alex rubbed his face with his hand, pulled the curtain back and was gone.

Joanne closed her eyes and willed Grace to come back to her.

GRACE

JULY 1975

The woman in the bed next to me spoke like a running stitch, a constant stream of words. She was sitting upright, her hair curled, lipstick perfect. 'You do look a little peaky. I was like that when I came round. I think they give you pretty strong pills the first night so you can have a proper sleep. You've slept all day.' She sounded almost accusing. 'I've been waiting for you to wake up.'

She slipped out of bed as if she'd done nothing more energetic than make a cup of tea, and slid her baby into the cot. Everything between my legs throbbed.

'I'm Jenny,' she said, reaching out her hand.

I was holding Joanne and didn't dare move a hand. I nodded down at her. 'I would shake your hand, but—'

'Don't worry, you'll get the hang of it. All of us girls here' – Jenny waved her hand grandly around the ward – 'felt strange at first. But the midwives are wonderful and we're all here to help one another. It reminds me of school. So much fun. You'll love it.'

I thought of Susie and swallowed. I couldn't have got through school without her. And she wasn't here now to help me through this.

Jenny slid her feet into a pair of pale-pink slippers with feathers, the type I'd always admired but thought too expensive to buy. 'Anyway, excuse me for a moment.' She pottered off down the ward, stopping to chat to some of the other women. I looked back at Joanne, still sleeping. My arms were numb with her weight, but I didn't dare move.

'Let's put Baby in her cot, shall we?' It was the young nurse.

I smiled gratefully. 'I need to go to the—' I nodded down below.

She nodded, her head on one side as she picked up Joanne with hardly a glance and tucked her into her cot. 'It'll be a little painful having a movement, but we've given you laxatives and I'll give you a jug. If you pour water over yourself as you're going, it'll dilute the urine and help reduce the sting.'

I looked down at my legs, lying uselessly on the bed. Suddenly, I wasn't sure how to move them. The nurse watched me and then started to pull them gently over the side of the bed. The floor felt reassuringly solid under my feet. I tested my weight and realised I could stand. We slowly walked to the bathroom, my stitches throbbing with every step. It felt like I hadn't walked for a long time. The last time would have been from the bath to the bed.

I'd only just sat on the loo when the crying started. Like the whine of a drill trying to hammer through solid wall. 'I think that must be Baby. You carry on here and I'll deal with her.' The nurse hurried out of the bathroom.

As I sat and poured the water over myself, a strange tingling sensation began in my nipples. I pressed them with my hands but it just made it worse. It only slightly distracted me from the searing pain below. I stared at the black, threatening clots of blood on the sanitary pad and pulled my gaze away. But I could see them out of the corner of my eye.

When I'd finished, I stood at the basin and washed the blood from my hands. In the mirror, a woman who looked like me stared back. I pulled a face and my reflection did the same, the grey crescents under my eyes trying to smile. The tooth I'd cracked was too deep in my mouth to see in the mirror, but my tongue probed at the unfamiliar outline.

I stood for a long time, watching myself. Eventually, the nurse came back. 'You have a hungry little girl there waiting for you. It's feeding time. We feed the babies every four hours. On the dot.' I walked gingerly back to the ward, holding on to her arm. The nurses were handing out bottles to the other women. Jenny was already feeding her baby. She looked like something out of the Kays catalogue.

The nurse helped me into bed and back on to the rubber ring, and then handed me Joanne. I slipped the rubber teat into her puckered mouth and she began to suck, vigorously pulling at the bottle but hardly opening her eyes. 'She's got a good appetite,' the nurse nodded approvingly.

'Just you wait until your milk comes in.' Jenny leaned closer and whispered conspiratorially, 'They'll give you tablets to dry it up, but my boobs were like two grenades about to go off. I couldn't touch them.' She laughed. 'The tablets take a little while to work, but when they do . . .' She wiped imaginary sweat from her powdered brow. 'I was so grateful.'

Joanne sucked at the bottle, milk dribbling down her chin, wetting the shawl. My boobs started to tingle again. The young nurse stood by, watching me.

'Miss Gull, how many times have I told you not to do it that way.' The older nurse was talking to a woman, younger than me, in the corner of the ward. 'You'll waste half the milk like that. And Lord help you, you'll need every penny you've got once you get home.' The girl looked flustered, shifting her baby in her arms. She kept her eyes fixed on her child, ignoring the nurse berating her. I felt sympathy for her but also gratitude that the nurses weren't focusing on me.

The young nurse dabbed Joanne's face with a cloth and repositioned the bottle so it leaked less. 'Hold it up like this,' she said quietly.

'Miss Gull, we have limited milk powder on this ward.' The other nurse was staring at the young woman, hands on her over-padded hips.

'Why's she got it in for her?' I asked the nurse, who was repositioning the muslin around Joanne's face to catch the milk she was dribbling.

She glanced at the matron and then back down. '*Miss* Gull,' she said.

'Oh,' I said, looking down.

'She's a right old battleaxe,' whispered Jenny.

The young nurse's mouth twitched and then retained its line. Jenny was so like Susie. The nurse finished with Joanne and turned her attention to the woman on the other side of me.

'She rules this ward with a rod of iron,' Jenny said, putting her baby back in the cot and standing by my bed, her hand on the metal frame. 'There was a baby here yesterday – before you woke up. Funny little thing it was. There was something wrong with it. You know.' She widened her eyes and I nodded, though I didn't really know what she meant. 'Disabled.' It was a loud whisper and the woman opposite, who was still feeding her baby, glanced up. 'They took it away in the end. Once they realised it wasn't quite normal.' She shook her head. 'Poor girl. She cried and cried after they'd taken it away and her husband came to pick her up. She was two years above me at school. I knew her a little. She'd waited ages to get pregnant too.' She turned away. 'You just never know what's coming down the line, do you?' She straightened her covers and glanced at her baby, who was happily cooing in its cot. 'I'm just going to pop out for a ciggie,' she added, as she slipped on the feather slippers and tip-tapped to the door. 'Could you watch her for me?' she added, nodding towards her cot, where her baby was already drifting into sleep.

Imagine going through all that and then they take your baby away. Away where? Was there a place for all the disabled babies? Misshapen. Without arms or legs. A woman on our street had had a thalidomide baby when I was a girl. Mum used to whisper about it with her sisters. It had died in the end.

Joanne had fallen asleep on the bottle and the teat had slipped out of her mouth. I still hadn't seen her eyes. Not properly. I tried to get off the rubber ring and put her back into the cot, but the fiery pain flared up. I imagined my whole undercarriage split in two and sewed up roughly with loads of puckers and gaps. A little like Susie's stitching at work sometimes when she wasn't concentrating. I wanted to get a mirror and put it between my legs to see what they'd done to me.

The young nurse helped me slide Joanne into the cot and I stood there watching her sleep, not willing to start the painful process of sitting back down. Everything below my waist hurt. I wanted to go to the loo again, but the thought of the pain made me shudder.

In the cupboard next to me, all my things were neatly arranged. On the top was a jug of water, a plastic cup, some tissues, the biscuits Mike had brought, which I didn't want, a book, my watch. He'd left the camera there by accident, the picture of the woman with the baby balanced on top of it. I tried to arrange them so they were all equidistant from each other. But then I realised that was silly. I should put the most important closest to me. I glanced at each item in turn, like in the game show Mike and I watched. Was the water more important than the tissues? If the water was important, then so was the cup. The watch could go at the back as I had the clock on the wall opposite. The book I wanted close to me. I didn't need the camera or the photo.

Why was I doing this? I pushed everything into one group and opened the cupboard underneath. On top of the small piles of underwear and a spare nightie was the baby book. All those months of flicking through the pages, waiting for something to write about. Now I had something to write about, I didn't know what to say. Still standing, I opened it and picked up the blue fountain pen.

My Birth

I was born at ______

On ____

At ____

I bit my lip. What day was it? When had she been born? A new nurse was passing, someone I thought I recognised. She had a kind, soft face and blonde hair. 'Excuse me. What day is it? When did I have my baby?'

'Mrs Bennett.' She smiled. 'I'm Sister Berry. I'm glad to see you up. I was there when you had your daughter.' She picked up the clipboard at the end of the bed. 'Now, let's look at the records and we can start to help you fill this out.'

I wrote down the details that she read out. Seven pounds six ounces sounded heavy. Six ounces of flour we used in cakes. With six ounces of sugar and three ounces each of lard and butter.

'She was born at five thirty-five in the morning on Friday eleventh of July,' she said as she put the clipboard back at the end of my bed. I put the pen down. I'd gone into hospital on the Thursday morning. Had it really taken all that time to have her? They promised me she'd arrive on the Thursday afternoon. 'Are you sure?' I said, looking up at her.

'Absolutely sure.' She smiled again. The strip lights glinted off her bob. I turned back to the book. I started to write July but couldn't remember how to spell it. Was it with an o or a u? It looked odd with a u, so I crossed it out and wrote Joly. But that was jolly, happy. Not the month. I crossed it out and wrote July. July, that was it. But the whole page looked a mess now. Scribbles everywhere. I tore the page out and scrunched it up, pushing it to the back of the cupboard.

The photo of the woman with the baby was still on the side. I turned it over and wrote:

Born: 5.35am, 11 July 1975 at Royal Sussex County Hospital, Brighton

Weight: 7lbs, 6 ozs

Why couldn't I have written that neatly in the book? I picked up the book again. Maybe nobody would notice there was a missing page. I had the information now anyway, on the photo, that was the main thing. Maybe we could stick it in the baby book. There was nothing else to say in the book. Her first steps, her first tooth, were all months away. Time stretched away like a never-ending spool of ribbon. I slid the book and photo back into the cupboard and looked down at Joanne.

Wrapped in her shawl, I couldn't see much of her. It was so warm on the ward, and she was so pink, maybe she was over-heating. I started to untie the ribbons of her bonnet. Mum had been right about the size, it was a perfect newborn fit. I'd never believed a baby's head could be so small. Though it hadn't felt small coming out.

As I slipped off the bonnet, two deep gouges started to appear on either side of Joanne's head. They were circular and symmetrical, the colour of a new bruise. Ugly against the pale beauty of her face. I stared, transfixed, and traced them with my finger. I could feel the indentations into her skull. Sickness thrust up inside me and I pulled the bonnet back on, my hands shaking as I re-tied the bows. What would Mike say? Mum?

'How are you feeling, Mrs Bennett?' It was the matron again. 'You still look a little washed out.'

I nodded and looked down at the bonnet hiding the terrible disfigurement. I wanted to ask her about it, but what if they hadn't seen it yet, what if they took her away?

'Let's get you back into bed, shall we? You need to rest.' She was rougher than the other nurse, gripping me too tightly as she lifted me on to the ring. It squirmed under my weight.

I stared straight ahead, not wanting to look at the baby in case Matron noticed the marks. She was still there, watching me. 'Do you have a magazine or something?' She started rifling in the cupboard and handed me a book. The cover was familiar, and I realised it was the story of the woman in the Scottish islands. I'd liked that story.

'Read this, Mrs Bennett. It'll help you rest. Everyone loves a good romance, don't they.' She smiled again and went to the next bed, where a much older woman was jiggling a crying baby up and down.

I opened the book and stared at the words. How long could I keep those marks secret? I needed to get out of here. For Joanne's sake.

◆ ◆ ◆

'You're not taking her away,' I said.

'But Mrs Bennett, all the babies are taken away at night.' There was a sharp line between the nurse's eyebrows. 'You feed the babies and then we take them to the nursery so you can rest. It happens every night.'

'I want to have Joanne here,' I said. 'She's my baby and I want her here.' She still hadn't properly opened her eyes and I wasn't going to miss it again.

'Mrs Bennett. Please. Let's put Baby back in the cot. You need to rest after yesterday's labour.'

I felt a wardful of eyes on me. It was dark now. The clock said nine o'clock. It must be night.

'It's all right, Grace. They'll bring her back in the morning.' Jenny's baby had already been wheeled away. She rested her hand on my shoulder. I shrugged it off. 'It's a good thing, my mum said. Means you get a proper night's sleep. You'll feel better in the morning.'

'Mrs Bennett, is there a problem here?' asked the matron.

I stood up straight. Or as straight as the stitches down below would allow. 'I want my baby here. It's wrong that you take them away. What if she's hungry or cold in the night?' What if they took off the bonnet and realised she was disabled? And then took her away.

Matron nodded at the nurse and murmured something I didn't hear. The nurse moved away towards the nurses' desk. Was she getting more people? Were they going to force me to give up my baby? Matron rested her hand on my arm. It was firm. She spoke clearly, carefully enunciating each word as if I were a particularly dim child. Like Mrs C did with poor Susie sometimes.

'I'm Going To Take Baby And Put Her In The Cot. It Doesn't Do Baby Any Good To Be Cuddled All The Time. Then I'm Going To Wheel Her Into The Nursery With All The Other Babies. A good night's sleep is what you need. I'm going to give you a little sedative to help you rest.'

I shook my head and held on to Joanne. She was beginning to stir. She opened her eyes and stared at me. Her eyes were dark blue. Mike had been right. Like the deepest water in the sea. Where the sun doesn't reach. 'Look, she's opened her eyes,' I said. 'She's beautiful.'

'I'm not surprised you've woken her up with all this fuss,' said Matron, but kindly. 'She's certainly a beautiful baby.' The other nurse had come back with something in her hand. She gave it to Matron.

'Open up, Mrs Bennett. Stick out your tongue. This will make you feel a little better and help you to sleep.'

I did what I was told, still holding Joanne firmly. Only when I felt the bitterness in my mouth did I realise my mistake. I tried to spit it out but swallowed it instead.

'I'm sorry,' I said. I felt her slip out of my arms. Suddenly, I was grasping at air. Matron was slipping her back into the cot.

A baby started to cry. 'I'm sorry,' I said, feeling myself start to cry too. The nurse was pushing Joanne slowly down the ward. Her face was scarlet, her mouth puckered like a buttonhole. If they found the deformity in the night, it might be the last time I ever saw her. The door at the end was opening. I could just see her raised hand, and then she was through the door and it had swung shut behind her.

'The baby blues are perfectly normal,' said Matron, lifting me on to the ring.

'Everyone has a good cry,' said Jenny. 'I sobbed and sobbed for England for the first few days,' she said with eyes so bright she'd probably never cried.

'Try to read, Mrs Bennett, just until the pill takes effect. It won't be long.' She gave me my book. The book fell open where the pen had been left. My pen. Someone had used it to scribble on the pages. I was going to get into trouble at the library when I returned it. They would fine me. Who had done it? Was it the woman next to me? Or maybe it was Matron. I thought of Joanne alone in a room without me. After all those months being inside me, she would be lonely. The tears built up again. I only ever cried at home when I had PMT. What was wrong with me? I tried to breathe slowly, counting my breaths as we'd done in the relaxation classes. I started to read. Annabelle was busy teaching her children to ride, the baby was being looked after by a nanny. I would never leave my baby with a nanny. Annabelle would have beautiful children – her pale skin and blonde hair with Rory's dark, brooding looks. They'd need lots of children, lots of boys especially. They all wanted boys first, the upper classes. He'd need someone to run his Scottish estate. Joanne couldn't do that. Or maybe she could. Susie was always saying that girls could do anything that boys could do. But I wouldn't want to be in the joinery department. *Keep the girls in upholstery and the boys in joinery I wrote in the margin.*

What have they done with my baby? Take her. Away. Escape.

Sleep pulled at my eyelids. I felt the book slip from my hands and waited for the thud as it hit the floor. But a hand reached out and slipped it on to my cupboard. Then there was darkness again. I looked for the stork but the sky was empty.

Chapter 12

Joanne

September 2021

'You're not from around here, are you?' It was the nurse Joanne had seen the day before, back for another shift. Her hair was almost white and her face lined, giving her a gentle, kindly look. 'I can't place your accent.'

Joanne smiled. No one had commented on her accent so much before, but then she realised she'd hardly left the north-east in her whole life. 'I'm from Berwick, right on the Scottish border.'

'Blimey,' said the nurse. 'That must be about as far away as you can get from Brighton and still be in England. I went to York once, for the races, but that's as far north as I've been.'

Joanne bit her lip. She'd never thought about that before coming to Brighton. Why had her father gone so far away? What had happened in Brighton with Grace that he'd needed to run to the other end of the country? 'I was born here but we moved up there not long after,' said Joanne, thinking of the picture of her parents standing outside the front of the cottage. They looked so happy, carefree. But a few weeks later, Grace had disappeared and she and Dad were miles away.

The nurse was reading the clipboard notes. 'So what brings you down here? Birthday bash? Hen do?'

Joanne laughed. 'Nothing like that. I'm trying to find out about my birth mother. I was born here but something happened to her after she had me. She ended up back in hospital and she died a while later.'

The nurse clicked her tongue sympathetically. She slipped the blood pressure sleeve around Joanne's arm and started tightening it. 'How did she die?'

'A head injury. All I know is that she died in the Egremont Hospital,' said Joanne. They'd looked at it on the map and they'd been planning to go out and see it before all this had happened. It wasn't far from Brighton.

The nurse looked up quickly. 'That's the old asylum,' she said.

Joanne screwed up her face. 'Asylum?'

The nurse nodded, releasing the pressure on the sleeve and slipping it off Joanne's arm. 'Yes, they closed it down in the nineties. It's derelict now, I think.' She walked back to the end of the bed.

'Are you sure?' Joanne's skin tingled in a way that was nothing to do with the blood pressure sleeve.

The nurse was writing on the clipboard. 'Definitely. I worked there in the eighties for a spell.' She looked up, frowning. 'It's a lovely spot. Surrounded by woodland. It was very advanced for its day.' She looked quickly back to the notes. 'When was your mum there?'

'She died there in 1977. But why would she have been in an asylum?' Even though she was lying down, Joanne felt her head spin. She touched her forehead.

The nurse slipped the clipboard back on to the end of the bed. She glanced over at the next patient. 'All sorts of people ended up in asylums in those days. There wasn't the support in the community that we have now, or the understanding of mental health problems.' She paused and turned towards the next patient.

Joanne pulled herself up in the bed. 'But why would a woman who'd just had a baby end up in an asylum? That doesn't make sense.'

The nurse glanced at Joanne without looking her in the eye and sighed. 'She could have had postnatal depression,' she said.

Joanne felt her chest tighten. 'Postnatal depression? But that's treated with a few drugs, isn't it? You don't get put in an asylum for postnatal depression? And anyway, it said on her death certificate that she died of an extradural haematoma.' The patient opposite her looked over, her eyebrows raised.

The nurse gave a too-quick smile and walked slowly back to Joanne. She sat on the side of the bed and took her hand. 'As you said, an extradural haematoma is the result of some sort of head injury and could have had many different causes. Perhaps she fell in the hospital? Things were different in those days, Mrs Shaw. We didn't understand things like postnatal depression in the same way that we do now. And we're still learning.'

'I need to find out what happened to Grace, to my birth mam. I feel everyone around me is lying about it.' Joanne looked up at the nurse, her eyes too bright. 'That people know. Dad knows. Mam knows. My two new aunts know. Susie, Grace's friend, knows. I feel I'm the only person in the dark.' She clutched at the sheet with her hand. Why would no one tell her anything?

'There will be records,' said the nurse. 'Somewhere, what happened to your mum will be recorded. They never throw that stuff away.' She stroked Joanne's hand. 'Though it is often kept secret for many years.'

Joanne knew there was a woman standing by the door. It was Grace. She was smiling at Joanne. She took a deep breath. Records, there would be records somewhere. She'd find out. Somehow. 'I'll start searching as soon as I get out of here.'

The nurse looked her in the eye. 'Be careful. Mental health hospitals were very different then to how they are now. You might not like what you find out.' She got up slowly from the bed, releasing

Joanne's hand. 'You have your own baby to think of now,' she said, nodding towards Joanne's bump. 'You need to rest.'

Joanne looked back over towards the door where she thought she'd seen Grace, but the figure had melted away. She was sure it had been her though, Grace, watching her.

Alex came to collect her later that morning, carrying their suitcase. 'I've spoken to Susie and told her that we're going home today,' he said, his jaw set. 'We'll catch up by phone.'

Joanne shook her head. 'No, I need to talk to her about Grace's death *now*.' She lowered her voice. 'One of the nurses here told me the Egremont Hospital, where she died, was an asylum.' His eyes widened. 'I need to know if Susie and my aunts knew that. And I need to know why Grace was in a mental institution. The nurse said it could have been postnatal depression.'

Alex took a deep breath. 'You can talk to them over the phone if you want to. I've got a taxi waiting outside to take us to the station. You need to rest and take care of our baby.' His eyes still held the memory of the blood on the sheets. 'And I've got a night shift later.'

Joanne had rarely seen him so determined. 'Our baby,' she said, her eyes narrowed.

Alex nodded. 'Our baby.'

'At least you can sleep on the train,' she said. She slipped off the bed. Joanne said her goodbyes to the other patients and the nurses, put her phone with its many missed calls into her bag, and walked out of the ward.

Alex was soon asleep on the train. His face now held an anxious frown even in sleep.

Joanne waited until his breath was regular before she slipped the phone out of her bag. She googled postnatal depression and read about the symptoms of sadness and a low mood, difficulty bonding with your baby and withdrawing from contact with other people. Was this what had happened to Grace? It didn't sound like the sort of symptoms to end you up in an asylum. But maybe things were different in those days. Grace's hospital records would have the answers.

Joanne googled hospital records and trawled through the results, picking up snippets of information. She sighed. None of the records had been digitised and most were closed to the public for a hundred years anyway. She glanced over at Alex, his head nodding along to the train's rhythm. Even if she could view them, she'd have to go in person to the Brighton Records Office, and yet here she was speeding away from Brighton to the other end of the country. Joanne googled the address and it came up on a map in the centre of Brighton – they were travelling further away from it by the minute. She moved her thumb and finger across the screen to show the whole map of Brighton. There in the top right corner, just outside the village of Helmer, was a red H for hospital and then 'closed' in brackets. The Egremont.

Joanne looked out of the window as the swathes of green morphed into the greyness of suburbia. The secrets of her birth mother's death were in Brighton. She bit her lip. She'd come back at the first opportunity.

GRACE

JULY 1975

Joanne was crying. I pulled myself up. I needed to see her, to hold her. The rest of the ward was quiet. Shrouded lumps lay in beds, blanketed by darkness. Even Jenny was silent, her curls spread across the pillow, her mouth still. The faint crying was growing louder. I needed to get to her. I imagined her in her cot, her mouth wide in distress, wondering where I was. I tried to turn on my side to get my legs over the bed but the pain held me down. 'Nurse,' I called. 'Nurse, help me.'

'Mrs Bennett. It's after midnight.' It was the night sister. 'Do you need the lavatory?'

I shook my head and gestured towards the crying. 'I need to get to Joanne. She's crying.'

She glanced towards the door. 'The babies are all asleep, Mrs Bennett. There's no crying.'

I shook my head. 'Help me up,' I said, pulling at the sheets to lever myself upright.

Her lips pursed but she gave me an arm and helped me stand. I tried to walk towards the door, but she was still holding my arm. 'Mrs Bennett, you can't leave the ward in the middle of the night.'

'But she's crying, Joanne's calling for me.' The baby was howling now, the sound echoing around the room across the sleeping women.

The night sister gripped my arm, pushing me back towards my bed.

'I need to see my baby,' I shouted, pushing past her and kicking a trolley with a force I didn't know I had. There was a crash behind me, followed by a loud bell. The shrouded figures were shifting in their beds, rising up like ghostly apparitions. I screamed and ran for the door, feeling the seam tearing.

Joanne was just the other side, her arms raised to greet me. Another nurse, a larger one, rushed through the door before I could reach it, gripped my arm and guided me back to bed. The sheets rose up and pulled me in. There was a bitterness on my tongue. The sheets covered me and drew me into the darkness. The bell stopped ringing. The baby was quiet again.

◆ ◆ ◆

Up and down the ward, shapes were moving under the white starch. The younger nurse went from window to window, opening blinds. Sharp boxes of light projected on to the floor. I pushed myself upwards and kept my eyes fixed on the door. The women were all looking at me. Sideways glances. Whispered words behind upright magazines.

Finally, the door swung open and the procession of cots appeared, all decorated with either blue or pink ribbons. Jenny's baby was first. Then the woman opposite. Then Miss Gull's poor mite. Then the woman at the end. Where was Joanne? Four more babies came through, none of them her. A fist gripped my heart. They'd taken her. They must have changed her bonnet in the night and discovered the marks. The door swung shut and I closed my eyes. I had to find her.

'Joanne,' I called, ignoring the other women's turned faces. I swung my legs over the side of the bed, gasping at the pain. My feet were on the floor when the nurse's cool hand touched my arm.

'Mrs Bennett, here she is.' Joanne stared up at me from the cot, her dark eyes unreadable. I felt suddenly giddy and had to sit back down. Thank God. Thank God. She was here. 'Now, this morning I'm going to show you how to top and tail Baby.'

I nodded dumbly as she set out bowls and cotton wool on the table. The nurse picked Joanne up and started to take off her shawl and cardigan. 'You start by holding your baby on your lap. You can strip them down to their vest and wrap them in a towel to keep them warm.' Not her bonnet. Not her bonnet.

The nurse's hands had long blue veins running from her fingers all the way up past her wrists. They disappeared under the starched cotton sleeves. 'You then dip the cotton wool in warm water. No more than ninety-eight degrees and test it with your elbow. But don't get it too wet, and gently wipe from Baby's eyes, nearest their nose, and work outwards. Use a fresh piece of cotton wool for each eye.'

Joanne screwed up her face as the cotton passed over her eyes. I tensed my arms, ready to grab her if the nurse tried to take off her bonnet.

'Then you take another piece of cotton wool to clean around Baby's ears, but don't clean inside them.' Joanne opened her eyes and followed the piece of cotton moving across her face. The nurse eased up the side of the bonnet, but not enough to see the deformity.

'Mrs Bennett, are you listening?'

I nodded and watched the words coming out of her mouth, rushing on like a never-ending reel of thread.

'Removethenappy,' she said, undoing the pin that secured it in place. The pin vibrated as she undid it. I couldn't take my eyes off it. 'Thenyoucleanbabysbottomwiththewarmwater.' The pin lay on the bed, its sharp end pointing towards me. I dragged my eyes back to Joanne's face and gathered my hands together in my lap.

The nurse's mouth was moving but my thoughts roared over the sound of her voice. I lifted up the corners of my mouth and nodded when she looked at me, her brow pleated. 'Takecaretodrybetweenthefoldsofskinandputbabyinacleandry nappy.' She picked up the pin and it caught the light.

'Don't hurt her,' I said.

The nurse glanced at me, her face drawn into a question. She slowly slid the pin into the terry towelling. I looked away and saw a red stain spread out from the nappy, heard the sound of screaming. Bile burned my throat. I swallowed it down and pulled my eyes back to Joanne. She was gurgling happily. The nurse had wrapped her into the shawl again. 'It's OK, Mrs Bennett.' Her hand was on my arm again. 'You're OK.' She placed Joanne in my arms.

'Tomorrow, I'll show you how to bathe Baby. You can try it yourself then. But for now, Baby is nice and clean.'

I looked at Joanne, who stared at me silently. What was she trying to say? We needed to get out of here. 'Can you show me now, about the bath?' The more I could learn today, the sooner I could leave and keep Joanne safe.

'I think this is enough for this morning – you had a disturbed night, didn't you? I don't want to overwhelm you.'

Overwhelm.

Underneath the shawl was the pin. I hated the thought of it so close to Joanne's skin. But at the same time, I couldn't stop thinking about it. Picking at the thought like a scab. Worrying it. Making it bleed.

I must have slept again. When I woke up, the front of my nightdress was soaking. Underneath, my breasts felt like two over-pumped footballs. They tingled when I touched them, my hands coming away damp. 'I'm, I'm—' I gestured down at my nightdress to the nurse who was watching me.

'I'll give you a tablet to dry you up. It'll feel a little uncomfortable for a while, but then it'll go.' Her eyes were kind. 'You can lay some cool flannels underneath your nightie, to reduce the discomfort, Mrs Bennett.'

How did she know my name? I stared at her as she walked back down the ward, her hips swaying.

Joanne was asleep, her hands raised either side of her head. I reached into the cupboard for my book. Annabelle was getting ready for a ball, brushing her blonde hair, slipping into a red silk dress. Rory was waiting for her, looking devilishly handsome in a dinner jacket. She painted her face, carefully outlining her lips in a deep red. Her mouth looked like a wound on her face. I underlined the important bits with my pen. I didn't want to forget them.

The nurse came back with a tablet and slipped it on to the table. 'For the milk,' she said, and turned away. I stared at the tiny circular pill. What if it wasn't for my milk? What if they wanted to take Joanne away?

'You should take it,' said Jenny, glancing over. 'It works quite quickly and will make you feel better.' She nodded towards my nightie, which was completely drenched through my bra. 'More comfortable.'

The pill vibrated. My head throbbed. I moved my hand towards the pill but it slid across the table away from me.

'Here,' said Jenny, picking it up. 'Honestly, it's the best thing ever.' She put it in my hand, where it glowed. She poured water into the plastic cup and handed it to me. The wheels of the catering trolley squeaked through the door. They were so loud I couldn't hear what she was saying. Why didn't they oil them? How could they bear it? I threw the pill into my mouth and took a gulp of the water. It felt like a golf ball going down my throat. I gagged.

The light slowly changed, from a light blue satin to a golden silk. Joanne stayed silent, watching me. I knew she was judging me for last night. For letting her go. Tonight, I wouldn't let that happen. I would hide her. The little hand of the clock pointed like a small quilting needle at the five. The big hand, a large knitting needle, was on the one. I stared at them for a long time, trying to remember the rule. Was the knitting needle the hour or the minute?

The ball was in full swing, with the most important people on the island, the best food and wines. I could see the austere castle, its turrets stretching into the warm summer night sky. The crowd of glamorous people dressed in kilts and long dresses dancing reels in the open courtyard. The trays of chilled champagne held by tall thin teenage waiters. The platters of haggis held high as they were piped into the grand hall.

The clock hands gradually moved around, meeting in the middle every so often as if in some slow dance.

The women started making up their faces. The bell rang. But it wasn't Mike this time. Susie and Mum threaded their way through the line and sat side by side like bolts of cotton by my bed.

I knew what I was supposed to do. I could see the other women doing it. Smiling and cooing. Holding the baby and showing it off. I made sure the bonnet was tied tightly on Joanne's head, and the blanket covered the ring beneath me so they couldn't see it. I didn't want to have to explain what had happened to me.

Susie had brought a camera. Her dad used to take it on holiday sometimes. He had a special cord to put round his neck so he didn't drop it in the sea. But when she saw my camera on the side, she picked it up and they took it in turns taking pictures of me. Me, Mum and Joanne. Susie, me and Joanne. Just me and Joanne. I kept smiling, though my mouth ached. Everything ached.

'How are you feeling?' Susie asked eventually when she'd handed the baby over to Mum. She glanced at me briefly as she asked the question, before looking back at the baby.

'I feel so . . .' What did I feel? Nothing. None of the excitement that I'd felt over the last few months. It had all seeped away, leaving greyness. Like the scum at the bottom of the pan after you'd drained vegetables. She looked at me again, her face upturned, expectant. 'Happy,' I said.

'I knew it. I knew you'd be an amazing mum,' she said, grinning. 'A natural. And she's such a beauty. Let's hope I have a girl too, then we can dress them like sisters, just as we said.'

Had we said that? The idea of pushing our matching babies along the road together felt very far away. Like something I could see in a shop window but not touch. Not afford.

Eventually, the bell rang and they disappeared back through the door at the end of the ward, taking the photos with them.

Part of Joanne was outside the hospital now, free into the world. Whatever happened there was proof she existed. I leaned against the pillows and closed my eyes but my mind raced around, thinking of all the things I needed to do. My things on the bedside table needed rearranging. Joanne would need changing soon. I needed to go to the loo before they brought the bottles for feeding. The baby book needed filling out. The book needed reading. They'd told me to drink lots of water to flush out my system, but I hadn't. I sat upright, my heart thumping in my chest. What should I do first? Joanne lay in her cot, staring at me.

The clock had done two more dance rounds when the colour turned into a reddish damask and then started to seep from the room, touching the end of the cot where Joanne now lay sleeping. I picked up my book and read. Annabelle danced all night at the ball. Not just with Rory but with other men too. But the words started to fracture. I read the same sentence about a reel but it kept slipping away from me, like a piece of eggshell in a bowl of cracked eggs. The closer I got to it, the more it jumped away. I tried to underline it with my pen but the words jumped around so I wasn't sure what I was underlining. I closed the book and then opened it again, but the words started to dance on the page. I let the book drop back on to the sheet.

The light disappeared completely. Matron's voice seeped through the door. I knew what was coming. With difficulty, I got out of bed and picked up Joanne from her cot. I smiled at her and she opened her eyes to stare at me unblinkingly. I lay back down in the bed and cradled her next to me. She was pink and warm. The pin started to vibrate underneath her shawl but I pushed it away. I wanted to lift up her bonnet and stare at the disfigurement, but I knew that someone might see it and take her away. To the place.

She stared up at me as I pulled the cover over her head. I picked up the book again and stared at the text, trying to follow each line, but my eyes couldn't focus properly.

Matron stood at the end of my bed. I stared into her eyes.

'They've already taken her,' I said.

Out of the corner of my eye, Jenny, her hair in curlers, was staring at me, her mouth open.

'Mrs Bennett. Please be sensible. I know you have Baby there.'

'Please leave me, Matron. I'm reading before bed. It helps me sleep.'

'Your book is upside down, Mrs Bennett.' Her voice was firm. 'Now, I'm going to take Baby and put her in the nursery for the night. She'll be perfectly safe with all the other babies.'

Her mouth was drawn together like an empty buttonhole.

'She's better with me,' I said, feeling Joanne's warmth against my leg.

Matron whisked the curtains around the bed and sat down on the opposite side from Joanne. I could feel Jenny's stares through the fabric. She'd be raising her eyebrows and gesturing to the woman opposite.

'Mrs Bennett.' Matron took my hand. Hers was warm and soft, but quite firm. Like Mum's. 'You're not quite yourself at the moment, are you?'

I looked down at my hands curled in my lap. They were my hands. I was real. 'I'm fine,' I said.

'I'm a little concerned about you. I want you to know that we're here to help you in whatever way we can. The journey of motherhood is different for every woman. For some, it's straight and easy. For others, it can be a harder journey, perhaps, at first.' Her eyes crinkled.

I nodded, though I didn't understand what she meant.

'It's completely natural to feel a little overwhelmed at first, to have a cry. Most women feel like that, so you shouldn't feel worried or embarrassed about it.'

'I'm not overwhelmed,' I said, staring at the mole on her cheek. I'd never noticed it before.

'I know you have a good family around you to help you, but we're going to use these next few days to provide as much support for you as we can, to help you for when you get home.' She reached into her pocket and took out a box of pills. 'These pills will not only help you sleep, but also make you feel a little calmer. The doctor recommended you take them.' The mole had a tiny little mouth. It was trying to tell me something, but I couldn't hear it.

The pills wriggled in her hand like maggots. I shook my head. 'I want to go home.'

'Mrs Bennett, you're not ready to go home. These pills really will help you.' She took one of the maggots and put it towards my mouth. I clamped it shut but she held it gently by my mouth. I felt it against my lips and stuck out my tongue to touch it. It wasn't a maggot after all. Just a pill. The mole on her face had disappeared. How strange. I opened my mouth and she slipped both pills in and handed me the glass of water. I took a gulp and they slipped down my throat. I felt them wiggle and thought of the maggots and shook my head. Pills. Not maggots. Pills.

'Well done, Mrs Bennett.' Her face was smiling. There wasn't a mole. She patted me on the head and then laid me down, as you would a corpse. 'Nurse,' she called.

The younger nurse slipped her head between the curtain folds.

'Please take Baby.'

Joanne was silent as they picked her up and laid her in the cot. The curtains billowed as the nurse pushed the cot through it, settling around us like the sheet caves that Emily, Gerry and I used to make when we were little. It felt soothing, like being wrapped up in a towel when you come out of the sea. I slid down on the pillow.

'That's right, time for a good, long sleep,' Matron said. 'You'll feel better in the morning. Everything's always better in the morning.'

The sheets enveloped me and the blueness turned darker and darker until I couldn't see anything at all.

Chapter 13

Joanne

September 2021

Alex went to bed as soon as they got home to grab a few more hours' sleep before his shift. Joanne walked around the little box room that would be the nursery. They had a new mattress for the cot now and Mam had knitted little zoo animals and attached them to an old mobile. Alex had hung it above the cot. She stroked the elephant and pushed the mobile around so the animals seemed to be racing around the room, the lion desperately trying to overtake the tiger who was running after the giraffe who galloped towards the elephant. One day there would be a baby in here, lying underneath watching this race. She smiled and stroked her bump. It was growing by the day. *Stay in there*, she murmured.

On the shelf was the envelope of photos, next to the baby book they'd started writing for their baby. She took it down again and looked through the pictures, staring for a long time at the one of Grace holding her on her sofa. Grace's expression was completely blank. Maybe she *had* been depressed? How could you tell? She slipped the pictures back in the envelope and back on its shelf.

Joanne looked in on Alex, who was lying on his back, snoring. She smiled and slipped downstairs, put the kettle on and tapped out the number for the Brighton Records Office. In a bored-sounding voice, the lady on the phone reiterated what the website had said. The records were only accessible in person and a request would have to be made in advance. Without thinking, Joanne arranged to visit the following week – the first appointment they had. She checked the calendar in the kitchen. Alex was working then. She knew he wouldn't be able to take time off again so soon, whereas the shop where she worked was much more flexible. She had some orders to make for the online store, but she could do that in the next few days. Even if the records office wouldn't let her see Grace's hospital record, at least she'd be near it. And she'd go up to the Egremont Hospital, to see where Grace had spent her final months. Years. She gulped. Susie and Aunt Gerry would help her, she knew.

Joanne put down the phone, poured herself a mug of tea, and immediately dialled Susie.

Her bright voice flooded through the phone. 'Joanne?'

Joanne smiled.

'Joanne? How are you? Alex told me about you being hospitalised. Gerry and I have been so worried.'

Warmth spread through her chest. They were her family, they were worried about her. 'I'm OK. They said the baby's fine, it was just changes to my cervix, apparently. Nothing to worry about, but it was really scary.'

'I'm sure it was. We're just glad you're all right and the baby's OK.'

'Thanks, Susie. But I was really sorry we didn't get the chance to meet again.'

'Me too. We'd love to see you. Perhaps we can FaceTime, the four of us. You, me and Gerry and Emily. Just until we have the chance to meet up.'

Joanne took a sip of tea. 'Actually, I'm going to be down in Brighton next week. Perhaps we could meet up in person again?'

'Oh my, yes. That would be lovely. Where are you staying?'

'I—' In all the excitement of making the appointment with the records office, Joanne hadn't thought about where to stay. She couldn't afford the B&B again on top of the train fare. And she couldn't go there and back in a day, it was a five-hour journey on the train.

Susie broke the silence. 'If you haven't booked anywhere, I've got a spare room, you'd be very welcome to it.'

Joanne pressed her hand on her belly. 'That would be brilliant, thanks, Susie. I'll be down on Tuesday if that's OK, early afternoon. I'll only need to stay for the night.'

'You're my best friend's daughter, Joanne, you can stay as long as you want. I'll invite Gerry along. We can have a family dinner.'

Joanne put the phone down and wrote 'Brighton' on the calendar. She looked at it and wrote 'family dinner' afterwards, a small smile at the corner of her mouth.

There was nothing in the fridge or larder, so Joanne slipped on her coat and walked out of the front door, closing it quietly behind her. The town she'd lived in all her life suddenly didn't feel so much like home. The streets pressed in on her. People she didn't know stared at her. The roads seemed so familiar but also so foreign that she wondered if she'd get lost. Susie's front room, its floral sofa and sleeping cats – Brighton, with its faded glamour, suddenly felt like the only place she wanted to be.

Joanne sighed and pushed through the plastic strips at the butcher's door. A couple of sausages would do for tonight for her, mince for Alex's spag bol tomorrow. Maybe some burgers for the weekend. A large woman waiting with two full bags for life hid whoever was at the counter. Joanne stood behind her, resting her hand on her belly. Maybe some stewing steak instead of burgers. It was cold enough for stews now. She'd get down the slow cooker. That would buy her some time, while she finished the hammered bangles. They were so popular now, she was making at least two a week. Maybe it wouldn't be long until she could afford to set up on her own. After the baby came.

The woman at the front of the queue reached forward to put the last of her packets in her bag. It was the familiar way she cupped her hand as she accepted the change that made Joanne's eyes widen. Mam. She leaned back against the wall's cool tiles, trying to hide behind the woman in front of her.

'Bye then, Tom,' said Lou cheerily, and she turned towards the door.

Joanne tried to shrink back further but there was no chance that her mam would miss her.

'Oh!' Lou's eyes widened. 'Jo.' She clutched her spare hand to her chest.

'Mam.' Joanne looked down at the pink-tinged sawdust on the tiles.

'You're back. Verity said you'd been ill down in Brighton,' Lou stuttered. 'I tried to call so many times.'

Joanne closed her eyes. Of course Alex would have told Verity – his mam – what had happened. And there were no secrets in this town. A blush rose up her neck. She should have answered her mam's calls. 'I'm OK,' she whispered. Then she thought of the secrets, her birth mother's secrets, that Lou knew but had refused to share. Her hands tightened into fists and she opened her eyes. On the wall behind Lou was a poster of the different beef cuts. Tom had disappeared into the back. Only the large woman remained in the shop, staring at them with her mouth open.

'Why didn't you answer my calls?' asked Lou. 'I've been so worried.' She clutched the neck of her jumper, scrunching it up in her hands. 'Is the baby OK?'

'I . . . I . . .' Joanne concentrated on the poster, mentally tracing the cow from the chuck down to its brisket, along the flank and then up through the sirloins. Lou had taught her the cuts as a little girl, standing in the same butcher's, when Tom's dad was alive. She'd told her to get there early on a Saturday and ask for a topside corner cut when money was flush and there was something to celebrate. 'I'm fine, the baby's fine,' she managed eventually, and looked Lou in the eye for the first time.

'Oh Jo, come here.' Lou reached her arm out to embrace her. But Joanne saw Grace's face, holding her outside the house on Windmill Lane. Lou knew what had happened to her but wouldn't tell Joanne. She turned and pushed back through the plastic strips into the street.

'Jo!' She heard Lou's voice echoing down the street as she almost ran home, the tears flooding down her face. Inside, she locked the door, ran upstairs to the box room and threw herself on to the floor by the window seat, sobbing into the newly upholstered fabric.

GRACE

JULY 1975

'Good morning, ladies.' The voice, and the sound of shoes squeaking on lino, pulled me through the layers of sleep. I turned on my side to see who it was and the sudden streak of fire between my legs brought me back to the ward. Joanne. Had it been yet another night? Every night seemed deep, and dreamless, and endless. When would they let me home? What looked like daylight filtered through the side of the blinds. I pulled myself up on my elbows. The hands on the clock had changed from a slow waltz into a blurry quickstep. I blinked and looked again, but they kept spinning. Too fast to read or be certain what the time was. What was happening to me?

Jenny was up and starting to put things in a bag. 'I'm going home today,' she said as she folded muslin cloths.

'Are you?' I said. Had she told me that before? 'How long have you been here?'

'Ten days,' she said, slipping a magazine into her bag.

'How long have I been here?' I asked.

'Five days, silly. You've got a few days yet and then you'll be going home too.'

Five days. I thought I'd been here since yesterday.

'When will they bring in the babies?'

'Eight o'clock.' She nodded towards the clock. I didn't want to look at it again. She tipped her head on one side, looking at me, her curls bouncing. 'In thirty minutes,' she said slowly.

I nodded and looked away. The corner of my book was poking out of the cabinet. I picked it up and opened a page at random. There were scribbles all over the page. Like those Egyptian letters we learned about in school. I turned over. The ball. A faint red blush in the west was all that was left of the day. But it seemed to be getting hotter, more humid. Women started fanning themselves, men dabbed the backs of their necks with napkins. Thunder rolled towards the castle from the north. The waiters started ushering people in from the courtyard. Annabelle had drunk too much champagne. She stayed in the courtyard with Rory and they looked up into the sky as the first drops of fat rain fell on their upturned faces. I could almost feel the coolness of the rain. It was so hot in this room.

Her kohl began to run down her cheeks. They laughed as their clothes dampened. Rory picked her up and twirled her around the courtyard, laughing into her hair. The letters started to move and I clenched my jaw. It hurt where I'd cracked the tooth. It was hard to make out. I closed the book and opened it again. The text was still. They were in the car, going back to their castle. It was silent, sleeping when they arrived, and Annabelle went to the nursery to kiss her sleeping children. In the corner of the room, where the nanny should have been sleeping with the baby, was an empty cot. The baby had gone. 'No!' I gasped. Annabelle was distraught, crying. Rory woke the servants and started to conduct a search of the castle. The nanny was also missing.

'No, they can't take the baby.' I heard the shout and realised that it was me. Like when Mike sometimes woke himself up snoring. Jenny was staring at me, her face ghostly. 'It's OK, Grace.' She started to come towards me.

I rubbed my hand over my eyes and then looked back at the book. The text danced again, the ts and the ds tangoing across the page. Jenny took it from my hands and slid it back into the cupboard.

'They've taken my baby,' I said quietly, starting to cry. I'd wanted a baby for so long and now I'd never have one. Mike would be so upset. How could I tell him? I knew they'd find out about the deformity eventually. I could never have kept that secret.

'Only for the night, silly. They'll be bringing them back in a minute. Eight o'clock.' Jenny's face was screwed up like a tissue. I saw her look at the nurse. They were talking about me. I just couldn't hear what they were saying.

'We have your baby here, Mrs Bennett.' It was the matron this time. She was holding a baby in a white shawl.

'No, no,' I said, putting my hands behind my back. 'That's not my baby.'

'Mrs Bennett, this *is* your baby. Baby Joanne. Here, put your arms out and hold her. It'll make you feel better.'

Joanne. We were going to call the baby Joanne. Or Justin if it was a boy. She slid the baby into my arms. I tensed, but then saw her midnight eyes staring at me. Joanne. I felt suddenly light, a silk thread floating through the air. Of course, Joanne. My baby hadn't been taken. That was the book. The fear drained from me, like waking from a dream that you can tuck back into your pyjama case and forget about until the following night.

They stood at the end of the bed for several minutes, watching me feeding Joanne. When they'd moved back down the ward, I folded up the edge of her bonnet. The indentation was there, sliced into her head. It was Joanne. I took a long breath and then let it out as slowly as I could, just like they'd taught us in those classes. I took another breath and looked at the clock. The hands slowed, but not enough for me to read. Why were they doing this to me?

Jenny was sitting fully dressed on the bed, feeding her baby. I knew she was watching me, even though she wasn't looking at me. When Joanne had finished with her bottle, I put her back into the cot and lay down.

A screech woke me. The catering trolley. The catering woman slid a plate on to the table. I put my hands over my ears to deaden the noise. The scrambled egg was congealed. It had soaked into the toast, making it mushy. I squeezed my eyes shut and pushed it away. There was a crash. I cracked open an eye and saw the egg crawling across the lino towards Jenny's old bed, trying to escape. The little cooked chicken finding freedom.

'Mrs Bennett.' Matron sounded like our old headmistress now. She'd get out the cane soon, just like she did with Susie. Those red marks on her hand. She couldn't hold her fork for days. I'd hated her for that. 'Please get back into bed.' Several nurses appeared and started rummaging around near my bed. What were they doing to me?

The starched sheets rustled every time I moved. I stared at the clock, then at Joanne and at the book that someone had placed in my hands. Whenever I opened it, I could only read a few lines before they started moving. Annabelle was devastated about the baby. They'd given her some sort of sleeping draught to calm her.

Rory and the men were out searching the grounds. The baby was called Joanne, or Justin. I closed my eyes. No, Joanne was my baby. She was lying in her cot, gurgling.

I opened them again. Mike was at the end of the bed, somehow smiling loudly. He sat on the chair and held my hand. The smell of oil was sickening. I turned away. 'Joanne's been taken.' I buried my face in the pillow.

Mike drew his eyebrows together, like bunched-up caterpillars. 'Gracie. Joanne's not been taken. She's here. Look, she's fine. Beautiful.'

I looked at her and felt the pin vibrating in her nappy. I dragged my eyes to him and nodded. 'Joanne.' I knew she was there. Who was the missing baby? I knew there was a missing baby.

'It's so loud,' I whispered. 'I want to go home.'

'Just a few more days, Gracie,' Mike said, trying to take my hands away from my ears.

There were no other men in the room. No other visitors. Why was Mike here?

'Mr Bennett, may I have that quick word?' Matron was standing looking at me.

Mike half rose from the chair.

'In my office.'

He stood up fully. 'Stay there, Gracie love, I'll just talk to the nurse.'

'Slight hysterical tendency,' she said to him as they walked down the ward.

I put my hands back over my ears. 'My baby's been taken,' I whispered, staring at Joanne. 'I'm allowed to be hysterical. I want to be at home.' Jenny had gone, I should go.

I started to take all the things out of the cupboard and put them in my bag. There was an order to it, a way of packing Mum had said, but I couldn't remember what it was. It started to hurt my head thinking about it, so I just threw it all in together.

I sat on the ring, my legs over the side of the bed, swinging them. The new Jenny was holding a tiny baby. She kept talking to me but I couldn't hear what she said.

Where was Mike? He'd been ages. Maybe he was waiting for me outside. He probably didn't want to have to see all these babies any more than I did. We needed to be at home together. I picked up my bag, walked past the baby in the cot and down the ward, pushing open the door at the end. It was another long corridor with rooms off the side.

'It's just a temporary nervous depression,' Matron was saying. 'A few more days here under our care and she'll be fine.' Poor woman, whoever it was. Nervous depression sounded like that king we learned about who was mad but then they discovered in the present day he'd only been mad because he had a urine infection. Gerry had a urine infection once, but then she'd always been a bit mad so it was hard to tell the difference. I shouldn't think that. She was lovely really.

The door opened and Mike appeared, frowning anxiously. Why was he in there with Matron? 'I've got my bag,' I said. 'I'm ready now.'

Mike put his head on one side. I'd seen him do that before, at school, when he didn't know the answer. But not for a long time. 'But Gracie, you and Joanne need to stay in hospital. It's only been five days. You need to be here longer.'

'But Joanne's been taken,' I said. 'We need to be out there looking for her.'

He stared at me and then looked to Matron, who shrugged. 'Come on, Mrs Bennett, let's get you back to bed. You need to rest. Give me the bag.'

I gripped the handles, making sure I'd put them over my wrists so she couldn't grab it off me. That was the mistake I'd made with the baby. I hadn't been holding her tightly enough and that was why I'd lost her.

'I'm going home,' I said calmly. 'I need to rest at home.' I started to walk down the corridor. I hoped this was the way or I was going to look really silly. Mike must have waited for a bit but then he was running after me, his shoes squeaking in quick beats.

'Gracie, you can't go home, you're ill,' he panted.

'You'd be ill if you'd been through what I've been through. And then to lose the baby. We should never have gone to that ball. I don't know why we went. What were you thinking?' He should take at least part of the blame, surely. I hurried on. The exit must be this way. The thought of lying in my own bed made me walk faster, despite the throbbing between my legs.

'Gracie, you need to go back to bed. The nurse said.'

I stopped and faced him. 'I know you're worried about me, and you're sad too. But I'll feel so much better at home. It's awful here. It's so loud, I can't sleep and the other women stare at me.'

'For God's sake, Grace.' His hand was gripping my arm. 'Pull yourself together. There's no way you're going to be allowed home behaving like that.' His eyes were like coal.

'Pull myself together. Like a torn seam.' I laughed. 'I have a torn seam and would like to pull it back together.' But every time I moved it unstitched itself.

My back hit the wall and another stitch unwound. Something dribbled down my leg. Mike was holding my arms either side of my head. His face was so close I could see the pores. They were sweating. No, it's only horses that sweat. Ladies glow, men perspire and horses sweat. That's what we'd been taught.

'If you don't start behaving, they'll never let you home.' His teeth were clamped together, his voice low. Dangerous. Was this Mike? What had they done with Mike?

'Everything all right, Mr Bennett?' The starch in Matron's skirt rustled. The man let go of my arms. Mike.

'Yes, Matron.'

She smiled at him and walked back down the corridor.

'I want to go home,' I said to Mike.

'I've told you, they won't let you leave this early. Ten days, they said, with a first baby.' Matron was watching us from outside her office.

'It's not a prison,' I laughed. 'We can leave whenever we want. Especially now we don't have a baby.' Mike's eyes darted towards me, but he didn't say anything. I knew he was struggling to come to terms with it. With the loss and the guilt. That's why he'd been so angry. I understood. I rubbed my eyes. She'd been a beautiful baby, even with those awful marks. Thank God he'd never realised she was deformed. It would have upset him.

'Stay here,' he said. 'Let me talk to Matron.'

He walked slowly back down the corridor, the grief weighing him down. I could see it almost pushing on to his shoulders. Matron stood with her hands clasped in front of her. I couldn't hear them over the whine of the lawnmower outside. Or maybe the sound was inside. Mike shrugged a lot and looked at me. Eventually, he disappeared back into the office. The seam below started to sag under my weight. There were no chairs so I sat down on the floor, my legs splayed out. The wall felt cool, solid behind my head. Comforting. I closed my eyes.

A baby was crying. My breasts started tingling. I pressed my hands against them.

'Gracie.' It was Mike.

I cracked open an eye. He was a silhouette against the overhead strip light. I thought he was holding my bag. But as I scrambled to stand, I realised it was the baby. 'We can't take someone else's baby home, just because we've lost our own,' I said. The front of my nightdress was drenched.

I saw him glance at Matron and look down at the baby. 'They said we can go home, Gracie. They want you to stay here so they can help you but if that's what you really want, then they'll let you go,' he said. 'They'll visit us at home.'

'Thank God.' I sagged back against the wall, tears welling up inside me. Home. Quiet, safe home.

'Mr Wood is coming to pick us up in his car. But you need to put your coat on over your nightdress.'

I looked down. It was completely see-through.

'Your husband has some more pills for you that will help, both for the milk and to make you feel calmer and more like yourself, Mrs Bennett.' Matron spoke quietly. 'The doctor will come and see you later today, and the midwife will come every day, twice a day if needed, until you're feeling better.' She put her hand on my arm. 'We wish you the best of luck and a quick recovery. We're here if you need to come back.'

'But the baby—' I said, feeling the fear rise up inside me, choking me from the inside. 'We can't take someone else's baby. It's not right.'

'Just leave it, Grace. Please.'

He never called me Grace. I put on the coat Matron held out, though I didn't recognise it. And pulled it across my swollen breasts. Mike was already halfway down the corridor. I tied the coat at the waist and followed him and the baby.

Chapter 14

Joanne

October 2021

Alex wasn't happy that Joanne was going back to Brighton so soon, and alone.

'How will you manage going all that way on your own? How are you going to get from the train station to Susie's cottage? What if you bleed again? The doctor said to rest. *I* say to rest. Listen to me.' He clutched his head.

'I'll be fine,' she said, raising her chin. 'I just need to find out what actually happened. It'll only be a couple of days.' She tipped the korma sauce into the pan with the chicken and onion and started to stir.

'But Jo, it's too far. It's not like you're going to Newcastle or something. It's all the way to London, across London and then another hour from there.' He sighed. 'You can't do that in your condition. Five hours on a train. It's madness. You need to look after yourself and the baby.'

'Could you please stop saying "in your condition",' said Joanne, getting the naan bread out of the packet. 'You make me feel like a walking womb. You've been like that since we started this whole

IVF thing. Like I'm just a thing to carry your baby. And not very good at it at that.'

'Oh Jo, I've never meant it like that.' Alex sighed, reaching down to get the rice out of the cupboard. He passed it to Joanne.

'No, but you've thought it, I know you have.'

Alex looked out of the kitchen window.

She sighed. 'I'm absolutely fine. The doctor said last week I was fine. Now, can you lay the table? I need to go for a wee again.'

Alex smiled at her, and touched her hair as she passed him and walked down the hall. As the kitchen door swung to, she heard him whisper, 'I just want to be a dad.'

In the morning, Alex insisted on carrying her bag to the train station to see her off. They stood awkwardly side by side on the platform, too early for the London train, with yesterday's argument weighing heavily between them.

'I told you we didn't need to leave this early,' said Joanne, looking at the information display.

'Better to be safe than sorry,' Alex said.

'Is that another dig about me going?' said Joanne sharply, looking at him sideways.

'No,' Alex said, shaking his head. 'I just like to be prepared.'

'I'm not going to be able to get to the grave tomorrow, so would you lay some flowers? Pink roses, like always.' Joanne looked down at her feet. It would be the first anniversary she'd missed.

'Eh?'

Joanne looked at him sideways. 'Have you forgotten what tomorrow is?'

Alex shook his head and looked away. 'The anniversary,' he said quietly. 'Pink roses, I will.'

She looked back at the bare concrete of the platform. The tannoy crackled. *Your attention, please. The next train to arrive at platform one will be the 09.42 service to London King's Cross.*

'Please take care of yourself, love, and the baby,' said Alex, casting a glance at Joanne.

She turned to face him. 'Of course I'm going to take care of myself. What do you think I'm going to be doing? I'm not going on a hen party.'

The tannoy interrupted. *Calling at Newcastle—*

'You know what I mean,' he said.

—Darlington.

'I'm doing everything I can for this baby. Everything. And all while I'm going through all of this with my birth mam,' Joanne said, tears beginning to fill her eyes.

—York.

'And I get nothing from you. Nothing. I'm just a womb on legs. That's all you care about.'

—And London King's Cross.

'Oh Jo, that's not fair.' Alex reached out for her, but she took a step back and folded her arms across her chest.

This train is formed of twelve carriages, the tannoy reported as the train eased into the platform.

'It's true though, isn't it? I know you're desperate to be a dad. I'm desperate to be a mam.' She shook her head. 'Perhaps you should have left me years ago and met someone else who's younger and could have a baby more easily.'

Alex looked at the platform.

Joanne's mouth dropped. 'You've thought about it, haven't you? Oh my God. You've actually thought about leaving me because I couldn't have a baby. After everything we've been through.' A cramp started at the base of her belly. Something behind her eyes tingled.

'Jo—' Alex pleaded, reaching out for her again. 'I never thought that—'

'No, Alex. Just no.' Joanne picked up her bag and went to the nearest train door, not caring if it was her carriage or not. She climbed on and walked down the train staring straight ahead, avoiding looking at Alex, who was walking down the platform alongside her. How could he have thought that? How *could* he?

'Jo, please listen,' he was shouting.

Customers are reminded to mind the gap between the train and the platform edge when boarding.

As she reached the front carriage, the train started to move off. She turned and, through her tears, watched Alex as he receded into the distance, a tiny figure standing at the end of the platform. Her phone started ringing in her bag. As the train went over the Royal Border Bridge and the river opened up below her, she sat in the corner seat, staring at her belly. Alex had always been there for her, or pretended to be there for her. But all along he'd been looking at other women, thinking about trading her in for someone more fertile. Had he even done more than think about it? The art gallery postcard flitted into her mind. What had he said about that? A patient or something. She tried to remember but the memory stayed out of reach. She switched her phone to silent, ignoring his calls and texts, and rubbed the tears from under her eyes. Thank goodness the carriage was almost empty.

By the time Joanne arrived in Brighton more than five hours later, her back ached and her feet were swelling, but she felt calmer. She checked her face in her compact mirror and adjusted her chunky necklace. Then she climbed slowly down on to the platform and started the long walk towards the ticket barrier. She'd slipped her ticket in and was just looking up to see where she could catch a bus when she heard her name called.

'Woohoo! Jo!' Susie was standing by the coffee shop, waving.

Joanne felt her shoulders drop and she walked over to Susie, who took her bag and gave her a quick hug. 'Quick, my husband's waiting on a double yellow just under the bridge,' she said, slipping an arm around Joanne to guide her to the exit. 'Are you hungry?'

'Starving,' said Joanne. 'I've only had a sandwich all day.'

'I thought I'd treat you to dinner. A new pizza place has opened up in the marina. John will drop us off there and pick us up later. Give us a chance for a chat.'

They sat outside in the last of the autumn sunshine looking at the boats jostling against one another in the marina. Around them, a teenage waiter was setting tables for the evening, adding a glowing candle to each table. It must be more for show; nobody would sit outside once the sun went down, Joanne thought. And then remembered how far south she was, and how much warmer it was. Despite that, Joanne felt at home. It was like how being with Mam and Dad used to be, she thought. Before she found the photos and started to unearth her dad's secrets. Before Mam started hiding things from her. Before Alex started looking at her as just a potential mother. Before everything changed.

Susie sat down in the chair opposite and handed over a menu. 'So what is it that you're down here for? You said you had an appointment somewhere?'

Joanne nodded and picked up the menu, glancing at the sections. To start, to follow, to finish. 'Yes, with the Brighton Records Office, tomorrow morning.'

Susie leaned back in the chair. 'What for?'

Joanne took a deep breath. 'What do you know about Grace's death?'

Susie suddenly studied the menu. Without looking up, she spoke. 'Why do you ask?'

Joanne watched her, biting her lip. 'I was always told my mother died having me. That's what Dad said,' she told Susie.

Susie's head jerked up, her mouth open. The menu shook in her right hand. She stared at Joanne intently.

'It wasn't until I found those photos at the bottom of a box of clothes and saw the pictures of Grace and me when I was born that I realised that wasn't true.' Joanne swallowed and looked down. 'My dad then told me that Grace had died when I was a few days old—' Joanne stopped, thinking of the death certificate in her bag. How much did Susie know? She was there, she must know what had happened.

Susie moved her chair around the table towards her. She took Joanne's hand in hers. 'Your dad is right in a sense. Grace did die in childbirth,' she said. 'She was never the same afterwards. Well, maybe for a day or so. But the birth changed something fundamental in her.'

Joanne screwed up her face. 'What do you mean, changed something?'

'What can I get for you?' The teenage waiter stood expectantly, a notepad in his hand.

Susie barely glanced up. 'Can you give us a minute?' He nodded and slipped away.

'Something chemical changed in her, I suppose.' She glanced at Joanne and then looked away.

'So when did she die?' Joanne asked, thinking again of the death certificate and 1977 and the nurse saying it could be post-natal depression.

Susie glanced at her and looked away. 'I don't know,' she said, clearing her throat. 'I last saw your mum when you were ten days old. They took her to hospital. I asked but Kathleen wouldn't say anything and nor would Mike, but later I came to think that she'd died that day. I was preoccupied by my own pregnancy. And then he suddenly left Brighton and no one knew where you were.'

Joanne's mouth watered and she wondered whether she was going to be sick. She reached into her shoulder bag to get a tissue and blew her nose. She could feel Susie's eyes on her. The brown envelope with the death certificate in it poked out of the top of her bag. Joanne wiped her nose and then drew out the envelope.

Susie narrowed her eyes and looked at it. 'What's that?'

'It's Grace's death certificate,' Joanne said, rubbing her hand across her forehead as she passed it over to Susie. She watched as Susie slid it out of the envelope and then held it at a distance, squinting to read it.

She blinked again. 'But this says she died in 1977, almost two years—'

Joanne nodded and waited, holding her breath.

Susie stared at the certificate for a long time and then handed it back to Joanne. 'I don't understand,' she said slowly. 'I never saw her after the ambulance took her away. I can't understand how she could have lived another two years and we didn't know nothing about it.'

Joanne put her hand on Susie's knee. 'Will you tell me what you know?' she asked.

Susie nodded and took a deep breath.

GRACE

JULY 1975

'I don't understand why we're doing this,' I said to Mike.

'Just humour your mum,' he said. 'She wants a picture of us bringing the baby home. It's for that book you bought.'

'But it's not our baby,' I whispered.

'Gracie, please stop saying that.' His hand gripped me too hard around the shoulder, his fingers digging into my bone. 'It is our baby, Joanne. Look.' He looked up and grinned at the camera.

I held the baby and forced a smile. It felt stiff in my arms, almost too heavy for me to hold although it was a tiny little thing. Joanne. But she'd been taken.

'Wonderful,' said Mum, pulling the picture out of the camera. 'You can go inside now. I'll wait for this to develop and then make some tea, though it'll be a bit thrown together. I wasn't expecting you out for another few days. I've brought some bits round from mine.'

I waited for her to take the baby and then followed Mike inside. Everything was as I remembered. Our lovely mustard sofa, the new wallpaper Mike and John had put up last year. The hands on the carriage clock on the mantelpiece were moving, but I could make out the time. Three o'clock. It must be the afternoon. I lowered myself into the settee carefully and leaned back. I breathed slowly in and out.

Mum came in with the baby and slid it into my arms, carefully placing her head in the crease of my elbow. 'Oh Gracie, I'm so proud of you. What a beautiful baby. She looks just like you. That hair.'

I laughed and she disappeared out of the room. The wall opposite had a damp patch on the wallpaper underneath the radiator. It looked like a map of France. Or was it Spain? I'd told Mike about it before and he'd promised to fix it. My arms were pinned down by the baby.

Mum came back in with the hospital bag and dumped it at my feet. 'She's still asleep,' she said, leaning over me. 'What a good little baby she is. I knew you'd be lucky. She's just like you was. Good as gold.'

She started taking things out of the bag. 'I'll put your and the baby's clothes away upstairs, but you might want these bits here.' She slid the baby book and my reading book on to the sofa next to me. 'And here's the photo. It's come out well. Let me take another, now that you're home. You and Baby on the sofa.'

I looked up at her as she clicked the shutter and then glanced at the photo on the side. Why had she wanted to take a picture of Mike and me with a strange baby? I lifted the baby book's cover, and the spine creaked. I blinked. Mike and I looked out of the first page, our faces full of joy, hope, life. I couldn't remember feeling like that.

'"We are so excited to be having a baby, to be having you, whether you're a boy or a girl",' I read out slowly. It had been a girl all along. '"I can't wait to hold you and look into your eyes—"' Joanne's eyes had been the most beautiful in all the world. So deep a blue you could swim in them and never surface.

I flicked through the pages with one hand, the other numb beneath the weight of the baby's head. There was the torn page. Then first tooth. First steps. These pages would forever be blank. Poor Joanne. I reached the blank pages at the end and unclipped the pen from the back of the book. How could I say what I felt about losing something so precious to me. And through my own fault. If only I'd never gone to that ball. Her fingers had been so small. I'd loved her in that short time, more than anything. More than Rory, more than Mum and Dad. More than Susie. I'd never get over it. We'd leave the island; it was so cold in Scotland anyway. I picked up the photo and started to write on the back.

My writing was scratchy, more like Susie's than mine. Why couldn't I write properly? How could I say how much I'd loved her in the short space of time she'd been with us? I used to write poetry at school. The teacher once laughed at something I wrote and made me read it out in front of the class. I'd hated her for that, but this poem was beautiful. Something Joanne could have read when she was older and known she was loved. The baby shifted in my arms and opened its dark blue eyes. Joanne. Was it Joanne? It looked like her, but she'd been taken in the castle. The map of France started to spread out. I took a breath and continued writing. The lines had to rhyme. They'd always told us the lines had to rhyme.

I was probably the best poet who ever lived. I would have been the best mother. If they hadn't have taken her. I was the girl who had invented a new type of poetry. I put the photo on the side, ready for them to read the poem later.

The settee pulled my head towards it. My body was heavy with sleep. But my mind was running, tripping over itself. I closed my eyes. But my mind wouldn't let go. It whirled around the poem, rewriting sections. I thought about picking up the photo again, but my arm felt too heavy to lift. My leg jerked and I lay back, waiting for my mind to switch off. My arm jerked, jolting the baby. I wanted to open my eyes to check it, but someone had weighted them down, like pennies on a corpse's eyes. My mind blinked and bleeped. It would not let go of the poem.

'Have this sandwich, Gracie, and a cuppa. It'll make you feel stronger.' Mum. 'It's important to eat in the first few weeks. It takes a lot out of you. Having a baby.'

The pennies rolled off my eyes. Crab paste. I crammed it into my mouth, chewing without a break. Bits fell on to the baby.

Mum wiped them off with the kitchen cloth. 'You are hungry. I bet they didn't feed you properly in that hospital.' The sandwich disappeared. Mum handed me a cup and saucer. I looked at it floating in the air. I tried to reach for it but it moved at the last minute. The pain was immediate. Heat. I leaped up. There was a thud on the carpet. Someone started to scream.

'Oh God, what happened? What happened? Oh Gracie.' Mum was kneeling on the floor. 'She's OK, she's OK.' She was standing up, the baby held against her chest, patting its back. Joanne. She was there but I felt very far away from her.

Mike and Susie ran in. 'What happened?' said Mike. 'Oh God. Is Joanne OK?'

'I think most of the tea went over Gracie,' said Mum, patting the sobbing baby.

'Gracie?' said Susie, kneeling next to me. 'Are you OK?'

My nightie was hot. I lifted it over my head and sat down. My thighs were bright red, the stain spreading up towards my stomach.

'I'll get a cold compress for the burn,' Mum said. She disappeared out of my vision, holding the baby.

Someone was screaming. I watched the redness spread across me and start to blister into little craters.

Susie ran out and came back in with a pile of flannels. She knelt and started to lay the flannels over me. I shivered. My boobs were huge, conical, encased in a thick cotton bra with small pads stuck down it to soak up the milk. My knickers came up to what was left of my waist, like an old man's trousers. Where were my clothes?

'What happened?' She laid the last of the cold flannels over my legs.

It felt soothing. Real. 'Thanks.' I smiled at her and she put her arm around me.

'Thank God the baby's OK.'

'We lost her.' I felt the tears prick my eyes again. 'It was all my fault. We went to the ball and when we came back—' I shrugged. I was bored of saying it.

'Gracie, what do you mean? Your mum has her.' She disappeared again. Mike sat on the chair opposite me, bent over. His head in his hands.

My eyesight started to narrow, the sounds became muffled as if I were about to faint. Then it burst into colour again as they both came back into the room.

'I'm sorry, love, I have no idea how it happened.' Mum slipped a fresh nightie over my head and I obediently lifted up my arms. 'Thank God it didn't touch the baby.'

Jangling noise filled the room, like a brass band gone wrong. The baby was on my lap and someone was pouring hot water all over it. I gasped and pushed it away off my lap. It rolled on to the floor.

'You OK, love? You're very pale.' Mum stood over me, her face pulled into a frown.

I nodded. The noise had stopped. I took a breath and then another one. It had gone.

'Baby's sleeping in her cot now. She went straight out after that fall. I reckon she'll be a good sleeper.' She smiled, but it didn't reach her eyes.

'She's beautiful, Gracie,' said Susie. 'She's all wrapped up like a mummy. I'm so happy for you.' They were all so happy, so happy. So fucking happy.

The jangling noise filled the room again. I covered my ears. 'Oh God, who's that?' said Mum, disappearing out of the room. Mike got up and stood next to Susie. They both looked at me.

'The doctor's here,' said Mum, popping her head around the door. Mike let out an audible breath. 'He just wants a chat with you.'

The hands on the carriage clock whirred. Mike and Susie left the room as the doctor came in.

His face was a battered piece of leather. His bulbous nose wiggled as he talked.

'HowAreYouFeeling?' he said, his words coming out in a rush.

His nose had two little eyes on it, watching me. I watched them back.

'TheMatronHadConcernsAboutYourWellbeing.' I knew he was talking to me but I couldn't understand what he was saying.

I winked at the eyes and one of them winked back. I giggled.

The doctor's other eyes stared at me. He kept asking questions I couldn't understand. So I just nodded or smiled.

Eventually, he stood up.

'I'veHadALookAtYourPrescriptionAndI'mGoingToChangeThePills.' He stayed by the door, talking to someone on the other side but watching me all the time. The door closed. I shut my eyes. The air changed, the sofa dipped. I opened my eyes and Susie was there. I turned so I couldn't see the clock or the map of France.

'Are you OK, Gracie?' she said as she took my hands in hers. 'You really don't look like yourself.' She opened her mouth, stopped and closed it again.

I looked at my palms, my fingers. They still looked like mine. 'I'm fine. Happy.'

'When did you last eat?'

Breakfast? Did I have breakfast? Mum had mentioned lunch but I couldn't remember what it was.

She stood up. 'I'll make you a cup of tea. You must be thirsty.' She disappeared out of the room.

The stain on the wall was getting bigger. It seemed to bend towards me as I breathed.

I got up and walked into the hall. Susie, Mum and Mike stood in the kitchen in a circle, their backs to me, whispering. There was another man there. He had the listening thing round his neck. The doctor. With the nose.

I couldn't understand what they were saying. Upstairs, the baby was breathing, the sound swirling down the stairs. It seeped into my ears and filled my head. I put my hands over my ears and slowly walked up the stairs.

The room was a deep red, the colour of blood, the sunlight easily penetrating the curtains. I should have double-lined them as Mum said. I leaned over the bars of the cot. The baby was asleep, lying like a chrysalis on the cotton sheet. She stirred and I backed away.

Her face looked like Joanne, but I knew she'd been taken. Rory had said. I rubbed my eyes. Mike's face swam into Rory's. I had two husbands, but they didn't know about one another. Maybe I had two babies too. No, I'd only had one baby. They'd said in the hospital. Joanne. Rory was disappointed, I knew. He'd wanted a boy, to head up the estate.

Her bonnet was skew-whiff on her head, covering one eye. A pirate. I tried to slide it back and then realised the marks weren't there. Those horrible deformities. I lifted the bonnet off her head and turned her on to her front. Unblemished.

This wasn't Joanne. I'd kept telling them that. Now I could prove it. I breathed in and out slowly, mimicking the relaxation classes. I'd thought I was going mad, but I'd been right all along. This wasn't Joanne at all. The baby stirred, its eyelids flickering. I willed it not to wake up.

They'd given me this baby as a sort of test, to see if I was allowed to have babies again. Then they'd give me Joanne back. I had to look after it. It was my duty. I would succeed. I would be the perfect mother to this fake baby. Then they'd let me have my real baby back.

Her cheek was soft, like a pale-pink silk.

I sat down on the rug and watched her chest rise and fall. A bubble formed at the corner of her mouth. With the next breath she blew it away. The bubble formed again with the next breath and was then blown away again. It formed and blew away. It formed and blew away.

It itched inside my knickers. I shifted on my bottom, but I couldn't help but scratch myself. They'd shaved my hair, hadn't they, when I'd had her. I scratched myself again and then crossed my legs so I couldn't do it any more. They'd tell me off.

Instead, I scratched my foot and went back to watching the baby sleep. My foot itched again and I scratched it. But the itch wouldn't go. An ant was working its way up my leg. I cried out and flicked it on to the rug. It puttered over the rolls of fabric, unperturbed by its change of environment. From deep crimson to light pink, it trundled along. Then suddenly it disappeared underneath the red terry-towelling jumpsuit. The one that had been Susie's. I waited for it to reappear and continue its journey. I crawled over to where it had last been, but I couldn't see it anywhere. The room was too dim. I turned on the light, the better to see the carpet. The ant had gone. I imagined it in the threads of the fabric, making a home with its ant family. Three ants sitting around a table having dinner. Then four ants. Then five. Then six. Then another family. Then a whole street of ants. A whole village. It quickly turned into a city of ants, all living and working, eating and shitting in the folds of the rug. I could hear them rustling. Now they were crying. We couldn't have this under our feet. It was wrong. The baby. They'd think I was a slovenly mother, letting all these ants near the baby.

There was a vibrating from the chest of drawers. I opened the top drawer and the pair of nail scissors shimmered.

Perfect. I started to snip the rug where the ant had burrowed. If I could stop this ant, then the whole city of ants would be saved. I snipped through the red towelling into the burgundy wool and through the scarlet cotton. But the ant may well have got further away. He was screaming now. Or maybe it was the other ants. They knew I was on to them. That their home was being destroyed. The screaming was so loud I had to hold one hand over my ear and press the other to my shoulder as I snipped.

The rag was flooded with more light. Even better. I saw a glimpse of the ant. Or maybe it was his son or his grandson. I started snipping towards it.

'Gracie, what are you doing?'

I sat back on my heels. Mum, Susie, Gerry, Emily and Mike were framed in the doorway. Five people. One person. Mike came in and took the scissors from my hand, sliding them into the top of the chest of drawers. They made a low-level hum. Mum walked past me to the cot. Susie knelt down next to me.

'Your beautiful rug,' she said, smoothing her hand over it. There was a huge patch where it was all cut and torn. I couldn't see the ant. They'd gone, thank God. I'd passed the first test. I stood up.

Mum was holding the baby, patting her on the back. Her face was purple and loud. 'Why did you turn the light on, Gracie? You woke the baby up.'

'I couldn't see the ants without the light,' I said. 'Look, I can prove this baby definitely isn't Joanne.'

Mike groaned. The screams dialled down into sobs.

'I didn't want to tell you at the time,' I said, looking at all five of them. 'Because I knew they'd take her away. Like they take disabled babies away.' Mike smoothed his hand over his head. 'But she was deformed. Joanne was deformed.' I let out a long breath.

'Gracie.' Susie held my arm. 'Don't be silly. She's the most beautiful baby.'

I shook my head. 'She had some marks on her head. On each side of her head—'

'Forceps,' Mum said.

'That's why the nanny took her. She was deformed. They took her to the place they take the disabled babies. Jenny told me about it in hospital.'

Mum's mouth was an empty circle. 'What nanny? What place? What are you on about?'

'Gracie,' said Susie, her eyes wide. 'Are you OK?'

'Look at the side of her head,' I said, pointing. 'The marks aren't there. The real Joanne had huge marks either side of her head. This baby doesn't have any.' I stroked her downy hair. 'She's perfect.'

I looked round at them, their mouths slack.

'They were marks from the forceps,' Mum said. 'They go after a few days.'

'I know this isn't our baby. I know it's a test, but I'm going to prove to you that I'm the perfect mother, so you'll let me have Joanne back.'

'This is Joanne. Our baby,' said Mike, gritting his teeth.

Why was he being like this? Maybe he was in on it? That was it. Rory was somehow conniving with the nanny. But why? Maybe he was in love with her, and they wanted to keep Joanne as their baby. He couldn't look me in the eye. He was having an affair with the nanny. Perhaps that was a test too. If I pretended I didn't know, then it would all be fine. I'd win him and Joanne back.

'OK, Rory,' I said.

Mike glanced at Mum, who was laying the baby down in the cot. She was just murmuring now. 'What's happening?' he whispered.

I knelt in front of him, clasping him round the waist. 'It's going to be OK. It's a test. If I'm the perfect mother to this baby, they'll bring back Joanne.' I winked at him. 'And I am going to be the perfect mother. I promise.'

'Grace—' he started.

'Annabelle,' I reminded him, tucking a trailing end of his shirt into his trousers. Grace was the other mother.

Mike leaned against the wall, pulling his hands through one another.

Mum knelt down next to me. 'Gracie—'

'Annabelle,' I said.

Mum looked at Susie and then back to me. 'Annabelle?' she said quietly.

'Annabelle,' I whispered. I sank to the floor and curled up on my side.

'Annabelle is the name of a character in the book she's reading,' I could hear Susie whispering. 'I read it just before her. It's about a woman called Annabelle and her husband Rory who live in a Scottish castle. They have four children including a new baby, but I can't remember what they call the baby—'

'What's this got to do with Gracie exactly?' Mum's voice cut through.

Susie was breathing loudly. 'I – well, in the book, Annabelle goes to a ball and when she gets back, the baby is missing. They search the whole castle and the grounds and they can't find it. Just like Gracie is talking about.'

I stayed quiet. At least Susie understood. I would succeed. I would be the perfect mother. I sat up.

Mum's face was all pleated together. 'What are you saying? That Grace thinks she's Annabelle?'

Susie glanced towards me and then turned away. She nodded. 'Maybe.'

'I am Annabelle,' I said, getting up. 'Of course I'm Annabelle.' There was so much to do. I needed to prove so much to them.

'I'm going to make a cup of tea.' Mike slunk out of the room, his head bowed. 'I think we need to call the doctor again.'

Mum nodded and stood in the door with Mike. 'There was a great aunt on Mum's side who went loopy after having a baby. I remember Mum telling me about her.'

'And?' said Mike, watching me.

'She ended up in the asylum.'

'And?'

'I didn't ask any other questions,' said Mum.

'We can't let that happen to Gracie. I'll go down to the pub and call the doctor.'

The front door slammed. They were trying to make out I was mad. I needed to show them I wasn't. I was very far from being mad. I was the perfect mother and I was winning.

Mum stood, her hands on her hips, watching me. 'What are you doing?'

'This chest of drawers is in a right mess,' I said, tipping the contents of the top drawer on to the rug. 'I'm going to tidy it all up so it's easy to find everything.'

'But Gr— you spent ages organising all these drawers,' she said.

'It's impossible to find anything,' I said, rummaging through the pile of muslin cloths and terry-towelling nappies on the floor.

'I'll help you,' said Susie.

'I'm fine,' I said. 'I need to do this on my own to pass.'

Mum and Susie looked at me. Susie yawned.

'You go home, love. I'll look after Gracie. You shouldn't be here in your condition, especially after working all day.'

'I don't want to leave her.' Susie looked at me sideways. Someone always seemed to be watching me, checking I was doing what I was supposed to.

'Rest, Susie. I won't leave her, even for a second.'

Susie touched me on the shoulder. 'I'm just going home for a bit, Gracie. But I'll be back in the morning to help.' I nodded. Mum switched off the light, but I could still see from the light on the landing, and stood by the cot watching the baby. I could hear her gurgling.

It was hard to work out what was the best place for the nappies. They needed to be on the top, but should they be next to the muslins or by the cream? I tried it in different combinations but I couldn't work out what they'd expect. Maybe I needed to practise changing the baby again, then I'd see what was best. The baby was lying still, its eyes closed.

'Don't wake her, love. Leave the baby sleeping,' Mum said.

I shook my head and picked her up, holding her gently under the head. That was all part of the test. It was very important to hold the baby properly, that's what they'd taught me in hospital. I laid her on the mat and started to unwrap the shawl. There were so many layers, like a complicated pass-the-parcel except without the gifts in each wrapping. She stirred but her eyes stayed closed. I was winning. Underneath the all-in-one I could feel the nappy pin shimmering. As I took off the final layer of shawl, the blood stain spread out and across the nappy. I screamed and backed away. 'Blood, blood.'

Mum was there, her arm around me. 'It's OK, it's OK.' She drew me in. 'There's no blood.'

No blood. The baby was OK. I was winning.

'Let's put the baby back in the cot,' Mum said.

I sat on the floor, watching the baby. Gerry brought me in a cup of tea but there was a skin on it, which I didn't like. It was important that I watched the baby all the time, that I was an attentive mother. Mum sat in the feeding chair. They whispered between themselves sometimes, but all the words streamed together. The light changed to a deeper and deeper red and then blackness. But I mustn't sleep. They'd take the baby if I slept. I started walking around the rug, counting the rolls of fabric. 23, 24, 25.

'Gracie, you need to sleep.' Mum was gripping my arm. 'Please. I'll stay here with the baby.'

I shook my head.

'The doctor said you need to sleep.' Gerry this time, on the other side of me. The walls breathed in and out. In and out. Rory was in the doorway.

I changed my breathing until I was breathing the same as the walls. In. Out. In. Out. The baby was doing the same in its sleep. It was clever. I kept walking.

They were whispering again.

'Annabelle?'

I turned. Mum stood there, smiling. 'The doctor said you need to take this, to keep your strength up. So you can look after the baby.' I looked at the pill writhing in her hand.

I nodded. They'd given me pills in hospital and they'd been right. My milk was dried up now. These pills would help me, make sure I won.

I swallowed it down, gagging at its dry bitterness on my throat. I walked back to the cot. 1, 2, 3, 4, 5 steps. The baby was asleep. Back to the chest of drawers. 1, 2, 3, 4, 5. Back to the cot. 1, 2, 3, 4, 5.

My legs were weaker. I'd just sit down next to the cot. They wouldn't mind, so long as I kept watching. I crawled over to the cot and held on to the side. The bars grew fuzzy and then merged into the wallpaper.

The curtains were open, the room bright. I struggled up to sitting, my eyelids heavy. The cot was empty. The baby. I must protect the baby.

Mum was sitting in the chair, feeding her. Was I allowed help? I had to be the perfect mother. I snatched the bottle from her. The baby started to cry. 'I need to feed her,' I said. 'Don't interfere.' The baby sucked the rest of the bottle and then started to cry again. I stood up and jiggled her up and down as the nurse had taught me with Joanne. It seemed to work, but only if I kept walking. I paced round and round the room, careful to avoid the dead ants in the middle. They wouldn't like that. Every time I sat back down on the chair, the baby's eyes opened. The same blue as Joanne's. A moment of peace and then the whine started up, like the drills in the joinery department. And I'd have to stand and pace again.

The clock was moving fast. It was clearly part of the test, but I knew that time was passing from the light. The gradual shift from darkness to light and back to darkness again. When I could no longer see the baby, they'd give me the pill and I'd lie down by the cot and sleep with her. After a while, they brought me in a camp bed, right up to the bars of the cot. No one was going to take this baby. They'd have to step over me to get to her. I knew that was part of the test. I'd lost one baby and I couldn't be seen to lose another. Sometimes Mum or Rory or Susie sat in the feeding chair. I knew Rory was in on it. Would he try to take the baby? How could I stop him?

I paced around the rug, patting the baby. Every time I passed the chest of drawers, the nail scissors vibrated. I pushed them away. Mum got up and went on to the landing and into the bathroom. Silence, then the grate of the chain. As I passed the chest of drawers again, I slipped the scissors into the pocket of my smock. They were silent. But I could feel the weight of them, nagging at me, pulling me down.

I laid the baby down on the mat and took the scissors out of the smock. The light glinted off them like a disco ball. The blades were sharper than I'd thought. I ran one across the top of my thumb. A thin line of blood glistened. Warmth spread through me. I sucked the trail of blood away. The baby gurgled and smiled at me. She was happy. I smiled back and pushed the blade deeper into my thumb. The initial smart was followed by peace, happiness. All was right with the world.

The bathroom lock flicked back. I slid the scissors into my smock. Mum came in.

'Is she OK?' she asked, coming towards us.

I sucked my thumb and nodded. 'I was just giving her a different view.'

'Well, she certainly seems happy,' said Mum, smiling at the baby, who was lying still, gurgling, on the mat. 'You're doing an amazing job, Gracie.'

I gave her a look but didn't correct her.

'Being a new mum is hard, but we're all here to support you.'

That was a trick. They were testing me. I had to do this on my own. I wrapped the muslin around the cut, then picked up the baby and continued pacing and patting. Pacing and patting. The baby was quiet, I was doing a good job. They couldn't fault me.

I had completed 227 circuits of the rug when Rory came in with a plate of food. The gravy was congealed, like the jelly in a pork pie. My stomach churned. I shook my head. I couldn't sit down, I'd fail the test. 'Gracie, you have to eat. I'll just leave it here in case you change your mind.' He slid out of the room. Mum went with him. They stood on the landing, whispering.

The baby started to cry. They'd hear it and then I'd fail the test. 'Shh shh.' I jiggled. 'Shh shh.' Fresh nappy. Full tummy. Not tired. What else could there be? I jiggled and jiggled but the volume grew.

'Everything OK?' Mum's voice was far away on the landing. 'Do you need me to help?'

They knew I was failing. They were going to take her. I'd lost Joanne for ever. Footsteps on the stairs. They were coming to take her. I couldn't lose Joanne. I couldn't fail. The scissors shimmered in my pocket, the walls panted in and out and then began to close in on us.

The screaming was loud, louder than the baby had ever made. Then I realised they were Mum's screams. And Rory's. Loud, loud. I'd failed, I knew that now. I needed to get away from them all. Rory grabbed my arm but I pushed him. The room was stifling. The walls so close, oppressive. I ran down the stairs into the street, where it was cooler. Rory followed and was holding my arm. I'd failed. I'd failed. They were going to take her. It was his fault. All of it. If we hadn't gone to that ball. His jaw felt soft, yielding beneath my fist. It made a good sound. I tried again but he held my hand and then pulled me into a tight hug. There was no love there. Just pinning me down.

Everything was loud. Clanging bells. Only the scissors were quiet.

Chapter 15

JOANNE

OCTOBER 2021

The waiter slid the drinks in front of us and walked away. 'The most important thing you must know,' said Susie, taking a sip of her smoothie, 'is that your mum was so happy to be having you. She was so excited about having a baby. We both were. We'd got married within a few months of each other and then here we were expecting babies at the same time. We both couldn't have been happier.'

Joanne pressed her fingers to her smiling lips. She knew how Grace must have felt.

'It all started to go wrong after she'd had you. Not immediately though. I visited her in hospital after she'd given birth and she seemed fine, happy and fine, despite having had a long labour. She was showing you off and quite rightly so.' Susie smiled. 'You was a gorgeous-looking little thing. Smiley and happy. Rosy cheeks.'

Joanne grinned. Nobody had ever said this before.

'Two days later, when I went again, she was different. She couldn't stop talking. That's how it started. She kept saying strange things.' Susie lined up the salt shaker with the pepper grinder. 'She discharged herself and you in the end. I remember that, because although the doctors were against it, they knew she really wanted to be at home. And her constant talking was quite disruptive on the ward.'

Susie stirred her smoothie with the straw. 'Usually you left after ten days, but she was home after five or six days, because she just couldn't seem to cope in hospital, with the strict routine. And she didn't want to be separated from you – they took babies away at night in those days. We all thought she'd be fine at home.' Susie paused. 'But she wasn't,' she added quietly.

That didn't sound like postnatal depression, thought Joanne. Grace clearly had no difficulty bonding with her baby.

'There was a pressure then, there probably still is, for women to suppress their feelings, swallow their emotions and get on with mothering. Grace tried to do that, but something was wrong. I think there must have been a chemical imbalance in her brain. She'd always had bad PMT, but this was different. She was different.'

Just like me, thought Joanne.

Susie looked up at the ceiling. 'She deteriorated really rapidly,' she said, 'as soon as she got home. She started trying to undo the rug.'

Joanne screwed up her face. 'The rug?'

'Yes, you know, the rag rug. In that picture you showed me. She spent her whole pregnancy collecting material for it and binding it all together. She was so proud of it. We both were. And then almost as soon as she had you, she started unravelling it.' Susie paused and looked down at her hands. 'I'm not a clever sort of person, but it was like the rug was her mind. She was unravelling the rug as her own mind was unravelling.'

The waiter reappeared balancing a huge pizza on one arm. 'One Pizza Margherita and one Meat Feast and a side salad.' He rearranged the table, moving the drinks and laying out the pizza cutters.

As soon as he'd gone Joanne nodded for Susie to continue.

'I remember your dad calling Kathleen – Grace's mum,' Susie said in answer to Joanne's questioning look.

Joanne nodded. Susie had mentioned the name before. She picked up a slice of pizza. Despite everything, she was hungry.

'Kathleen was on her way round anyway, to help out. She'd been in and out of your house since you'd come home from hospital. But Mike ran out to get her, he was that desperate. Your grandmother stayed in the house with Mike and tried to cope with your mum. Your aunts were there too. But they couldn't cope.' Susie shook her head and closed her eyes.

Joanne put her hand on Susie's arm. Without looking, she knew that if she glanced towards the door, she'd see Grace standing there.

'I went round and tried to reason with her, but she wouldn't listen to me. She couldn't listen by then, I don't think. The doctor came eventually and gave her some tablets, I don't know what they were. But it calmed her a bit. It all seemed to be OK again.' Susie touched her gold necklace, running the chain through her fingers. 'Mike went back to work – men did in those days, there was no paternity leave – and Kathleen, your aunts and I took it in turns to be with you. That weren't unusual in those days,' said Susie, looking up. 'Not like now, when a new mum is just left to it on her own. Then, everyone in the community rallied round, cooking meals, helping out. Your mum seemed OK for a day or two. She kept cuddling you, she couldn't seem to let you go. She wouldn't sleep. I remember that. But we didn't think it was too odd. Just a new mum being protective.'

Susie looked down at her hands. She was twisting her gold wedding band around. 'But then, by the afternoon of what must have been the tenth day, she was talking continuously again, running up and down the stairs, pacing around your room. She—' Susie glanced up at Joanne. 'She seemed to see things that weren't there. She thought she was someone else. Kathleen, Gerry, Emily and I were all there, trying to help her and look after you. But we couldn't. It was too much. Grace was a different person.'

Joanne glanced at the door but it was just a family waiting for someone to show them to their table. Disappointment twisted inside her. She turned back to Susie.

'The doctor came and gave her more pills. Huge, they were. I remember that. He said they'd knock her out. And if they didn't work, he didn't know what else to try. And again, they did work for a little while. Grace was quiet and sat with you upstairs. We all took it in turns to be with you. I was there with Gerry in the evening and then Kathleen came for the night shift.' Susie stopped.

The noise from the restaurant receded. The air between them was very still. Joanne waited, hardly daring to breathe.

'I knew that things were changing when I left. But I was so tired—' Susie dropped her eyes to her uneaten pizza. 'I'd been with you all day and evening and was just so tired. I was over seven months gone by then, just stopped work. I didn't even say goodbye to your mum. Just let myself out and walked the few yards home and collapsed into bed.' She shook her head and rolled her lips on each other. 'I'll never forgive myself for not saying goodbye properly. I should have done more. She needed me and I should have been there.'

Joanne took her hand again. 'Don't blame yourself, Susie, you weren't to know what would happen,' she said quietly. 'What did happen?'

'I heard the screaming from my house. I must have been in a deep sleep. John leaped out of bed and I ran after him out of the house, just in my nightie. Grace was in the street, covered in blood. She was shouting, saying he'd tried to hurt her—'

Joanne thought of her father and his reluctance to talk about Grace's death. But Susie had pretty much said he'd had nothing to do with it.

'Your dad was trying to hold her, but she kept hitting him. His nose was bleeding all the way down his shirt—' Susie paused and glanced to the side of Joanne, not quite looking at her face. 'You was screaming too, from inside the house. I could hear Kathleen shouting for an ambulance.' Susie looked away.

She picked up a slice of pizza and stared at it like she couldn't quite remember what to do with it. 'Eventually, the police came and the ambulances and they took your mum and – it was so awful.' Susie dropped the pizza and covered her face with her hands. 'They wouldn't let your dad go with her. He followed behind in another ambulance.'

Joanne closed her eyes and covered her face with her hands. She felt Susie's warm hand on her leg.

'Are you OK?'

She looked up, swallowed and nodded.

'I know it's a lot to hear.' Susie rearranged her cutlery. 'I went home but I couldn't sleep. Every time I dropped off, I saw Grace or you.'

'Where was I?' asked Joanne.

Susie looked away. 'I don't remember. Maybe with Gerry or Emily.'

Joanne nodded. That made sense. After all, Susie had been with her all day.

'Mike came back to the cottage a few hours later, looking defeated.'

Joanne's heart ached as she thought of her dad. Selfishly, perhaps, she'd always somehow thought his life had begun when he arrived in Berwick, but he'd had a whole other life here.

Susie continued. 'He locked himself in his room and he didn't come out for ages. Kathleen, Gerry, Emily and I took turns looking after you. Eventually, your dad appeared, but he was a broken man.' Susie shook her head. 'He went to work and said little. I asked him where your mum was, but he just shook his head. He was mono-syllabic by then. Had totally shrunk into himself. Kathleen didn't seem to know either, and Mike wouldn't talk. Nobody seemed to know. I asked a nurse friend of mine, but she said Grace wasn't at the General. She'd just disappeared. In the end, I guessed she'd died the night they took her away.' Joanne struggled to swallow. 'Though there was no funeral, not even a memorial service. I should have asked more.'

Susie sighed. 'And all along, she was just in a hospital up the road. I could have got the bus there. I could have visited. We all would have done. If we'd known. To think Kathleen died not know-ing what really happened to her daughter.' Susie clenched her fists.

Joanne closed her eyes. Why had her dad kept all this secret? It wasn't his fault it had happened. And what was wrong with Grace? It didn't sound like postnatal depression. She was seeing things that weren't there. Joanne glanced at the restaurant door again, where quite a queue had formed, then twisted her wedding ring around her finger.

Susie looked at Joanne. 'She was there for two years in that place?'

Joanne nodded. 'It seems that way.'

'I just can't understand it,' said Susie, shaking her head. 'Why didn't we know? Why didn't Mike tell us what was happening?' She rubbed her face, and suddenly looked much older.

'Anyway, one day, I went round to Mike and Grace's to look after you as normal and Kathleen was there, crying. She said he'd taken you. He'd just gone. All the furniture was still there, except your cot. He'd just taken a few clothes and that was it.' Susie shook her head.

'Was that when he came to Berwick?' asked Joanne. The tim-ing made sense.

'We didn't know that at the time. He just took one of the vans from work and left. We never heard from him again, never knew about you. Until that Facebook post the other week.' Susie shook her head. 'Years, the cottage was empty. We all waited for him to come back with you, but he never did. Mike was an orphan by then, with no family around, so there was no one to ask. Even John, his best man – my husband – didn't know. He'd literally disappeared into thin air. Of course, there was no internet then, no way of finding him. Kathleen and I went to the police, but they said there was nothing they could do. He was within his rights to take his daughter away.'

'Abandon Grace. Start a new life,' whispered Joanne.

'He didn't abandon her,' Susie said. 'Grace was very ill when she left here.' She took a deep breath. 'The landlord eventually took your mum and dad's place back, and then another family moved in. I never got used to seeing someone else going through the front door.' Susie sighed. 'Kathleen and I stayed friends. I thought of you and thought that you were growing up somewhere, not realising you had a grandmother and aunts who loved you. People like me, who loved you.'

'He took me, but he left Grace,' said Joanne, pressing her lips together. 'He left her at the Egremont. In an asylum. For two years.'

Susie nodded slowly. 'I suppose I never knew about that asylum then. Never even knew it existed. If Kathleen did, she didn't tell me.'

'But to leave his wife, my mother, in an asylum for all those years. Leave her to die.' Joanne paused. 'It's unforgivable.'

Susie rested her hand on Joanne's shoulder. 'Your mum was very ill, Joanne. She – she did things that were out of character. She was a danger to herself. To you.' Joanne looked at Susie quickly. 'A danger to everyone,' Susie added.

'But he just left her, abandoned her—' Joanne blinked back the tears.

'I know. It's hard to understand, but don't judge him, Joanne. He tried his best. It was a terrible time for everyone. It was awful that he left, but maybe he felt that he didn't have a choice, after everything that happened.'

Joanne thought back to her mam talking about her dad arriving in Berwick with a tiny baby, how quickly he'd got together with Lou, even while Grace was dying in an asylum. She curled her lips. Tomorrow, she'd find out from the records office exactly what had happened to Grace in that place. Then she could go home and challenge her dad about why he'd never told her.

'C'mon, you look tired. Let's pay up and get you home,' said Susie, taking out her purse.

Later that evening, after she'd chatted with John, her dad's old best friend, Susie showed her to the little guest room. 'You should have everything you need, but if there's anything at all, just ask. You're family.'

Joanne smiled and put her bag down on the floral duvet cover. The room was cosy – two pink lampshades on the bedside tables cast a warm glow. Modern sketches of Brighton landmarks – the Palace Pier, the Pavilion, the old West Pier, and the new i360 tower – were stuck on the wallpaper with Sellotape.

'My daughter did those,' said Susie. 'I know you two never met, but you were always supposed to be best friends. Just like your mum and I were. She knows all about you. It'd be lovely to introduce you.'

'That'd be nice,' said Joanne automatically.

'Her husband would get on well with Alex, I think. How is he doing? I was surprised he didn't come down here with you.'

Joanne thought of Alex standing at the edge of the platform that morning. 'He's fine,' she said. She was staring at the huge rug that covered most of the floor, disappearing under the bed. It was made of hundreds of different types of multicoloured fabric bound together. Joanne knelt down to touch it. 'Is this . . . ?' She looked up at Susie, finding her throat felt suddenly thick.

Susie nodded. 'Mike left it behind. I couldn't bear to see it be given away to someone who didn't know your mum. She'd spent months making it.'

Joanne smoothed her hands over the uneven surface, imagining Grace rolling each piece of fabric and binding them together. 'I thought she'd destroyed it when—' She looked up at Susie.

Susie clutched her necklace. 'I managed to put some of it back together. The main damage is in the middle, hidden by the bed. The bits I couldn't repair. My sewing was never as good as hers.'

'I'm so glad you kept it.' Joanne stood up, her eyes filling with tears.

Later, she lay in bed imagining the torn fabric under the bed. What had been going through Grace's mind to make her want to destroy something she'd spent so long creating? Her phone buzzed with another message from Alex. She turned it off and tried to sleep, the baby heavy in her belly.

GRACE

JULY 1975

The clanging of bells grew louder and louder. Mike gripped my arms by my sides, holding me tight. He was shouting at me, spit hitting my cheeks. I kicked and kicked his shins, hearing my toes crunch against his bone. How dare he? How dare he? It was all his fault. His idea. I lifted my knee and thrust up and forwards. He yelped and crumpled to the ground. Release. I turned to run but now Dad was there, his face bunched up like puckered fabric.

'Grace, stop it. Stop,' he shouted. He never raised his voice. He grabbed my arms and held them against my chest as if in prayer. Then drew me into a thick hug, holding me against the pale-blue stripes of his cotton pyjamas. He hadn't done that since I was a little girl.

'It'll be all right. It'll all be all right,' he murmured, as if I were the baby, not Joanne. The sky was panting like a dog, faster and faster, the vibrations filling my head.

Someone was screaming. Lights flickered on up and down the street, curtains pulled back. 'Shut up, you lot,' shouted one of the neighbours. 'Some of us have to work tomorrow.'

'It'll all be all right, Gracie, you'll be all right,' Dad whispered in my ear, his breath hot against my cheek. 'You're just not yourself.'

I pulled back, his acrid smell making me sick. But he wouldn't budge, holding me tightly.

Mike was beside me again, half bent over, holding my arm. 'Gracie.' I yanked my head away from him. The sky panted around me.

'Get her a paper bag.' Emily. Shouting.

The clanging intensified and the street was filled with swirling blue light, drowning out the dark.

New hands grabbed me, this time from behind. I leaned forward and sank my teeth into the soft flesh, a metallic taste on my tongue. Free. Susie was standing, staring. I ran towards her but was grabbed again from behind, my arms pulled behind me. A popping in my shoulder. Red fire flickering down my arm. My cheek against the road. An old lolly stick in the corner of my eye. A Zoom or an Orange Maid.

More clanging bells. 'The baby, the baby,' someone shouted. Was Joanne safe? I tried to turn my head, but all I could see were shiny black boots. The other clanging bells started off again, jarring my head.

A face bent over me, I wrenched my neck forward to smash against it. Another soft, crunching noise. A grunt. Something warm on my face.

'Fucking bitch.'

A sharp redness in my leg and then a cloud of black released over me.

Joanne.

Chapter 16

Joanne

October 2021

'Have you got an appointment?' The receptionist at the records office tapped importantly at her keyboard and sighed with a tinge of disappointment when she found Joanne's name on her screen. Perhaps she enjoyed the power of turning people away, Joanne thought. 'Wait there. Edna Gardner will be with you in a moment.'

Joanne and Susie perched on the mismatched plastic chairs in the small reception area. Leaflets about domestic violence and modern-day slavery were fanned out across the table. On the wall, dusty oil paintings of long-forgotten dignitaries stared down at them. The carpet tiles were stained by decades of spilled takeaway coffee.

'Joanne Shaw?' Edna Gardner didn't look much younger than the building, but her round face was split by a smile. Her glasses, held on a purple chain around her neck, bounced against her enormous chest swathed in a lilac jumper. 'Come this way.'

Joanne and Susie followed her down a narrow corridor into a small office. They slipped into the two chairs positioned opposite a huge corner desk that looked like it had been there since at least the 1980s. Edna picked up the glasses and positioned them on the end of her nose, and looked over them at Joanne and Susie. 'How can I help?'

'We're interested in looking at the hospital records for my birth mother, Grace Bennett. She died in the Egremont Hospital in 1977 and I want to find out how and why she was there.'

'Ah,' said Edna, sucking her teeth. 'I'm afraid hospital records are closed for at least a hundred years. To protect people's privacy. I'm sure you can understand. They should have told you that on the phone when you booked the appointment.'

Joanne dropped her head. She'd known in her heart that it had been a waste of time. She'd never find out what happened to Grace.

Susie leaned forward. 'But you don't understand. It's not just simple curiosity. We need to know what happened to her mum' – she glanced at Joanne – 'so we can make sure that Joanne gets the right care in her pregnancy and the first few days of being a mum.'

Edna wrinkled her forehead and looked at Susie. 'What do you mean?'

Susie stuck her chin up. 'I was her mum's, Grace's, best friend. After she had Joanne in 1975, she became very ill.' She took a deep breath and said quietly, 'Mentally ill.'

Edna tilted her head sideways.

'She had some sort of postnatal breakdown. She was taken away by ambulance and we never heard from her again. Shortly afterwards, her husband, Mike, disappeared with Joanne here. I never heard from them until recently, when Joanne got in touch.'

Edna was silent.

Joanne swallowed. 'It took me a long time to get pregnant, even with IVF, and I lost several babies. I got pregnant again on my last try and I'm now past the danger phase. Well, almost. I'd always thought my mum had died having me, but I then found out she died in the Egremont Hospital two years later. I need to know what happened to her.' Joanne looked up at Edna. 'Please. If she was ill after having me, it could have implications for me and my baby.

This is our last chance with the IVF. Please help us.' Joanne realised she was clasping her hands together as if in prayer.

Edna sighed and looked down at her desk. She spent a few moments lining up her notebook with her pen and the tissue box. Then she moved her triangular name plate to line up with the top of the notebook. 'There are occasions when we do release records,' she said almost inaudibly. 'But I'd need a letter from your doctor and an official request for the records. It will take weeks. I can't just—' She shrugged.

Joanne could feel a lump developing in her throat and looked down, focusing on the laces of her trainers.

'But we don't have weeks, don't you see?' Susie was leaning forward, her hands gripping the side of the desk. 'Joanne's due in a few weeks, we need to know now what was wrong with Grace so that Joanne can prepare. And she lives at the other end of the country. She can't keep making this journey in her condition. Please, please understand, Mrs Gardner. Just let us see the records. We won't take them out of here. Just let us look at them. Then Joanne can get her doctor to request them formally when she gets home.' Susie's eyes were bright.

Edna looked down again and then took a deep breath. 'I want to help you, I really do. But those records are confidential for a reason. You will need to request them through your GP. If he explains the situation, it can be fast-tracked and you should have them within the month.'

'A month,' repeated Joanne. 'In a month I could have a baby.' She started to cry. Everybody just seemed against her getting to the truth.

'It's bloody ridiculous,' shouted Susie, standing up. 'I get that you have rules but this is so important. We need to know now. Sod the rules.'

Edna looked down. 'I'm sorry,' she said. 'I wish it was different.'

'So do I,' said Susie, helping Joanne up. 'She's got a right to see those records. It affects her and her future child, and you, you penpushers, are just stopping her.'

Susie stormed out past the receptionist, almost dragging Joanne behind her.

On the pavement, she gave a big sigh. 'I'm sorry, I'm just so angry about it. It's so unfair.'

'I know,' said Joanne, sniffing. 'I thought we might actually get somewhere today.'

'Let's get a cuppa,' said Susie, pointing towards a cafe opposite. Joanne nodded and they pushed open the door, a jangling bell announcing their arrival.

They sat down at a table with steaming mugs of tea. At another table sat two young women. Briefly, she thought one of them looked like Grace and seemed to be staring at her. But as soon as Joanne met her eye, the woman looked away. She didn't look like Grace at all.

Suddenly, she felt horribly overwhelmed by it all. Her hands shook and she swallowed to try to keep the tears away. 'I just want to find out what happened to her. Just thinking of her in a place like that. It's so awful. Awful.' Susie put her arm around her shoulders but said nothing.

After a while, Joanne turned to Susie. 'I'd like to visit it, see where my mother died.'

'It's derelict now,' said Susie. 'There won't be much to see, but I can get John to drive us up there now if you like. Just to see the outside. Before your train. It might help.' She squeezed Joanne's arm.

GRACE

JULY 1975

It was completely silent. Not Sunday morning quiet. Dead silent. As if the end of the world had come, and I was the last creature on Earth. No distant rumble of traffic, no whispered conversations from rooms nearby, no impatient whistle of the kettle, not even the chirp of birdsong. I opened one eye. I was in the spare room at Mum and Dad's, but they'd painted it all cream. I reached out but the walls were soft, not the usual pockmarked plaster. I dragged myself up. The walls yielded slightly under my fingertips. It looked like a type of painted leather. I wondered what was underneath to make it soft. Maybe the same material we used at Brunswick. Why on Earth would they do this? Dad must have been up all night.

They'd taken away the bed as well. There was just a mattress on the floor. The grey serge blanket was unfamiliar too. I'd never known Mum to have these. 'Mum?' I called. 'Mum?' My voice started and ended at my mouth.

I tried shouting 'Muuuuuuuuum.' The sound just stopped. I screamed but the noise barely left my mouth before it was sucked back in.

The rest of the room was empty. Just me and the mattress on the floor.

I lay back down. The only light came from a fluorescent bulb in the ceiling, encased in a metal cage. The insect carcasses inside cast threatening shadows on the walls. It was so unlike Mum not to have swept them up. She had such a thing about dead flies. Maybe she'd bring in one of those yellow sticky tapes and attach it to the ceiling. Gerry, Emily and I were always so horrified by the sight of the flies trapped on it. Some even ate their own legs to escape.

As I took a deep breath, the ceiling moved towards me. I blew out and the ceiling retracted. I practised it several times, watching the ceiling breathe in and out with me. It was comforting, like Mum sitting next to me, her arm round me, our breathing in the same rhythm. I thought about calling for a cup of tea but I knew they'd bring one eventually. I closed my eyes. The ceiling breathed out loudly.

Minutes, hours or days later, I opened them again. Everything was exactly as I'd left it. Like when you return from holiday and are amazed that the same familiar things are in the same familiar places.

But in the corner of the room there was a pale lump that hadn't been there before. It separated into two things and then merged into one lump, then separated again. Maybe there were two things. I wanted to find out what it was, but it was too far away. I tried to call out for Mum, but my tongue was stuck to the roof of my mouth. She would come in and bring it closer. I waited but she didn't come. The taller lump might be a cup of tea. I had to get to it.

My arms shook as I dragged myself up and then used them to pull myself across the floor. Everything felt heavy. Numb. A third of the way there. My legs felt like dead meat as I pulled them across after me. I pinched my thigh – it felt solid like a rubber hose – but there was no pain. Halfway there. The ceiling panted with me. Two-thirds of the way. My arms burned. Almost there. There were two things. It wasn't a cup of tea but water in the type of plastic beaker we had at school. I took a gulp and the water streamed out of my mouth, running down my face. It couldn't get past my tongue. I worked at my tongue, trying to prise it from my mouth, swilling the remaining water around my mouth. Little by little it loosened and eventually came away. It felt foreign in my mouth. Swollen. I licked my chapped lips, wincing as the water seeped into the cracks and the inside of my mouth, and wondered how I'd stop myself biting it. I kept my mouth open, my teeth far away from it. The last few drops of water dripped out of the upended beaker on to the floor. I smeared them on to my fingers and wiped them across my lips.

Next to the plastic beaker, the other thing was square and soft and white and in the middle of it was something creamy yellow. I had the vague thought that it was something I needed to put in my mouth, but it smelled of the bottom of the wash basket. I stacked the beaker on top of it and left it for Mum to collect.

Somehow, it was easier to get back to bed. It seemed shorter and I knew the way this time. The ceiling wheezed with me as I pulled myself along. I collapsed on the mattress, my arms aching, my dead legs strangely pulsing.

The dream was so vivid. My eyelids snapped open like the kitchen blind, springing up. Fear drenched my body. I was shaking. But I couldn't remember what the dream was. The silence was loud now. I clapped my hands so I could hear over it and that felt better. It was nice to have some sound for company, apart from the ceiling. And all that did was breathe quietly, or noisily. I kept clapping and started to sing 'Colours of Day', the hymn we'd sung at school.

We'd sung that at almost every assembly, Susie and me. It was my favourite and Mrs Hart's too, but Susie preferred 'Lord of the Dance'.

My hands conducted my voice. I would have liked to tap my feet but my legs still didn't seem to be working. Susie had got into trouble for what the headmistress called 'dancing on her bottom' in the hall. Apparently, that was disrespectful.

I shifted into sitting and a sharp pain down below pulled at me. Underneath my dress was the biggest pair of pants I'd ever seen. Proper grown-up pants. Like Granny used to wear. They were unbearably itchy. I started to scratch at my pubic hair through the fabric. It felt good, but there was something there. I opened up the pants and inside was a giant sanitary towel saturated with blood. It had leaked down my thighs, creating a mirror image of blood stains. Like the butterfly drawings we made in art.

An image flashed on to the wall. Me covered in blood. It was all over my hands, my chest, drenching my dress. Then it was gone. I gasped and closed my eyes, letting my dress fall. I wouldn't look at the knickers again.

When I peered through my fingers again, my dress was clean. There was no blood. I lay back down. I'd tell Mum when she came in that I needed a new sanitary towel – my monthly was much heavier than usual. The ceiling breathed in and out with me, soothing me to sleep.

Chapter 17

JOANNE

OCTOBER 2021

Helmer was the sort of place featured on the front of boxes of Sussex fudge. A main street dotted with a butcher's, a baker's, an ironmonger's and a greengrocer's – a colourful display of fruit and veg. There was a local bookshop and a buzzy little cafe, all dominated by a Norman-style church, alongside which there was a large church hall with bunting flapping in the breeze. Joanne sat in the back of the car as they crawled along, the air punctuated by bursts of excited screaming from the local primary school's playground.

'I seem to remember it's just outside the village on the left,' said John, turning round to smile at her.

'I can't believe you came here regularly, yet you never mentioned it,' said Susie yet again.

'Heating engineers visit all sorts of places,' John reminded her for the tenth time. 'I must have been in every building in Sussex. And the asylum wasn't a place you wanted to remember.'

Joanne saw the look that Susie gave him and glanced down at her hands. Asylum was a horrible word. But maybe it was more of a refuge for Grace.

They left the village behind and came into open countryside, a wooded hill rising to the left. From the top of the trees Joanne could just about make out a Victorian water tower.

'Look, there it is,' said John, pointing. 'I knew it was just outside of the village. Now whether we can get past the gates is another matter.'

Trees canopied the road and it was suddenly dark. John slowed down. 'I'm sure the turning was along here somewhere.' The trees and undergrowth formed a wild tangle and it seemed impossible that there could be a path.

'Stop!' said Susie. A few yards on, the words 'Egremont Hospital' were just about visible on a faded wooden sign. Someone had added 'for lunatics' underneath in marker pen. A modern, offi-cial sign read 'Keep Out'.

John swung the car into what looked like it had once been a grand driveway. Nature had almost completely reclaimed the space, its green tendrils encroaching over the tarmac, leaving only a nar-row stretch of road for John to navigate. They edged up the path for several minutes, the ground rising sharply, expecting at any moment for it to open up to reveal the hospital. A sharp bend ended with metal security fencing and signs promising cameras and guard dogs.

'You literally go round the bend to get here,' said John, laughing.

'John!' Susie gave him another look.

'Sorry.'

Through the iron mesh fence, an austere brick building rose up in front of them, the boarded-up windows of the ground floor gazing blankly. Bars decorated almost all the windows of the first floor. Behind the main building was a taller one, a cross on the top indicating a chapel. A water tower stood to the left. What were once probably pretty gardens for patients to relax in had turned feral, as if they were intent on taking over the house, stealing through the windows.

'Looks like it's all closed off,' said John, turning off the car engine.

Joanne and Susie got out of the car, slamming the doors. Joanne went up to the fence and linked her fingers through it. Even derelict, it was a beautiful building. The sort that developers would probably kill to get their hands on. But perhaps nobody wanted to live in an old asylum. It was a picturesque place to end your days in. Even if you were too young.

'I've found a gap, Joanne, here.' Susie was standing on the other side of the fence. 'Look, someone's already been here. Probably kids.'

Joanne squeezed through the gap with difficulty and joined Susie.

'Are you really sure you should be doing that?' said John. He was standing by the car, smoking. 'Especially in your condition, Joanne. Trespassing's illegal.'

'We just want a closer look,' said Susie, putting her arm on Joanne's. 'We won't go inside, just have a look through the windows.'

John rolled his eyes. 'I'll wait here.'

They pushed through the tall weeds, broken glass crunching under their feet. The main entrance was a huge stone arch, the year 1884 engraved above it. A small wrought-iron balcony looked down on them, two smaller windows behind it. How had her mother felt when she first walked through here, thought Joanne. Or maybe she hadn't been in a fit state to think anything.

Joanne gripped Susie's arm as they climbed up the stone steps and under the arch. Two stone benches lined the wall of the open porch. Above them, faded notices advertised a hospital dance and a fundraising quiz night. She lowered herself on to one of the benches and breathed deeply. The air felt very heavy here, as if it were holding on to something.

Susie stroked her shoulder. 'How do you feel? It must be strange for you, being here. Knowing that—'

Joanne nodded. 'And for you too.' She looked at the solid wooden door. 'I suppose it's locked?'

Susie walked towards it and gently pushed. She gave a small cry as it creaked open to reveal a brown tiled floor.

Joanne stood up and moved next to her. They looked at each other, their eyes wide. 'We could just have a little look. Just to see what it's like. We don't have to go all the way in,' said Joanne.

Susie nodded and pushed the door fully open. It moaned.

In the gloom of the entrance hall, they could just about make out two ornate staircases curling upwards and joining at the top, like dancers. A series of doors, each half wood, half glass, were positioned on either side. Clutching Susie's arm, Joanne crunched over glass and other debris towards the closest one, feeling her heart thump. The baby was very still, her bump tight.

She pushed open the door into an enormous room filled with light. The windows here had escaped being boarded up, but not the attention of vandals. There was hardly a solid pane left in the lattice windows and a chill breeze hurried across the glass-strewn tiled floor of the almost empty room. The radiators had long rusted up.

'Look!' said Susie, leaving Joanne's side to step across to a grand piano, which listed uncomfortably to one side. She touched the keys and a note echoed around the room. Coils of ivy reached through the broken pane, their sights seemingly set on the piano. A bird had made its nest among the strings. The wood and ivory was slowly being drawn back to nature. At the end of the room were double doors, the glass in the top panes miraculously almost intact. They pushed them open and found themselves in a smaller room. Stainless-steel work benches were against the walls, while in the middle a large oak table was covered in broken crockery.

'The kitchen,' Joanne breathed. She glanced back at the previous room. 'That must have been the dining room.' Had her mother sat and eaten in there?

Ignoring Susie, who was poking around in what looked like an oven, Joanne walked back through the dining room and into the hall beyond. She tried the next door. It led into what must have been the laundry – there were lines of industrial washing machines, their mouths gaping open. One window was completely missing and the floor was covered in moss. She stepped across glass to the washing machines and peered inside one of them. Resting on the bottom of the drum was a black slip-on shoe, the type Joanne had worn for PE lessons. She picked it up. The rubber bottom was worn and mildew was devouring the fabric. It wasn't the sort of thing you would wash, so why was it in the washing machine? Unless someone had climbed into the machine and lost it in the process? She shivered and backed across the room, closing the door.

They crossed back into the entrance hall. The door opposite led to a corridor so long that Joanne couldn't see the end. The ceiling had fallen in places and littered the floor. She could see through to the sky. What was left of the paint and plaster peeled off the wall, taking the graffiti with it. One side was boarded-up windows, while closed doors punctuated the other. They held their breath and looked at one another, listening, but the only sound was the cooing of the wood pigeons. Proo. Proo. The building seemed to be quietly waiting.

They walked slowly down the corridor, avoiding the larger piles of rubble, and pushed open the first door.

Joanne gasped and covered her mouth with her hand. Eight metal-framed beds lined the walls, with cream curtains still partly drawn around some of them. Most had mattresses, and there was even the occasional pillow and a screwed-up sheet at the end. Three huge arched windows lit the room. Bars ensured that, while the light reached in, nobody could get out.

'It's like they've just left,' whispered Susie.

Joanne nodded and walked into the room, stepping across peeling white paint and plaster. The mattresses were damp to touch and the mildew had begun to spot around the Egremont Hospital logo. Underneath the end of one bed, a pair of blue leather shoes waited to have feet slipped inside them. Had her mother stayed in this room? She glanced under the beds but there were no personal items left, just the beds and the one pair of shoes, which looked like a man's. At the end of the ward, a small table held an old-fashioned grey telephone. Joanne picked it up and listened but there was only silence.

'I'll go and have a look and see what's in the other rooms. You OK here?' asked Susie.

Joanne nodded. If it wasn't for the bars, it wouldn't be a bad place to stay, she thought. High ceilings, airy. Only eight people to a room, by the looks of it. A nicer room than the ward she'd spent the night in the other week. She walked around touching the ends of the beds, drawing back the curtains. Perhaps her mother had done this too, when she'd woken in the morning. Got out of bed, drawn back the curtains. That was if she'd been well enough. How did they treat people with postnatal depression in those days? She bit her lip. There was so much she didn't know.

She walked out of the room and wandered down the corridor, glancing through the doors that Susie had opened. Most of the other wards were identical. Abandoned beds, some with mattresses, some just bare springs. Curtains half torn down from their tracks, either by patients or by vandals. Strange pieces of twisted metal, which might have been an old-fashioned hoist, lay contorted on the ground. The only sound was the painful creaking of the silver birches outside. Susie's head appeared out of a room much further down the corridor. 'This place is huge,' she shouted. 'This corridor must be almost half a mile long. They would have had hundreds of people here.'

Joanne shivered, and hurried to join her. She suddenly didn't want to be alone in this sad, silent place. Together they explored the rest of the rooms, finding them all similar. At the end of the corridor, a door led out into the gardens. It was ajar and leaves and small branches had blown in, banking up on either side of the cor- ridor. There were the remnants of a nest. The corridor turned right and there was a series of smaller doors. Joanne pushed the first open but it hardly moved. She grunted and pushed harder, wincing at the sharp stab of pain in her side.

'Here, let me,' said Susie, giving it a huge push. The door swung open, revealing a small, low-ceilinged, windowless room. They both stepped inside, looking around them in the gloom, the only light seeping through from the corridor. Joanne switched on her phone torch and swung it around the small space. The door swung closed behind them and an oppressive silence filled the room.

'A padded cell,' whispered Susie. 'I didn't realise places like this actually existed.' She ran her hands along the wall, where tufts of horsehair had forced their way through the cream-painted leather. Paint peeled off the ceiling, flaking on to the floor.

Joanne stood in the centre of the room, looking up into the rusted metal cage around the broken light fitting. Even the silver birches were silenced. 'Imagine being left in here,' she said, the walls absorbing the sound of her voice. There was something about the room that felt comforting. Like being cocooned in a womb.

'I can't imagine anyone would have spent much time in here. It was probably just used for the most violent patients,' said Susie, putting her hand on Joanne's arm. 'Grace wouldn't have been in a place like this. She would have stayed on the wards we saw. With the lovely windows overlooking the gardens.'

She sounded like an estate agent.

Joanne leaned against the walls, her legs and belly aching. On one side of the room, the floor was clear of damp and paint scrapings. Joanne suddenly felt exhausted. She sat down, sliding her legs out in front of her. From this angle, the room felt bigger. The small, T-shaped window sliced in the door drew in a weary light. She imagined sitting here, being watched. Or maybe the patients who were in here were too far gone to realise where they were or what they were doing.

To her right, the padding ended above the floor and there was a gap of several centimetres. Joanne ran her fingers along it. Had it always been there, or was that the result of years of decay? Joanne shone her phone torch at the gap and noticed some scrapings. She traced the tangle of letters with her fingers, imagining crazed patients desperately scratching out their names and messages with whatever they had to hand. 'B E T', she spelled out. Was that meant to be Betty? There were other indecipherable scratchings, which could have been unintentional. Then the unmistakable curve of the number nine. She swung her phone torch closer and followed the line along and there, in the tiniest script engraved into the cement, were the numbers 1, 9, 7, 6. It was clear. As she turned around to move closer, a sliver of pain ripped through her belly. She gasped and breathed out slowly as she rubbed her fingers on the cement to get rid of the dust.

'Look, Susie, it says 1976. Grace would have been here in 1976. She could have written this.'

Susie stood above her. 'Anyone could have written that. Anyway, what are you doing down there? It's filthy.' She held out her hand and Joanne took a long look at the numbers and then allowed herself to be hauled up, grimacing at the pain. She looked around the padded cell and then squeezed her eyes shut.

'Come on, let's keep looking around,' said Susie, backing out of the room. As she opened the door, the creak of the trees filled the room. Joanne hadn't realised how much she'd missed the sounds from outside. It was a relief to take Susie's hand and be led out.

They walked down another never-ending corridor. Susie found some bathrooms but there was something about the rusting metal hoists that made Joanne's stomach turn. She left Susie to it and continued to the end on her own. The final room looked like an office, with six desks, and a glass door leading to another room with one larger desk. In the gaps between the piles of paperwork scattered across the floor, Joanne could see a swirly blue carpet, the type they'd had in their front room at home before Mike and Lou discovered laminate flooring. A scuffling behind her made her jump and she gasped, her heart thudding.

'Sorry,' said Susie. 'Didn't mean to startle you. This place is incredible, isn't it?'

Joanne nodded, clutching her chest. Across the long wall, five rows of matching framed pictures were screwed to the plaster. The glass in the frames was almost all smashed but the screws were rusted into the wall, which was presumably why nobody had bothered to take them off.

Most of them seemed to be formal staff photos, with people in different uniforms standing in front of the hospital's entrance, their faces faded by age. 1893. 1895. 1901. 1908. 1912. 1923. 1933. The women's skirt length rose as the years went by, eventually turning into trousers in the 1980s. Joanne sidestepped, following the images along the wall.

Underneath the formal photos, a group of older men played football on a muddy pitch, one ignoring the ball and instead standing stock still and posing for the camera. Egremont First V1

1946 read the caption. In another a woman in a long flowery dress appeared to be singing accompanied by a man in a suit on the clarinet and another at the grand piano they'd seen in the main rooms. Christmas Concert 1952. In a third a group of patients stared fixedly at a television inside a wooden cabinet. The screen appeared to be blank. The new television lounge someone had written underneath.

But it was the next picture that made Joanne gasp out loud. Grace. It must be Grace. She stood grinning at the camera in long flares with a flowery top and some kind of bandana trying to keep down her curls. She was raising the hand of another similarly dressed woman above their heads. Next to them, a man in uniform was holding a box of what could be chocolates that he seemed to be about to give them. Eurovision Song Contest 1976, the label read.

'Susie, look,' said Joanne, smearing the grime off the picture so they could see better.

'Oh my goodness.' Susie clasped her hands to her mouth. 'Oh God, that's her. That's Grace.'

'I can't believe it,' said Joanne. 'She looks fine, happy.'

Susie nodded. 'It looks like she won the contest. Not like Grace at all, she would never have put herself forward for something like that.'

They stood staring at the bleached-out photo for a long time before Susie carefully picked out the slivers of glass. Joanne helped her until she caught her finger on an edge, a blush of crimson spreading across her palm. 'Careful,' said Susie. Joanne sucked it clean.

'There,' said Susie, giving Joanne the picture.

Joanne stared down at it. If Grace was so happy why was she still here in 1976, a year after she'd had Joanne?

The two women examined all the other photos but there were no other ones of Grace.

Susie reached down and picked up the piece of paper on the desk nearest to her, which was mottled with mould. '"Reginald Wells has been physically aggressive towards a female patient this a.m.",' she read. '"Patient seen by MO. No signs of bruising or pain after fall. Following incident, Reginald spent time in coercion chair." I wonder what a coercion chair was,' said Susie, her forehead wrinkling. She dropped the report back on the desk and picked up another.

'I wonder if there's anything here about Grace?' said Joanne, shuffling through the remaining few reports, but there weren't any names she recognised. She opened the top drawer of the first filing cabinet, expecting it to be empty. 'Oh,' she said. Uniform manila folders sat between alphabetical dividers. The top drawer ended with an Emmeline Baker. Joanne opened the second drawer and almost immediately saw the name Grace Bennett. The pain in her stomach stabbed again and she pushed away the thought that it might be serious. She was finally going to find out something about her birth mother.

Joanne and Susie looked at each other, their eyes wide. Susie snatched up the report, and spread the content over the desk. The pages were badly mildewed, black and blue spots obliterating whole sections. Joanne flicked through the first few pages, which just seemed to list contact details and next of kin.

'Here's the delivery.' Joanne ran her finger across the first few lines. '"Admitted 9 a.m. Bath taken and castor oil and orange juice administered."' She made a face at Susie. 'Yuk.'

'Oh, we all had it in those days,' said Susie. 'Disgusting stuff.'

'"9.30 a.m. enema." Oh my God. She had an enema.' Joanne made another face.

Susie laughed and looked back at the document. 'Ah yes, she was induced. I remember now. She'd gone over her due date and the doctors were worried. But lots of people were induced in those days,' she said, looking up. 'I was induced a couple of months later and it was fine. They said it was for convenience. So you could go into labour after your husband had gone to work and have the baby by teatime and visiting hour.'

Joanne rolled her eyes. 'Thank God that's changed. It sounds like the birth was quite quick. Look, the contractions come thick and fast. I can't read the next bit.'

'But she didn't have you until the following day.' They read down what they could decipher in silence. 'Oh, you were breech,' said Susie. 'I hadn't realised that. No wonder it took so long.'

'These days, Grace would have had a C-section. I wonder why they didn't then.'

Susie shrugged. 'Different times.'

'Episiotomy. Forceps.' Joanne made a face. 'Why would there be forceps if I was breech?'

Susie shook her head. 'I don't know. It all sounds quite dramatic, doesn't it? There seem to be lots of people involved. Blood loss. Third-degree tears. Retained placenta. Stitching.'

'Bloody hell,' said Joanne. 'This sounds awful. What does it say there?'

'I can't read it,' said Susie, taking off her reading glasses. 'But the main thing is that you were healthy. Look, you're seven pounds six ounces, a good weight. You passed all the newborn tests. You were fine.' She read down. 'And you slept well. So Grace might have suffered badly, but it hadn't affected you.'

Joanne nodded. 'Oh look, she had a blood transfusion.'

'I never realised any of this,' said Susie. 'I knew it had been a long labour because we were waiting for news all day and then all the following night, but Grace said it was all fine. That she was happy.' Happy, that word again.

'Dad visited the following day,' said Joanne, pointing. 'And then you the day after.' Joanne looked up and smiled at Susie.

'Yes, I came with Grace's mum. It was quite a palaver getting permission. They tended to only allow husbands, but I was so desperate to see her.' Susie sighed. 'And honestly, she seemed fine. She said how happy she was. She looked well, you've seen the photo, I had no idea about any of this.'

'"Patient talking incoherently and continuously. Sedative administered 12th July 9.15 p.m.",' Joanne read out. '"Patient disruptive",' she continued a few lines down. '"Refusing to hand over baby to nursery."'

'I think I said, in those days, the babies slept in the nursery at night so the mums could recover.' Susie paused. '"Patient confused in the night. Second sedative administered 2.10 a.m."' Her voice caught. 'This must be the start of it. I can't read the next bit.'

Joanne's mouth suddenly felt dry. '"Lactation suppression medication administered."' Joanne screwed up her face. '"Patient confused and disorientated. Seems overwhelmed and unable to follow instructions. Talking incoherently. Sedation given." Then look, later that day, "Dr Tuck prescribed lithium carbonate."' She looked up.

'What's that?' asked Susie, but Joanne was already googling it.

'It's a mood stabiliser. Fair enough.' She sighed. 'They increased the dose again – and look, again here, the following day. "Patient becoming delusional, refusing to accept baby."' Joanne's eyes were wide. 'What?'

Susie let out a long breath. 'Grace was just confused. She'd been reading a book about a woman whose baby was kidnapped and she started thinking she was a character in the book, I think. That's the only way I can understand it. She thought you'd been kidnapped and the baby they replaced you with wasn't you, if you get what I mean.'

Joanne said nothing.

'Once she discharged herself' – Susie nodded towards the document – 'she became convinced that you had been given to her as a test, to see if she was fit to be a mother.'

'Why did she discharge herself?' asked Joanne.

'She told Mike that it was because everything was so loud in the hospital, that she couldn't cope or sleep. I remember him coming to pick you and Grace up. It was such a surprise. We weren't expecting you for a few more days. Kathleen ran around trying to get everything ready.'

They turned over the page but it was almost completely covered in mould. 'The doctor at home gave her chlorpromazine,' read Susie.

'That's an antipsychotic,' said Joanne, looking at her phone and then back at the records. '"Patient exhibiting clear symptoms of postpartum psychosis."' She looked up at Susie. 'Postpartum psychosis,' she whispered. 'I've heard of that. There was something on the TV about it ages ago. It's a terrible mental illness that affects a tiny percentage of women after they give birth.' She exhaled. 'So you were right, she did go a bit crazy after the birth. Literally crazy.'

Susie nodded, her eyes heavy. 'I didn't know about the illness then but I knew she wasn't herself, your mum, after she had you. I just thought she needed some pills or something, short-term treatment. Not to be incarcerated.' She shook her head. 'Postpartum psychosis.'

Joanne bit her lip and reread the words. Postpartum psychosis. Was it hereditary? Could she end up the same way? She'd seen and felt Grace watching her over the past few weeks, even though rationally she knew she couldn't really be there. Joanne shivered and turned over the page, but the next two pages were unreadable. The mould spores obliterated everything bar the occasional word which made no sense. They turned over the past few pages which became slightly more legible.

'Look,' she said. 'This must be when she was in the hospital. "Report from visit of Michael Bennett, husband, 29th July 1975." So he did visit.' She flicked over one more page. 'And again here. Another visit in early August. And again on the 15th.' Joanne felt suddenly lighter, almost giddy. Her dad hadn't abandoned her mother in an asylum. He'd visited regularly. 'It looks like he visited monthly, even when we were in Berwick. He brought me with him – look, it says there.' She flicked through more pages. 'But the visits stop in May 1977. I wonder why?'

She read on. '"Patient placed in seclusion following incident during visit. Patient requested husband not visit." So he did want to visit. It was Grace who told him not to. Oh God.' Joanne covered her face with her hands. Susie slipped her arm around her shoulders.

'Oh Joanne, love. Poor Mike.'

'I've said some awful things to him, Susie. And I never apologised. I was so angry that he'd kept all this secret. But he was just trying to protect me, wasn't he?' Joanne dropped her head.

'Yes, I think he was. Your dad's a good man. He went through a lot,' said Susie. 'He loves you. I bet he's been so worried about you.'

Joanne nodded and looked back down at the document. How could she have suspected him?

'It's so annoying that we can't read so much of it,' she said, tracing her finger across the black mould.

Susie looked sideways at her and then looked away.

Joanne let out a long breath. 'I can't believe that this has been left here all these years. And all these other records. Anyone could have found it.'

'But we found it,' said Susie gently, closing the report and putting it under her arm. 'We know more than when we came in here. By sheer luck really.'

Joanne nodded. 'Now we can request the official version through my doctor and hope that that's been kept better than this.' She looked around the room where the wind was ruffling Reginald Wells' report on the other desk. The air was cold and close. 'Let's go,' she said.

GRACE

JULY 1975

'Gracie.' Mum was calling me. 'Mrs Bennett.' The voice was far away. I pulled myself up and tried to follow the sound. It seemed to come from high up, on the opposite side of the room. She wasn't there, but I could hear her. Who was Mrs Bennett? 'Mrs Bennett, come to the door and put your arms through the gap.'

What gap? I pushed myself into a sitting position and looked towards the lumps. They'd gone. Mum must have taken them away and now she was here. 'Mrs Bennett, come to the door and put your arms through the gap.' Did they mean me?

I dragged myself towards the voice and it felt easier than the first time. My arms felt stronger underneath me. Where the lumps had been was a door I hadn't seen the first time. Not the normal spare-room door, but a different one. Dad must have put it on when he painted the room cream. I banged the door, but it didn't open.

'Stand up and put your arms through the gap.' My legs still looked useless, lumps of flesh trailing behind me. But when I tried to move them, they actually did what I asked. Slowly, I edged myself upwards, into kneeling, then crouching, and then slowly standing. My legs creaked but held my weight. The ceiling let out a long, slow breath.

Just above my eye height was a gap in the door. It hadn't been there before. Mum's voice barked through it again. 'Put your arms through the gap.' She had her cross voice on. I pushed them through the hole, and on the other side Mum grabbed them and pulled them towards her. 'Mum,' I complained. 'That hurts. I'm having to stand on tiptoes.' But she held them firm. I tried to twist and pull my hands back, but they'd been fastened to something.

The door swung open and I was thrust backwards, against the wall, the open door stopping me seeing anything. Footsteps walked into the room.

'Mum?' I said. 'Can I have a cup of tea? I'm thirsty.'

She grunted and then started to close the door again so she was behind me. I turned my head but she stayed out of sight.

'No funny business now. You kick your legs and I'll put you in a leg lock as well as the arm lock.'

Arm lock was what John's brother did to him all the time at school. He never did it to Susie or me though. 'No, Mum.'

A sharp prick in my leg. The sting travelled up my leg and into my belly, my chest, my heart, further up into my brain. I started to swoon and then Mum appeared and held me. Dad was there too. They laid me on to something that wasn't the mattress. The light changed and then the noise hit me. People shouting, scream-ing, grunting. The wheels of the trolley squeaking. Plates being slammed on the table. Pens scratching on paper. Cars revving their engines. Birds screeching. Even the trees groaned. I closed my eyes and focused on the ceiling breathing with me, following each in breath and out breath. 'Mum,' I called, but she didn't answer. The landing between the spare room and the bathroom seemed to go on and on.

Eventually, the trolley slowed, the wheels turning from a shrill shriek to a dull moan. Then they stopped and the bed jolted. The ceiling breathed louder here, and mingled with the breaths of other people. It smelled of bleach. Mum cleaning again. I opened one eye and peered through my eyelashes. I was in Mum and Dad's bedroom but there were other people here too, other beds. Four beds opposite me and three next to me. Why had they let these people into their home? Dad had changed the windows too. The square boxes had been stretched into huge arches, like a cat stretching.

Mum was talking to another woman in the corner. 'Mum,' I called, but she ignored me. The woman next to me was lounging on top of the bed, dressed in a green satin floor-length evening gown. Her hair was pulled back into a victory roll. She must be a friend of Mum's. 'Hello,' I said politely. 'I'm Kathleen's daughter. Grace.' I reached out my hand, but it was bandaged. I didn't remember hurting myself.

'How do you do,' she said, slipping out of her bed and taking my hand. 'I'm Marjorie. It's a pleasure to meet you, Grace.'

Of course. Marjorie. Hadn't Mum mentioned a friend called Marjorie once? How nice to invite her to stay. Her dress looked glamorous, but as she took my hand I realised it was stained in places and threads had been pulled. Hair was escaping from her pins.

Opposite, another woman waved enthusiastically. 'That's Catherine,' said Marjorie. 'Lady Catherine. Top-drawer bonkers, if you want my opinion.' She winked and I laughed.

'So what you in for?' she said.

I smiled. 'It's my home,' I said. 'I was going to ask you the same thing. I don't think we've met before?'

Marjorie laughed. 'Well, at least you've accepted it early. Catherine there is under the illusion that she's the lady of the manor. She bosses the staff around no end. Get her into the ball-room and she starts doing the waltz.' She waved her hands in the air. 'Mind you, I'm a mean dancer myself. Won prizes, I did.'

I turned away and looked for Mum. She'd disappeared. Maybe she'd popped to the loo. Someone else, dressed as a nurse, was looking at me. 'How are you feeling, Mrs Bennett?'

'Mrs Bennett?'

'Grace,' she smiled, showing her teeth.

'Where's Mum?' I said, looking towards her bedroom door.

'Your mum will be along soon, I'm sure. We do have a visitor for you. But I just want to check you're ready to see visitors. I don't want to have a repeat of the behaviour when you arrived here.'

I stared at her. Who was this woman to tell me how to behave in my own home? I was almost certain I wasn't rude to her. I was never rude. Suse would tell you that. Her lips were pressed into a line, but the downy moustache above waved like rushes in a river. I waved back and she narrowed her eyes.

'Grace? I'm warning you. Any funny business and you'll be back in seclusion.'

'If you mean the spare room, then I'm quite happy with that,' I said to her. 'Oh and—' I dropped my voice to a whisper. 'I need another sanitary towel. My monthly's going on much longer than it usually does.'

She raised her eyebrows and turned away.

'Be careful with that one, dear. She's not one of the nice ones.' I turned back to Marjorie, who was sitting, legs crossed, on the side of her bed, dangling a green slingback shoe on one foot and a beige loafer on the other. And she had the nerve to say that Lady Catherine was bonkers. 'She's always looking for an excuse to punish patients.' Who were these people? I couldn't imagine Mum and Dad inviting them to stay.

I lay back on the pillows and studied the ceiling. It breathed slowly, evenly. Calmly. It made me feel quiet, following its lead. Marjorie was talking but I closed my eyes and ignored her. Someone was moaning. A trolley squeaked. The door banged.

'Grace, here's your visitor. I'll just pull the curtains round to give you some privacy.'

Mum at last. I smiled and opened my eyes as the sludge-green curtains billowed around us like parachute silk. A man stood there, with dark sideburns. He wasn't smiling. 'Grace?' he said, his voice threaded with worry. The ceiling breathed faster and faster.

Blood started spurting out of his shirt, drenching it. It ran over his chest, down his trousers. He put his hands on it and rubbed it across his face and head. Someone was screaming. I put my hands over my ears. 'No, no,' I said. 'Stop. Blood.' But he still stood there. His blood was pooling on the floor. I started to clamber off the bed towards Marjorie. It would reach me soon. Too much blood.

The man backed away through the curtains, which billowed around him like a bedsheet on a washing line. The screaming wrenched through the air. The man tripped on something and fell into the blood, half under the curtain. Then the curtains flew up and the rude woman was back, but with other women this time. Something was strapped over me. 'I warned you, Grace, I warned you.' It was that woman again. Harsh voice.

They dragged me over the man where he was scrabbling in his own blood. Why weren't they tending to him? That poor man. My feet couldn't touch the ground – it was like being on the big wheel, swinging my legs into the abyss as they took me along. I kicked my legs and laughed.

'Give her the full dose this time,' Harsh Voice said. There was the prick in my leg. As the door of the spare room swung to, I could see Mum in the corridor, shaking her head. She was disappointed in me, I knew, for showing her up in front of the guests. I'd have to apologise later.

Chapter 18

Joanne

October 2021

Joanne was standing at the door of the train as it pulled into Berwick station, tightly gripping the handrail. She looked up and down the platform as she got off, but there was no sign of Alex. She hadn't told him what train she was on, but still . . .

She followed the steps down from the platform and walked along the river. It glided silently next to her in the evening darkness. The hot summer was just a faint memory now. The cold nipped her face as she walked, working its way through her layers. The buttons of her coat could only just about do up. She'd have to get something bigger to get her through the next few cold months. She could feel the weight of Grace's secret.

She glanced down her own street as she passed it, just about making out the shape of their house. Alex would probably be at the hospital starting his night shift by now, the house waiting for him to creep in just after dawn. Three streets on, she walked away from the river, slower now, to her dad's front door. Light crept around the curtains in the front room. Joanne glanced at her watch. They'd be watching TV now, sitting in their separate armchairs, mugs of tea on the table, her dad owning the remote.

She hesitated outside. Given everything that had happened, everything that she'd said – Joanne winced at the memory of her dad's face – could she just walk straight in? That was if the door was even unlocked again. Next door's net curtain twitched and Joanne imagined Mrs Stewart standing behind it in the darkness, waiting for something to talk about in town tomorrow. She quickly pushed the door and felt her shoulders drop as it yielded. The mix of old dinner – fish? – and woodsmoke – they must have lit the fire already – drew her in.

She closed the door quietly behind her and stood in the hall. A game-show jingle blasted through the open door to the front room. There was a scraping, the sound of her father putting the poker back on to the rack. Joanne waited for the springs in the armchair to go as he sat back down. He'd been promising to sort out the creak since she left home twenty years ago.

In the hall mirror, she saw some of her curls had come loose from the hair grips. She tucked them back in, watching her reflection. Her cheeks were pink, her eyes wide. She crept quietly down the hall. Patrick's and her own school portraits charted a journey from sweet four-year-olds, grinning with excitement at the school photographer, to camera-shy teens. In the final one, just before the door to the front room, Patrick stared out through his acne while she was trying to hide behind her hair. Joanne touched her fingertips against the glass of her sixteen-year-old face. She'd thought life was hard then. Struggling with GCSEs, hating her body, constant friendship shifts, wanting to move to the city. But it felt nothing as seismic as now. Her own mother had literally gone mad having her. And to think Joanne had once thought her dad had killed her. That was what she'd felt but had been too afraid to name. She shook her head as if to cast the thought away.

The game show blared louder as she pushed open the door to the front room. Two faces swivelled towards her.

'Joanne, love.' Lou was immediately on her feet, her smile not quite meeting her eyes, a quick raised eyebrow at her dad.

He stood up behind her, rubbing his hand over his jaw. 'You OK, love?'

'Alex not with you?' said Lou.

'He's working,' said Joanne.

'Cuppa?' Lou was already bustling out of the room, not waiting for a response. There was no occasion in her world that didn't require a cup of tea.

Joanne hugged her dad hard, her bump squeezed between them. 'You OK, love?' he said again, his eyebrows weaved together.

She sat down on the sofa and he clicked on the remote control, silencing the game-show host. Joanne cleared her throat. 'I went down to Brighton again. To look at the records,' she said.

Mike was looking at his hands. He nodded. 'Alex said you'd gone.'

The kettle's whistle filtered through from the kitchen and quickly died.

'We were worried about you, I—'

Joanne got up and stood next to Mike. 'I'm so sorry, Dad, that I said those things. I know what happened. I know it wasn't your fault. I can't believe I ever thought it was.'

'Oh, Joanne.' Mike stroked her cheek, just as he had when she was a little girl. They remained standing there for a minute, the house silent.

Eventually, Joanne looked up. 'I went to the records office. They wouldn't let me see the records, said it had to be official, through my doctor. But then Susie and John took me to the hospital where Grace was. It was all there. All the records were there. I know what happened.'

A flush began to spread up Mike's neck. 'You know what happened?' He ran his hand across his face. 'What did it say?' There was a slight tremor in his voice.

Joanne sat back on the sofa. 'It's all in Grace's record. Some of it's all mouldy and difficult to read, but I got the gist. Having me made her go crazy, didn't it?' Her voice faltered just saying the words.

'I don't think we'll ever know what really happened, love. Or why it happened. What else did the records say?' Mike shifted in his chair.

'She had postpartum psychosis. It wasn't anyone's fault. It just happens sometimes.' Joanne's shoulders sagged.

Lou came in with a tray of tea and biscuits. 'I'll just leave these here with you. I'll be in the kitchen—'

Joanne got up again. 'Don't be silly, Mam. This is as much about you as it is me and Dad. Stay.'

'Oh, Joanne love. I've been so worried about you.' Lou and Joanne hugged, Lou stroking the back of Joanne's hair.

Joanne's voice was muffled against her mam's shoulder. 'I'm sorry I've been such a cow. I know you were just protecting Dad.'

'Don't be silly, chick.'

They sat down together on the sofa. 'I was just telling Dad. We found the records in the hospital where Grace was. Such a fluke.'

Lou turned slightly to glance at Mike. 'What did they say?'

'That she had psychosis, brought on as a result of having me. It's really old and difficult to read in places but there's enough there that I understood.' Joanne reached inside her bag and took out the folder. She handed it to Mike. 'Here, Dad. You should read it. It's your history as much as it's mine.'

Mike's eyes darted towards Lou and then the folder. Eventually, he took it from her and picked up his glasses.

Lou swallowed and started pouring the tea, her hands shaking. She gave Joanne a cup. 'You've grown so much over the past few weeks.'

Joanne laughed. 'I won't be able to fit through the door soon.'

'And everything's OK with the baby?'

Joanne sighed. 'I've had more cramps and a little bit more bleeding, but nothing as dramatic as before.'

Lou gasped. 'What did the doctor say about that? Surely cramps and bleeding isn't normal?'

Joanne looked down at her hands. 'I didn't want to worry anyone. It's only a little bit of blood each time. And the cramps aren't that painful. Not like before.'

Lou shook her head. 'Jo, love, you should tell the doctor.' She took hold of Joanne's hands. 'You know you should. You've come so far. What does Alex say?'

'It's fine, Mam. I'm fine. Now I know the truth about all of this' – she waved her hand around the room – 'I'll be fine. I'll relax, I promise.'

'I was so worried that all of this anxiety would—' She glanced down at Joanne's bump.

Joanne pressed her lips together. 'I know. But it's OK. I can focus on the baby now.'

Mike put the folder down on the table and sighed.

'Dad?'

His eyes were soft, sad. But there was relief in his voice. 'It's strange, seeing it all written down after all this time,' he said. 'I didn't ask many questions then. It was a terrible place, that hospital.'

Joanne watched his face twist. 'I'm sorry, I didn't mean to—'

'No, you have a right to know. I just didn't want—' He gestured down at her belly. 'Not while—'

Joanne bit her lip. Lou slid her arm around Joanne.

'I wanted to get her out, but once you're in a place like that, they won't let you. And they told me that she'd never recover. That I was better off leaving her there and getting on with my life, looking after you.' He gulped. Joanne felt Lou shudder next to her.

'They said there was no cure for her,' he said again. 'That she would need sedation for the rest of her life. They told me I should leave.' He looked down at his hands. 'I visited for a long time, but they said it just upset her. I took you with me once but—' He glanced up and looked at Lou. 'I didn't take you again. It just upset Grace too much.'

'But why did you leave Brighton, Dad?' Joanne asked. 'You knew people there, we had family. People who loved you and me.'

Mike smoothed his hand over his face. 'Everyone knew us. Everyone talked. They'd seen what happened – it was all very public. I went to work and they were talking about it. How Mike's wife had gone mad. How—'

Lou coughed. Mike glanced at her and looked away.

He looked at Joanne and grimaced. 'I didn't want that for you. I didn't want you to be known as the daughter of the woman in the . . . the asylum.' He took a shuddering breath.

Joanne reached across and took his hand.

'Grace's family all rallied around to look after you.'

Joanne nodded, thinking of Gerry, Emily and Susie. And the grandmother that she'd never known. 'One day, I just couldn't take it no more. I don't think I knew what I was doing, really. I just packed a bag for you and me and nicked a van from work.' He looked up at Lou. 'That van was stolen, the one I brought here. I don't think I ever told you that. I'm sorry.'

'It doesn't matter, love, you had good reason,' Lou said, her voice quiet.

'I started driving north, away from the coast, from Brighton, from everyone we knew, from the memories. I drove and drove, all day. Only stopping to feed and change you – Kathleen had shown me how. I was quite good at it by then. I don't remember the journey, really. I remember driving past the sign that said "Welcome to Berwick-upon-Tweed, the northernmost town in England".

Perhaps I knew then that I couldn't go any further. That I was as far away from Brighton as it was possible to be. Maybe fate thought so too, because the van broke down on Castlegate. There was a problem with the chassis. Fortunately enough, there was a mechanics' just along the road. I went there and—' He looked up at Lou, who smiled sadly.

'I remember you coming in that day,' said Lou. 'I was doing my homework in the office. Dad said a wild chap had asked to use the lift. The lads were all talking about it. I walked out and there you were, with a screaming baby in your arms. The lads all rallied around the van and suddenly I was holding the baby.' Lou swivelled to face Joanne. 'You. I don't know how it happened. We didn't have anything for you there, so I walked round to Christine Weaver, who had a young baby, and she changed you and I fed you a bottle. Then we came back.'

'I'd fixed the van by then and thought I might stop for the night. One of the lads offered me a sofa.'

Lou nodded. 'Jimmy, that was. And my sister looked after you that night.'

Mike grinned. 'One night turned into a few nights on that sofa. Then I got a room in a boarding house. Mrs Redman on Palace Street. And then I was offered work at the mechanics'. And so we stayed.'

He looked around the room, his eyes stopping at Joanne. 'I kept in touch with the hospital. I don't like to call it an asylum. I went down to visit Grace regularly. The hospital was trying some new treatment.' He shuddered slightly. 'I thought perhaps that if it worked and Grace got well, we could settle up here where no one knew us. But she—' He shook his head.

'And then one day they wrote to me and said she'd died. I've still got the letter.' He glanced at the ceiling. 'So matter-of-fact. And that was the end.'

'It said on the death certificate and in these notes that she died of a head injury,' said Joanne. 'Did you ever find out more about how?'

Mike closed his eyes. 'No,' he said eventually. 'No, I didn't want to know. I didn't like that place. That hospital. She didn't belong there.' He looked at Joanne. 'She really died, the person I knew, your mum, when you were born. I thought it was easier to tell you that as you grew. I didn't want you knowing all—' He waved his hand at the report on the table. 'I met your mam' – he looked at Lou – 'but nothing happened between us, not till Grace had died. I couldn't do that to her. Even though—' He shrugged, then reached forward and gripped Joanne's hand. 'I knew we could have a good life up here. That Lou would be a good mum to you. Not to replace Grace. No one could ever replace Grace, but that she'd bring you up as her own.'

Lou nodded. 'I never saw any difference between you and Patrick, love, I hope you know that.'

Joanne smiled. 'Of course, Mam, I know that. So Grace is buried down in Brighton, like you always said?'

'Yes,' said Mike. 'The hospital arranged it when she died. There's a little cemetery attached to the hospital. We buried her there.' Joanne tried to picture a cemetery next to the Egremont, but it was so overgrown it had been hard to see anything.

'We?' Joanne questioned.

'Me and the hospital matron,' Mike said, knotting and unknotting his hands. 'She was a bully of a woman.'

'You didn't think to get in touch with Grace's family – her sisters, her parents?'

Mike sighed and ran his hands across his head. 'I should have done, I know. But by then I hadn't seen them for two years. I didn't know how to tell them. The hospital never asked, because I was her next of kin. Nobody else had visited while she was there—'

'Nobody knew she was there, Dad,' Joanne said, louder than she intended. Lou put her hand on her arm.

'I know. Kathleen was the only one who knew. She didn't want people to talk, to know that her daughter was in an asylum. It would have broken her.'

'So you said nothing.' Lou squeezed Joanne's arm.

Mike nodded, but didn't look at her. 'I went to visit her grave every year. I still do. To remember her.'

'He does, love,' said Lou. 'He always takes himself away at the end of June. I never asked why, but now I know.'

Joanne blinked back her tears. 'Next year, can I come with you?'

'Of course you can, love. We don't have to wait until her anniversary. We can go whenever you like.'

She looked between her parents. 'I know this has been difficult, me discovering all of this. But I'm glad I know everything now. That it's all out in the open.'

'Yes,' said Lou, glancing at Mike and then looking away. 'I'm glad too.'

'There are some things you should have, now that you know,' said Mike.

Joanne stared at her dad, her eyes wide. He got up from the sofa, walked over to the bookcase and took out a book. He stared at it for a long time before handing it to Joanne.

'After Grace died, the hospital sent me this,' he said, twisting his hands into a knot. 'It was the book she was reading when she had you.' He rubbed the back of his neck. 'That she got confused about.' He sighed. 'She never finished it. I thought she might in the hospital. When she got well, but—'

On the cover, a woman swooned into a man's arms. 'An Adventure in Irasa,' Joanne read out.

'Irasa.' Irasa. Irasa. She'd read that name before. Then it came to her. On one of the Polaroids – the rushed handwriting at the end, that was Grace's. She'd written about this book.

Joanne starting flicking through the pages. 'Susie told me about this. Grace got confused and thought she was a character in the book?' The first few chapters were untouched but, from the middle onwards, there were scribbles in Grace's blue fountain pen. It started with some paragraphs being underlined, or notes at the side. Yes! He stole her. Towards the end, the writing became like hieroglyphics and then just more and more pages entirely covered in with blue ink. She closed the book and looked at the cover again. 'You know, I've seen this before. Years ago. I was going through the shelf for something to read and pulled it out.' She glanced at Lou. 'I thought it was yours. I can't believe it's been here all this time.'

'It's a library book, but we had it for years. A reminder letter came a couple of weeks after you were born. I meant to go in and explain but then we were up here and it didn't seem to matter any more.'

'I don't suppose they want books like this now anyway. Tastes change,' said Joanne.

She stood up and went to the window still holding the book. Opposite, Mr Dixon was on his doorstep, the door pulled to behind him, surveying the street. He brushed a piece of dirt off the step with his shoe. Her birth mam's book. She finally had something belonging to her birth mam. Upstairs, the baby's chest of drawers was full of the jumpers and cardigans Grace had made for Joanne when she was a baby, together with the new ones Lou had made recently. All ready for Joanne's own baby. Now she had something that had actually belonged to her birth mam, or at least something she'd borrowed. A proper connection to her that she could touch, feel, smell. Read. *Oh, this? It was Grace's, my birth mam's*, she imagined saying.

The chair springs squeaked as Lou shifted. Joanne could feel Lou staring at her, that concerned look on her face. Waiting for the opportunity to say something comforting, something calming. She'd be entwining her fingers, the way she did. The spring creaked again. But out of the corner of her eye, standing at the mantelpiece with her back to the fire, was another figure. Smaller, with long, dark, curly hair that matched Joanne's own. Dark eyes watching her. Grace.

Joanne was rigid, taking tiny breaths into her lungs, not wanting to do anything to disturb Grace. She'd hoped to see Grace at the Egremont Hospital, but she had been strangely absent and hadn't even come to her in last night's dreams. Instead, those dreams had been of her back in the hospital, walking along the deserted corridors searching for the baby she thought she'd lost.

Lou was talking, but Joanne focused on the minutiae of Grace's face, the way the top of her lip changed from dark to pale pink to the white of the start of her upturned nose. The dark brown eyes smiled at her. Her hand rested on the mantelpiece, the standard lamp shining off the gold band on her ring finger. She was looking at Joanne's belly and seemed about to say something.

'There's something else, love.' Joanne's head swivelled to Mike as he stood up again from the sofa.

Joanne turned back to the mantelpiece, but Grace had gone. She searched the space where she'd been, walking over to place her hand on the mantelpiece exactly where Grace had rested hers. She was sure it felt slightly warm.

Mike took an envelope out of the sideboard, handing it to Joanne. He and Lou were watching her. She sat back down on the sofa, half an eye on the mantelpiece, waiting for Grace to reappear. 'Are you going to open it, love?' said Mike.

Joanne nodded. Inside the envelope was a cross-stitched bookmark, the sort she'd made with a kit with Lou when she was a child.

It was tucked inside a card – an outline of a Christmas bell which had been carefully coloured in.

Which child had drawn this card? She didn't remember doing it, and Patrick certainly hadn't, she'd have remembered. Joanne opened it. 'Wishing you a merry Christmas and a happy 1977. Love, Grace.' Grace. But Grace would have been an adult, a mother, in 1977. The handwriting, in pencil, was completely different from what she'd seen on the Polaroids. A child's simple handwriting, not even joined up.

The baby was very still inside her, her stomach felt hard. It hadn't been a happy 1977 for Grace.

'This is from Grace, to you?' she said to Mike.

He smoothed his hand over his head as he nodded. 'Yes, they sent them just before Christmas, the second year she was there.' He paused and looked at his hands. 'I thought that because she was able to write, and had got back to her beloved sewing, she was getting better. That she'd come home.'

'Oh Dad, oh God. I'm sorry.' She put her hand on his and squeezed it. She looked back to the bookmark. What a precious thing to have. 'There's just one more thing I'm curious about.'

Mike and Lou jerked their heads towards her. 'Yes, love,' her dad said, his voice not quite steady.

'Susie mentioned that you and Grace had written a baby record book, like the one that Alex and I are putting together for this baby.' She stroked her bump. 'I wondered if you still had it. Susie didn't know what had happened to it.'

Mike sighed. 'That's gone now,' he said, shaking his head. 'Kathleen, that's Grace's mum, threw it out after Grace went into that hospital. She'd scribbled all over it, and torn out most of the pages. It was a mess. She took out the photos Grace had stuck in. And somehow they got into that box of baby clothes we gave you.'

He smoothed his hand over his head and stood up. 'Scuse me a minute.' He disappeared out of the door.

Lou's eyes followed him and then turned back to Joanne. 'It's a lot for him all this, talking about it'

Joanne nodded. 'And you, Mam. All of us.'

She looked back to the book, slipped the card and bookmark inside and put it with the hospital records back in her handbag. 'I'll take this home,' she said. 'Have a look through later.'

Lou put her hands on Joanne's shoulders. 'I'm glad you know,' she said. 'To put your mind at rest.'

'I'm going to take those hospital records to my doctor and see what he thinks. Whether postpartum psychosis is hereditary. Whether there's a chance that I could—'

'Oh love, I'm sure you'll be fine,' said Lou, squeezing Joanne's shoulders again. 'Grace's was an extreme reaction and she had always had bad PMT, whereas you don't. And even if you did, treatment is so different these days. But do talk to the doctor, just to be on the safe side.' She drew Joanne in for a hug. 'And talk to Alex too. I know things are a bit strained between you two. This could give you both an excuse to clear the air.'

GRACE

NOVEMBER 1975

We sat slumped on Mum and Dad's three-piece suite, waiting for them to come in and switch on the telly. The ones who were a bit slower had to sit on the hard upright dining chairs they'd brought in, but Marjorie and I had got lucky today and had prime position in front of the telly. Lady Catherine was sitting bolt upright on the other end of the settee, avoiding eye contact with everyone. She was getting snootier and snootier by the day.

Mum came in and smiled at everyone. 'You all ready?' She opened the telly doors and switched it on. It was the end of the news, which Lady Catherine adored but no one else liked much. 'Just wait till the end and then it will be *Porridge*. Hold on and I'll bring the sweets.'

She disappeared out and I could hear her in the kitchen, rummaging through the cupboards and talking to Dad. He never joined us, I hardly saw him at all any more, he was so busy at work. The door opened again and she appeared with a basket of small white paper bags, twisted at the top. She moved around, handing one each to everyone – Lady Catherine, Marjorie, Miss Randall, Penny, Betty, Margaret, Mrs K. The bag felt heavy in my hand. I peered through the folds of paper and saw a quarter of sherbet lemons. My favourite. Mum always made sure I got my favourite. Harsh Voice gave us liquorice sometimes, which was disgusting.

The newsreader was reading the closing headlines. A cod war between Iceland and the UK. The Group of Six were meeting somewhere in France. A lunar eclipse was expected. The prime minister was talking about a Buy British code. Lady Catherine started grumbling as she always did when the news ended. Mum closed the curtains and turned off the light. I liked it in the dark. It was the only time that I felt Mum or Harsh Voice weren't watching me. You could be anonymous in the dark. Have your own thoughts that no one else could guess at. You could pick your nose. Bite your nails. Roll your eyes. No one could see. But when the screen went dark, you had to eat the sweets by feel alone.

The doors of HMP Slade filled the screen and everyone was silent apart from the crunching of sherbet lemons.

'Suck, don't chew,' someone said. Maybe Betty.

'Shhhhh,' said everyone else.

Norman Fletcher came on the screen and started his familiar walk through locked doors and dim corridors.

Betty read out the title. '"The Harder They Fall."'

'Shhhh,' said everyone else.

Lennie Godber appeared in a red tracksuit. My heartbeat started to race.

'Oooooh,' said Marjorie.

Everyone giggled.

There was something about Lennie that I didn't quite like. All the other girls loved him. Marjorie would have a poster up of him if Mum'd let her. It was the dark sideburns, maybe. He made me shiver. I couldn't quite look at him square in the face. I just looked at his tracksuit and waited until Fletcher came on the screen, packing up his drafts pieces.

We watched in silence as Lennie and Fletcher talked about a boxing match. Lennie bounced around on his toes. I closed my eyes. Mr Mackay's Scots brogue filled the room and I opened them again. Lennie had gone. I breathed out slowly and popped in another sherbet lemon.

Fletcher was summoned to see Harry Grout, whose cell looked more luxurious than Mum's sitting room. He was trying to rig the boxing match. Dad liked boxing sometimes, but Mum hated it. I hoped she didn't come back in the room and turn it off, once she realised what this episode was about. She was funny like that. Always changing her mind about things. Especially now it was just me at home, and Gerry and Emily had left. I got the brunt of her temper.

The door opened and I stiffened, waiting for Mum to change the channel. But it was just her friend Lucy. Who Marjorie called mad as a box of frogs. She was a bit odd. She never really mixed with the other guests, so I didn't feel I needed to make an effort. She marched to the telly and switched it off, closing the doors with a flourish.

'What are you doing?' bellowed Lady Catherine. 'How very dare you switch off the television.'

'We're watching that,' said Penny, standing up. 'Put it back on.'

Lucy stood with her back to the telly, her hands on her hips, and looked at us all in turn. 'Would you please leave my office. I have a very important meeting in five minutes.'

'For God's sake,' muttered Marjorie. 'Not again.'

My mouth filled with the zing of the sherbet and I coughed.

Lady Catherine was squaring up to Lucy. 'Turn it back on *now*. We're going to miss the boxing match.' Betty was trying to get past her to open the doors.

'This is my office,' screamed Lucy. 'Get out. All of you. Just fucking get out.' The shouting reverberated off the walls. I put my hands over my ears.

'I'll go and get Mum,' I whispered to Marjorie and ran out of the room.

Chapter 19

JOANNE

OCTOBER 2021

Joanne sat on the sofa reading *An Adventure in Irasa*. She'd got halfway through last night, before sleep washed over her. It reminded her of the romance novels she'd read as a teenager, when all she'd wanted was a man to whisk her away to something more exciting. Scottish castles, aristocrats and balls. But there was nothing special or out of the ordinary about it. Why had Grace become so obsessed with this particular story? Or was that part of the psychosis? The scribbles in the margins, the text underlined so emphatically the pen had gone through into the following page, made her heart ache. The hieroglyphics seemed such a visible manifestation of Grace's mind unravelling that it hurt Joanne to see them.

She flicked through the pages, determined to finish it before the doctor's appointment.

Alex's key rattled in the lock and she slipped the bookmark into the page and laid the book on the table. Her heart raced at the thought of seeing him, in a way that it hadn't for a long time.

'Hi,' she said, standing in the doorway of the front room.

He stopped in the hallway. 'Hi,' he said, looking at her with his head on one side. He took his jacket off and hung it on the hook, throwing his gloves and hat on the shelf.

'I'm back,' she said.

He nodded and walked towards her. 'How was it?' He didn't reach out to hug her, like he normally would. 'You didn't respond to any of my messages.'

'It was hard, but I'm glad I went.' The silence was loud between them. 'Do you want a cup of tea?'

'No, thanks,' Alex said. 'I better get to bed.' He went to walk up the stairs.

'I've got a doctor's appointment in an hour,' she said. 'Nothing bad,' she added, as his head swivelled round. 'I thought you could come with me.'

'OK,' he said. 'I'll get changed then. And I'll have that tea.' He disappeared upstairs.

◆ ◆ ◆

By the time she'd made the tea, he was in the front room looking through the book. 'What's all this?' he asked, pointing at the scribbles, as she came in with the mugs. Joanne explained and then went on to talk about what she'd found out in Brighton.

'Oh, Jo,' Alex said, touching her shoulder. 'That must have been awful.' He moved across the sofa and drew her into his arms. 'I should have been there with you.'

His scent was usually so familiar to her that she couldn't smell it any more. But now, she remembered what it was like to be hugged by him for the first time. To smell him for the first time – the muskiness mixed with a faint hospital smell that he could never seem to scrub off, but was so part of him. She clung to his arms and rested her head on his chest.

'I'm sorry we had that row before you left,' he said, over the top of her head. She smiled, her eyes closed. It felt good to hear those words.

'I'm sorry I accused you of that,' she murmured against his chest. 'Let's forget about it and just focus on the next few months.'

Alex drew back. 'No, Jo,' he said, holding her away from him so he could see into her eyes. His gaze was intense. 'We need to talk about this.' He looked around the room. 'About all of this.'

A thudding started in Joanne's belly, which she knew was nothing to do with the baby. What was he going to say? She shook her head. 'Whatever it is, it doesn't matter. Let's just move on.'

He was looking at her intently. 'No, I can't move on. We've never really talked about it all. Everything we've been through over the past ten years. We've always just moved on' – he made inverted commas in the air with his fingers – 'and brushed it under the carpet.' He looked away from her. 'I'm always talking to patients about therapy – after they've been diagnosed, during chemo, when they get a terminal diagnosis – but we never had therapy, even though what we were facing was huge.'

Joanne turned her mind back. 'We were offered it,' she said. 'After we lost the baby late on. And then the second time, and when we first did IVF.'

'We should have taken them up on that,' said Alex, scratching his beard. 'Things between us would have been different.'

'It felt like admitting defeat to go to infertility counselling. I just always hoped we'd have a baby in the end. I couldn't talk about the idea that we might not.'

Alex took hold of Joanne's hands. 'Somewhere along the way, we've become too obsessed with the idea of being parents,' he said quietly.

Joanne snatched her hands away from his and folded them in front of her. 'What do you mean?'

'It's taken over our lives, over us.' He paused, looking around the room. 'When we met and then married, we had lives and dreams. And having a child was part of that, but it wasn't the whole thing. I wanted to become a nurse consultant and I'm on my way to that, but I could have done more if I hadn't been so obsessed with the baby idea. I wanted to do that triathlon, remember, with the idea I might train for an Ironman, but we were worried it would mean I'd be away when you were ovulating, or needed me for the IVF, so I never went for it.'

He was right, Joanne realised suddenly. Their lives had been on hold for years. She took his hands. 'When we met, I wanted to have my own jewellery shop.'

Alex nodded. 'You were already making loads of jewellery for craft fairs and stuff, and selling online.'

'I just wanted to stay working in Mandy's shop because I thought it was easier until after I'd had the baby. That was ten years ago and here I still am.' She looked at the small piles of jewellery boxes stacked in the corner. 'Still doing small numbers of online orders, and still working at Mandy's and no further on.'

Alex took a gulp of his tea. 'And it's not just that. It's about us as a couple.'

Joanne felt her heart slow. An image of the postcard flitted into her mind. 'We don't need to talk about that.'

'We do, Jo.' He looked straight at her. 'We stopped talking about anything else that wasn't having a baby. We used to do stuff together, and somehow it just stopped.' He leaned forward and stroked her cheek. 'I never thought about leaving you because we struggled to have children. Please don't think that.'

She looked down at her hands, curled in her lap.

'I was worried that if we didn't have children, we'd end up resenting one another and be unhappy. But I never thought about leaving.'

There was silence in the room and she stayed still, looking at the flaking red nail polish on her thumb.

'That postcard you found in the book. The Cézanne painting.'

She scraped a bit more of the nail polish away.

'It was from a patient—'

'You said.'

'An elderly patient. It was her and her husband's favourite painting. They saw it in London and it sent them on a trip across Europe to search for Cézanne's other paintings. She gave me the postcard before she died.' He paused. 'To me, it just showed that it was possible to have children – they had three children and loads of grandchildren – and still have interests other than family. I spoke to her about us' – Joanne looked up at him – 'and she said how important it was to have stuff other than children to focus on. I think we lost that along the way.'

Joanne took a deep breath. 'I think we have,' she said. 'But you've been just as obsessed about having a baby as me. More so in the last few weeks.'

Alex looked down. 'I know. I know I wasn't there when you needed me for this stuff about Grace. My mam told me off for letting you go to Brighton—'

It was unlike his mother to be on her side, Joanne thought. She usually couldn't wait to criticise her for something.

'I ignored this big thing that was happening to you, because I was just so worried that having come this far, we'd risk losing it all again. And when you had that bleed in Brighton—' Alex covered his face with his hands.

'I know.' Joanne sighed and reached forward to hold his hands. 'I have been obsessed. First with having a baby for the past ten years, and now with this whole thing about Grace. You're right, that we need to spend time not thinking about the baby and just doing something for us. Getting back to who we were.' She looked back at the little cardboard boxes. 'And once the baby is a few months old, I'll look at properly doing something with the jewellery and get my own shop.'

Alex took her face between his hands and kissed her. His beard brushed against the side of her cheek, and she was reminded again how rarely he'd kissed her on the lips recently. 'I thought we could go out for dinner at the weekend, when I'm off nights.'

'I love you,' she said, kissing him again.

'And I love you.'

◆ ◆ ◆

Joanne and Alex had spent hours in doctors' waiting rooms over the past few years. Always waiting for news. So often bad news that when the good news had finally come, on the last round of IVF, it took them a long time to take in what the doctor was saying. Although most of the IVF appointments had been in the hospital, the staff at the GP surgery knew them well.

'Morning, Mrs Shaw, Mr Shaw,' said Mrs Waters, her jade beads swinging against her lime-green scarf as she stood importantly behind the reception desk. Behind her, a wall of manila folders held the town's medical history.

'Not long to go now,' she added, nodding at Joanne's protruding belly.

Joanne smiled at her and took a seat. Alex gripped her hand. Even though patient records were supposed to be confidential, Joanne wondered if Mrs Waters could not resist a quick rummage now and again. Just to confirm suspicions she already had, of course. She imagined her holding court at the WI, regaling the others with stories of the surgery's patients' various interesting medical complaints, her bosom trembling as her stage whisper carried well beyond her open-mouthed audience. Or maybe Joanne was being unfair. Joanne had gone to school with Sophie, Mrs Waters' daughter. And she'd always been very kind to her. There'd been that time on the trip to Lindisfarne, where Toby Morris had managed to stab her in the arm with his home-made Viking spear. Mrs Waters has been the one to take her to hospital and wait until Mam had come.

'You OK?' Alex murmured.

She dipped her head and then rested it on his shoulder. She was glad they'd talked. And she knew they would again. She needed to tell him how alone she'd felt when she was doing the IVF. And how that joke he'd once made about injecting her had really upset her, however much she'd laughed it off at the time. But all marriages went through ups and downs, Mam had said. It had been a test and they'd passed. Maybe not with flying colours, but they'd got through it. And perhaps they were stronger now and they'd get through whatever life had in store for them further down the road.

'Joanne Shaw.' Dr Petzold was a neat little man who still wore a three-piece suit to work even though all the other doctors had become more casual over the years. He stood smiling at the end of the room, waiting for her to collect her bag and, with Alex's help, lever herself up. Dr Petzold had been the first person they'd approached about her failure to become pregnant. She remembered sobbing in his surgery when she'd gone to see him after the third miscarriage. Even Alex had cried then. He'd seemed as delighted as they were when Joanne had finally passed the five-month point this time round.

Alex followed her into the windowless consulting room.

'How are you feeling?' Dr Petzold asked as he shut his door behind her.

'Oh, really well, thank you, Doctor,' she said, as she dropped into a chair. There was no need to mention the pain.

'You look well,' he said, nodding, his eyes smiling. 'You have, what, eight weeks to go?'

'That's right,' said Joanne. 'It's flying by now.'

'And you're all sorted at the hospital. You've done the tour?'

Alex nodded. 'Yes, we're all set. We've chosen the infirmary. It just felt the safest option.'

'Whatever works best for you both. The team there are hugely experienced, and they know your history, of course.' He blinked rapidly. 'So how can I help you today?'

Joanne swallowed. 'I've recently found out that my birth mother – I think you know that my mam isn't my real' – she shook her head – 'biological,' she corrected herself, 'mam,' she said, looking up at him.

Dr Petzold nodded.

'Well, I've recently found out that my mother suffered from postpartum psychosis after I was born.' Joanne took a deep breath. 'I want to know what the chances are of me having it too.'

Dr Petzold frowned. 'Are you sure it was postpartum psychosis and not depression?' he asked.

Joanne nodded and reached into her bag. She handed him Grace's medical record. 'These are her medical records. It's quite clearly some form of psychosis and from what Dad described, it was definitely that.'

He took the report, placed it on his desk and reached for his glasses. Then he silently read through the documents, turning over the pages slowly. His frown deepened, until two lines were firmly etched between his eyebrows. Joanne caught Alex's eye and looked away. Eventually, he took off his glasses and looked at Joanne. 'Where did you get this report?' he said. 'It hasn't been well looked after.'

Joanne briefly explained about discovering the photos, the visits to Brighton, meeting Grace's family and the recent trip to the records office and then the asylum.

'It sounds like you've had a difficult few weeks,' he said. 'I hope you haven't been overdoing it? You know how important it is to rest.' Dr Petzold glanced at the report and looked away, staring at something behind Joanne. 'Much of this record is so water damaged, it's impossible to read,' he said. 'Did they say in the records office that there was a copy there?'

Joanne nodded. 'I think so. They said it would need to be requested formally by my doctor and that that could take weeks.'

'Your birth mother was clearly very seriously mentally ill,' he said. 'But postpartum psychosis is rare. It affects one in one thousand new mothers—'

There are about twelve thousand people living in Berwick, thought Joanne. *Say half are women. And another half of them are childbearing age. That's three thousand women, so three women in this town alone have had postpartum psychosis in their lives. In Newcastle, that would be nearly a hundred women.* That didn't feel that rare. Joanne held her belly.

'We don't know what causes it, but we do know that it's more common in women who have a diagnosis of bipolar disorder or schizophrenia.' Dr Petzold looked down at the records and ran his fingers across a long, mouldy section. 'And of course, fortunately that's not something you need to be concerned about.'

'Yes,' said Joanne, glancing at the clock. There couldn't be long left in the appointment.

'But is it hereditary? Because Joanne's birth mother suffered, is there more of a chance that she could?' Alex asked.

Dr Petzold leaned back in his chair and cleared his throat. 'It's not an area where I have an enormous amount of experience. As I said, cases are extremely rare—'

Alex leaned forward. 'And?'

He adjusted his waistcoat slightly. 'I believe that a family history of mental illness, particularly postpartum psychosis, is a risk factor,' he said, looking from Alex to Joanne. 'But a very small one. I doubt you'd even reach the threshold—'

Joanne's shoulders slumped. She'd known all along, in her heart.

'But as I said, it's incredibly rare. I really don't want you spending the last few weeks of your pregnancy worrying about this, after everything you've been through.' He undid the top button of his waistcoat, and then quickly did it up again. 'You said yourself that your maternal aunt had three children and didn't experience any problems, so it doesn't necessarily follow. I'm sure that you will be the same.'

Joanne nodded at him mechanically. It suddenly felt very hot in the room. She moved the hair off the nape of her neck. 'How will I know if I have it?'

'Well, you may not realise that you're ill. You may feel manic, or low, or restless or confused. But don't think about this. Focus on the next few weeks. Everything is going well, isn't it? I had a look at your record and you're sailing through. No more cramps or bleeding?'

Joanne shook her head and looked at the floor. Blood had polka-dotted across her knickers when she woke that morning. She'd bundled them up and put them in the kitchen bin so Alex didn't see them in the washing basket when he came in from his shift. That happened most mornings now. But not the major bleeding. And no cramps, just a little pain now and again. So that was OK, wasn't it?

'There's nothing to worry about then. Soon you will have a beautiful baby.'

The clock clicked on to the hour. How long had they been in here? Too long, probably.

'What I will do, Joanne, Alex, is to write to the maternal mental health team for advice and see if we can set up a meeting with the midwifery team and the obstetrician at the infirmary in the next couple of weeks. I will make sure that this is on your record, and we can put together a care plan with you. So if you do have any issues after the birth' – he shook his head – 'and I'm sure you won't, this is just a precaution, we'll be able to treat it straight away. It will also help your family' – he glanced at Alex – 'to look out for any signs so they can alert us. Don't forget, treatment is very different now to what it was in the seventies when your birth mother had you.'

'Yes,' said Joanne. 'They don't just lock you in asylums now. One final thing.'

The doctor looked up at her.

'Grace's cause of death was recorded on her death certificate – and on those hospital notes – as an extradural haematoma. But all the detail about her death is missing, attacked by the mildew.' Joanne nodded towards the report. 'What could have caused an extradural haematoma?'

Dr Petzold sighed. 'An extradural haematoma is a build-up of blood in the space between the skull and the outer membrane covering the brain. It's most commonly caused by a head injury of some kind. It'd be impossible to know without having the complete notes. You may never know.'

Joanne leaned on his desk and pushed herself up. 'Thank you, Dr Petzold, I appreciate you talking me through this.' Alex stood up beside her.

Dr Petzold's smile didn't quite reach his eyes as he also rose to stand next to her. 'Please don't worry, Joanne,' he said, gently touching her arm. 'I want you to enjoy this time. You deserve it after everything you've been through.' He picked up the record and went to hand it back to her, and then stopped. 'Do you mind if I get a copy of this? I'd be interested in seeing if I can get a full copy. To see if we can learn anything that may help you.'

'Of course,' said Joanne. 'The woman at the records office said that they'd be able to release the full record if they got an official request.'

They walked with him back into the reception area, where Mrs Waters was dealing with a growing queue of patients. Joanne sat down to wait for the doctor to finish the photocopying. Alex sat opposite her and took her hands. 'That was positive, wasn't it?' He said it as more of a question than a statement. Wanting her reassurance. She nodded and looked at her hands. Her fingers were swollen now. She couldn't take her wedding band off, even if she wanted to.

Dr Petzold brought back the records. Alex thanked him. *One in a thousand women*, Joanne thought. She stroked her bump and closed her eyes. A cramp started to build.

GRACE

MAY 1977

The tablets rubbed gently together in my hand, the off-white against the dirty brown. 'An extra one for you today, Grace.' Harsh Voice was smiling, a sliver of green wedged between her middle teeth. 'We have a treat for you later.'

I smiled back. 'I haven't forgotten it's the Eurovision Song Contest today, if that's what you mean,' I said. Marjorie and I had been making our outfits for weeks. We were determined to defend our title.

'An even bigger treat than that,' she said, watching as I swallowed the pills. I opened my mouth and lifted my tongue and she turned away, rattling the medicine trolley down the line of beds.

'Save your kisses for me,' sang Marjorie, twirling around in the purple outfit she'd made. Or rather I'd half made. Her stitching would have made Mrs Cornford livid.

'Stop singing that,' I said, laughing. 'I've written down the words for you.'

'I know, I know,' she said, picking up the exercise book.

'C'mon then, let's practise, so we're ready for tonight.' I sat on the side of her bed. 'Who d'you wanna be this time, Lynsey?'

'I'll be Lynsey,' she said, flicking her hair. 'You start.'

I cleared my throat and sang jauntily, just like we'd seen Mike Moran do on *A Song for Europe*.

'Rock Bottom,' crooned Marjorie. She had a surprisingly good voice.

Lady Catherine slow-clapped in the corner. But Mum smiled as she walked towards us. 'I can't wait to see you two in action this evening. You're both sounding very professional.' The blush moved from my chest up my neck to stain my cheeks. Mum hardly ever praised me in front of the guests any more.

'Now, Grace, we've got a very special visitor for you today. Mike, you remember Mike?' Her eyebrows held a question. I remembered her talking about Mike. Who was he? The caretaker, perhaps? No, that was Mr James. Was he the guest in the other half of the house, the new part? That I'd danced with the other week? She wouldn't be pleased that I couldn't remember, so I nodded brightly.

'Good, good. Now, Mike is bringing Joanne with him. Do you remember we talked about Joanne?'

Her eyes flitted over my face. It was a test. I'm sure she'd never mentioned anyone called Joanne.

Marjorie sang, and Mum held up her hand and glared at her. She giggled.

That extra tablet was making me feel light-headed. I closed my eyes. *Joanne. Joanne.* I reached out to touch the memory, but it slid away into the darkness. But I knew it was there, in the folds of my mind. *Joanne.*

I opened my eyes and nodded at Mum. 'I know a Joanne.'

She let out a long breath. She was pleased. 'Good. Now, let's see how today goes. It could be the beginning of your return to society.'

I stared at her. She made me sound like a debutante.

'Now, come with me. You can wait in the day room.'

I slid off the bed, humming. Marjorie and I would win again tonight, I was sure of it.

The day room smelled like wet dog. Mum slid open the window an inch and then walked out. I stood by the streaky pane, watching the birds flit between the silver birches. What were they? Swifts? Swallows? What did they say, *one swallow doesn't make a summer.* Well, there were plenty of them, so it must be summer. But the breeze was still cool on my face, like a freshly washed cotton sheet blowing against me as I hung it up on the line. I breathed in and out slowly, like they'd taught me to do. Big breaths. Big breaths.

The smell changed. A chemical tang. I turned and there was the man who looked like Lennie Godber, standing next to Mum. He was smiling in a mechanical sort of way, worry in his eyes. This was Mike, yes. Not Lennie. He was on the TV, Mike was a different person. 'Hello,' I said, coming towards him.

'Hi, Gracie,' he said, standing awkwardly in front of me. Then he suddenly put his arms around my shoulders. I stood there as he pressed himself up against me. Mum was nodding at me to do something. I put my arms on his back and squeezed and he seemed to gasp. 'Oh, Gracie,' he said, burying his head in my shoulder.

I patted his back and drew away. His eyes were full of tears. I'd said something wrong but Mum was smiling, her eyes soft. I breathed in and out slowly.

Mike took my hand and led me to the settee. How much longer was he going to hold my hand? His was clammy, like a damp tea towel. 'I have a surprise for you, Gracie.' He watched my face, waiting for a reaction. I lifted my lips into a smile and waited. 'I've brought Joanne with me to visit you.'

Someone started breathing heavily. *Joanne. Joanne.* I sorted through my memories but Joanne slid out of reach. She was always almost there, but then flitted away. I could almost see her. The door opened and Mum spoke to whoever was on the other side.

'Mike,' she said, nodding towards the corridor. He patted my hand and got up, disappearing out of the door. I sat listening to the heavy breathing. It was comforting, whoever it was.

The door opened wider and the man stood there again. Mike. This time, he had a little girl with him. She had a halo of curly brown hair, smoothed under two kirby grips but escaping at every curl. I touched my own hair.

'D'you remember me telling you about this special lady we were going to visit? Well, this is her. This is Mama.' He led the little girl to me. Her socks were wrinkled around her ankles but her red flowery dress was pretty, made by someone who knew what they were doing, though the hem was wonky. A broderie anglaise collar would have looked better than the plain white one.

The little girl stood in front of me and Mike lowered himself on to the sofa. 'This is Joanne, Gracie. She's a bit bigger than when you last saw her.'

Joanne. Joanne. The breathing was getting louder. I looked up, away from the girl, and realised it was the ceiling pulsating, breathing in and out with me. I hadn't heard it for a long, long time.

The girl looked at me. ''Lo,' she said.

'Hello,' I said automatically. 'How are you?' She looked at Mike and stuck her thumb in her mouth. He picked her up on to his lap, where she swung her feet against the settee.

'She's pretty,' I said. 'I like her hair.'

'She's got your hair.'

I touched my own hair. 'Yes.' Despite the clips, hers was covering part of her face. I reached over and tucked it behind her tiny ear so I could see her face better. Running up the side of her neck was an angry gash. The top had silvered but the rest looked like a badly sewn seam, bulging red and pink. The ceiling was panting.

'Gracie?' Mike's voice was higher now. 'Gracie?' Blood oozed out of his clothes and on to the girl, covering her hair and neck. It pooled down on to the floor. She started to scream. I scrambled back, knocking my foot against the table. I cried out. 'Help, blood. Help me. Stop. No. Help.' I ran for the door but it flew open. Mum stood there with Harsh Voice and two others.

'Give her an extra dose and put her in seclusion,' said Harsh Voice. They gripped my arms as I tried to point. 'Blood. Everywhere.' The blackness fell over me. I remembered Joanne now.

Chapter 20

JOANNE

NOVEMBER 2021

'They'll be here in a minute,' said Alex, walking into the bedroom. Joanne was sitting at her dressing table, dusting blusher on her cheeks.

'I won't be long,' Joanne said, picking up her mascara.

Alex stood behind her, resting his hands on her shoulders. 'You've never looked more beautiful than you do now, y'know. Pregnancy suits you.'

Joanne looked up at him. She knew he was making an effort, and she still appreciated it. He was making lots of small gestures. 'I do love being pregnant. It took us forever to get here but I'm so grateful we did.' A small frown began to dance in her eyes. 'It's just the next bit I'm worried about now.'

'But love, you're fit and healthy. You'll be fine. And there's always the drugs if it gets too much.' Alex dropped a kiss on top of her head.

'I don't mean the birth,' said Joanne quietly. 'I mean afterwards. What if I fall ill like Grace?' She nibbled at the inside of her cheek. 'She was completely normal until she had me, then she went psychotic and was locked away until she died. What if that happens to me?'

'Come on, we've done the research,' said Alex, wrapping his arms around her from behind, his chin resting on the top of her head. 'It's so rare it's hardly worth mentioning, but that's the point of this meeting with the doctors, isn't it, in case the worse does happen – so we're all on the lookout for it and know what to do.'

Joanne looked at his face above hers. His seemed so open, happy, positive. Hers was pinched, drawn. She already felt that something bad was going to happen. She hadn't seen Grace for weeks, but kept looking out for her, convinced it showed that she was going mad. She touched the scar on her neck. It seemed more obvious somehow. She picked up a pink chunky necklace and slipped it on.

A car horn sounded outside. Alex stood and looked through the net curtains. 'They're here,' he said, giving Joanne an arm to get up.

'I swear you grow more every day,' said Lou, grinning, as she gave Joanne a hug by the car. 'You're properly blooming now.'

'I'm blooming big,' said Joanne, smiling as she lowered herself into the back of the car. 'Let's hope I can still fit in this when I'm in labour.'

'I can always put down the seats and you can lie in the boot,' said Mike, turning round from the steering wheel, grinning.

'Mike!' said Lou. 'She's not a piece of luggage.' She poked him in the ribs as she slid back into her seat. Alex helped Joanne wrap the seat belt across herself.

'This can be a practice run for the big day,' said Mike. 'Though if we wanted to do it properly, we should try it at different times of the day to see what the traffic's like.'

'Dad, I'm sure it'll be fine, whatever time of day it is. The infirmary's not far.'

Joanne caught Mike's eyes in the rear-view mirror and saw her own worry reflected in them. He looked away and started the car.

After spending ages trying to find a parking space, they waited in the clinic reception for almost half an hour. Nobody said anything until they were called into the consulting room.

'Thank you all for coming. I'd like to start by setting out the purpose of this session. We call it a care plan meeting and it's an opportunity for us to get together as a group to make sure everyone is aware of the potential risks and to agree a care plan for the birth and your care afterwards.' The doctor looked around at everyone. 'Planning well for postpartum psychosis can help Joanne and Alex and their family accept that, although an episode is a very slight possibility, you have the best support and treatment plan in place. This will ensure that, if you do develop it, everyone around you is prepared, and you can get early treatment and recover much more quickly.' He cleared his throat. 'Now, let's take it in turns to introduce ourselves so we all know our role in the care of Joanne here and her baby. I'm Dr Law and I'm Joanne's obstetrician, here to support you during the birth and afterwards.' He smiled again. His teeth were so white, the overhead strip light seemed to glint off them.

Of the five medical people in the room, Joanne only recognised Dr Petzold and the midwife with the bird tattoo on her ankle, who she'd seen right from the beginning. They exchanged smiles as she introduced herself. Then there was a man with longish wavy hair, who was the psychiatrist, and a woman in her twenties from the community mental health team, who wore the type of elasticated trousers advertised in the back of the Sunday supplements.

Mike and Lou sat silently, glancing at each person as they spoke. Alex slipped his arm around Joanne's shoulders. Joanne took out a notebook. She didn't want to miss anything.

By the end of the meeting, she had four pages of notes covering early warning signs for postpartum psychosis, her birth plan, medications, preferences for hospital treatment if she did develop it, actions to take if she didn't develop it until she got home, and who would make decisions on her behalf.

'Partners are the best barometers,' said the midwife. 'Alex knows you and knows when you're not all right. When I come and see you after you've had the baby at day one, five and ten – and I'll probably pop in in-between – I'll make sure I speak to Alex too, make sure he's happy that everything is normal.' She smiled at Joanne, her tongue piercing catching the light.

Dr Law closed his file. 'I hope this has all given you some reassurance, Joanne,' he said, checking his watch. 'As I said, it's incredibly rare. I doubt you'll be affected – having a familial history of postpartum psychosis doesn't officially meet our threshold. We usually only go down this route if the expectant mother has herself had psychotic episodes or a mental health diagnosis.' Joanne thought of the times she'd seen Grace. Did that count? She'd never told anyone. 'But it's always good to be prepared. Forewarned is forearmed.'

Joanne nodded. 'It has, thank you.'

Dr Petzold leaned forward. 'The environment in which you're having your baby now is nothing like your birth mother had,' he said. 'I know you're going to be absolutely fine.'

'Oh, that reminds me,' said Joanne. 'Dr Petzold, did you find out anything from my birth mother's records?'

The doctor glanced at Dr Law. 'Um.' He swallowed.

Joanne leaned forward over her bump. 'You remember, you took a copy of them when I came to see you at the surgery a few weeks ago.'

His eyes darted around the room. 'I did.'

Joanne waited. 'To see if you could get an undamaged copy,' she prompted. Had he forgotten?

Opposite her, Mike rubbed his face and looked down. Lou closed her eyes and put her hand on his knee.

A sheen of sweat appeared across Dr Petzold's forehead. 'Joanne, clearly your mother was very seriously ill and wasn't herself at that time. I don't think her experience, and her records, have any bearing on our conversation here.'

Joanne bit her lip. 'So you didn't manage to find out anything else?'

Dr Petzold straightened his already straight tie. 'Well—' He glanced down at the folder on his lap.

Joanne's face greyed and seemed to sag. 'Oh. Oh, you did.' She looked to her dad, who looked away. Joanne turned to her mam, who clutched her necklace, her skin wrinkling against the gold chain. She gave Joanne a small, sad smile. Joanne swivelled in her seat to Alex, who moved closer and rested his hand on her shoulder.

'What did you find out?' he said to the doctor.

Dr Petzold rubbed his hand on the back of his neck and looked at Joanne directly for the first time. 'The damaged sections referred to a period of time after your birth, when you were at home but before your birth mother was taken into hospital,' he said quietly.

'So you found something else out?' Joanne said, running her tongue over her lips. She opened her notebook again.

The doctor gave a small nod. 'They had a complete original in the records office which they sent me last week.' He glanced at Mike and looked away, and then opened his file.

Joanne waited, her eyes bright. The room was completely still. Even Dr Law had stopped rustling his papers.

Dr Petzold adjusted his waistcoat and looked around the room. 'It – it seems that Grace was sectioned because she—' He glanced down at the photocopied record. 'She attempted infanticide.' He rushed his words and then stroked a non-existent beard.

There was a moment of complete silence. The temperature in the room seemed to drop.

Joanne blinked rapidly. 'W-what do you mean? Infanti – oh!' She covered her mouth with her hand. 'Oh God, oh God.' She bent over her belly, hiding her face with her hands. A heaviness filled her chest. It was suddenly difficult to breathe.

Alex clutched his neck with one hand and reached for Joanne with the other.

Mike gave a small moan.

Lou squeezed Mike's leg and then stood up and moved over to Joanne. She crouched in front of her and took Joanne's hands, slippery with tears, away from her face. 'She was ill, love. Your mam loved you. She wasn't herself. Don't even think—' Lou shook her head and looked at Dr Petzold, her eyebrows raised.

'Your mam's right,' he said, his voice trembling. 'Infanticide is incredibly rare. I don't know the exact statist—'

'Grace tried to kill me.' It wasn't a question.

Mike looked at Lou. She gave him a small nod and held on to Joanne's hands.

'Grace wasn't herself, love,' he said. 'She was desperate to be a mum. She loved you so much, but something happened. Something chemical—' He looked at Dr Petzold, his palms upwards. 'I can't—'

The doctor started to talk, but Joanne cut him off.

'How?' she asked. 'How did she try to—' She folded an arm against her belly.

Mike got up and walked towards the door. Just as Joanne thought he was going to leave the room, he turned and walked back to the chair, gripped the top of it and turned around again. 'We didn't realise how bad she was. Kathleen was worried, I knew that. She wouldn't leave you alone with Grace. She made sure one of us – me, Gerry, Emily or Susie – was with her always.' He turned and looked straight at Joanne. The sudden feeling of heaviness in her chest moved through her body into her arms and legs.

'I was there when it happened,' he said, almost inaudibly. 'It was my fault. We were upstairs in the bedroom. Grace was holding you, pacing up and down. I asked Kathleen to talk outside your room and left you alone. We knew there was a pair of scissors in the room, but we never dreamed—'

Joanne gasped and squeezed her eyes shut.

Mike's eyes glazed over and he stared into space. 'We'd only had them up there because one of your nappies had frayed and I wanted to trim it. Stupid, really. She'd been cutting that blasted rug she'd made.' He took a deep breath. 'We – Kathleen and I – heard Joanne start to cry and Kathleen asked Grace if she was OK. Then there was a huge scream. Blood-curdling. I'll never forget it. I sprang for the door. She was holding you, and you were both covered in blood.'

Mike nodded at her neck. 'Your scar. You didn't fall into a barbed wire fence.' He swallowed and turned to look out of the window. 'It—'

'But I remember that happening. I remember the pain. The barbed wire cutting into me. The blood,' Joanne said, staring at Mike. She did remember. It was so clear, she could see it happening. She'd tripped over a tree root with her wellies. They were a size too big – hand-me-downs from the family next door. She'd caught the barbed wire as she fell, and it had sliced her neck. She'd felt the heat of it, then the warmth of the blood trickling down her neck on to her T-shirt. *It was the blue dinosaur one*, she remembered now. *Mam had tried to soak it in salt, and then lemon juice.* But it hadn't come out and she'd never worn it again. That was what had happened. She *remembered* it.

Mike shook his head. 'We told you that that's what happened. We described it to you. That's what you're remembering. But that's not what happened.'

Chapter 21

JOANNE

NOVEMBER 2021

'I'm sorry, love, I never wanted you to find out.' Mike pulled at his chin and ignored the cup of tea Lou had poured. 'It wasn't your mother who tried to kill you. It wasn't her. She was ill.'

Joanne nodded and took a sip of tea, leaning against the cushions. It felt good to be back home, away from the sterility of the hospital, the professional curiosity of the doctors and midwife, Dr Petzold's obvious embarrassment. The horror of it. She couldn't remember how they'd got home. Alex slipped an arm around her shoulders and pulled her to him. Joanne let her head fall on his shoulder. It was awful, but at least she knew now.

'Your dad and I have been talking about it,' said Lou, sitting down on the other side of her. 'I had no idea until he told me the other week.' She shook her head. 'Now I understand why he was so worried when I was pregnant, why he was so funny afterwards and then didn't want to have any more children after Patrick.'

Mike nodded. 'I just couldn't risk it all happening again, it was so awful. So unexpected. My mum had warned about the baby blues – and that's what we thought it was initially, but this was something else.' He cleared his throat. 'I never wanted you to be burdened like, with that. And I didn't want people to look at you differently because of it. Only Susie, Kathleen and the sisters knew what had actually happened in the cottage. And John, of course. But I knew it would get out somehow. People talk. Somehow someone would find out and it would be all over the village. That's why I needed to get away.' He looked up at Joanne. 'I couldn't have you growing up somewhere where people knew that your mum had tried to—' He took a deep breath. 'Tried to kill you.'

'I understand, Dad.' Joanne gave him a small smile. 'You did what you thought was best, for my sake.'

Mike nodded. 'I'm sorry I lied to you, love. I just didn't want you to be burdened by that. And especially when you're expecting.'

'I know, Dad.' Joanne levered herself off the sofa and gave him a hug.

After they left, Joanne went upstairs and sat at her dressing table. She called Susie and told her what had happened at the care plan meeting.

'Oh Joanne, I'm so sorry you had to find out. It must have been such a shock.' Susie's usual bubbly voice was infused with anxiety.

'It was, but at least I know it all now. Why didn't you tell me?'

The line went quiet, and Joanne thought they'd been cut off. But then she heard Susie sigh.

'It wasn't my secret to tell, Joanne,' she said slowly. 'I think your dad felt it was better that you didn't know, and I had to respect that.'

'Yeah, I know.'

'But remember, it wasn't your mum who did that – she was ill. Your mum loved you, so so much.'

'Thanks, Susie.' Everyone kept saying the same thing. That Grace had loved her, that it was just one of those things. Her mind had unravelled. It didn't help.

'Just remember, you have family down here now. Don't forget about us. And tell your dad I'm sorry, and I'm glad he's doing OK. John and I would love to see him.'

She ended the call and took off her necklace to look at her scar, as she had done every day of her life. She traced it with her finger from the base of her neck, winding lazily around almost to her ear. This mark had defined her life – the taunts in the playground that had morphed into the subtle glances in the shop when customers thought she wasn't looking. Alex had asked about it on their first date, which meant there almost hadn't been a second one. She'd always explained what had happened to anyone who was bold enough to ask directly – the memory cementing in her mind with each retelling.

Now she stared at the scar and tried to unspool that memory. But it was stuck fast. She remembered the barbed wire so clearly. The feel of it as it pierced her skin. The surprise of it, how her body tingled then went cold. The sky had been that deep blue you sometimes get on the Northumberland coast in summer. The blue dinosaur T-shirt. It had sat in a bowl soaking for what felt like years. But that must have been something else. There was no barbed wire.

Alex knocked on the door, something he'd never done before. 'OK to come in?'

She didn't answer and he pushed open the door slowly, peering round tentatively. She caught his eye in the mirror. 'You OK?'

She nodded automatically. He stood behind her, his hands resting on her shoulders as he had that morning. Before she had found out. Before. There would always be the before and after.

She saw him looking at the scar and she touched it again, as self-consciously and with the same curiosity as if she'd just seen it for the first time. He leaned down and kissed just behind her ear, and then dropped tiny kisses along the length of the scar until he reached the base of her neck. 'I've always thought it was beautiful, that it made you more beautiful, made you *you*,' he said.

He was trying hard, she thought. Trying to erase Dr Petzold's words. Her dad's words. Infanticide. His face when he told her.

She looked at Alex in the mirror. They stared at each other for several seconds. Eventually, she spoke. 'How can I trust myself to ever be alone with the baby? After everything we've been through to get here, what if the same thing happens?' They'd waited for so long for this moment and now she was absolutely terrified of becoming a mother.

Chapter 22

Joanne woke in the early hours of the morning, needing the loo. After she'd stumbled to the bathroom and had a wee, she realised the sensation hadn't gone away. Something felt heavy. Like a full bladder. Her belly was tight, like a drum.

She lumbered downstairs into the kitchen, feeling as if she were carrying a football between her thighs. The baby had dropped. Engaged. That was the word the midwife used. It felt lower, anyway. She put the kettle on and looked into the garden. Darkness shrouded everything. She couldn't even make out the little Wendy house Alex had spotted advertised on the community noticeboard. But it was there somewhere, waiting for its owner. She touched her belly.

It was a little after 6 a.m., not even a hint of dawn in the sky. Not long now until the shortest day. Then the year would turn and the nights would start getting lighter. She'd be sitting down here feeding a baby by then, watching the sun come up.

Joanne poured the boiling water over a teabag and added some milk. The feeling that she needed the loo was still there and she wondered if she was going to wet herself. Better stay in the kitchen rather than risk the carpet in the front room. She sat down heavily at the kitchen table, cradling the tea and watching the blackness beyond the window pane. Only a week until the due date. Joanne bit her lip. Almost there. She prodded her belly. The baby was very still.

A sliver of light sliced across the garden from next door, reflecting off the metal table and chairs, now covered with rotting leaves. Pete at number 4 must be on nights. He'd be coming in now, making tea and having a fag before heading up to bed. The light changed and she imagined him standing in the doorway, looking out into the garden. Ange didn't like him smoking in the house.

There was now a dull ache between her legs and Joanne shifted on the bench, spreading her legs wider and leaning forward. In a few months, she'd be sitting at that garden table in the sunlight, rocking the baby to sleep in her arms. Next door, Pete finished his fag and turned off the light, darkness enveloping the garden again. Joanne blew out a long breath. The ache began to ease and she leaned back, her shoulders dropping.

She took a sip of tea and waited, looking at the clock. Was this the start of it? She glanced at the ceiling, and thought about waking Alex. But what if it was a false alarm? He might as well sleep while he could. And first babies were never early. That's what Mam had said. She could have another three weeks to wait before they induced her.

The ache began again, or was that just the niggle she'd been getting in her back? No, it was definitely something else. She pushed her bottom against the back of the seat and leaned forward, focusing on breathing. It built up and then began to ease again. What was that, five minutes? If that was a contraction, then it was OK. For now.

She'd go and wake Alex if it happened again. But when it came again, she found she quite liked sitting in the dark. Silent. Alone.

The swell grew – she managed to remember to breathe, as the woman in those funny classes had told them – and then it died down again. She didn't want to wake him, because then he'd put on the light and it would all change. Joanne waited until it had finished and stood to put the kettle on again. But when it boiled, she didn't fancy a cup of tea but reached for the hot-water bottle and filled it up. The next contraction hit her just as she'd finished screwing on the cap, and she clutched the edge of the work surface. It didn't feel safe here. She dropped to her knees and went on all fours. She heard a growl and wondered where it had come from.

It was cold on the floor, wearing only Alex's oversized T-shirt. She thought about the throw in the front room and how nice it would feel wrapped around her with the water bottle on her back. That was where the pain seemed to be. Maybe it wasn't labour after all. Just that back pain coming back. She didn't want to bother Alex over a bit of back pain.

She waited for the ache to go – they were definitely getting worse, maybe she should tell someone – and then she crawled through to the front room. She pulled the throw off the settee and wrapped it around her, putting the hot-water bottle down the back of her knickers. That was better. Then another contraction hit her. 'Alex.' Her voice sounded choked, it wasn't making the proper sound. 'Alex.'

Suddenly, it didn't feel warm and safe in the dark. She tried to crawl to the door but was stopped by another contraction and gripped the side of the coffee table, grunting. The cordless phone on the table caught the street light's glare. Joanne reached for it and pressed the speed dial.

Lou's voice was warm, reassuring. 'Joanne? You OK, love?'

She could only grunt in response.

'Is Alex there?'

No sound would come, apart from another grunt.

'I'll be over right now.'

Joanne slumped on the floor and waited for the pain to ease. Then she crawled back to the settee. It felt safer there. Her head sank into the velour.

There were footsteps on the stairs and then Alex was there, stroking her back. 'Why didn't you come and tell me? Your mam just called. How far apart are they? Remember, they said at five minutes apart and lasting sixty seconds we'd need to go in.'

But Joanne just shook her head and closed her eyes, feeling the next surge come again. It gripped her and she fell into darkness. When it died down, she heard Alex on the phone.

'Yes, I'm going to bring her in now.' Silence. 'I don't know, but it seems bad. She can't speak.'

He lifted her up under her arms and was slipping something around her shoulders. She couldn't open her eyes. She could hear Grace in the background, and she sobbed. She was going mad after all. Having the baby was going to kill her, or was she going to kill the baby? But then she realised it wasn't Grace but Mam's voice. Mam was holding her other arm. Someone had put shoes on her feet and she was being half carried to the front door. The cold air made her suddenly shiver and double over as another wave hit her. She stopped, dropped down and clutched the bonnet of the car, growling through it. Someone was stroking her back but it was irritating, and she reached behind to push the hand away.

Eventually, she opened her eyes and used the bonnet to push herself up. The sky was a brilliant blue. How had it got so light? 'Wassa time?' she breathed.

'It's almost ten,' said Alex, his voice far away. Surely it was only just after six. Pete had just come back from his night shift.

Then she was inside the car, on the back seat. Alex was trying to put her seat belt on her, but she pushed him away and stayed on all fours.

'You go in the front, Alex, next to Mike. I'll stay with her.' Mam's voice.

Then soothing strokes. 'You're all right, love. It's all going to be OK.'

The pain built up again and she tensed, waiting for the peak. They were getting longer, the contractions, if that was what they were. She gripped the back of the seat and felt the growl in her throat. It was her making that noise. Then she felt the first sign of easing. Still unbearable, but a little better. Then a little better.

She took a deep breath and opened her eyes again, blinking in the light. The car started to move off towards Bridge Street and the house grew smaller. 'This is it, isn't it? The baby's coming.' She turned to look at her mam.

'Yes, the baby's coming, Joanne. You're doing really well.' Lou stroked Joanne's back. 'We're going to the hospital now, it's time.'

'What if I change? What if I go crazy like Grace?'

Lou shook her head, smiling. 'You're not going to go mad, Joanne love. But you will be changed. When we next drive back down this street, you'll be a mam with a baby in your arms.'

Joanne nodded and then closed her eyes, gripping the back seat as the surge grew again.

Chapter 23

Joanne

June 2022

It was just family left now. And Susie and John. But they were almost family, Joanne thought.

'We should start clearing up,' said Lou, glancing at the empty cups and glasses which covered every surface of the sitting room, together with bowls of crisp fragments. It was the first time she'd spoken for hours.

'I'll do it,' said Susie, leaping up. 'It won't take us long. You—' She looked at Lou but didn't finish her sentence and instead started picking up glasses.

'I'll help,' said Lou. 'I need to do something.' She rolled up the sleeves of her black blouse to the elbows and took four cups into the kitchen. Joanne followed her with some of the old wine glasses. One rim was stained with fuchsia lipstick. She didn't remember anyone wearing fuchsia lipstick. And who wore fuchsia lipstick to a funeral anyway?

In the kitchen, John stood smoking at the garden door, still stiff in his suit. The platters of sandwiches had been demolished, though there were still a few tuna and sweetcorn left. Joanne picked one up, smelled it and put it down. She wasn't hungry though she hadn't eaten all day.

'Your dad would have loved today,' said Lou as they walked back to the front room.

She was right, Joanne thought. All his favourite people in one room, a bit of drink, plenty of food. 'That's the irony, isn't it? You never get to attend your own funeral,' she said. Funeral. A horrible word.

They collected more glasses and went back to the kitchen where Susie had organised John, Alex and Patrick into a washing-up production line. The twins' shrieks echoed though the back door into the kitchen. Sometimes their noise set her teeth on edge, but today, when everyone seemed to be speaking in whispers, she appreciated the normality of it. They didn't understand that their grandad had gone. They probably thought heaven was like Lindisfarne, a place you go on holiday and come back two weeks later. But Dad was never coming back. She slid the dirty glasses on the counter next to Alex.

He gave her a small smile. She'd felt his eyes on her all day, holding her hand when he was close, sliding a tissue into it during the service. He'd been like that ever since Dad collapsed a month ago, and through those long days in intensive care sitting with Lou to the soundtrack of beeps and whooshes, forcing air into his lungs and monitoring his vital signs. And he'd been there, with Patrick, when the machines finally slipped into silence. Her rock.

She went back into the front room. Lou was wiping down the mantelpiece where there were wet glass rings. 'People should have used the mats,' she said. 'We put them out to make sure this didn't happen.'

'There's no harm done, Mam, it'll come off.' Lou put down the cloth, and pressed her fingertips under her eyes. Joanne swallowed. There was a start of a wail from upstairs.

'I'll go,' said Joanne, taking the stairs two at a time. What she'd learned over the last six months was that if the baby was left to cry she worked herself up into a fury which was difficult to recover from. But if she got to her quickly, she could easily be pacified.

In the baby's room, the summer sun filtered through the window on to the rag rug that was stretched across the floor. It felt like it had always been there now. All those evenings of unravelling the destroyed middle part and stitching it back together, rolling and binding the fabric until you would never guess what had happened.

She'd known Lou had been concerned about her intense focus on the rug in the few months after Grace was born. Whenever the baby slept, Joanne had got her latch hook out. 'I know it wasn't my fault, what happened to Granny Grace,' Joanne had said. 'I'm not repairing the rug to make up for it. I just thought it would be nice for baby Grace to have something of her namesake, like the cot.'

Lou had nodded and Joanne had ignored the worry in her eyes. She'd known that her mam had been right, as she usually was. She had been trying to make amends to Granny Grace, as she'd started calling her. The whole 'birth mother' term had felt so unnatural. Had felt like it was relegating Lou to some sort of runner-up position. But you can't apologise for being born and for what happened when you were just a baby.

Granny Grace sounded matriarchal. As if she were looking over her, caring for her. A guardian angel of sorts, like it felt she had been when Joanne thought she'd lost the baby in the hospital in Brighton, and then again in those first early weeks after Grace was born and when she was almost delirious with sleep deprivation.

Seeing the rug spread across the floor now, its colours grey in the half-light, Joanne felt that it was one of the few things that were part of her shared history with her mother. She knelt down and picked Grace out of her cot.

'Hello, chick,' she said. 'You had enough of sleeping? Want to join us downstairs?'

With Grace balanced on her hip, she opened the curtains, and the light caught the side of the silver photo frames on the dresser. The first was of Mike, Grace and baby Joanne standing outside the cottage in Seadean. The photo which had started her whole journey. The second was Mike, Lou, Joanne, Alex and baby Grace, taken in the garden here, not long before Mike's collapse. Precious memories. 'We'll make sure you always remember your grandad,' she said to Grace as she pressed her fingertips to her lips and then placed them on her dad's grinning face. 'Miss you', she whispered. 'I miss you every day.' Would this feeling of loss, desolation, ever lift?

Downstairs, Lou was still wiping down surfaces in the front room. Her face lifted when Joanne came back in with Grace. 'How's my baby?'

Grace reached out for Lou and Joanne handed her over. The three of them sat down. The front room was tidy now. You'd never have guessed that sixty people had crammed into the house and garden earlier to say goodbye to Mike.

'At least your dad got to see this little one born, and you safe and well as a mum,' said Lou, stroking Grace's downy head.

'Yes, I'm glad of that. But she'll never remember him and that's really sad.' Joanne could feel the tears rising and swallowed. She didn't want to set Lou off again. She shouldn't have had those two glasses of wine. It had eased the ache a little at first but made the tears come easier now.

'We'll tell her all about him when she's old enough,' said Lou, holding Grace up so she was resting some weight on her feet. 'And thank God the truth came out about everything while he was still alive to talk about it,' she said. 'I think after hiding everything for all those years, he was glad of the chance to talk about it all. He was at peace when he died. And that's the most important thing.'

'I want Grace to know about her family, all of her family,' said Joanne, thinking of the journey she, Mike and baby Grace had taken down to Brighton just before Mike had collapsed. Standing in the hospital's cemetery in front of Granny Grace's grave, Joanne had thought that this was the first time she'd been with her birth parents for more than forty years. And now there was a new generation leading the way.

The twins came tearing into the room, chasing their rescue dog who had a gardening glove in his mouth. 'Benji,' screamed one, trying to rugby tackle the dog to the ground. Lou lifted Grace out of harm's way. Benji dodged the child, knocked over the coffee table and raced out of the room, with the twins in hot pursuit.

Joanne laughed and rearranged the rug and table. 'I don't know how Patrick and Jenny cope with those two. I find one exhausting.'

Lou settled Grace back on her lap and held up her toy rabbit. 'One day, all of us adults will be gone and it'll be the twins and Grace who'll be taking on the family name and customs.'

Joanne looked round at the room, at the photos of her mam and dad on the mantelpiece and at Lou holding her third grandchild. Her dad was gone, and gone too soon and too suddenly. There was a huge gap which would never be filled. But somehow, with Susie and John and her aunts in her life, and the truth about Granny Grace out, the family left felt more whole.

Epilogue

Joanne

Six Months Later

It was a classic Boxing Day feast. Platters of turkey and ham. A plate of bubble and squeak next to a bowl of creamy mashed potato. Spiced red cabbage. Coleslaw. Crispy pigs in blankets. Some rather tired-looking Brussels sprouts. Susie had baked enough sausage rolls to feed all of Berwick, while Gerry had brought what she claimed was her world-famous chutney. As she passed it around the table, her husband quickly picked up the jar of piccalilli and scooped some on to his plate instead.

Joanne put some chicken and pasta into the plastic bowl in front of the baby, along with carrot sticks.

'Gah!' said Grace, throwing a carrot on to the grass.

Everyone laughed.

'She really is the spit of her namesake, isn't she?' said Emily, handing Grace a breadstick, which she started to chew enthusiastically. 'You can tell from the hair that she's going to look exactly like Joanne and my sister. I'm sorry, Alex, it may say Shaw on her birth certificate but she's a Bennett through and through.'

Alex finished topping up everyone's glasses. 'Oh, I know I have as beautiful a daughter as I do a wife. I won't get a look-in!'

'Did you never think about having children?' asked Joanne, and suddenly regretted it as Emily flinched. 'Sorry, that's a terrible question. I used to hate it when people asked me that, especially when we were trying so hard to get pregnant and it wasn't happening.'

'I don't mind talking about it, not with family, not with you,' said Emily, taking a sip of wine. Her husband Steve laid a hand on her arm. 'The truth is that I wasn't well as a teenager and in my early twenties. They didn't take it seriously then, not like now. They just put it down to bad PMT. But I was depressed for many years. I couldn't seem to shake it off.' She took a mouthful of salad and chewed it slowly. 'Grace also had bad PMT, as you know. The doctor who came to the house when she was ill mentioned that women with bad PMT can go on to develop postpartum depression or even psychosis, that the two things can be linked.' She stopped and looked around the garden.

'After seeing what happened to her.' Emily glanced at Joanne. 'What happened to you and to poor Mike, I just couldn't risk the same thing happening to me.'

Joanne fiddled with her napkin. 'I understand. That must have been a difficult decision for you both.' The ramifications of Grace's illness had been so much wider than she'd first realised.

'Can you pass a beer out of the esky,' said Steve, nodding towards the cooler next to Lou. She reached in and handed one to him. 'In some ways, I don't think we realised what a big decision it was at the time. We had so much going on then, our lives were so full. It's only in the last few years as our friends' children have had grandchildren we've realised that loss.'

Emily stroked Steve's cheek. 'Which is why it's so wonderful that you've come over here. That we get to meet you properly and have little Grace in our lives. Our grand-niece.'

'Let's raise a toast,' said Steve, holding up his can of beer. 'To family.'

Everyone raised their glasses, Joanne clinking hers against Alex's and then Lou's before reaching across the table to touch Steve's can and Emily's wine glass. Grace gurgled and picked up her beaker, waving it in the air. Everyone laughed.

'I'd like to raise another toast,' Joanne said. 'To those of us who can't be here.' Joanne glanced at Lou, but her face was unreadable.

Emily nodded. 'To absent friends and family,' she said quietly. Everyone raised their glasses again.

'Christmases are always a time of reflection, aren't they, a time to think about previous Christmases?' said Emily. 'I remember a Christmas back in England when I was a teenager when the electricity went off and Mum only realised when we got back from church and the turkey was supposed to have been cooking for four hours.' Emily laughed at the memory.

Grace started to grizzle, throwing another breadstick on the ground.

'So what happened?' asked Joanne, handing her a piece of carrot. 'Did you manage to have a Christmas dinner in the end?'

Emily nodded. 'Mum took everything round to Susie's mum's house – all the food, chairs, plates and everything. We all crammed round the table somehow. It was chaos. Mike's mum was alive then, and she helped out too.'

'Wasn't that the year Grace was a vegetarian?' asked Steve. 'I remember you talking about it.'

Joanne leaned forward.

'Oh God, yes!' said Emily. 'I'd forgotten about that. Mum was so angry about it. No one was veggie in those days. She cooked Grace an omelette for Christmas dinner. But she'd cooked her an omelette every night for weeks. It was the only vegetarian dish she knew.'

Grace broke into a proper wail.

'I think I'll just put her down for a sleep,' said Joanne, standing up. 'She's tired from the heat and the attention all day.'

'D'you need a hand, chick?' said Lou, pushing her chair back.

'I'm OK, Mam,' said Joanne, walking past the back of her chair and resting her hand on Lou's shoulder as she passed. 'You relax and enjoy the meal.' She went inside and climbed upstairs, holding the grizzling Grace against her chest.

Grace stopped crying as Joanne tucked her in in the travel cot at the end of the spare bed she and Alex were sleeping in. She reached around for the little pink rabbit that she liked to hold. Joanne picked it up and slipped it into her grasping hand. She pulled down the blackout blind that Steve had so thoughtfully installed for their arrival and watched Grace's eyes get heavier as she sucked on the foot of the rabbit. *God help us if we ever lose that, we'll never get her to sleep*, she thought.

There was another roar of laughter from outside. Joanne studied Grace's face to see if she'd woken. But she was clutching the rabbit, her eyes tightly closed.

Joanne tiptoed away from the cot and sat down in front of the dressing table, looking at her scar in the mirror in the gloom. For years she'd hated it, cursed herself for her clumsiness for slipping into the barbed wire fence. She'd seen it as an ugly tear on her neck, a gash to be hidden. No necklace had ever properly covered it, so as soon as she was old enough Joanne had started learning to make her own.

For years, she'd covered it with these necklaces, or with tightly wrapped thin scarves when it was colder. But in the year since she found out how it had come to be there, she'd hardly covered it at all. Somehow, knowing how it had happened had transformed it from a scar to hide to a symbol of remembrance, a visual link with her birth mother. It was the last thing Grace had given her.

Joanne fiddled with the new rings she was wearing. The weight wasn't quite right. The flower emblem was too heavy and kept dragging the ring around. She'd have to change that in the next version. That was why it was always good to trial out jewellery before she sold it, she thought. That way, customers were always happy with the end result.

If she'd been told this time last year that within twelve months she'd have sublet part of Mandy's shop for her jewellery and be supplying shops in Alnwick and Kelso, with an enquiry even coming in from a shop in Newcastle, she'd have said it was utter madness. Especially after her dad's death. But she'd thrown herself into it after he went, and the business had really taken off and was so flexible she could just about manage to do it around Grace's nap times and Alex's shifts. Now that he'd finally got the promotion he'd been working towards for years, his hours were slightly more predictable. She'd seen some interesting designs in a shop in Sydney on Christmas Eve that might work quite well for the UK market. She yawned. She was still tired from the long flight and the busy lead-up to Christmas selling at the craft fairs.

A reflection in the mirror made her glance up. Behind her stood Granny Grace, wearing a blue polka-dot dress, her dark curly hair making her face pale. Joanne's heart thudded but she managed a small smile. She'd thought she'd never see her again. Grace's hands felt light on Joanne's shoulders – her fingers were tiny, Joanne noticed, like a child's. Joanne breathed shallowly so as not to disturb Grace, who slowly traced the scar from Joanne's throat to her ear, as if seeing it for the first time. Then she bent over and kissed it once, as a mother would kiss her small child's graze better. Her lips were unexpectedly warm on Joanne's skin. Joanne held her breath, willing Grace to look her in the eyes. As she looked up, she smiled at Joanne and bent over and kissed her on the top of her head.

She'd never told Alex or Lou that she could see Granny Grace sometimes. She knew that would have been on their list of Things to Look Out for with Postpartum Psychosis. And she'd known really that Grace wasn't there. She was just conjuring her up, willing her to be alive to tell her her secrets and then to hold her hand through those early days. She hadn't needed that reassurance for a long time. The photograph on the mantelpiece was enough.

The landing creaked and Joanne automatically turned. It was just Lou. She stood in the doorway and whispered, 'Did she get down OK?' Joanne knew without looking that Grace had gone.

She nodded and Lou padded across the rug, glancing in the cot, and stood behind Joanne, putting her hands on her shoulders, just as Grace had done. Joanne shivered and took a deep breath. She knew she wouldn't see Grace again now. That kiss had been goodbye, for both of them. They didn't need each other in that way any more. But her scar would always bind them together.

'I'm so proud of you, chick,' whispered Lou. 'Not just for giving me such a beautiful granddaughter, and for being such an amazing mam. But also for creating our new family after your dad died. I know it's been a tough few months for everyone, but this new section of the family has given us all a new lease of life.'

Another bark of laughter from outside. When her dad was alive, reigniting the friendship with John had been the making of him. She'd never thought about it, but her dad had always been a loner. He had people he worked with and the people at the Rotary, but he'd never had close friends. He wasn't the type of person to go out for a drink with anyone. Maybe because he'd had a close friend in John and had left it all behind when he left Brighton. After he died so suddenly, Susie and John and her Aunt Gerry had scooped them up as they floundered in their grief. With everything she'd already been through with the IVF and the discovery about Granny Grace, Joanne couldn't believe they were being tested again. But this new friendship, and that of their old friends and neighbours, had helped them reshape their lives without Mike.

The invitation to spend Christmas with Aunt Emily in Australia meant they avoided a sad and lonely one in England, where Mike's absence would sit heavily.

Joanne turned to face Lou in the half-light. 'Are you still OK about this? Being away for the first Christmas without Dad? Being with Emily and Steve.' She nodded towards the noise.

'Of course, chick,' Lou said quickly. Then she stopped and sighed. 'At least, I was worried when the invitation first came through. I worried about being away from everything familiar. But what would we be doing if we were home? With Patrick and his family away, it would just be you, me, Alex and the baby, and Mike's absence would be huge. We'd be moping around. Here, it's all new and exciting. I feel his absence but it's somehow easier, even yesterday on Christmas Day.'

'I feel the same,' said Joanne. 'It is better away from home, and with people who knew and loved him and want to talk about him. It keeps him alive somehow.' She looked sideways at Lou. 'And you're OK that we're with Granny Grace's sister?'

'I wasn't at first. I thought it was wrong to rake up the past. That I'd lose you, and Mike.' She wiped her hand across her face. 'I always saw Grace, the memory of Grace, as a sort of competition, I suppose.'

'Mam?' Joanne's forehead pleated together.

Lou gave a quiet half-laugh and looked at the floor. 'He loved her first. If she hadn't got ill, then he'd still be with her. I was always the second choice. And as much as I loved you, I knew that she'd been your mam first. She was your real' – her voice hardened around the word – 'mam.'

'Oh, Mam.' Joanne turned and looped her arms around Lou's neck and pulled her close. 'You're as much a mam to me as Grace was. More than she was, really, because we have all those years and years of memories together. You were always there when she couldn't be.'

Lou looked down at her, her eyes full of tears. 'It's wonderful to hear you say that. I was so worried I'd lose you with all this. To Grace's memory. Silly really.'

Joanne could see the worry deep in Lou's eyes. 'Biology is a part of being a mam, but it's much more about being there. Day in, day out. Loving someone and being there for them. That's what being a mam is.'

'After Mike died, I thought I'd be an intruder in your new family, but everyone has been so wonderful, so kind and welcoming.' Lou sniffed and swallowed.

Joanne got up and gave her a proper hug. 'You will always be my family,' she said. They walked towards the door together, checking Grace was still asleep, their arms linked.

Emily's voice shouted up from downstairs. 'What are you two doing up there? Having a mothers' meeting? We want to raise another toast.'

Joanne and Lou smiled at one another. Lou raised an imaginary glass. 'To you, for being a wonderful mam over the past year.'

Joanne raised an imaginary glass in turn. 'To you, for being a brilliant grandmother. And an amazing mam to me and Patrick.'

Two flushes of pink appeared on Lou's cheeks. 'To all of us mams. You, me and Granny Grace.'

'However we became mams.'

They clinked their imaginary glasses and walked back downstairs and out into the warm Australian sunshine.

ACKNOWLEDGEMENTS

After I had my third child in 2009, I found life quite a challenge. My new baby cried almost continuously and wouldn't be held by anyone but me, my toddler was jealous of the attention the new baby was getting and my seven-year-old son was put out by them both and acted accordingly. I couldn't drive and was reliant on public transport – not easy with a double buggy. Going anywhere with the three of them was nigh on impossible and suddenly my world felt very small. I started 'hearing' the new baby talking to me – saying, among other things, that she didn't want to be here.

I took her to A&E several times, explaining that she was dying. The baby was checked over and was physically fine – albeit colicky. These repeated visits were put on my record and at my next postnatal check-up, the health visitor had a little chat with me and asked if I was coping. I was outraged. Of course I was coping. I had a good job, was a mum of three and a person who always copes.

In reality, of course, I wasn't coping. I was physically and mentally exhausted. I kept waiting for the baby to sleep through the night but it was to be over fifteen months until she slept more than five hours in a row and four long years until she slept through the whole night. I kept waiting for her to be weaned, but she hated all food on sight. It took more than seven months before she'd even drink expressed breast milk out of a bottle.

I laugh about those months now, but at the time I felt desperately, paralysingly sad. There were days when I found it hard to get out of the armchair.

I was lucky. I had a good network of friends and family, my health visitor was on the case and I had plenty of support. I came out the other side and, while having three young children was often challenging, it was never again paralysingly so.

Postnatal depression affects more than one in every ten women within a year of giving birth. Meanwhile, postpartum psychosis affects around one in one thousand women, and although it's a dangerous disorder – with a 3–4 per cent of risk of infanticide or homicide and a 4–5 per cent risk of suicide – most women recover without harming anyone. But the stigma of mental illness – particularly for women with babies – continues to make it difficult to speak openly about.

Those early months as a mum of three stayed with me and I knew that I would one day write about them. That time came when they were all teenagers and sleeping well into the morning – and even afternoon.

There are many people who kindly helped me with this book.

Janet McGinn, for talking about life in Brighton and Sussex in the 1970s.

Keith Upward, who worked in the Jaycee furniture factory in Brighton and talked about the city at that time.

Chloe Ronaldson, a local Brighton midwife, for insight on the treatment of postpartum psychosis today.

Jenny Martin (and her friend Judith Gilmour) for explaining what having a baby was like in the 1970s.

Hove Writers, run by the brilliant author Jo Furniss, who read some early drafts of this book. Likewise, the writers on the Advanced Writing Workshops run by the Creative Writing Programme in Brighton, which provided excellent feedback on the early chapters.

The team at Kemptown Bookshop in Brighton where I did many of the edits for the book, particularly those writers who joined me for the monthly #5amWritersClub.

Dr Hilary R. Nash, my brilliant GP friend, for answering my questions about postpartum psychosis and other health things.

My wonderful agent, Sam Brace from PFD, for all her encouragement and support in getting this story out into the world.

My editors, Mike Jones, Victoria Oundjian and Maisie Lawrence, from Amazon Publishing for their brilliant suggestions for the story and careful editing.

The #writingcommunity on X for encouragement to keep writing in the first person. You were all right, it took time, but it came and now I love it. Grace wouldn't be Grace without being first person.

The November mums – Angela Meade, Daisy Gupta, Debbie Daskivich, Franziska Stahlknecht, Hannelore Bout, Helen Howcroft, Jag Strachan, Judith MacBean and Sarah Lynch – for helping me through those first few difficult months as a mum of three. Getting out of the house on some days was lifesaving. The ten of us – whose babies were all due in November 2007 – remain great friends to this day.

Sian Thomas, whose third baby also didn't sleep and who was a great support in those early years, and continued to be as our children got older and into very different sorts of scrapes.

Rachel, Jo, Doo and Hilary for being such fabulous cheerleaders.

Richard, who was the first person to read the first draft of this story, and for all your encouragement always.

Jude, Zara and Katy: without you there would be no story. Thank you for all being such wonderful, individual humans. I'm so proud of you in your different ways. And relieved that you all now sleep through the night.

If you are worried about postpartum psychosis for you, or someone close to you, there is a wealth of advice and support available from the NHS https://www.nhs.uk/mental-health/conditions/postpartum-psychosis/ and Action on Postpartum Psychosis https://www.app-network.org/what-is-pp/app-guides/

BOOK CLUB QUESTIONS

If you're choosing to read *The Missing Mother of Rose Cottage* in your book group, then a massive THANK YOU. I love the idea that people are reading my book, but far more exciting is that you're sitting around talking about it with cups of tea or glasses of wine. Here are some pointers for your discussion, which I hope are helpful. If you haven't yet read the book, then stop reading this now. There are spoilers ahead!

1. How did *The Missing Mother of Rose Cottage* make you feel?

2. Alex and Joanne have great difficulty in having a baby and their lives are almost put on hold for several years. How does this affect their relationship? And how would it have been different if they'd managed to have a child earlier in their marriage?

3. We hear a great deal about how Joanne feels about her infertility, but we also get an insight into how frustrated Alex feels. Did you have any sympathy for him as a character?

4. Motherhood is a key theme throughout the book but all the mothers struggle to some degree. Grace falls pregnant easily but has postpartum psychosis afterwards. Joanne never knew her birth

mother and is raised by her stepmother and then struggles to get pregnant herself. Lou raises another woman's child as her own, only to then have to face her daughter trying to find her own birth mother. Gerry and Emily are so traumatised by their sister having postpartum psychosis that they decide not to have children. Susie is pregnant with her own child when Grace falls ill and then raises her without her best friend, a constant reminder of what could have been. Discuss each woman's experience of motherhood.

5. Mike thought he was doing the right thing by not telling Joanne (or his second wife, Lou) what happened with Grace after she gave birth. Do you think he did the right thing? How would Joanne's life have been different if she'd known what happened to her birth mother?

6. Joanne sees visions of Grace during her pregnancy and in the early days of being a mum. How did you interpret these visions?

7. Grace's story in the 1970s is written in the first person, while in the present day Joanne's is written in the third person. How did this affect your experience of the characters? Did you prefer one character over the other?

8. Treatment for postpartum psychosis is very different now from the 1970s. Do you think this story could take place now?

9. If the book was to be made into a film, who do you think would play the key characters – Grace, Mike and Joanne?

Chapter 1

JANUARY 2019

Emma's phone rang as she was peeling potatoes for mash. She glanced at the screen but didn't recognise the number so ignored it, cutting the peeled potato in half before adding it to the pan.

Her son James wandered into the kitchen, headphones clamped to his ears. He grabbed a carton of milk from the fridge and lifted it to his lips.

'James! Use a glass,' she said, nodding towards the cupboard.

He rolled his eyes but poured the milk into a glass and sat down at the kitchen table. 'How long till dinner?'

'Thirty minutes,' she said. 'How was college?'

James shrugged and looked at his phone. 'Same, same.'

'Best bit of the day?' coaxed Emma. She remembered asking the same question when she used to pick him and his sister Libby up from primary school. Best bit of the day? Worst bit of the day? What did you have for lunch? She learned that after receiving a standard response of 'fine', they would compete on who could describe the most outlandish things that had happened. Now they were both teenagers she was lucky if they answered at all.

James didn't look up. 'I scored a couple of baskets in practice and coach asked me to join the first team.'

'James, that's amazing.' Emma smiled and rested her hand on his shoulder. A faint blush crept up his neck. 'You must tell Dad when he gets in.'

James nodded and focused back on his phone.

'How many sausages do you want?' Emma asked, slipping them out of the packet on to the grill tray.

'Six?' he said hopefully.

Emma laughed and got a second packet out of the fridge. 'D'you want any help with revision later? I could go through those index cards with you, ask you some random questions?'

'Yeah, okay,' he said.

Really she should try to finish off the survey for the new development. She'd only got halfway through before she'd had to leave to pick up Libby and take her to street dance. That was always the challenge – trying to fit what was a full-time job into part-time hours. But Emma loved her afternoons off. Since James started school, she'd only worked from nine to three, meaning she could pick him and Libby up every day and spend the rest of the afternoon with them. Even now they both tended to do their own thing – James at basketball or out with friends, Libby hanging around in town – she still liked being at home when they arrived and they knew she was there if they wanted her. She could finish the survey after she'd helped out with the revision.

Libby came in and sat at the table. 'I saw you with that girl at lunch,' she said to James.

James narrowed his eyes and mouthed, 'Fuck off.'

'I saw that,' said Emma. 'It still counts as swearing even if you don't say it.'

James rolled his eyes again slightly and looked back at his sister mouthing something Emma couldn't interpret.

Her phone rang again and she glanced at the number. It was the same one as earlier and she still didn't recognise it. She was about to answer when Nick came through the door.

'Hi, gang,' he said. 'Nice to see everyone here rather than hiding in your rooms.'

'The draw of dinner rather than my company, I think,' laughed Emma as he pulled her into a hug. 'How was your day?'

'So, so.' He screwed up his face. 'Client meeting was a compete fiasco. I spent most of the rest of the day trying to sort out the mess.'

'Oh, darling, I'm sorry. Why don't you change? Then dinner will be ready.'

'Fab, I'm starving.'

'Libby, James, could you lay the table, please, while I serve up?'

There was a general grunt of disapproval but they both slowly got up and reached for plates and cutlery as Emma started putting pans of steaming mash, peas and beans on the table. Nick joined them and Emma dished up, making sure to put plenty on Libby's plate. She had been looking too thin recently.

They were halfway through dinner when Emma's phone rang again. She put her fork down. 'I know we say no phones at the table, but I just want to check it's not that number again. Someone keeps calling me.'

'One rule for us . . .' said Libby.

'Libby,' said Nick. 'Enough.'

It was the same number. Emma clicked 'Accept' and said 'Hello?' as she walked out of the kitchen, closing the door behind her.

'Hello, is that Emma Bowen?'

There was something official about the man's tone of voice that made her heart beat slightly faster. 'Speaking.'

'My name is Mr Eals. I'm calling about Margaret Chapman – your mother, I believe?'

'Yes?' Had she had a change of heart?

'I'm sorry to inform you that Margaret died earlier today. It was very peaceful.' The voice was soft.

Emma felt her throat constrict. She held the phone against her chest, unable to speak. Almost immediately tears spilled down her face. Mum was dead. She'd always thought they might reconcile. She'd rushed to her mother's bedside several times over the past twenty years of her illness, as she had gone in and then out of remission. She'd become so used to her recovering that she thought they'd always have time to make things up.

She swallowed with difficulty and raised the phone to her ear. 'Hello?' she said.

'Hello, Mrs Bowen.' The voice was quiet, understanding. Someone who was used to delivering bad news. 'I realise this will be something of a shock for you. May I suggest we talk tomorrow morning, once you've had time to digest the news. We can then talk about the official arrangements. Is there a good time for us to speak?'

'Any time,' Emma managed. 'Thank you, Mr Eals.' Emma ended the call. She opened the kitchen door again and looked at Nick and the children around the kitchen table. They were laughing. Three faces turned towards her.

'All okay?' said Nick.

'It's Mum,' said Emma, her voice broke. 'She died earlier today.'

'Oh, Em.' Nick was on his feet, holding her as her knees started to give way. He guided her back to the table. 'What a shock.'

Both James and Libby stopped eating. Libby got up and put her arms around her mother from behind. 'Sorry, Mum. We love you.'

'Thanks, Libs,' said Emma, wiping her eyes.

'I'm sorry too, Mum,' said James, frowning at her.

'I think I'm going to go upstairs for a while,' said Emma, getting to her feet. 'Leave you to finish off here.'

'I'll come with you,' said Nick.

'I just need a moment on my own,' said Emma.

'I understand,' he said, giving her another hug.

Lying on her bed, she let the tears come. But what was she crying for? She and Mum had never got on. She felt guilty that she hadn't been there at the end though – especially when she'd dashed up to be with her the other times they'd thought she was near the end. Had she died alone? No, Mr Eals had said it was peaceful so there must have been someone with her. *As her only child, it should have been me*, Emma thought, crying harder.

But their relationship had always been strained. Even as a young child. There was a feeling of slight relief that it was at an end, and it made Emma feel even more guilty.

Later, when Nick came up, she sobbed into his chest. 'I don't know why I'm crying so much. I didn't cry like this when Dad died and we were always so close.'

Nick stroked the back of her head. 'I think it's because you're mourning the relationship you never had.'

And that was it exactly, Emma thought.

Chapter 2

Betty

March 1937

Betty lay in the bath, her white legs flushing a blotchy pink in the scorching water. The passage light leaked around the edges of the bathroom door, merging into the glow from the streetlamp, fractured through the frosted glass window. The mirror perspired in the heat, dripping into the basin.

She took another gulp straight from the half-empty bottle balanced on the corner of the bath where the mould bred between the tiles. Her face twisted at the gin's bitter burn, but the bottle was cool against her cheek as she pulled a breath into her tight lungs.

Her mother's knitting needle balanced on the cloth used to wipe her sisters' faces. As she leaned forward to feel the pointed tip again with her finger, the water sloshed over the sides of the bath, on to the floor. The muffled sounds of her sisters finishing off their tea in the kitchen next door mingled with her mother's muted scolding.

There wasn't much time. *Not for me, not for it. He.* Betty was sure it was a he. *He would look just like him. But not grow up to be the coward his father was. He'd have a proper job where he'd have clean hands, a smart suit and a bowler hat. Live somewhere posh like Epsom, not in this tiny tenement.*

The hum of buses grinding up Battersea Park Road past St Saviour blurred with the shouts of the men clocking off, heading to the pub, and the yelling of the boys playing football by the dim streetlights.

She reached forward, over the tightness of her belly, and grasped the knitting needle, then let it float on the surface of the scalding water until it sunk beneath the water line, turning almost gaily downwards. The intense heat made her drowsy. It was difficult to move.

The pain won't be bad. Not as bad as standing there, looking the best I've ever looked, wearing that beautiful dress, waiting for him. Father pacing up and down. Then realising he wasn't ever going to come. That awful journey back home.

Angry steps sounded.

'You've taken all me bleedin' hot water. There ain't none left.' Her mother was at the door, shaking the handle.

'I won't be long, Ma.'

'Least you could do is be 'ere helping me with this lot, not dilly-dallying in there. Betty?'

'I'll be there in a minute.'

'What you doing in there anyway? Dolling yerself up? Got yerself another fancy man already, 'ave yer?'

'I won't be long, Mum.'

'Bloody hurry up. Cheek taking all that water. Nothing for yer pa when he gets home.'

The sound of steps moved away, and Betty imagined her mother, her thin, faded housecoat wrapped around her ample frame, stomping back into the tiny front room. There was a shout from next door, the sound of a child being slapped and then whimpering.

The knitting needle had settled, resting across the dark mound of her pubic hair. She stared at it. One small movement. Over. Quick.

She closed her eyes. She had no choice.

Chapter 3

Emma

January 2019

Emma yawned. It had been such a long drive to Morecambe to the solicitor's office. She wasn't used to driving that far and she felt guilty for leaving James in the middle of his mocks. And work. She'd never finished the condition survey. And it was due today. She sighed and looked around the small solicitor's office. The window ledge hadn't been dusted for years. A dried-out spider plant was caked with decades of grime. The reception area, which doubled as the secretary's office, was chilly. There was a heater under the desk of the woman who had only reluctantly glanced up from her pile of paperwork to welcome Emma. She didn't look much younger than the building.

Behind the secretary's desk, Emma saw a figure emerging from a narrow corridor. Mr Eals, her mother's solicitor, looked even more dilapidated than his office. His dark eyes were sunken into his face, barely visible below untamed eyebrows. The hand he held out to greet Emma was equally hairy. Already a short man, he was bent over, as if from the weight of people's troubles he had shouldered over the years.

He was smiling. 'Ah, Margaret's daughter, Mrs Bowen. I was hoping we would meet. It's a pleasure.'

'Good to meet you too, Mr Eals.' They shook hands and he ushered her back down the narrow corridor, years of spilled coffee staining the carpet tiles. The back door was open, the chilly draught riffling the stacks of paper lining the corridor and breezing into Mr Eals' small office at the back of the building. The windows here were high up on the wall, so there was no view of whatever lay behind the office. But even if there had been big windows, Emma suspected the old solicitor would have found a way of covering them. Every single surface in the room was buried under piles of manila files held together by elastic bands, labelled in the same spidery script. The top of a mahogany glass-fronted bookcase, which was full of impressive-looking legal tomes, was stacked to the window ledge, and even the chair opposite the old desk had several newer-looking folders on them. Mr Eals slid them on to a pile on his desk and indicated where Emma should sit. He eased himself past another tower of files and sat on a well-worn leather chair opposite her.

He was watching her, the tips of his fingers pressed together, his elbows resting on the cluttered desk. 'You do look like your mother. I suspect everyone says that.'

Emma smiled. 'Not many of my friends knew her.'

The contours around his eyes rippled as the old man returned her smile. 'Your mother was one of my longest-standing clients. I'm sad that this day has come. As a solicitor, you follow a client through their lives, intervening at the crucial points. Births, marriages, divorces, deaths of relatives, house purchases, and, then eventually, death. It's the natural order of my professional life.'

'So you had known Mum a long time?' Emma didn't recall her ever mentioning Mr Eals.

'Yes, since her twenties. She was one of my more interesting clients,' he said slowly. 'Now, have you got the death certificate we discussed on the phone yesterday? It is a relatively simple estate so, with a fair wind, we should secure probate in a couple of months.'

Emma drew the envelope out of her bag – she'd got the death certificate from the town hall that morning – and handed it over to the solicitor. He took out his glasses and put them on his nose before examining the death certificate closely. He nodded gravely. Then he raised his arms to the sides of the chair and used them to push himself upwards, until he seemed to judge that his knees would be able to support him. He moved slowly over to a pile of files in the corner nearest Emma and selected an enormous series of folders second from the top. It was held together by blue elastic bands, straining against almost a foot of paperwork. What on earth had her mother needed to discuss over the years?

Mr Eals dropped it with a thud on to the desk with the look of a man surveying a job well done. He rolled off one of the elastic bands and slid in the death certificate.

'Thank you for arranging to get this so quickly and for offering to sort out her possessions. As I said on the phone, the will makes a number of stipulations about certain items. I always think it's better for relatives to manage that. It saves unnecessary solicitor's fees and allows for what the Americans like to call "closure".'

'I think I'd have to go through years of therapy to get closure with my mother,' Emma said with a grimace.

She'd meant the comment light-heartedly, but Mr Eals paused and looked down at the file, stroking it.

'I'm not a religious man,' he said quietly, 'but I believe there's a phrase in the Bible about walking a mile in another man's shoes. Until we have done that, we will never understand what it's like to be the other person.'

Emma glanced down at her hands and realised she was twisting her wedding ring around her finger. She placed her hands on the desk and looked up at the old solicitor, who was watching her over his glasses. She nodded. Emma had no wish to walk in her mother's shoes. Their relationship had been difficult at best.

He eased a couple of sheets of paper out of the file. 'I have your mother's will here,' he said, passing it across the desk, 'so you can see what needs to be done.'

On the top sheet *Last Will and Testament* was printed in large bold letters across the top.

'*This Will is made by me Margaret Chapman of Flat b, 487 Marine Road East, Morecambe on this day Monday the 21st of January 2019*,' she read.

Emma looked up quickly. 'This will was made the day before she died,' she said, her eyes wide. 'Didn't she have a will before, or did she change it?'

Mr Eals hesitated. 'Your mother made some small changes to her will just before she died, but it was easier to make a new one than add them in as a codicil.'

Emma frowned and looked down at the document. Her heart started to thud. Why would Mum change her will just before she died?

The solicitor continued. 'Now, after the usual blurb about revocation, executors – that's me' – he looked up – 'and funeral directions, you'll see there's a section entitled "Specific Gifts".'

Emma traced her fingers down the page. There was a list of items that her mother wanted distributing to different people. Books, ornaments, jewellery, a coin collection. Nothing that Emma particularly remembered.

'All these items are in her property,' Mr Eals said, 'and I've arranged a courier to come to collect them later today to save you having to distribute them yourself. Some of them are going to other parts of the country, although a couple are local.'

Emma reached the end of the list and gasped. '*The Girl in the Midnight Maze*. She wants the painting to go to someone called Clare Richens. But—'

'Yes, your mother's friend Clare lives close by. I've included her address and phone number on this sheet,' he said calmly, slowly sliding another piece of paper across the desk. 'If you prefer, I can cancel the courier and you can deliver it yourself?'

'But *The Girl in the Midnight Maze* is ours. Our family's. It can't go to a stranger. I love that painting, it's beautiful,' Emma said, suddenly finding it difficult to swallow. She thought of the little girl dancing in the moonlight in the centre of the maze.

The secretary appeared at the door with a tray cluttered with a teapot, cups, and a milk jug. She laid it gently between them and set out the cups either side of the tray. Mr Eals reached forward and carefully poured milk and then tea into two cups, both covered in roses, and slid one across to Emma. She picked it up, her hands trembling, and took a sip.

With his fingertips once more pressed together in what she realised was his habitual pose, Mr Eals spoke quietly. 'I'm afraid that's what Margaret's will says. She wanted the painting to go to Miss Richens.'

Even though Emma hadn't seen the painting for years, for much of her childhood it had hung in the sitting room of their family home in Sussex, watching over her as she grew. When she was tall enough, she would reach up and follow the labyrinth with her fingertips, trying to find an escape route for the girl in the white dress locked within the shadowy prison of green hedges.

Her shoulders dropped and she looked back to the will. She hadn't thought there would be anything controversial in it. How naive. Mum had always loved any opportunity to be contentious.

'There is also the matter of her property itself. If you turn to page two, clause seven . . .' The solicitor paused and looked up at her.

Emma flicked over the page, scanned down and read out loud. 'To Elizabeth Margaret Bowen I leave my property Flat b, 487 Marine Road East, Morecambe.' She looked up at the old man. 'She's left her flat to Libby?'

Mr Eals smiled. 'Yes, to your daughter. Your younger child, I believe?'

Emma covered her mouth with her hand. 'But Mum hated Libby,' she said, rereading the text.

'Hate is a strong word,' he said calmly, slowly opening a drawer and extracting a set of keys. 'These are the keys to your mother's flat. I'm afraid it's been empty since she went into the nursing home a few months ago, but I've been keeping an eye on it.' He reached up and scratched his neck inside his starched collar. 'I think you'll find it all in order.'

Emma nodded, staring at the keys. Some had a carefully labelled tag, written in an unfamiliar hand: *communal door, front door, meter cupboard.* A small brass key was unlabelled.

'The residue of your mother's estate goes to a selection of charities, as you'll see on page four. If you can box it all up and label it, I will arrange for all of that in my role as executor. I can perhaps book another courier to save you taking it to the various charity shops she stipulated.'

Emma nodded blankly and then blurted out, 'What was it she changed the day before she died? The property going to Libby or the painting going to' – she looked down at the will – 'Clare?'

The old solicitor shook his head. 'I'm afraid I'm not at liberty to disclose the content of her previous will. I'm sure you understand.'

Emma nodded again, her foot tapping the floor.

'Now, this final document' – he slid a sheet of paper across the desk – 'details her funeral wishes. The music, readings and so on. Margaret had been in touch with a funeral home and made all the arrangements herself. You will just need to contact them and arrange a date.'

Emma scanned through a short list of music and the contact details for a humanist celebrant. *How very like Mum to want something different to the norm.*

'If you need anything else, do get in touch.' Mr Eals pulled himself up by the arms of the chair and stood. 'I will be in contact about the probate in due course.'

She also rose, clutching the keys. 'Thank you for your help,' she said automatically and followed him out of the room, her throat tight with repressed emotion.

ABOUT THE AUTHOR

Photo © 2025 Dani Brown

Cathy trained as a journalist and wrote about everything from HR and supply chains to football finances and port strategy before moving into public relations. In 2022, after having spent a lifetime pottering around bookshops, she bought Kemptown Bookshop in Brighton, where she has created a community hub that supports local authors and aspiring writers. In 2023, she took on joint management of the Creative Writing Programme, the leading independent centre for creative writing teaching in the south-east of England – the course that set her on track to be a writer. When she's not writing (or reading), Cathy loves pottering in other people's bookshops. She lives in Brighton with her three children and two rescue cats.

Follow the Author on Amazon

If you enjoyed this book, follow Cathy Hayward on Amazon to be notified when the author releases a new book!
To do this, please follow these instructions:

Desktop:

1) Search for the author's name on Amazon or in the Amazon App.
2) Click on the author's name to arrive on their Amazon page.
3) Click the 'Follow' button.

Mobile and Tablet:

1) Search for the author's name on Amazon or in the Amazon App.
2) Click on one of the author's books.
3) Click on the author's name to arrive on their Amazon page.
4) Click the 'Follow' button.

Kindle eReader and Kindle App:

If you enjoyed this book on a Kindle eReader or in the Kindle App, you will find the author 'Follow' button after the last page.